"'Do you ever suppose what makes a picture look pretty might be the parts of it you can't see? The hardship behind it, I mean.'" Spoken by a woman who knew how to love an unlovable man and find happiness in an almost unlivable life. What stays with the reader long after they have finished *Brighten the Corner Where You Are* is the brilliantly captured voice of Maud Lewis—as innocent and tender as it is knowing and tough. Carol Bruneau's depiction of the artist and her world is as joyful and colourful as a Lewis landscape."
–K. D. Miller, author of *Late Breaking*

"Dazzling! A poignant imagining of Maud Lewis's life; as colourful and joyous as Lewis's art, as bleak as an abandoned garden in February. Bruneau's vivid imagery and deceptively simple prose create a portrait of a woman so full of pluck, talent, humour, and compassion that it will never leave me."
–Lauren B. Davis, author of *Our Daily Bread* and *The Empty Room*

"*Brighten the Corner Where You Are* convincingly and beautifully illustrates the world of Maud Lewis, as told from the artist's perspective. Singular, strong, and remarkably observant, she narrates her story with wit, agency and spark, holding beauty above all throughout the successes and challenges of her lifetime. An unforgettable character portrayal, Maud's companionable voice will stay with readers long after the last page."
–Emily Urquhart, folklorist and author of *Beyond the Pale* and *The Age of Creativity*

"Everyone who has known Bruneau's stunning work from her award-winning beginnings, who has admired her unwavering commitment to her art, marvelled at her characters, her ability to get to the heart of relationships, to explore, to reveal the complexity of our humanity, has been waiting for this book. In this masterful telling, the world will get to know Maud Lewis as never before.... We've badly needed a vision like this. Bruneau holds both beauty and sadness in her magical hands."
–Sheree Fitch, author of *Kiss the Joy As It Flies*

"In Bruneau's talented hands, the story becomes a fully realized narrative.... Lewis is presented as a woman of strength and sass, a chain-smoker who detested being seen as a victim (even when she clearly was), and who desired romance and simple pleasures. But perhaps most importantly, it is clear that Bruneau respects Lewis as an artist and a human. *Brighten the Corner Where You Are* is a welcome addition to the Lewis legacy."
–*Quill & Quire*, starred review

"Read *Brighten the Corner Where You Are*, slowly, listen quietly! It is a gem of despair, of hope for those who believe they can't face another day of adversity. The writing is as kind as it is painful, as beautiful as it is sorrowful, as dark as midnight footprints. Bruneau has Maud in the palm of her hand, holds her there lovingly like a summer rose until her dying day. And lets her bloom again for all to see the beauty we may have missed."
–Beatrice MacNeil, author of *The Girl He Left Behind*

"Carol Bruneau's new novel really is a "wildwood flower"—plain and beautiful, tough and tender. And her Maud Lewis is a joy to keep company with."
–Cary Fagan, author of *The Student*

Praise for Carol Bruneau

A Circle on the Surface

Winner, 2019 Jim Connors Dartmouth Book Award

"A quietly brilliant novel."
–*Quill & Quire*, starred review

"Told with a meticulous eye for detail, Bruneau's voice is simple, elegant, arresting. A portrait of a partnership in peril, *A Circle on the Surface* lingers for days after its final page is turned."
–*Toronto Star*

"Reminiscent of Kate Chopin's *The Awakening* in both style and approach, Carol Bruneau's *A Circle On the Surface* captures the complexities, right up through to its tragic, memorable ending, of a woman's role in 1940s Nova Scotia."

–Donna Morrissey, author of *The Fortunate Brother*

"A compelling, unforgettable story of how World War II came to Nova Scotia, *A Circle on the Surface* reveals the sea changes for Enman and Una, a couple about to start a family. Delving into the depths of their lives, Bruneau gives us a powerfully haunting novel."
–Anne Simpson, author of *Speechless*

"Carol Bruneau's latest novel holds your heart right to the last, devastating sentence. In the tender lives of Enman and Una, naïve love and profound loneliness are infused with universal

questions: peril and mortality, how and why we love, and the unknowable mystery of a human soul. A compassionate and beautiful read."
—Carole Giangrande, author of *All That Is Solid Melts Into Air*

"*A Circle on the Surface* is a vivid, sensitive, often aching, imagining of a small Nova Scotia community looking fearfully out to sea during the Second World War. The sense of period and place is impressive, but the characters and situations are timeless. Bruneau mines each minute, observing in exquisite detail. The book is an unsparing but nonjudgmental portrait of a community and of a marriage facing threats from without and within. Bruneau creates memorable characters, presented in all their complexity and contradictions in a clear-eyed way, and then she goes that important extra step of truly inhabiting them."
—Mark Blagrave, author of *Lay Figures*

"C*A Circle on the Surface* brilliantly explores the complexities of family dynamics with well-crafted characters and a most engaging story. She deftly portrays the lives of Maritimers affected by World War II and after as they emerge from a time of darkness into an ever-changing modern world. Once again, Carol Bruneau proves herself to be one of Atlantic Canada's finest novelists."
—Lesley Choyce, author of *The Unlikely Redemption of John Alexander MacNeil*

"Bruneau's novel abounds in rich language that is often connected to the emotional state of the characters.... The author's use of imagery also creates a profound sense of place: the sea in particular is ever-present in the lives and dreams of the characters."
—*Understorey* magazine

A Bird on Every Tree

Shortlisted, 2018 Thomas Head Raddall Atlantic Fiction Prize

"Bruneau's writing rarely calls attention to itself, but this is a bravura performance.... This is no mere exercise in voice: this is a reflection of a writer utterly in touch with her stories—not only what they are, but how they are, overlooking nothing in her craft. Bruneau is a master."
–*Quill & Quire*, starred review

"Each of Carol Bruneau's stories is not so much told as meticulously shaped with exacting and mesmerizing attention to every gorgeous detail. Bruneau submerges the reader entirely in the physical and emotional worlds she so vividly evokes."
–Lynn Coady, author of *Hellgoing*

"Carol Bruneau is the Mavis Gallant of the North Atlantic. Her narrative voice is an extraordinary blend of elegance and grit, the characters and their observations both pragmatic and elegiac. These are stories of a diverse range of people...all told with startling detail, lyrical prose, and uncanny insight into those moments which break us apart and those which hold us together."
–Christy Ann Conlin, author of *Watermark*

"12 beautifully crafted short stories. Her exceptional prose reveals how much there is to discover in the everyday.... Bruneau does not settle for cliché. Her prose is accessible and lean as she flits into her characters' lives."
–*Publishers Weekly*

BRIGHTEN THE CORNER WHERE YOU ARE

A Novel Inspired by the
Life of Maud Lewis

CAROL BRUNEAU

Vagrant
PRESS

Vagrant Press is an imprint of
Nimbus Publishing Limited
3660 Strawberry Hill St, Halifax, NS, B3K 5A9
(902) 455-4286 nimbus.ca

Printed and bound in Canada

NB1544

Editor: Whitney Moran
Cover and interior design: Jenn Embree
Cover image: Original notecard by Maud Lewis. Copyright © Bob Brooks. Used with permission.

This is a work of fiction. While certain characters are inspired by persons no longer living, and certain events by events which may have happened, the story is a work of the imagination not to be taken as a literal or documentary representation of its subject.

Library and Archives Canada Cataloguing in Publication

Title: Brighten the corner where you are : a novel inspired by the life of Maud Lewis / Carol Bruneau.
Names: Bruneau, Carol, 1956- author.
Identifiers: Canadiana (print) 20200264982 | Canadiana (ebook) 20200265024 | ISBN 9781771088831 (softcover) | ISBN 9781771088848 (EPUB)
Classification: LCC PS8553.R854 B75 2020 | DDC C813/.54—dc23

Nimbus Publishing acknowledges the financial support for its publishing activities from the Government of Canada, the Canada Council for the Arts, and from the Province of Nova Scotia. We are pleased to work in partnership with the Province of Nova Scotia to develop and promote our creative industries for the benefit of all Nova Scotians.

For Jen Powley and to the memory of Maud Lewis

CONTENTS

"Do not wait until some deed of greatness you may do,
Do not wait to shed your light a-far,
To the many duties ever near you now be true."
–"Brighten the Corner Where You Are" by Ina Duley Ogdon
and Charles H. Gabriel, 1913

1.

I'VE BEEN
EVERYWHERE

The first thing you need to remember is that I'm no longer down where you are, haven't been down your way in years, in what you people call the land of the living. You could say I'm in the wind, a song riding the airwaves and the frost in the air that paints leaves orange. As the rain and the sunshine do, I go where I want. The wind's whistling carries me, takes me back, oh yes, to when the radio filled the house with Bob Wills and his Texas Playboys singing "My Life's Been A Pleasure." Though I'm not sure I would go *that* far. Freed of life's woes, these days I see joys that, in life, I just guessed up. If you know anything about me, you might be thinking, oh my, that one's better off out of her misery. Which might be true, but, then again, might not. But I dare say, without the body I dwelt in and the hands that came with it, I wouldn't have gotten up to half of what I did in your world; I'd have spent my days doing what you do. Where'd be the fun in that?

The best thing about up here is the view. Now, I'm not so high up that folks look like dirt specks and cars like hard candies travelling the roads. Nor am I so low down that you can reach up and grab a draught of me in your fist. Up here, no one gets to grab on to anybody, or be the boss. No shortage of bossy-boots down your way, folks only too certain they know best. So it was when I lived below, in a piece of paradise some called the arse-end of nowhere. I wouldn't make that kind of judgment myself. Mostly I kept to myself; for a long time doing just that was easy. Out in the sticks there are lots of holes to hide down, until someone gets it in their head to haul you out of yours. Next, the whole world is sniffing at your door, which isn't always a bad thing. Like living in the arse-end of nowhere isn't a bad thing, pardon this habit of speech I learned down your way. Habits die hard, even here. Except here I get away with whatever I want, which is a comfort and a blessing. Comforts and blessings mightn't be so plentiful where you are. Here, for example, a gal can cuss to her heart's content and who is gonna say boo?

And that view! Now I can see backwards, forwards, straight up and down instead of sideways or tilted, I can look at things face on the way, before, I just guessed things up and painted them in pictures. When it suits me, I hover at gull-level where hungry birds cruise the shore for snacks, or at crow-level where the peckish seek treats spilled by roadsides. Food aside, it's grand up here. I see the fog tug itself like a dress over Digby Neck and the road travelling south to north, pretty much tracing the route that took me from birth to this spot up here. Apart from the coastline's jigs and jags, as the crow flies north to south is a fairly straight line from the ridge where my bones lie to where I grew up.

Those who don't know better call this otherworld "glory." But, looking down at the green of Digby County stretching into Yarmouth County, a patchwork of woods and fields set against the blue of St. Mary's Bay, I'd call this part of your world "glory." *If* I were the churchy type, which I am not and never was. Though I did enjoy a good gospel song if it was the Carter Family singing it. Some days a good old country song was my lifeline to the world. Each melody crackling over the airwaves got to be a chapter of my life, its sweet notes looped in with the sour ones.

Churchiness aside, I know attention when I see it. Folks flocking to see my paintings, paying big dollars for them. Imagine if they'd paid me back then what they pay now, travelling from all over to see my home. Though that would be pissing in the wind, wouldn't it? For you can't take nothing with you. You land here as naked as when you land where you are. All the money in the world won't change it. Yet I wouldn't have minded being sent off properly. Wearing my ring, I mean, all polished and shiny and on the right finger, and everything right with the world. A badge of honour, say. Maybe if I'd heeded my aunt's Bible talk—not about turning the other cheek to have someone smite it too, but about being wise as a serpent, gentle as a dove—things would've played out different. My husband had serpent-wisdom galore, I was the dovely one. But if I'd got the serpent part down pat, who's to say I mightn't have turned half cur and bitten the hand that fed me?

But, about that wedding band. Marriage means where the one party flags the other party takes up the slack, making the couple one big happy serpent-dove. According to such logic, my man and me ought to have been two sides of the same dime tucked in a jar for safekeeping: equals. I let on that we were. Why I did is for me to know and you to find out. Your world will always have folks who take advantage of those with no choice but to let them. Up here, things even out. No one owns a thing; not the earth, sunshine, rain, or fire, and most certainly not the wind.

And in the end, what sweetness it is to enjoy a blue moon and just paint it in your mind's eye, no need to fumble with a brush! It's easy to love something named for a colour. Though other things about being up here mightn't be to everyone's taste, people don't exactly line up for tickets to get here, do they. If you're the type that's all go go go, the pace is hurry up and wait. As for reunions with loved ones, well, I am still waiting, but I haven't given up hope, no sirree. And there are other things to like about this so-called glory. The insects don't bite, unlike the no-see-ums that plague you every season but winter. And there are cats aplenty, don't let anyone tell you cats aren't allowed, as if up here is your chesterfield. You just can't see or pat them. Their purr might be what you hear when a motorbike goes by or a boat with a make-and-break puts out to sea.

Even better than the view is the moon's company, as stead-fast as memories you cannot shake. The moon doesn't care who tramps over her face or journeys to her dark side. Let her keep her secrets, I say. Though she doesn't mind shining her light on ours, and under her shine things buried and thought missing come to light, even things we reckon are gone for good—with an exception. For I have been searching high and low for that ring, the gold band I once put on with pride. When I could still wear a ring. The ring that belonged to me, even if it wasn't always mine. What a shitload of stories *it* would tell if it could, if anyone laid their fingers on it. Where it got to is a mystery, the way *here* is a mystery. Then again, where you are might be a mystery too, memories the only things we have that are certain. Bearing a weight all their own, they wax and wane. Like my pal, they hang around, old and full-blown or new and shy, whether they are pictures we paint of ourselves or pitchers of us that others pour out.

If only I could put my finger on when and where I last saw that ring. Thinking of it takes me back to a bright March moon, a night more than fifty years ago now, a night so long ago those men that first walked on her still had three years to go before stepping foot there. The moon pouring down her light is what springs to mind first. Pretty as that March night was back in 1966, I've spent a long time trying to forget it, and to forget about mud and dirt and footsteps and things on and in the ground. Buried things. For, as you will learn soon enough, things buried and unearthed are the undoing of us all.

All around me that night the county slept sound as a bear in winter, so it was in the wee hours beneath that moon. It was one of those cold, clear nights after a thaw, when frost silvers the meanest buds and you think the pussy willows have got a jump on April—until a snowstorm blows in and covers everything.

One step forward, two steps back. That was spring in our neck of the woods, never mind where you found yourself.

To this day, I have no clue what time it was I awoke. My husband had brought me upstairs hours before. From the nearby woods an owl screeched, but that was the only sound. It was either too late or too early for the crows to be up, not just any crows but the ones setting up house in our yard. The lady crow had recently stolen my fancy.

My man got up. His sharp, sudden moves near pitched me from the bed. Wide awake, I listened to him scuttle across the floor and shimmy down through the hatch. The stairs shuddered under his weight. I heard him scuffling about below, heard the rustle of him grabbing his jacket and his boots left warming by the range. The door creaked open and banged shut behind him. His footsteps stirred the gravel out front, slouched along the side of the house before they grew faint. Off to wake the crows and lure my favourite with a crust of bread, set to win her affection? (I do believe Everett envied my friendship with Matilda, never mind she was just a crow.)

I thought with a start he must be off to the almshouse, was after taking the shortcut out back—see how the mind plays tricks in the dead of night? He had not worked over there in three, going on four years by this time, which was roughly the last time I'd seen my friend Olive, the warden's wife, when she finally realized it was no place to raise her boys. With a shiver of relief, I heard the creak of hinges from the shed nearest the house. It was where Ev liked to partake of his TNT cocktail, homebrew in the years before we had money, and then store bought later on.

Save that sharp creak, it was so quiet you could have heard a field mouse stir, the poor creature come in from the cold seeking a crumb or a smidge of warmth. Then, way out back, down by Seeley's Brook or beyond it in the hills, a coyote yowled. Its cry echoed close but somehow distant at the same time. Yet from the pen by the shed came not a peep. Any other time Ev's old mutt, Joe, would yap for a treat, especially if he spied someone else getting what he thought was his due—Joe was third or fourth in a long line of Joes, and he would bark his head off, it's a fact. But not a yip sounded. Maybe Ev had obliged him before he could start a ruckus. For Ev loved that dog, loved spoiling him. Would have spoilt Matilda the crow, too, I do believe, if Matilda hadn't set her sights on me.

From out back I heard another creak, then a thick, padded silence. The draft coming into the loft stirred the oilcloth Ev had tacked to the rafters. It was water-stained and worn but you could still see the sailing ship I'd painted on it. Filling its sag, the draft put wind in the sails. A muffled clang rang out, another and another, a clang like metal hitting rock. The sounds came in through the attic's tiny gable window and echoed under the rafters. There was little to the roof's pitch or its shingles and boards to dampen night noises or hinder the cold. The air in the loft held onto them, made them its own.

I wasn't the sleeper I am now—not because of the cold, I was as used to the cold as a body gets. If I had trouble sleeping it was on account of my old companion, pain as loyal a bedmate as any man. Of course, it's hard to sleep, alone or with company, when you lack the comfiest bed to lay in. Not that I am complaining, there's no point complaining now. On this March night heavy with frost, I could have bunked down closer to the range, curled up on the daybed at the foot of the stairs. I would have been closer to my window then, ready to watch for Matilda coming to perch there after dawn.

But Ev had carried me up to the attic, one step at a time, and lifted me through the hatch. What good wife leaves the marriage bed to sleep alone?

Roused by the clangs, I let curiosity get the better of me. You know what they say about curiosity and cats. Concern for my husband was at the top of my mind. It was no mean feat to unfurl myself from the covers, slide out from the bed on hands and knees, and crawl across the cold, rough boards towards the hatch, a square hole a little less dim than the rest of the floor. Squared careful as could be on all fours, I went through the hole arse-first, taking each stair the way a tiny child would—the only way to manage their slant, especially in the pitch black. If I had taken the same amount of care later on I'd have saved myself grief, maybe even lived longer? On this occasion, I wasn't even seized by the urge to pee, only the worry that something was wrong, that, like it or not, Ev might need me. But by the time I had reached the last stair from the bottom, my ladder-list of priorities had rearranged itself a little.

It was a chore getting up off my knees and onto my feet, but I managed. Downstairs was brighter than the loft, only because of the moonlight leaking in through both windows.

It cast spiky shadows of the flowers on both sides of my window-pane, beaming in around their shapes on the glass. A paleness cracked in around the door, which stood unlatched and ajar, the draft from the road nudging it against the jamb. Any other cold night I'd have used the bucket under the stairs, and saved myself the trip to the outhouse. But on this frosty night worry pressed me forwards, said I ought to try killing two birds with one stone: have a pee and see what Ev was up to.

I felt my way past the range; there wasn't a ghost of warmth from the fire's embers. By the light of my husband's window I gripped the back of his chair, sank one foot after another into my slippers, yanked my coat down from the hook, and squirmed into it. Pushing the door wide, I launched myself over the threshold onto the wooden doorstep, from there onto solid ground. Its iron cold pressed through my soles. It was frosty enough to warrant mitts. But even with my sleeves pulled down over them, my fists were so clumsy-cold reaching up I couldn't even think of pegging the door shut behind me. Luckily it was a windless night, bitter but still. The stillness made each sound carry so. One good bang of the door and, oh yes, Ev would have come running.

He'd have been there like a shot, thinking that we had been burgled or I had taken a spell.

Well, he didn't come. I followed the clangs, picking my way around back. The clangs were ringing out faster and heavier, echoing louder. I reached the outhouse, managed to climb inside and do my business, then made my way as quick as I could down the little slope behind it, past the old swing hanging useless from a tree branch. When I glanced back, the house shrank away like a boxy little ghost. From the swing it was a hop, skip, and a jump to Ev's collection of sheds and lean-tos. Over the years, these had sprung up like toadstools around the one he did his drinking in, which was big enough to keep a car in. It was his hidey-hole from my nose-minding eyes, he would joke, if ever we got to tripping over each other in the house. Next to this shed was a tool shed stuffed with his treasures.

The clangs kept ringing upwards from the back lawn, though I still couldn't see him. Back then that patch of yard was tufted in summer with thick dewy grass, now it's all grown in with alders. At the time I speak of, it was half hid from the house by spruce and a twisty old apple tree Matilda and them had nested in one spring but abandoned for a big, tall pine handy the road. I stopped and stood in stripy moonlight listening to the *ting* of what I knew was a shovel gouging stones. Ev would be mad if he knew I'd gotten up and come down the stairs by my lonesome. Knowing it, my smarter self should have just slunk back to the tool shed, rested for a bit, then slipped back up to the house. Of course, a person could've disappeared in that shed, camouflaged by bits of fishing line, tire treads, rope, busted lobster pots, and cans, cans, and more cans, some empty and some still with paint. I could have let myself pass for flotsam and jetsam, what the sea spat up that month and all the months and years before. Or I could have just hightailed it best I could back to the house before he saw me.

For the last thing you wanted was to startle or annoy Ev, see his surprised look screw up into a scowl. Land, the things that would pour from his mouth if he thought you'd been watching him, especially if he was nursing a bottle or a tin full of money! *"What the hell? You spying on me? I'll learn you a thing or two about spying."*

But, lulled by the stillness, and my own curiosity I must admit, I crept closer, paused on a little rise of bare turf. There he was, leaning into his task. He grunted as he drove the shovel into the dirt. I was just close enough and angled just right to see his face full on, the determined look on it. A hot chill shimmied through me. He would have my hide for taking the stairs on my own. And the sight of him digging up the earth in the moonlight brought back a night but a year or two after we'd married, something I had promised myself well and good to forget. For what was the use of worrying about a thing you could do nothing about?

Whatever Ev was up to burying now, he could have waited for a solid, steady thaw to make the task easier. His impatience filled me with wonder. The same wonder held me there, froze, with just the length of a few yardsticks between us. My husband was a hard worker but never one to waste effort. Bent over his work now, he could have been a scarecrow, if scarecrows talked. For he was cussing under his breath. Cussing the rocks, tree roots, and frozen dirt. So much for him replacing me in Matilda's affections, I thought. Most birds liked a gentler touch. Each clang of the shovel's rusty blade could have jarred her and the other feathered ones from their sleep. I imagined her sassing him back, leading a chorus of rocks, roots, and turf all giving him what-for.

At his feet, something glinted in the moonlight. It was glass, what looked to be a preserving jar. Even from a distance I recognized it as the one my secretary had dropped off that afternoon, a jar of homemade mustard pickles. I hadn't managed to get a taste but those pickles must have been some good, seeing how fast they'd disappeared. It was too nice a jar for storing worms—was Ev digging worms to go smelting? I wondered. Strange time to do it, waiting till sunup would've made more sense. With the ground hardly thawed, the robins hadn't even arrived from down south. Ev aimed to beat them to a juicy tangle of worms? Wouldn't put it past him, I thought. Ev was always trying to outdo someone or something. This included himself and the care he took with our money.

Of course, it's easy to be critical. And it ain't nice or useful to spy. I'd learned early in my life: what you don't see won't pester you. But, stepping back a ways from the moonlight, I stayed put on the rise and watched through the spruce boughs. Somehow, Matilda and her murder stayed asleep. After leaning heavy on the shovel, scooping and flinging away frost-spiked soil, Ev stooped to roust up with both hands a rock that didn't want to give. Curiosity made me bolder, and the fact of what I'd done. If I could climb down those stairs, I could climb back up them too. I leaned into a stitch of moonlight for an even closer look.

Wiping his brow, Ev straightened up, yanked his cap forward, then scraped it backwards on his head. He took up the shovel, dug a bit more, then flung it down again and lifted up the jar. I didn't need to tilt myself backwards to see something lining the bottom of it glinting, shiny and dull. If they'd been awake, Matilda and her cronies would have been all over it like one big flapping black shirt. Ev brought the jar to his lips—for one last lick of pickle juice or to kiss the jar for good luck? Crouching down, he planted it deep in the hole. He shovelled then kicked dirt over top of it, and clods of grass. His face had the same dull grey, frosty look as the trees and bushes around us.

I wanted to call out, I should have called out, but his look stopped me. Not a twig or creature stirred. It was always better to hold my tongue. I watched him do a comical little two-step, tamping down the dirt under his boots. It made me think of Joe burying bones or Matilda hiding peanuts from the blue jays. Of course I thought of people, too, in movies and songs and whatnot, burying things to keep what they didn't want known out of sight and out of mind.

I breathed in a good big gulp of air, its hint of spruce gum a balm on my lungs. But as I did so I wobbled and stamped down hard on a fallen twig. It was no bigger than what I'd seen Matilda and them building their nest with, but the snap it made cracked the stillness.

Ev near dropped the shovel, looking up. His surprised holler rent the darkness, fiercer than cawing could have done. His eyes gleamed as they fixed on me. "You! What the jeezus are you doing out here?"

The yard and the woods dimmed to the same solid chill that lit all through me. What had possessed me to be here? I was in for it now.

"How the jeezus did you get down them stairs? Did I say you could leave the loft? How'd you get back here without me seeing you? The hell you think you're doing, scaring me like this. Checking up on me. Like a goddamn bloodhound. You could have fell! Git back to the house, git back there now, before you bust something and catch your death of ammonia."

Even years later, after I landed in hospital the last time, dying of that illness, do you think Ev could say the word *pneumonia*? But he was right, I should not have ventured down the stairs let alone outside in the dark. I should have stayed upstairs where I belonged, and I sure as heck shouldn't have been watching him like this. And yet curiosity gripped me. Out the words popped, as unbidden as could be:

"What in God's acre are you up to, Ev?"

Unleashed this way, my tongue betrayed me, as it had a few times before. The question startled Ev so bad he swung the shovel like a bat. The tops of his boots flubbed against his shins as he strode near. "What did you say, woman?" For half a second, how foolish, as he stood over me and I forced my gaze sideward, I half feared he would bring the shovel down on my head.

He peered down into my face and I could smell the liquor on him. "Look at your husband when he's talking to you!"

With him standing there on the rise, I could not have done so if I'd wanted to. Of course, Ev had never landed a blow or laid a hurtful finger on me, not intentionally, and never would.

But there is a first time for everything, I remembered someone saying on the radio, as Ev grabbed ahold of my sleeve. He must have felt me trembling. "I asked you, what did you say?"

"Nothing, Ev. You are hearing things, I didn't say nothing." I bit down on my treacherous tongue. Instead of staring at his chest I cast my eyes downwards. Matilda! I called out in my head, Wake up! Git down from your nest right now and witness this! Whatever happens, which of us do you want for a friend, him or me?

Only then did my fool brain come unfroze enough to remember that Matilda had begun brooding and would not leave the nest even if she wanted to.

Ev gave my arm a sharp tug, then let go. He barked out a laugh. "My, my, aren't you the cat's arse. Smart! Smart as all get-out, coming out and spying on your husband. Traipsing down here in the dark, coulda fell and broke a leg, then what? Missus Smarty Pants, thinking you can come and go as you please, all hours, risking life and limb."

Of course he was right. If I busted something, how would we manage? I kept my trap shut. Keen as I was to get back to the house, don't assume I thought his words didn't merit an answer. It wasn't the first time one of us had got riled up over nothing. Plenty to get riled up about in twenty-eight years of marriage. But, like the crows, I'd learned the value of keeping mum. Best just to bury the hatchet, like they used to say. As for burying stuff, you could count me just as guilty as Ev, I suppose, the two of us like Joe and all the dogs that came before Joe squirrelling away bones for later, always later.

A later that seldom came, I have since learned, until you found yourself fresh out of time.

Ev stayed put, gaping at me. Imagining Matilda's saucy cry, I finally summoned the playful gumption to speak, and more gently this time. "What were you planting, anyways? Funny time to be planting. Awful cold, still so early in the season."

But my playfulness didn't help.

"You crazy thing. Crazy as a bag full of hammers. Coulda landed flat on your arse. Then you'd have been done for. Planting, all right—planting whatnot, for me to know and you to forget about. Creeping downstairs in the dark, so he'p me, you'll get planted." He grinned as he spoke, and shook his head indulgently.

Now, let me back up a little in my telling of this: it had dawned pretty quick what was in the jar, from what I'd glimpsed. A small silver collection: nickels, dimes, nothing dearer, perhaps, than quarters, no fifty-cent pieces or silver dollars. Silver with a coppery hint of gold? The dim gleam of a new penny or two was surely not the gleam of my ring. Yet I had merely caught this glimpse, mind; there could have been more. Paper. Tightly folded dollar bills or a message, the sort more usually poked inside a liquor bottle and cast into the sea. But I didn't suppose Ev would take such pains over disposing a note—unless it was an IOU for a debt he wasn't ready to call in *or* forgive and forget, but wished to lay to rest until such time as it was useful. A love letter, a farewell note, these amounted to the same for Ev, given that he couldn't read.

I imagined Matilda stealing such a note, lining her nest with it.

Now, suppose that glint *was* my ring, the dearest, costliest thing the two of us had to call our own in all the world? Of course, it had been a dog's age since I had worn it. For years now, my old paws had been way too swelled up to get it past the nail of any finger on either hand. Just because I didn't wear it never meant I had no use for it.

"Now git back up to the house before I plant *you*!" As he hefted the shovel, Ev's laugh was a hiss. I heard something stir in the bushes, a raccoon maybe. Swinging the shovel, he marched ahead, then stopped to heave it in amongst the loot in the tool shed.

As I watched the back of him bob towards the house—the red checks of his jacket dark as pitch—the sight made me brazen again. Reckless. "You eat all them pickles or what?" My voice carried as clear as the moon just beginning to pale overhead. "They'd have been nice on beans. We could've made them last a while. Secretary might need her jar back. Might think poorly of us just keeping it."

He laughed over his shoulder. "That one? She's got jars coming out her arse, I'll bet. Wha'd I tell you about en'ertaining her? Huh?"

I coughed out a laugh that was hollow-sounding even to me, but didn't say anything. Ev hardly gave a cock-a-doodle-doo about other people's possessions. But he cared what they thought, and by that I mean letting them know we needed their help as much as we suffered their kindness. On the little slope close by the privy he spun round to face me, stumbling in his boots. "What's so goddamn funny? That one takes advantage. Taking your paintings, paying four dollars for one she wanted, plus some old pickles for a tip? A real nice painting, too, wasn't it, like you done for her other 'friends.' Make her and the rest of them mucky-mucks think you and your pitchers come cheap. Next they'll be writing and askin' us to give 'em away. Oh I got folks like her figured out, don't worry. Sure she's helpful. Sitting on a pile of cash where them four bucks come from."

Never mind the dark, he didn't wait for me to catch up.

More pickles, more money, more whatnot. Much as Ev didn't care about other people's stuff, there wasn't a person on the planet had less than us, he sometimes fixed on thinking. Like Matilda and her murder living off what nature afforded, Ev and me lived off of the kindness of people like my secretary, and before her, Olive Hayden and her husband. He just wanted a bit more for himself, like people owed him.

15

I admit, now and then his habit of want left me wanting.

"Just let it go," I called, only half under my breath. "What good is a pile of cash to any one of us, when the time comes." When the reaper comes, I meant, what comes for all and sundry one day, rich or poor, a nicely feathered nest or not. Poor you, I thought half aloud, thinking anyone owes you the sun or the moon. Like hell they do, I wanted to say, unless once you're out of everyone's sight, even the birds', each person gets his or her comeuppance.

Though I wouldn't hold my breath on that account. Back then I hardly knew what I was talking about. As far as come-uppances go, I'm still waiting for one, fingers crossed. It could be like waiting for a big hammer to drop, but so far, up here in this otherworld, there's no sign of one. As for being out of sight, give it time and we all slip from sight, some faster than others, after we're planted. Not to be morbid. And given what happened to Ev later, I'm just as glad I never mentioned the reaper that night. Not to be superstitious. But sometimes giving voice to such notions can be an invitation, opening the door to things best kept shut out.

2.

LET THE
LOWER LIGHTS
BE BURNING

Before *I took it into my head or had reason to keep an eye on any* man, I would watch Mama at the piano. Her fingers danced up and down the keyboard accompanying herself like Mary Pickford in *Sparrows* as she trilled "Shall We Gather At The River." She was so happy when she played, the house could've burnt down around her before she would notice something amiss while singing to me. The words "the beauteeful, the beauteeful rivvver" took me right back to when I was a little girl, before I knew about the curse and fellas and spooning and all that.

I remember a beautiful blue-green bird came to visit our house in Yarmouth. He was no parrot, he wasn't all the colours of the rainbow. But in my imagination the glister of his feathers showed flashes of pink, violet, and gold. Before he flew away forever, I used to dream of finding a gilded cage for him, the way I would dream sometimes of raising my head high, having it turn like an owl's. In my dreams, the beautiful bird talked more than Matilda ever would or could. He would sit in his cage atop the piano and sing the sweetest song while Mama played and I turned the page for her each time she called out "Turn!" But when she missed a note and said "Darn," he would repeat, "Darn darn darn." In real life, I would peer into his tiny black eye, get swallowed up by it. In a dream he tweeted my name, "Maud Maud Maud," but then chattered, "Cripple cripple cripple" till I opened the door to his cage and watched him fly away. No bird or human needed to speak these words for them to echo in my head.

When I turned fourteen and quit going to school, I could have used that bird to keep me company. But by then he had flown from our yard never to be seen again. You could say Mama and me grew even closer, sad to have him gone, missing the joy he provided.

Back in those golden days, though, I used to love going on our family picnics. Father would borrow a horse and buggy from Phillips Moving for the day and off we would go, all four of us, through the countryside down Arcadia way. On the grassy bank of the Chebogue River, Mama would spread an old quilt for a blanket and we would sit and feast on egg sandwiches, jellied chicken, biscuits, and cake.

My brother, Charlie, would throw rocks into the gently swirling current. In between snoozes, Father would tell us stories. Holding me on her lap, Mama would comb snarls from my hair with her fingers. Her hands smelled of the rose-water and glycerin she rubbed on them after working in the garden. Our picnic spot looked out over the village, Arcadia's houses and stores backing onto the river where fishing boats with bright red, green, and blue hulls bobbed on the incoming tide. At low tide you could see the stilts and staging the wharfs and houses were built out on. High tide covered them up, the river acting like a dress—a dress, say, that could hide the leg braces cripples wore. The leg braces the doctor had recommended for me.

"Nonsense. My girl will wear nothing of the kind," Mama told Dr. Wheedie. "She's only nine years old, you said she could grow out of this...trouble she's got."

You see, I was born pretty much okay, my chin only tucked down a little, my hands like anybody else's. After I'd started school and it looked like my chin was not going to raise itself from my chest like people hoped and my knees and ankles and wrists and knuckles started to swell—with pain for no good reason—she had taken me to see him. She worried I wasn't growing the way I should be.

"She gets the very best, Doctor. Not a day goes by she doesn't get milk, cream, butter, eggs, fish, meat."

"Her trouble could be any number of things," the doctor said. I heard words like *arthritis* and *rheumatism* and others that made Mama shake her head in wonderment.

She began taking me there oftener, though the doctor just repeated these things every time. He prescribed Aspirins and suggested a brace for each leg. But I didn't want to wear those braces kids with club feet wore, for pity's sake. Mama didn't want me to either.

"Perhaps your daughter will grow out of it, this condition she has. Children do. Grow out of things. As long as she manages to get to school, there's nothing really to worry about."

It was Dr. Wheedie's polite way of saying there was nothing he could do to fix whatever I had. Whatever it was didn't keep me from trying my hand at the piano, being just like Mama.

This one sunny day in Arcadia, as I sat with Mama on the picnic quilt, Charlie threw a ball, expected me to catch it. "Butterfingers!" he yelled when I missed. "Stupid!"

"Charles!" Mama cried and hugged me to her so fierce I thought I would smother. I wasn't a baby, by now I was eleven going on twelve. Though maybe I didn't look it, being on the small side. Wriggling away from her, I stuck out my tongue at Charlie. "Sticks and stones will break my bones but names will never hurt me!" My singsong cry woke Father from his nap. "Charlie!" Then Father's voice softened. "How 'bout a game of catch, then we'd best grab the reins and get a move on, eh, Mother?"

Mother, he called her, not Agnes or Mama or Dear. I helped Mama fold the quilt, pack the picnic things into the basket, and put them in the buggy. Then she lifted and held me up high enough to feed the horse sugar cubes she'd brought for our iced tea. She was robust for a lady, and taller than Father.

I forgot Charlie's taunt until we had put the village behind us and came upon a grim-looking building big enough to be a school. It was painted white and had three storeys and a hip roof, and rows of windows like sad eyes staring out. A tangle of wild roses grew out front. In the side yard long lines of laundry flapped in the breeze. In the field just up from the road, men, women, and kids were bent over, picking rocks.

"That's where you'll end up, Maudie," Charlie said, matter of fact. "That's where cripples go."

"Charlie!" Father's voice was a bark. Charlie laughed and dug his elbow into my ribs, then tickled me so hard I thought I would pee. But I wasn't laughing. I couldn't laugh. The feeling in my throat was like having a bee stuck there trying to escape.

Mama's eyes burned. "For goodness' sake, Charlie. Jack?"

"Over my dead body." As Father spoke, Mama cuddled me closer. "Over my dead body you or any one of us will end up in a place like that, sweet pea. Now shut your mouth, son. I'm warning you, not another word."

We carried on in silence. By and by, Mama pointed to some daylilies growing by the roadside. She opened her mouth to speak, and I knew she wanted to stop and pull up some roots to take home. The lilies were yellow, rarer than the orange ones in our yard. But before Mama could say anything, Father cracked the whip and told the horse "Giddup!"

"You have nothing to worry about, my darling," Mama breathed into my ear. "People in places like that don't have a soul in the world to care for them. Otherwise they wouldn't be there. No wonder the ones off their heads get that way, no one to love them."

I couldn't resist calling out, "Like *you*, Charlie!"

"Takes one to know one. 'Don't try to understand me, just love me.' That's you, sis."

Father lost his patience. "Charlie. That. Is. Enough."

Then Charlie pulled something from his pocket, put it in my hand. "Here you go." I could tell he was sorry for teasing. It was a moon snail shell just big enough that when I held it to my ear, I heard the sea inside. Mama started singing "Arcady is Ever Young," her best imitation of Elsie Fox Bennett's twittering soprano. *"Far away in Arcady/Summer never passes/Warm the wind that wanders free/Thro' the bending grasses."* Cuddled up to her, I knew I would want for nothing so long as I had her and Father. Before we knew it, we were clip-clopping up to the Lewis Fountain for the horse to get a drink.

But a parent's protection only goes so far, see. It wasn't that I hated learning, or that the kids were mean, or that they mocked me—if they did, they seldom did it to my face. In the schoolyard I did my best to keep up at skipping rope, playing chase, hide-and-seek. Increasingly, instead of skipping rope I skipped class. Mama told the teachers my absences were due to growing pains.

"It's not like she's got polio," the doctor said.

Some days when I was playing by myself in the garden, girls a grade or two ahead of me would peer over the fence between our yard and the Thibeaus' on their way home from school. They would holler out, "Hey, Odd-may Owley-day! How come you won't look up? Are you scared of us?" As if yelling my name out in pig Latin would block Mama or my brother from hearing them. I figured they only came around because they had a crush on Charlie. One had a dad who was boss at the woollen mill; she was the worst, saying "neck" so it rhymed with "sick." "Lift your chin off your nick! Cripple!" The rest chimed in, "Nick nick nick," till I wanted to nick them with Mama's garden claw. I wouldn't have, of course. Mama came out waving her trowel. "You girls get going! You should be ashamed. Don't let me catch you here again!" The girls hightailed it then, cutting across Hawthorne and behind the barn and in back of the shops on Main.

I thought their taunts bothered Mama more than they bothered me. If I was bothered, I kept it to myself. That day, Mama was peeved worse than when folks she considered friends were slow paying Father for his work. That day she seemed mad at me. "Well, I never. Maud, come here! You're better off in the house. Why you'd want anything to do with those brazen pups is beyond me."

Not that she meant this in quite the uppity way it sounded. In her very next breath, she said how sticks and stones will break your bones but names will never hurt you. That line was one a little old bird could've repeated in its sleep.

Mama got out her box of pastels. They were still special to me, though many were broken and the ones in our favourite colours, blue, brick-red, and green, were worn to nubs while the beige and grey looked brand new in their paper wrappers. I tried to peel the paper from the tip of a reddish-orange one, to draw honeysuckle. But my fingers got clumsy when I was worked up. Mama's anger upset me more than anything the mean girls could have said.

"Tell me you didn't do something to irk those kids. You know, if you'd speak up for yourself it would make *my* life easier." She seized the pastel and peeled it for me, passed me some cardstock. Then she sighed and stroked my arm. "For pity's sake, imagine if we drew the world like it is. Wouldn't be much fun, would it. Here, amuse yourself while I make us tea."

Her words made me buckle inside. For the first time ever, I defied her. "Mama. If tea stunts your growth like Teacher said at school, how come you let me drink it? How come some kids drink it and grow straight and tall?"

Mama's eyes glistened. She seemed to sink into herself. "Oh, my darling—next time anyone says one mean word to you, you tell me, and I'll have Father get after them and their parents, too."

Just what every fourteen-year-old gal wanted, her papa going after her bullies, hoping to reason with them.

"Mama. They'd tease me all the worse then."

Never minding what I had said about tea, Mama served me some in my special cup. The cup was a deep purply pink with prickly china flowers on it painted gold, and fancy script that said "For A Good Girl." My grandmother Isabella, Father's mama, had given it to me for my twelfth birthday, the same way *her* mother had given it to her. "The Dowleys are nothing if not good." Mama winked, she'd got over her bad mood. Maybe Granny Dowley reminded her of her sister Ida, reading the Bible and that. The same birthday Granny Dowley gave me the cup, she had shown me the page in *her* old family Bible where she'd written my birthdate, *March 7th, 1902*, in her big, spidery hand.

Mama gave herself the cup that was hand-painted with violets. She said it reminded her of the countryside around

South Ohio, where she and Father lived when they first tied the knot, before they moved to Yarmouth. *"Quiet? Nothing out there but a church, fields, and a couple of houses. You couldn't get me to town quick enough."*

The tea was milky and sweet, the way I liked it. I forgot about tea doing bad things. Calmed, I set to drawing while Mama watched. The turquoise pastel was so short I could barely hold onto it, but it was the only colour that would do.

"My, that's a pretty bird you've done. What sort of a bird is it?"

"An indigo bunting, have you forgot?"

"Clever girl." Mama picked up my picture, held it by the window to admire it. It was as if I'd brought the real bird back to her garden. "You'll do better staying home, believe me."

And she was right.

After that I fixed on copying pictures I found around the house—pictures on candy boxes, cookie tins, calendars, and in magazines. Charlie made fun of me. "What's the point, taking all that time to copy what's already there? I've got a Brownie camera can do the trick in jig time, only like the movies, black and white."

"Dumb bum. It's the colours I care for."

"What, you can't picture them in your head?"

"'Course I can. Bah."

But drawing and painting and copying the world from pictures of it didn't mean I liked being housebound. From the parlour, I watched girls littler than me skipping double Dutch in the street, boys stealing jump ropes to lasso them like horses and play chariot. Just watching this, I felt the swelling in my ankles spread like an invisible bruise. If I could have drawn the pain, purple would've done.

One day I did go outside, and after a while tried to join in. A mean girl tied her jump rope to my foot, said she'd invented a game, did I want to learn? She had another girl take the rope's other end. When the Boston ferry blasted its horn from the dock, they yelled "Tug-o'-war!" My feet flew out from under me, landed me flat on my rear. The shame I felt was hot and sudden as the flash of a knife. Their friends came and made a circle round me. "Ring around the rosies/pocket full of posies/ashes, ashes, we all fall down!" Their voices were shrill and sweet. But instead of tumbling down and squatting with me, they ran off, though not before the sight of bare shins, ankle socks, and scuffed saddle shoes got burned into my head.

One pair of shoes had no toes. The kid wearing them wasn't just bad but was poor. I'd heard Father say her family had "bad debts." Being poor was bad, being rich was good, everyone knew. I caught the poor girl's eye before she darted off with the others. It was funny they let her play with them. Poor thing, you could end up in the poorhouse, I almost cried out. I wondered if Granny's Bible or Aunt's had anything to say about poorhouses, as they sounded like places of punishment, which the Bible seemed big on. Hell: being poor *and* bad was sure to land you there, while being rich and good would spare you from it.

As for the teasing and mockery dealt to me, looking back I figure it was good training for being married to Ev. Like Mama used to say, What doesn't kill you makes you stronger.

Before you know it, I'll have been gone as long as I was alive down your way. Then again, time means diddly on this side of the veil, and no matter which side of the veil you're on, it plays tricks. Down where you are, people smile at my pictures and say,

"It's like she lived two hundred years ago, what never-never land was *she* dreaming of?" Let them wonder while perusing my pretty scenes of villages, coves, and woods where even in bleakest winter leaves don't fall from trees but glow red and orange. Sometimes my days below *felt* like two centuries, mind you. But time does equally odd things in so-called glory.

That night Ev buried the jar out back happened more years ago than I can count, even if I had fingers to count upon. I have an idea that what he buried that night wasn't the half of what-all he planted out there over the years, and I don't just mean potatoes and turnips. Wondering what precisely was in that jar haunted me for a good long while, and haunts me still. Was there money that had come in the mail the day before? Except for this and the other odd niggling worry, I am carefree as the bird in Wilf Carter's song, I'm my own person. No more pain, no more guilt—free. And there's the view, like I was saying, grander even than Matilda's or any view I could have guessed up if I had lived a thousand years, below, I mean. Of course, it helps not being required to turn my head or look sideward at everything; certain things used to slip by me on account of that. Some might say it's a pity that in life I lacked the luxury of flitting hither and yon, like a Matilda unburdened of her young, taking in the sights. No telling where I would have got to—maybe as far as Saint John, New Brunswick, or Boston, or New York City, or even to Nashville, Tennessee. Who knows where a crow can get to?

But Matilda is neither here nor there. Yes, at the moment, I fancy myself a herring gull taking in the bay below, the marshes and mudflats. Or a goshawk soaring over Seeley's Brook, glittering like a garter snake in the reeds back of where the house stood. It isn't too shabby being a bodiless bird. The only sad part is life's earthbound part, the leavings of life as it is lived, I mean. Such leavings make me think of a clam squirting brine at people bent on digging the creature up and eating it rather than letting it be.

You've heard it said, so-and-so is happy as a clam. And so I was, just ask Olive. And maybe there's a logic to the body ending up buried like a clam after the clamming up we do in life to save face and keep peace. There's nothing pretty about a clam, innards full of grit, its foot like a man's dirty old dick. Its shell, though, tide-scrubbed white, there's a thing of beauty with uses galore. Even better is a scallop shell, its mother of pearl a lovely surface for a picture of a bird or a cat. Washing up on the shore, offering themselves as canvases free for the picking, shells never cost me and Ev a cent—perfect for painting on when boards were scarce or my hands hurt too bad to do a full-size painting. Tourists snapped up my shells, locals did too, even if they said they could paint just as good themselves.

I mention shells because I sold one the morning before that March night Ev buried the jar. Sure, my inkling of what he was up to harked back to that day's business, which was capped by Secretary dropping off the pickles. I was glad to see her though I was worn out. I'd been up since dawn making myself useful.

I call her my secretary because she was exactly that. She answered letters when I couldn't, and she was the help who handled the mail orders. She would come by regular to take my finished paintings to the post office in town. She had two little boys, and before they grew up she sometimes brought them along. They'd play on the swing and watch Fred, the trout Ev kept in the well, swimming round and round and snapping at flies. Once her boys stopped coming, she would stick around long enough to take a quick cup of tea before driving off with paintings to wrap and stick in the mail. Ev and I would have got nowhere without her help, I know it. Without mail orders, we would have relied on drop-ins and been at the mercy of drive-bys. For there are two kinds of customers in the world, the curious and the self-satisfied, buyers and tire-kickers.

A little squall blew in as Secretary's car pulled up that chilly March day, just before suppertime. The orange sun shone through a swirl of snow that lasted but a second yet scattered the crows. By the time my helper knocked on the door, the snow had quit.

I was tired, like I mentioned. I guess my tiredness showed when I let her in.

"Aw, shoot, I shouldn't have got you up." She was apologetic, stepping inside. "Ev's not around, is he?"

I slipped back into my corner by the window, happy my secretary didn't expect to be entertained. I had a slew of paintings almost ready for her to take, and Ev had stuck them in the range's warming oven to dry. I couldn't help notice her nose wrinkle as she glanced that way, at the basin of dishwater standing on the range-top and the opened tin of meat waiting to be sliced up. At least our cold spring kept the flies at bay. I suppose maybe she caught a whiff of the rabbit Ev had keeping in the breadbox. I saw that she'd come bearing a present, a jar of something.

"Keeping all right, are you, dear?" Her voice was warm, yet she spoke with a shiver as she loosened her scarf. Its wool caught on the sparkly brooch pinned to her coat. I glimpsed it from the corner of my eye. I think she said her boys had given it to her.

"Now why on earth wouldn't I be?"

Then I remembered the piss-pot needed emptying. There the bucket stood, just below the shelves with the breadbox for storing food. It was kind of comical how Secretary gave it a wide berth—well, as wide as she could—looking for somewhere to set her pickles. There wasn't a square inch not taken up with something; Ev and me had run out of space for our treasures ages ago—old *Couriers*, cookie tins, magazines, dishes, rags. She set the pickles on Ev's chair. Not the best spot, as it suggested the pickles were for him and not for the two of us to share. I didn't say nothing to her, of course. Even the nicest people like to talk, and I feared she thought Ev had no time for her. People get ideas, gad knows where these ideas come from. And there is no telling what people will say if they think you're playing with half a deck.

Secretary was a nimble woman in her blue woollen coat. I guessed she had come from some meeting or other in town or at church. Maybe it was her nice clothes that made Ev wary. She stood on tiptoes to get the pictures out of the oven above the range top. She took care not to let the front of her coat touch the stewpot Ev had left simmering.

I gazed out the window. Another snow squall had started up. "Will you stay for a cuppa?" Flakes twirled past the panes, and even though I wasn't certain there was water in the kettle, it only seemed right to invite her.

"No, no—I'll leave you be, and if I skedaddle quick I might get these in the mail before they close." The post office was a good five or six miles away, in the middle of Digby, past Conway. Far enough that we relied on Secretary using her car.

"Look at that snow. Won't stay on the ground, though. Won't affect the driving." Secretary liked to talk, but not too much. I could picture her before a room full of church women or helping her boys with their homework. The boys keeping still, listening. I smiled and nodded at the clock by the stairs. Its hands were stuck on the same old time they'd been stuck on for ages. Its cuckoo-bird was permanently shelter-less, put out of its house.

"Quite the drive for you. All the ways up there and back. I appreciate it, I do."

I had the addresses ready, scraps torn from the corners of envelopes folks sent their letters in, requesting this or that: cats, oxen, deer, what have you. I'd strung the scraps together on a big safety pin and got up and set them atop the boards in my secretary's arms. Then I laid the obits section from a *Courier* overtop everything to keep the snow off.

But Secretary made no move to go, cradling her burden. "My, you've been busy." And she smiled.

Of course she wouldn't take a cent for helping us out, so I didn't offer one. Ev kept promising to pay her back for the postage as soon as a new batch of cheques rolled in. I left this up to him since he was in charge of the money. He knew better than me about the business of money, that you never knew when it or the work that brought it in would dry up. Even though he hated bankers, he had an in with the one at the Royal Bank in town, a Mr. Sutherland.

Still Secretary lingered, and eyed me in a funny way. I wondered if she was wondering how much we owed her. But that wasn't it.

"You okay, Maud? You don't seem yourself."

"Why, who else would I be? I'm okay. No complaints." I laughed to prove it. Truth was, I was more than just tired. I was wondering, well, ruminating, about some folks who had dropped in that very morning. Couldn't get them off my mind, heck knows why.

"Oh, before I forget." Secretary set down the paintings and dug in her purse. She pulled out a tiny tin of Aspirins and slipped it onto my table-tray.

"Reckon you'll think I eat those like candy." I gave a great big chuckle. But I was thinking of Ev entertaining those people, a family who'd stopped by with their boy and two little girls. They'd been all eyes taking us in. You could say I was fretting about them, just a bit.

"Sure you're not feeling poorly? You don't seem—"

"I'm fit as a fiddle, don't you fret." I glanced out the window, then at the door.

If I seemed poorly, it was just that I expected Ev home any minute and he would have something to say about Secretary and me lollygagging the afternoon away. But I couldn't tell her that.

"Well, I guess that's that." Maybe she'd expected me to ask after the boys? As she gathered up the stack of paintings, I saw that the wind and snow had quit again. When she let herself out, the world outside the door glowed blue and gold.

Matilda's mate, Willard, perched on the mailbox across the road. He watched Secretary leave. I'll bet he had his eye on her brooch. She looked so nice in her coat with its little fur collar, and I remembered the first time we met. My secretary and I, not me and Willard.

One early summer's day not too long after I'd come out to Marshalltown, I had taken myself out by the roadside to pick a bouquet of dandelions sprung from the ditch. One ankle had seized up, then the other, and next I knew I was flat on my arse, so close to the asphalt that if he'd been there Ev would have had a fit. No matter how I tried, there was no graceful way of getting back to my feet, even rolling onto my knees. Sinking down again I figured I'd have to set there till Ev came home from wherever he was, unless some good Samaritan appeared first.

Just as I'd thought this, a car had come along and slowed down, a car I had seen going to and fro, a lady driver who Ev said lived with her husband up the road. "Oh, steer clear of them two," Ev had said. "They think their poo don't stink, you don't want nothing to do with folks like that." Lo and behold, the lady had stopped and got out and walked towards me, calling out, "Everything all right?" Like it wasn't too unnatural to be sitting in a patch of dandelions by the road, and so I couldn't be completely off my nut—that is, I wasn't from the almshouse cheek by jowl to our place. Of course, I didn't like asking a stranger for help. The last thing I wanted was a stranger's pitying look; worse, that roll of the eyes that means you are not where the person thinks you ought to be: Why, shouldn't you be locked up somewhere, somewhere like next door?

But no, this lady had bent down and held out her hand, gentle as could be, and I'd let her pull me up. Even after I'd steadied myself, she kept ahold of one hand and her arm at my waist to prevent me stumbling again.

"Land, first I spotted you I thought, that's a bear in the ditch!" She'd laughed, kind of embarrassed, like she had said the wrong thing. "Then I thought, that's no bear, what bear dresses in a pretty flowered skirt? None that I know of. But seriously, it gave me a fright. I hope nothing's sprained."

"Didn't mean to scare you. Sorry about that." And I had felt my face turn as red as her lipstick. By then she'd said her name, Kay MacNeil, and how she would see me in the window and her husband was always saying she should drop in and make my acquaintance. "But I didn't like to intrude, knowing you have enough on your hands with Everett." She still hadn't let go of me. Polite as could be I withdrew my hand, and she'd slid hers into the pocket of her peplum jacket. It was a nice green gabardine. Her skirt matched perfectly, a getup such as a teacher would wear or a bank teller. "Well, I'm so happy to finally meet you," she'd said, and the sunny look in her eyes was different from when others, like Ev's old mother, said the same thing and you weren't sure they meant it.

Now, on this blustery March day, I peeked out from behind the curtain at Secretary going to her car and the crow sitting there—of course it was Willard not Matilda, I knew on account of his size and the brazen way he stayed put, hoping for a cookie or a peanut or whatever else might get tossed his way. Secretary had nothing to throw to him. I watched him watching her start the engine. He squawked in disgust and flew off empty-beaked. Just like a man, I thought, and allowed myself another chuckle, a chuckle I enjoyed this time. Only then, still peering out, tilting myself way back, I spied Matilda up in the pine tree. I could just see the top of her head poking from the nest she and Willard and last year's brood had only finished building a day or two before.

Watching Secretary drive off I confess my heart sank a little for all of us, with regret that she couldn't have stayed a bit longer, and for Matilda. If Matilda wasn't in for it already, soon enough she would be, tethered to the nest while this year's eggs incubated. Then she wouldn't be swooping down to visit any time soon, she would be playing the stranger even more than I did.

See, I wasn't blessed with the gift of gab. Even if Secretary had stuck around, I'd have run out of things to say, the same as I used to with Olive if and when the indolent and lunatics in her care allowed a moment's peace. I liked how Matilda and I didn't need words to stay friends.

Oh boy, could *she* keep a secret!

"You like that bird better than me," Ev had joked once, watching Matilda peck at a lump of pork fat he threw outside. Instead of hopping up onto the sill outside his window, she hopped right up onto the sill outside mine and perched there for a full minute. She looked right through the pane into my eyes. I swear she could see the picture taking shape in my head, of yellow finches and apple blossoms. She must have liked what she saw, because she gave the glass two sharp taps with her beak.

It wasn't hard to see why the bond between her and I left Ev feeling slightly ruffled.

"For frig sake, I'd like you too if you fed me. That weren't but a bit of rancid fat I threw her. Easy come easy go."

No shortage of things ruffled poor Ev's feathers.

He got really ruffled at people who came and went without buying anything, and at those who he said made you feel beholden. Over the years, he had not grown kindlier to Secretary; he seemed to forget all she did for us by handling the mail orders. He couldn't have done it, with just a bicycle to get around on. I doubt he could have lugged a stack of paintings all the way to town without them getting ruined. Not to mention the fact that he couldn't decipher or write the addresses.

And yet, ever since the day—so long ago I forget now what year it was, 1948? '52, '55?—some fairy godmother had brought us a radio, he seemed to think Secretary turned me into a slacker. Oh, he liked to tease. "You got to earn your keep, girl. Sit around shooting the shit, listening to the radio, you and that woman. Like a pair of white lawn darkies, you'd make good ornaments but that's about it."

I hated Ev's jokes aimed at people over Jordantown way, and I expect Secretary would have bristled at them also. I let him know it, too, how these jokes didn't sit well with me. "Now Ev, I reckon most folks step into their drawers same as we do, one leg at a time, whether they're brown or yellow or white. Or green, for Pete's sake."

"Oh, g'way. See? You're listening to that one again. What else does she have to say? She ought to mind her own business."

"Reckon our business is her business."

"Her beeswax, then. Mind her own beeswax, I mean. Her husband ought to keep better tabs on her. Where's he at when she's gadding about? It's a man's business knowing where his wife is. If he ain't minding her, who is? Why isn't she home with her kids?"

It was after the days of him showing off the first couple of Freds swimming in the well that he said this. "Because they are grown men?" was my reply. Ev could come off sounding cranky, sometimes even silly—just his way of making himself heard. Like Ev himself said about Joe, his bark was worse than his bite.

Still, something made me glad that March afternoon it was Willard and not Ev watching Secretary come and go. I was happy Ev had made himself scarce, wherever he had got to. Never mind that rabbit needed cooked, never mind the piss-pot

needed emptied, though as far as I could tell its hum was softened by the smell of wood and tobacco smoke.

Speaking of tobacco, have I mentioned what's *not* to like
about being in glory?

Well, for starters there's no cigarettes. No chocolates,
molasses kisses or ribbon or clear toy candy either, and you
would be hard pressed to find a gingersnap cookie, or a hairnet
or jewellery. Though of course you can live without these things,
and the latter are but vanities.

But, getting back down to earth, by the time my secretary
hit the road with those orders, I was bone-weary and glad to
have the house to my lonesome for a spell. As I said, she was
not the only human who had come to call that day or that week,
a day and a week that unfolded like most others, aside from the
fact that daylight stretched longer and longer past supper hour
into the evenings. The orange sunlight beaming into my corner
meant another hour or two that I could have made myself useful
and started on another painting.

Something about spring's lengthening days made me wish
the sap that flows in trees flowed likewise in a person's veins.
It just wasn't so. Like my aunt Ida used to say, the spirit might
be willing but the flesh is weak. As weak as the day was long.
For right after breakfast that same morning, Ev had set my
sign outdoors like always, hung it by my window. I do believe
Ev had spring fever, so keen was he to get started on the day's
business. I had barely scarfed down my toast and a cup of tea.
Even though most mornings went like this, this one seemed different, somehow. Of course it helped business if I stood outside
with a painting, held it up as cars sped past. Today he brought
his chair out so I could sit now and then.

"Gonna be a good day, Maudie. I feel it in my bones, see?
Make yourself comfy, set there and don't forget to wave to them
folks whizzing by. Just give 'em a nice wave, make them slow

down and stop, turn around if they have to, come and have a look-see. Let them sniff around—I'll be out back. Gimme a shout and I'll come and give 'em my spiel. Any tire-kickers only in'erested in wasting our time, don't worry, I'll give them what-for."

Once I got settled on the chair he handed me the sign. We'd made it from a child's blackboard, a piece of twine salvaged from the mailman and strung through holes in both upper corners. I had painted it up nice, taking real pains to make it attractive. *Paintings, for sale,* I had lettered on it, and *M. Lewis,* adding a sprig of apple blossoms, four bluebirds, and a big yellow butterfly to brighten it up.

Ev looped the string over my head and round my neck to keep the sign from sliding off my lap. "You warm enough?" He rubbed his hands together. Despite the sun shining down from the clear March sky, the wind coming off the bay sent a rawness into my bones, never mind I was bundled tight as a sausage in its casing. Under my red sweater and coat, I had my apron on over top of my blouse and skirt. Even with my toque pulled down low, in a matter of minutes the wind gave me an ice-cream headache. I could've used mitts, and pulled my sleeves down over both fists. If I'd been wearing my ring it would have snagged the wool. Ev breezed close, rubbed both my hands between his to warm them. I like to think if I had been wearing the ring he would have run his thumb over it, even fondly. In a rush he yanked up my sleeves, rolled them up one by one. "It ain't that cold, now. You want folks to see your hands."

"Think I'm like you?" I laughed as I said it, made my voice as sweet as a song sparrow's. Just as I spoke an oil truck barrelled past spitting gravel, and I doubt Ev heard me. The roar shook Willard from his roost on the topmost bough above Matilda in her nest. For two whole days, those birds and their

yearlings had kept me entertained, flitting back and forth ferrying twigs and grass and more pieces of twine dropped by the
mailman. Back and forth they went until the nest was finished.
A good solid one I hoped it was, that would withstand spring
storms and the heavy snow that was bound to come between
now and Eastertime.

"Fuckin' maniac, slow down! Driving like he owns the
fuckin' road." Ev shook his fist at the driver, way too late. I don't
suppose the fella noticed him in his rear-view mirror. It didn't
matter as Ev launched into a rant. "If everyone burnt firewood
and not oil you wouldn't have nuts like that flying by." Though
I couldn't look up that far, I knew the sun made Ev squint, I
could hear it in his voice. I knew the crowsfeet round his eyes
gave him a kindly look but figured the twinkle in his eyes
themselves would be a sharp glimmer. "Jesus, you wouldn't have
a snowman's chance in hell, would you, crossing that goddamn
road. Wouldn't even be a deer in buddy's headlights."

There's some who would say the silver dollars Ev had for
eyes, so to speak, caused any such glimmer. But I knew that
glimmer was out of concern for me, not to mention the cold.
Sure, on occasion I had glimpsed a look in his eyes that wasn't
coldness so much as it was hunger. It was a look I figured could
be softened with patience—a good big dollop of patience, sure,
which meant keeping my lip zipped and the warmth of my heart
never too far from his.

"Now get to work." He nudged me, teasing again. "Don't
you let the next one pass without stopping, hear?"

Ev sauntered off to junk up the last of the winter's firewood
and disappeared around back.

Having saved a morsel of toast, I reached behind the sign
on my lap, dug the crust from my pocket, and tossed it. Willard
swooped down, snatched it, and delivered it up to Matilda. So
sweet. It reminded me of Ev bringing back my smokes from

Shortliffe's Grocery up in Conway. From my perch, if I tilted my shoulders way back and looked straight up, I could just see the top of Matilda's head poking from the nest. If all went well, a couple of weeks before Easter there would be babies. By the end of April it would be up to Matilda to turf those babies from the nest and teach each one of them to fly.

Wasn't that a mama's job, seeing that her kids figured out how to make it in the world on their own gumption? I figured a woman like Secretary was good at that.

The chair I was parked on wasn't so different from the crows' nest, it struck me. The possibility of Ev's teasing struck me too. *Don't go inside till you've drummed up a bit of business.* Now, apart from the oil truck, the vehicles travelling the road that morning were few and far between. It was months before the tourists would make their yearly migration to this neck of the woods.

Confirming Ev's wisdom on home heating, wood smoke sweetened the air. I suppose the neighbours, fewer and farther between than cars, were snugged up nice and cozy to the wood stoves in their homes up and down the road and on the ridge yonder. A picture of this formed up in my head, a cozy scene of people sitting around a kitchen table. Though I wasn't much for visiting, I could imagine it—a smaller kitchen, I mean, than the one next door where Olive had put the harmlessly insane to work peeling potatoes.

I heard Ev's axe ring out behind the house, just as the mail truck rounded the curve and pulled in by our box on the opposite shoulder. The mailman was early. He waved to me and called out hello and stuffed something in the box. He jumped back in the truck and drove off just as my man came scrambling up from the backyard. Ev rubbed his palms together when he spied the box's little red flag sticking up. I always was touched by how happy he got when the mail came. My teeth chattered a blue streak as he scooted across the centre line, gleeful as a kid, and lifted the mail from the box. He held something up to the sun, grinning over at me like he had won a prize, and crossed back over to our side.

I was too busy keeping myself warm to feel much excitement. I started to get up. "There's not much doin', Ev. Hardly anyone going by. That's enough setting for now, don't you think?" But Ev wasn't listening. He was too busy ripping open the envelope, pulling out the letter inside. I could feel Matilda and Willard and last year's brood watching from the trees. At that moment, a pulp truck came trundling by, travelling way too fast, the driver not giving so much as a wave. When I looked back at Ev, he was pushing something into his pants pocket. A place there was little risk of Joe sticking his snout or a crow its beak—or me reaching in with my fingers, not at this age.

He flung the letter at me. "Here you go." It was on a single sheet of creamy paper. At the top was a lady's name written in a hand like Secretary's, that tidy and perfect, and an address down in Massachusetts. *Dear Mrs. Lewis*, it went. *Your painting arrived in good shape and I want to tell you it looks very nice in my sunporch. The children get a kick out of it because of the snow on the ground and the green trees and hills and the little man in his cap with his horses hauling logs. I told them maybe winter in Canada is not quite so cold as we think. Maybe it's not all igloos and polar bears up there.*

This gave me a chuckle because not a summer passed without Ev and me seeing Yanks speed by, fresh off the ferry from Maine, with skis on their car roofs. Skis in July, while the rest of the tourists, the ones from Uppity Canada, paid good money to drive around with dead lobster traps atop their vehicles.

"What are you laughing at?" Ev's voice wavered up to me, near drowned out by the grab of car tires pulling in at that moment. I tucked the letter into my coat pocket to finish reading later on. Ev beamed a smile at the man behind the wheel.

There was a woman beside him, three little kids in the back seat. The man rolled down his window and Ev leaned right in. "You come at the right time. She's right here, see her?"

The man got out of the car first, then the woman did. She opened the rear door and two small girls and a boy hopped out. Nodding to them, Ev kept up his patter. "Well, ain't you in luck. You even get to shake her hand. Don't worry now, what she got ain't catching. I mean if that's your worry, having little ones and all." He hustled over and raised up my left arm, like a referee raising a boxer's. "Take a look. Them hands ain't too pretty, I know, but once you see her pitchers you'll know what beau-tee-ful use she puts them to."

The two little gals, one just a smidge taller than the other, were dark-haired and cute as buttons. They reminded me of chickadees, dressed alike in dark brown, yellow, and cream-coloured outfits. Ev's eyes lit up, of course. He got a kick out of little children, especially the girls. His eyes worked their way from one girl to the other, then up and down the mother. She was quite a young thing herself, with dark hair like her daughters', and sapling-slender legs in her dark green slacks. You couldn't see the rest of her shape under the plaid car coat she had on—not even Ev could see it, I wager, despite his having eyes that could see through wood if need be! He pushed ahead, waving the visitors towards the house. "Don't mind the missus, she's slow as cold molasses and don't walk so good, I'm afraid. Come in, come in!" He held the door open for them, with all my decorations painted on it. In the bright sun its birds, butterflies, and red, yellow, and blue tulips looked a little winter-weary and in need of fresh paint.

Almost worse than standing out by the road with the sign was having perfect strangers—any old Tom, Dick, and Harry— come into our home like this. Especially kids I didn't know. I felt their curious eyes scour me and each corner of the place where I had shored up my happiness—with Ev's help and with his blessing, of course. But the circle of sunshine behind my window was the one place in the world that felt like mine and mine alone. There, I was as free to roam as the dust that speckled the sun's rays coming in.

I watched out of the corner of my eye as the pretty young missus eyed her husband and smiled. The husband glanced at her. His voice was peeved, impatient. "*You* said you wanted to stop, Shireen. Have a look."

The woman eyeballed me, embarrassed. "If it isn't any trouble?"

Well you're here now, aren't you, I thought.

Eager to please, Ev spoke right up. "It ain't no trouble a-tall. Missus likes her fans stopping by. Have a look, you folks pick a painting; the young fella here, he can help you choose."

I shot Ev a glance. Most everything we had on hand was set to fill the orders for Secretary to pick up that afternoon. He must have forgot. "Missus might even let you pick two, won't you, Missus? Youse take your time looking, Mom, Pop, and Junior, no need to rush. I'll babysit, sure, I'll take these fine young gals off your hands for a bit. Gals, how 'bout we go out back and see my dog and my pet squirrel, how's that? You can see our fish, Fred. If you're real lucky, you might meet my pet crow."

I guess Ev had forgot that Willard and Matilda had better things to do than entertain children, human ones. Assuming either crow was Ev's to call his pet.

"Me too! I wanna come too!" That was the boy, he must have been nine or ten years old. His sisters couldn't have been more than seven and eight. Someone had been busy making babies.

"Copycat!" Both girls sassed their brother. "Dumb arse! Stupid! Stunned!" The bigger one stuck her tongue out.

So much for them being cute as chickadees; all three kids were already getting on my nerves. I hated the way they kept gawking at my hands. Why weren't they in school? Nobody moved for the longest time, they were too busy ogling the stairs, the washboard leaning there, the little bell I'd wrapped in cigarette foil dangling from the drawn-up blind at my window. The bucket with its lid on.

"Hang on, hold your horses—you two stay with us." The mama gripped the girls' hands, gave me a look. I don't know if it was pity or what. The littlest one was caterwauling. "I want to see the squirrel." The bigger one jeered at their brother. "You're not invited. You can't come."

Their squalling hurt my ears. Filling the place with its ruckus, it made it feel like the roof would burst off any second. By now my head was pounding.

"Now hold on." The mother sounded huffy. But before she or the father could stop them, both girls scampered out the door with Ev. They passed by my window, Ev holding each one by the hand. I had to chuckle: after the first five minutes of cuteness wore off, he didn't even like kids *that* much. We had never talked much about having any of our own; except for a disappointment, it hadn't been in the cards for us. Yet here Ev was like the Pied Piper, only without a flute and not to chase away critters but show some off. Left behind, the boy tried to run outside too but the father grabbed on and held him by the wrist. "If you go too we'll never get out of here," I heard the mother hiss. Of course the boy was chomping at the bit to follow his sisters, you couldn't blame him.

"Listen to your mother." That was the father. "They'll only be a second. Whyn't you go wait in the car, we'll get going, maybe there's ice cream somewhere nearby."

"I wanna see the crow. Does it do tricks or what?"

I couldn't tell if the boy was asking me or his parents. I just shrugged, then turned my back to let them do whatever it took for them to decide what they wanted. But the mother wasn't having any of this. "I don't like it," she said in a loud whisper, sounding worried. "You can see crows any old time." I wanted to say, Not crows like Matilda and Willard, you can't. But she slipped outside, to fetch the girls, I figured, so they could be on their way. More, or maybe less, polite, the father and son stayed put. I guessed the boy was a handful, even more than his sisters, which gave me pause. What would *I* have done with a boy like that?

"I just want to see *his* crow."

I just wanted them gone. But business was business.

"Folks nice enough to stop generally buy something. I'm afraid, though, these pictures here are spoken for." I gave the father a smile, and dug through a pile of old cards and that for something to sell. "Hate to see anyone leave empty-handed. She *is* a mighty fine crow, if I do say so—"

Ev came in then, a bit out of breath. "Got her trained good, too. Why, she'll even talk back to you—"

"I want to see it, I want to see the crow—I want to *hear* it—!"

By now I had had it up to *here* with the boy's carry-on. I was even more fed up with the father's tolerating it, though at least he kept his eyes to himself. Truth be told, I was a bit miffed at Ev, too, for making Matilda out to be a plaything for his, for their, amusement. Most of all I felt miffed at the whole family for acting spoilt, and the mother for acting uppity. Then I felt bad for the father who must have meant well, well enough, taking the trouble to stop, trying to please them all. What a good father did, I guessed.

I grabbed the ashtray off my table-tray. It was a scallop shell painted with a cat on the inside. I dumped the butts into a dish, gave the shell a wipe, and handed it to the boy. It could have used a proper rinsing but the boy didn't seem to mind. A smile crept over his face. He kind of reminded me of my brother, whom I had not seen or thought of in years and years, not since before I'd got married. I wanted to mention this; I wanted to say, Hey, what do you know, when I was your age me and my brother got along like a house on fire, we were like two peas in a pod, that tight. Though there were only two of us, not three like you and your sisters. But I sure as heck didn't want to prolong their visit.

Doing my best to follow the boy and his father outside, before I could open my mouth to speak the mother yelled from the car, "Get in here now." She scowled like she was weaned on a pickle, more than fed up. The girls were in the back seat. One of them was raising hell, crying. I could hear her, though I could barely see the top of her head where she leaned against the window. The noise was enough. I imagined her mouth open like a fledgling's squawking blue murder, demanding lunch.

"Jesus Murphy. So much for excitement." Ev cursed something bluer under his breath, spat on the ground. The rest of them piled into the car like they were late for the ferry or something. I sank down onto the chair, glad it was there.

Just before they sped off, the mother wound down her window and threw something. Coins bounced and spun on the asphalt, I would say scattered but that would make them sound plentiful. Ev dashed out into the road to snatch up what was there. Luckily there was nothing coming or he'd have been a goner. He held out the money in his palm, making sure I saw it. A quarter, a dime, and a nickel. Forty cents, ten cents shy of the fifty cents we charged for an ashtray. But it was better than thirty cents, twenty cents, ten cents, or no cents a-tall. Mostly just glad that the couple and their travelling circus were out of our hair, I made excuses for the mother's tightness. "Oh well, what the heck, that ashtray *was* used. And those kids are some handful."

Ev wasn't so forgiving. He kicked the gravel and stomped into the house. Sitting on the chair, I heard him inside, banging pots. After a little while, the smell of the fire and eventually the molasses-y aroma of beans drifted outdoors. I wanted nothing more than to go in and get warm but stayed put, my sign propped against my shins. It was best to leave Ev in peace while he did what a wife should have been doing, fixing lunch and that. Of course, keeping busy calmed him down, I wanted him to be good and calmed down before either of us made a peep, putting the family's ruckus behind us. The smell of roasted tin-can soon wafted outside. By and by he came out holding a saucer. It had a nice big spoonful of beans inside a folded-over slice of porridge bread. He pulled two humbugs from his pocket, laid them beside the bread. "Here—you have 'em. Those spoilt brats wouldn't take them. Imagine, kids that won't eat candy." Gentle as could be, he set the saucer on my lap. "There you go, for your troubles. Don't be saying I don't feed ya." He was joking, of course. I'd never said such a thing. Why would I? And who would I have said it to, Matilda?

I quit shivering long enough to make my voice steady and sweet as pie. "Got a cuppa tea to go with that, Ev?" But I could tell he was still in a snit; it was like I hadn't spoken. Without another word, he slouched off out of sight. I heard the shed door creak down back and Joe's yip and Ev going, "Good boy, good boy." I guessed he was down there doing what he did, having a nip of something or other from the liquor commission. After a while he came up to the roadside pushing his bicycle. His hands looked dirty, there were muddy smudges by his pants' pockets, which looked to be stuffed with something. "I'm gonna go to the bank, see what's what." I wasn't too sure what he meant by this. Everett made it no secret he had no time for banks, or bankers. I supposed a trip to the liquor store, what folks nowadays call the NSLC, was likely in order.

The beans' sweetness made me want more. I should have saved some bread for the crows but couldn't keep from polishing everything off. The only thing that could have improved the flavour would have been sweet mustard pickles, which I couldn't have known my secretary would be bringing when she came to collect the orders. The humbugs made a nice dessert, their peppermint-and-butterscotch taste mixed with the woodsy smell of Ev's pocket. I couldn't imagine why those little kids would turn their nose up at such a treat.

Ev leaned his bike against the house, then took my saucer and brought it inside. Stepping back outside, he kneeled to inspect the rear tire. He groused that it needed air, then glanced up at me on my chair. He eyed me with a kind of awe. At my stupidity, perhaps.

"Well what are you setting there for? You look froze. Christ, woman, are you that stunned? Lounging when you've got work to do. Lord love a duck, them orders aren't gonna fill themselves. You think those pitchers of yours paint themselves? Huh?"

Try as I might, I couldn't stop thinking about the mail I'd received before the morning's kerfuffle. I guess I was full of beans—it was the beans that made me pipe up, any other time I wouldn't have. Maybe the thought of those squalling youngsters just kept on getting my goat. Maybe because all the morning had brought in was forty cents, my tongue got loosened, against my better judgment.

"What else was in that envelope, Ev?"

He eyed me like I was talking crazy, was touched by the sun beaming straight overhead. It did nothing to warm things up, alas. I tugged my hat down lower.

"What's that? What fool envelope you talking about, now? What the heck are you waiting for anyways, Christmas? Jesus.

Set there long enough and you'll catch cold. Git off that darn chair, have yourself a cup of tea and a fag, and get cozy. You want to be nice and warmed up before you start painting." He said it the same way he said some mornings, "Git up and start eating. What do you think this is, a diner? I don't got all day to wait on you."

Before I could budge from the chair he steadied the bike, no longer too concerned about that tire, and flung his leg over the crossbar. Straddling it, he pushed off on one pedal and, without saying goodbye, wheeled out onto the pavement. Heading left, he moved slow and wobbly at first, then getting up to speed, he sat straight as a preacher and pedalled as fast as a man half his age in the direction of Digby. I watched until he was a dot that grew lean as an exclamation mark before he disappeared altogether. He might be gone now for hours or days. I never really knew how long his excursions would last until he came home—it might be that night or two nights hence. Once the almshouse shut and his work there ended, he didn't have to keep regular hours. But as long as there was wood handy and the fire didn't die I could sit in my corner uninterrupted, get a painting done and maybe start on another, whatever it would take to fill back orders.

Yet, as quick as Ev vanished from sight, a weariness overtook me. It was all I could do to haul myself over the threshold, let alone drag the chair inside with me. So I left it out there on the gravel, the sign hung over the back of it.

3.

WORK, FOR THE NIGHT IS COMING

How many years had Ev and me been at this business of ours? Too many to count, it seemed. Ever since a nice man from Yarmouth had come and snapped pictures of us, people kept writing to ask for paintings. They'd taken a liking to my pictures of cats, oxen, horses, boats, lighthouses, wharfs, and happy-looking couples tooling around the countryside in roadsters during apple blossom season. A smiling man at the wheel of an old black jalopy, the lady riding shotgun. The human version of Willard and Matilda. *The Wedding Party*, I called that particular scene, which I admit I was kind of partial to, though the farther Ev and me got from our newly wedded bliss the harder it was to copy the picture with the same delight. You might know how it is with lengthy marriages. It's not that familiarity breeds contempt, or that fish gets old after a time. But sharing your life with the same person day in and day out for near thirty years does feature the odd yawn and less-than-starry-eyed moment.

And think of it: I had been painting and Ev had been begging, borrowing, peddling, caretaking, and scrounging a living for as long as we had known each other.

A lot longer, in fact.

Now, if it didn't get too cold in the house and Ev kept himself busy elsewhere, I could lose myself in my work, even copying pictures I had copied a thousand times. When my hands pained too bad to paint, I could amuse myself reading over letters people sent, like the one that had come earlier. I could play a little game with myself imagining the folks who wrote them, picturing their houses and their faces, their children, their pets. I even tried to imagine their voices, how they might sound.

As I dug out today's letter, started to read it again from the top, I imagined the lady speaking the words in her Yankee accent, the way she probably said "ah" for "ar." As in—if she owned a cow, say—"Got a heffah, you can have ah, if you want ah." I pictured her sitting in her sunporch, maybe it had a nice big fireplace made of beach stones, and my painting on the wall, and the spring sunshine streaming in through the windows, warming it so the smell of paint and turpentine was a genie escaping its magic bottle, a genie waking up after the ride in Secretary's car, then a downhill jaunt in the mail truck, then onto the ferry to rock its way across the Bay of Fundy, then onto a train and into another truck and maybe the lady's car before reaching its final destination, her place.

The picture would be a little piece of my life in Marshalltown, Nova Scotia, making itself at home in her big, beautiful house.

There's a reason they call turpentine a spirit, I guess.

I wondered if the woman was lucky enough to have a crow like Matilda to watch, and to watch over her. Maybe not, as not everyone is so fortunate. Though I could have been wrong about this; maybe she had a whole flock of bird friends. Maybe I'd get Secretary to ask about this when I had her write the woman back.

By now, the fire Ev had banked to warm the beans had dwindled to near nothing. Halfway through reading the letter, I pocketed it again to go and lift a burner lid and poke in a few splits of kindling. The scorched bean can sat there licked clean; Ev had given it his best, it looked like. There was enough water in the kettle to save me traipsing out back to the well, dipping, hoisting, and lugging the bucket back to the house, hoping Fred didn't come with it, all the while wondering if that kindling could fuel enough of a fire to make ice water boil. It was a further trek to the woodpile, a pile which grew shorter as the days lengthened.

The fire was amply strong to heat the kettle's dregs, water enough for a cup of tea. It was a bit of a chore reaching the tea bag Ev had hung to dry from the line strung above the range. It dangled like a mermaid's purse pegged between two of his socks. I almost needed to climb on his chair to get at it but managed to flick the bag down using the fly swatter. Flinging it into my tin mug, I hoisted the kettle, poured in the water. There was a speck of milk in the tin on Ev's windowsill. When the tea looked as brown as could be, I tipped the milk in. Ev was particular about milk. I suppose it came from his upbringing, his notion that a person should only have so much, which made sense when you thought about the cows, poor beasts, giving all that milk and for what? I carried my tea to my table-tray and once I was settled behind it on my little cane-seated chair—all without spilling a drop, mind—I picked up reading where I had left off. *P.S.* the lady had put below her name, *Please find enclosed five US dollars which should cover costs, plus a little extra.*

I remembered Ev holding the envelope up to the sun, just before that pesky family drove in.

Maybe he had gone to town to see about getting that Yankee funny money turned into the real McCoy, Canadian bucks? It was a worry how those greenbacks of theirs all looked the same, aside from the numbers on them. I hoped that whoever helped Ev at the bank would be honest. It hurt to think of folks taking advantage of him on account of his poor schooling, which wasn't his fault. This troubled me more than his habit of pocketing cash without letting me count it first.

It was hard to get mad at Ev, harder to stay mad at him. Before he left, he'd set everything up so nice. My sardine tins were topped up with paint, just so, the turpentine in its alphabet soup can. My clean brushes stood bristles-up in their peanut butter jar. "*Waste not, want not,*" I remembered my father saying a long time ago, and these words remained words to live by, through feast or famine, as Ev would warrant at any time. The green paint barely needed a stir; Ev was way ahead of me in readying things, his way of helping speed the work along. He had guessed at my plan to colour in hills, grass, and spruce trees he'd helped me trace on a slew of boards, scrap wood, really.

Waste not, want not.

I had teased him once: "You've got so good at this soon you won't hardly need me, will you." Nudging his arm, I'd leaned in to feel the warmth of him through his sleeve against my cheek and to breathe in his woodsy, smoky smell. Ev's smell was a complicated smell occasionally muddled by the smell of drink, part and parcel of his man-body's smell of sweat. I imagined the lady in Massachusetts imagining me unfolding her five dollars. How easily Ev had taken to handling the money I brought in—doing like our vows had said all those years back, for richer or poorer, in sickness and in health, what's mine is yours, etcetera. Yet something about those five dollars disappearing didn't sit quite right; it stuck in my craw, and I scolded myself over it. It wasn't like Ev and I were in competition for the money. It would have felt clearer, fairer, if the lady had addressed her letter to both of us.

After I'd teased him, Ev had given me a bashful shove. "Oh g'wan, it's you they want. Not me. But if I can he'p you, I guess that's what I'll do." Putting his face close to mine, he had smiled his smile, playful and bashful both, with that twinkle in his eyes. The twinkle that kept me wondering why, just *why*, are some folks born with horseshoes up their rears while others, like Ev, are not? I appreciated his eagerness to help fill the orders, but didn't like how it made me feel, half useless, a malingerer. No longer up to snuff, I mean. The way my father might have felt when cars replaced horses and rendered his fancy harness work not just quaint but a frill.

Unnecessary.

We all need to feel needed, it's a fact.

And I dare say this points to one huge drawback to being up *here*: the fact of being useless on top of being invisible. Especially when the king and queen bees of usefulness down *your* way make sure some folks already feel this way, useless and invisible, like nothing beyond those uppity ones' noses matters any-old-how.

As for being useful, in life I could do things Ev could not do and other women, women with good hands, clothes, legs, and hairdos, couldn't do either. I tucked the customer's letter into the Pot of Gold box with all the other letters thanking me for work received, then guzzled down my lukewarm tea. The letters proved the point: what I did was make grown adults get over themselves and their troubles, even if just for a moment, and smile, just smile. Even when the down-below world taught them, See here, there's just this one way of looking at things. Like the whole world was an old photograph.

But I had known since forever that it's colours that keep the world turning, that keep a person going.

Thinking this happy thought, I rummaged for my cigarettes, found them buried under the latest *Courier*s Ev had got off the neighbours. He said you could tell a lot about people by what they put out for trash. I would have liked to visit these people, see for myself how they lived and what they were like. But it was true what Ev said: walking that highway would be taking my life in my hands. *"What, you're gonna play chicken with an eighteen-wheeler? Not over my dead body, you ain't."*

The paper matches were right where they were supposed to be, beside the kerosene lamp. Ev kept the box of wooden ones on his window shelf by the range. I lit up and for a second, with no one but myself for company and only Matilda and her murder outside, the peace that wrapped itself round me was as good as a thick woollen shawl. Curled inside such coziness, I blew smoke rings and watched them mix and mingle with sunbeams. These poked through the windowpane, setting the tulips' red and gold aglow. Angling in above the flowers, the sun glinted off the bells tied to the window blind's pull. I fancied its shimmer and glow might be some person's foretaste of glory. Ending in dimness, the smoky rays resembled the fingers that reach down from storm clouds on dull days. Fingers of light my aunt would ascribe to the hand of her Almighty God.

I took a couple more puffs then butted out, saving the nail of the cigarette for later. Using my left fist to brace my right one gripping the brush, I dipped the brush's sable-haired tip into the forest green, knocked off little drips of paint against the tin's razor-sharp edge, and fighting to keep steady, brought it to the board's surface. I pushed the bristles as gentle as I could against the wood's grain, filling in inside the pencil lines Ev had helped trace using the cardboard cut-outs he made. Helping to guide my fists holding the pencil, he said this was the best way to get the work done. It worked all right with square and straight-lined things like houses, barns, wharfs, even the decks of boats above their plimsoll lines, but wasn't so good for fine curves and details, the hills, treetops, grass-edged roads and ponds that needed done.

But, who was I to complain?

Holy frig, he would have said. *Do it yourself, then.*

We both of us knew working by my lonesome I would never, ever fill all the orders. Feast or famine: that about described the life of an artist. Though it took surviving more than one long famine before I ever dared call myself that, an artist.

After I filled in all the green on the first board, I stopped and lit up the rest of my fag. The smoke tickled my throat, cooled my lungs. I imagined them like a hot air balloon lifting me up and out of myself, a whoosh of relief that warmed my ears and filled my belly. I leaned forward on my chair, rested both elbows on my table-tray, and near drifted off. Had I done so, I'd have landed face-first in my picture! But, enjoying the final drag off my cigarette then slowly crushing it out, I straightened up. Ash blotted out the gull soaring inside the spare ashtray I'd rustled up. I could've kicked myself for letting that other one go to that kid for less than asking price. No wonder Ev had left in what some might think was still a bit of a snit.

Regardless, I needed to finish off at least one painting before daylight wore out. It was hard to work once the shadows stretched longer. My window faced sou'-east while Ev's faced sou'-west. When he was around, the setting sun shed light for him to cook by. Even in early summer, the sun working overtime to dispel the house's dimness, the evening light wasn't right for painting. Daylight was precious, I don't need to tell you. Yet it was all I could do just then to keep my rear end planted in that chair and not stumble over to the daybed at the foot of the stairs. I wanted nothing more than to lay myself down for a nap. But

Ev would've had a conniption coming home mid-afternoon to find me out cold.

Every now and then stray brush hairs stuck to the board, damned if I could pick them all off. They spoilt the smoothness I favoured when I could get it, depending on the paints Ev rustled up. Of course, thanks to that kind man from my hometown and the photographs he'd taken of us, by this time people who meant to encourage me were sending real artist's oils. Imagine! Among these folks was a nice man up in Ontario by the name of John Kinnear, who had heard about me and taken a fancy to my work. I had no way to repay his kindness except by trading my paintings for the paints he sent. Secretary helped with all this. But every silver lining has a cloud, and being famous, as Ev was convinced I was, is not all sunshine and all-day suckers. Putting out the number of boards people expected meant using whatever paints Ev could lay his hands on, not much different than when him and I started out. Fame takes you full circle, maybe. I had to use what I could get. Beggars can't ever be choosers, like Ev said.

If people from all over creation want pictures to pretty-up their winter houses and summer homes, la-de-da, they too will just have to take what they get, I figured.

Have another smoke, I told myself.

Lighting up, propping the ashtray between two paint tins, I thought once more of the family that had stopped by that morning. I imagined that boy rubbing his finger over the shell's painting to feel its smoothness. I imagined them driving, maybe pulling into Yarmouth by now to catch the ferry to Bar Harbor or Portland, Maine—or simply arriving home, entering a mansion with lofty ceilings, bay windows, and a widow's walk atop a steep pitched roof, and a cute little lap dog, not a mix dog like Joe, jumping up to lick everyone's faces. I imagined the mother hanging up everyone's coat, the father giving her a kiss, the boy going off to read a book or play with a toy truck or whatever boys nowadays did, the girls running up a long, polished staircase to a vast pink bedroom to play dolls.

Imagining all this gave me a second wind. It only lasted for a minute, though.

Say that crowd's life was nothing like this. Say that family had just kept driving, farther and farther from home, wherever home was. Say those kids didn't even belong to that couple, the couple were babysitters fixing to drop those three little christers off somewhere and keep going. Maybe the real parents were dead, those kids had no mama or papa to coddle them. Of course, I was thinking of my Ev growing up next door, back when the almshouse was actually a poor farm, and his ne'er-do-well father and his mother were stuck there. Not only poor Ev, but all the other folks locked up there over the years through no fault of their own. At least my people had had means, unlike Ev's people. Hard as things could be, I'd had a loving mama and father a lot longer than many folks do. Though seeing a mother live to old age like Ev's had was no blessing either, not when a life is more or less lived like a sledge being hauled daily from a gravel pit.

Remembering Ev's ma made me feel for my ring. I wished to high heaven it would have slipped over any one of my knuckles. I'd even tried, to no avail, pushing it onto my pinky with a slick of wet soap, and, when that didn't work, a bit of pork grease. And I pictured the ring in the little box where I'd put it for safekeeping—the box my brooch had come in, a tiny palette with dots of red, blue, and yellow glass for paint, a present from a lady who wrote about me. Oh it was a sad day when I said goodbye to wearing my ring, but a happy one when that brooch arrived in the mail. I had tucked the ring into the nest of cotton batting inside the brooch's tiny box and hid it in the narrow basket by my windowsill. The basket was a pretty thing made of split ash by an Indian lady over Bear River way, though I couldn't begin to tell you how I came to have it. I can't remember everything, you know.

Running my fingers over the basket's pinkish strips of shaved wood, I snapped out of myself long enough to add the finishing touches to that first picture, along with my John Henry. *LEWIS*, I stroked in, real careful. My hands were too tired to put in *MAUD* and the usual dot after it, but my last name would do. I got up off my chair and hobbled to the range and somehow made myself tall enough to reach up and shove the picture into the warming oven to dry. Stepping back, I staggered a little, almost reeled off my pins. What a scare that would have been, poor Ev coming home to find the door blocked, a body sprawled behind it. I steadied myself, turtled over to the daybed and stretched out.

I had no sooner got comfy, lying there with a smoke in my hand, when I heard a car draw up outside. Seconds later came the knock. It took me a while to get the door. It was a lady come to pick up the cat painting I owed her, the one of Fluffy all white and grumpy. She gasped when she saw me, like she was seeing a ghost—or maybe an angel, yours truly haloed with smoke, hands and apron properly dappled with green paint. Carmelita Twohig, she was, a spinster from up past Deep Brook somewhere, not too far away. She was a dried-up stick of a woman, a bearer of bad news, more often a tire-kicker than a buyer. A person more likely to rain on your happiness than smile upon it. The fire in the range had all but gone out, and Carmelita Twohig brought the cold in with her. Her eyes darted around in wonder—at my decorating, I suppose. Then she looked at me half miffed.

"You poor little dear. Where's your man?" were the first things out of her mouth.

"My husband, you mean?"

With a single eye-swoop, my visitor took in the whole place.

I was able to look up enough to see it. Her eyes came to rest on my apron. Perhaps the paint clashed with its pink rickrack trim? Carmelita was dressed neat as a pin in a green-and-black tweed coat, her hair done up like a bird's nest. Her face was powdered and its surface seemed to crack as she spoke. Her voice was almost pained.

"He's left you here? All by your lonesome? Well. Don't take offence in my saying he's a queer duck—he *is* a bit of one, isn't he."

"What?" I was gobsmacked at the gall of her to barge in then talk so uppity. I chuckled a chuckle that was strictly of the nervous kind. Carmelita Twohig made it sound like Ev and me both owed her some sort of apology.

"Only duck I've got." I only meant it as a joke.

The woman turned pink as the pickled beet juice stuck to a dish atop my magazines. She looked around for somewhere to sit—the nerve of her, uninvited. There was just my painting chair and Ev's and the chair outdoors with my sign on it. After a full minute, she invited herself over to the daybed and plunked herself down.

"Sorry, I shouldn't have said. Whatever your husband might be, it's not my business. But if you need help—" Her pitying eyes raked me up and down as I backed onto and sank into my chair. I felt her gaze come to rest on my shins, where both stockings had slid down around my ankles. Stifling a wince, I bent and flipped through some paintings leaning like record albums against the table leg. My mind skipped back to the days when the wind-up phonograph had stood in that spot, to the wax cylinder we had played on it. It was years since our phonograph had died and that unknown person, bless their heart, had left us a radio. A radio was a lot finer company than a Carmelita Twohig could provide or would merit—though nothing could stand in for for that old record, or the old songs from the movies

Mama and I had loved. But then that radio had brought me a world of music, country music I mightn't have heard otherwise.

I still imagine the Hawkshaw Hawkins, Hank Snow, and Hank Williams records I'd buy if I could, and if they had a machine up here in the otherworld to spin them on. Then we'd be talking glory—cooking with gas, like you people say.

Carmelita's eagle eyes fixed on me as I searched through the paintings. Thinking of my secretary buffered me some. I thought of the day she had found me by the road and helped me into the house. She'd paid no mind to the bucket by the stairs or the clutter, just helped me sit, fetched a hankie for me to wipe my nose on. I'd scraped both knees on the gravel, so she'd wet a cloth and dabbed them clean. The last time I'd felt such a gentle, kindly touch was when Mama was alive and I was still a girl—or maybe later, when I used to get my hair done.

"I'm pleased to meet you, Mrs.—?" it hadn't taken a lot of gumption to say to her.

"Oh. Call me Kay."

"O-Kay. You can call me Maud." Then we'd both laughed, me all dusty from the ditch and her dressed so nice, clearly on her way to town.

"Well, I won't take no more of your time," I'd said. "Didn't mean to trouble you."

"No trouble at all—the store's not going anywhere. Would you like tea?"

Like I was a guest in my own house. "Only if you're making it." I'd laughed. "Only if you'll stay and have some yourself."

A far cry, that visit was, from the visit with the spinsterwoman who sat before me now. Miss Carmelita Nosy Parker Twohig eyed me like there was no tomorrow. I couldn't help but wonder what she had at home to make her act special. The look on her made me butterfingered. Her eyes were on my shin, a black bruise from a few days before when I'd bumped myself on the opened oven door.

"Yours is here, don't worry." Paint a picture of my leg, it might last you longer, I wanted to say, wishing she would quit her staring. "You wanted one with the white cat, right?"

"Nasty bruise. I don't suppose you did that yourself."

"No, a donkey jumped out an' kicked me."

The Twohig woman didn't laugh, she had no sense of humour. Still she gawked, her eyes made that bruise burn. When I finally put my finger on her painting and handed it over, she looked stunned. She held the picture out, studying it. Her eyes had a shine I was used to seeing. A do-gooder's self-satisfaction: pity with a pinch of guilt thrown in. The spinster lady opened her tidy black purse, took out two pink two-dollar bills, and laid them down atop the cookie tin I saved buttons in. Four dollars was the price Ev had agreed on quite a while back. I wasn't about to haggle for one more dollar, have Carmelita Twohig eyeball me any longer than necessary. Since Ev wasn't there, I took the bills and slipped them inside my blouse. It would have been nice if there'd been another dollar to go with the two. Never mind, four dollars was better than none. The bills felt shammy-soft tucked under my shirt, next to my bosom.

I dipped my brush in the turpentine, wiped it on a rag, hoped the woman would take this as a hint to shove off. I just wanted her to git. But she was in no hurry to.

"You should have that bruise looked at. If there is anything I can do to—"

Avoiding her eyes, I made my voice humbug-sweet: "Now why would a body need your help?" I wished I hadn't let her in, wished Ev had never taken her order. "All right. It wasn't a donkey kicked me, it was the range that jumped out and did it."

"Good heavens." She sounded flustered, impatient, when

I was the one whose patience was being tested. Then she had the gall to say, "I don't know why you defend him like you do. Everyone knows what he's—" Her high and mighty voice trailed off.

If she had not been a paying customer, then and there I would have told her to git. I'd of sicced Joe on her. You aren't married? I longed to say. Will no one have you? Though my heart frosted over at her rudeness, my voice melted through.

"I have got my reasons," I said.

Miss Twohig hugged her purchase, looked away. "Ever think of doing dogs or roosters? Make a nice change. I mean, cats *are* best." Then her eyes drifted to my hands—my left one, namely—and I glimpsed what she was thinking. Sure enough, she blurted out, "If he's your husband, how come he never put a ring on your finger? If you're not married to him, why put up with—?" She looked around and I saw where her gaze came to rest, on the chamber pot or whatever you prefer to call it. You could walk right out of here, what's stopping you? the woman's eyes seemed to say. People do not need to speak to say the damnedest things. Now she looked mortified, at herself I hoped.

Proper thing, I thought. Must be nice, deciding for other folks what works for them and what doesn't. So, just the once, I spoke up. "*You* ain't married to him, why the interest?"

Clasping her purchase to her chest, Carmelita Twohig studied the mat that lay between our feet. You could still see the roses hooked into it, despite the wear. Then she opened up her purse again, took out a quarter, and planted it atop my table-tray. "For you." Her voice was regretful, almost apologetic. "I hope you'll spend it on yourself, and don't spend it all in one place." She gave a little laugh. Then, muttering her goodbye, she beat it outside, quick as lightning. I heard Willard and them cawing and flapping around, like crows do. Watching her go to her car, I saw two yearlings swoosh down past her head, Willard supervising from atop the mailbox till she got in and drove off. As they flew back up to roost in the trees I felt for the spinster's bills, making sure both were safe. I set the quarter out where Ev would see it someday, maybe, next to his shaving brush.

By now it was near chilly enough to see my breath, yet my face burned. I kept thinking of how I should have answered the woman back. How I should have pointed out that I had painted more than my lion's share of dogs, horses, oxen, and swans, not just cats and bluebirds. I wished Secretary had been there to set the woman straight.

Let me tell you, I was that glad when Secretary's car pulled up soon after—like a gift from above, only ten minutes too late. She was coming from town, like I told you before, to pick up the orders and put them in the mail. She'd passed Ev on his bicycle a few miles up the road near Conway, she said, all in a rush. She pulled the pickles from her bag, mentioned she'd bought them at the Baptist church bazaar in Barton. She cut herself off. "Is something wrong, Maud? Gosh, are you okay? Is it Ev, something's happened?"

"Nothing a good night's sleep won't fix. Don't mind me." I smiled at her, and thought how in this neck of the woods, maybe in the whole of Nova Scotia, it was just a given that everyone knew everyone else, at least anyone who got around a-tall. I longed to complain to her about the Twohig woman. But, dollars to doughnuts, she and Carmelita Twohig were acquainted, or at least knew of each other.

I opened a tin with one last toffee in it, held it out to her. Like I said, folks talk. One person's word against another spreads like wildfire, and just because Secretary was a helpmate didn't mean she was above this. She wouldn't take the candy. I slipped it onto my tray for later.

Secretary was also the type who didn't sit still, always busy helping somebody out—I suppose it was the mother in her.

"Now don't you fret about me, hear?"

Glancing over at the candy, she gave me the eye. "My, you look hungry. Could I fix you a bite to go with the pickles, before Ev gets home?"

I'd have liked that, I'd have liked her to stay for a spell, but we both knew she had best skedaddle before Ev arrived. "Well thanks. That's nice of you. But you've done more than enough just stopping by. Don't want to hold you up. We'll enjoy your pickles, we sure will."

Her eyes darted to the window. She was watching for him, I knew, anxious to grab the orders and be on her way.

"Can I offer you something for your trouble?" A card, an ashtray, a trinket of some sort, I meant, though I had none of these to give. And of course she would say no, she helped us out of the goodness of her heart. True to this goodness she shook her head, then hesitated.

"You can tell me, you know. Whatever's on your mind. And what's with those birds? Good Lord. Glad I'm not superstitious, 'one crow sorrow' and all that. Now, if something's not right... you can trust me. I won't say anything."

"Ah, you got better things to do than listen to *this* old crow's worries." I gave a playful snort, glimpsed her smile. She had the kindest eyes, my secretary did. As she bit her tongue, I admired the string of pearls around her neck. The pearls gleamed like a person's eyes in the gloaming of nightfall. "It's just, well, someone was here asking why don't I paint something else for a change. Something besides cats."

"Pfft." Secretary rolled her eyes. "Who was? Do I know him?"

"Her. Oh no, a tourist is all." A tiny fib. White as Fluffy and just as harmless.

"Early in the season for those Uppity-Canadians-from-away,

isn't it." She snickered, as amused by summer people as Ev and me were. "Like what, though? What did she mean, this 'someone'? Is there something else you'd like to do?"

Fly to the moon? I thought, giving her question but a moment's pause. I gazed out the window. "Crows. If I had more time, oh yes, I might like to try painting crows."

"You've got plenty to draw from, that flock outside," Secretary said, following my gaze. "They're smart, crows, but not exactly cheery. They might be a little dark"—Secretary drew in her breath—"but, why the heck not? You paint 'em, I'll post 'em. I don't doubt for a second they'd catch on. Now, you're sure there's nothing I can fix for you?"

I shrugged and gave her a big smile. Leave it to my helper, she had boosted my spirits more than I could've hoped for. She smiled right back, gave me a hug, and before I knew it was on her way. The only signs she'd been there were the pickles in their jar and the shrunk-down stack of paintings.

4.

A GOOD MAN IS
HARD TO FIND

*Hours after my secretary left, dusk fell deep enough to justify light-*ing the lamp. The kerosene's smell brought back memories of kids in school years ago, kids poorer than I could have imagined being back then, their hair slicked down dark with spirit to kill the nits. A smoky draft filled the lamp's chimney, greyed its glow. I pined for company, not company you had to talk to but the company that was on the radio. Voices swooping in over the airwaves from as far away as Boston and, sometimes, if the radio and the airwaves were extra canny, from all the way down in West Virginia. But there it sat on the shelf, dead as a doornail.

Ev had tried replacing the batteries, but no dice. I could hardly remember the last time it worked. But I remembered clear as a bell the day the radio had appeared, just sitting there on the doorstep. Just like I remembered Secretary's set-to with Everett, which happened pretty much at the get-go. Dropping in not long after my tumble in the ditch, she had bustled around and lit a fire to boil water, as Ev was off somewheres. First I had thought, what, she thinks she owns the place? Then I'd felt grateful. It felt a bit like having Mama come visit, if Mama could've returned from the grave. Except with this woman there was no need to explain. About Ev and me, I mean.

"My husband has known your husband quite a while" was as much as she would say, and that Ev was "a character." But she had put me at ease, adding, "What man isn't, behind closed doors? What goes on in the home stays in the home." So she could see right off how things worked with Ev and me, seemed happy enough to leave it at that. This was a comfort, because I didn't need someone coming in and rocking the boat. Marriage being a dinghy you don't want to stand up too straight in, lest it capsizes.

She had gone ahead and rinsed out two cups, found the tin with the teabags. "You're company, you shouldn't be doing the work," I said. Sitting in Ev's chair, she'd sipped her tea, bright eyes smiling as she turned her head this way and that, admiring what-all I'd painted here and there.

"Well, there's something else you and I have in common. We both love birds and flowers." Her voice was warm as honey standing in sunshine. Tickled pink, I never asked what the other thing was we had in common. Being married, I guess. Blushing, I'd smiled into my teacup. Kept smiling as Ev's boots disturbed the gravel outside and the door scraped open. Then there he'd stood, caught by surprise, me having company.

"This is Kay," I'd blurted out before he could speak.

"I know who she is." Ev had slouched over, scowling, and lifted the lid to find the teapot empty. "Well ain't that sweet. Man of the house comes home and not so much as a cuppa for him." My visitor had spoken right up. "If we'd known you were coming—" Setting down her cup, she had eyed me like she was that sorry for him getting riled up. "I was just driving by, Ev. Thought I'd check on Maud after that fall she took."

"I bet you were. That's Mr. Lewis to you. I reckon you'd best get back in your car and keep driving. There's nothing wrong with Maudie, she don't need your help." I'd held my breath, braced for his "Now *git*." Instead, he'd turned on his heel and left. My visitor had shrugged and shot me a curious look. Trembling, I'd listened to his footsteps fading. She'd patted my wrist, real gentle, and again I thought of Mama.

"Anything you need, Missus Lewis, you can call on me. I am happy to lend a hand."

And I had thought, well isn't that the ticket—finding yourself flat on your lonesome arse one minute, then having someone so kind and helpful over for tea the next. But then her voice sounded less like Mama's than the teacher's at school the year I had quit: "You must find the time long. It's good you've got your painting to keep you occupied." Then she'd asked, "But is there anything that could make your days more enjoyable?" I'd said my days were plenty enjoyable but since she'd asked, music—music would make nice company while I painted. But before she could answer, Ev had come thundering back in.

"You still here? Your husband kick you out or what? Don't you have kids coming home from school? When I was in school—"

My visitor had shot him a nervy grin. "You got as far as what, grade three, Mr. Lewis?" Her sass struck me dumb. Ev's face had looked blanched, a pale spot high in each cheek.

"Long enough to learn my ABCs. And my Ps and Qs." The pride in his voice helped me find mine.

"That's right, Ev did, too."

Maybe my tone was high on its horse. For my guest had looked a little upset, gathering up her purse and saying goodbye. And I realized too late, this is a person who needs to be helpful, the best kind of helper. I'd figured that was the end of it, though, our friendship squelched before it barely got started.

Imagine my surprise when, a few days later, Ev went to fling the water from washing the porridge pot out the door and there was something on the doorstep. No note, no nothing. It was a small rectangular box the colour of a crow's egg, but without the brown and grey blotches, and it had dials on it. Imagine my surprise again when Kay turned up at the door that afternoon, dolled up in a pretty shirtdress. "Got something for you," she'd said, stepping past Ev. She had a tin of King Cole tea straight from Saint John and a can of cookies with butterflies on it. She set them both on the table. Her eyes lit right up at the sight of the radio. "You like it?"

It was nothing like the radios I had seen in the Eaton's catalogue, with wooden cabinets like the old Edisons had. To show her how it worked, I turned a knob and a crackling noise jumped out. Kay took the radio from me and turned the dial till a voice sprang out loud and clear. The voice had a twang like you imagined the villain Mr. Grimes having in Mary Pickford's silent movie, the one with her playing the piano that Mama and I had loved so.

"There, you can tune in to pretty much anywhere has a signal strong enough."

I was well and truly tongue-tied, but when at last I could speak I asked what I owed her for it. Even if she'd said twenty-five cents I knew I couldn't pay. I looked at Ev and he shook his head. Kay looked at him as she spoke. "It wasn't from me. Even if it was, I wouldn't charge you a cent." Ev's grimace lifted, his eyes brightened. "Don't look a gift horse in the mouth. Oh, and Lloyd, that's my husband, had nothing to do with it either. Though he did provide batteries."

Then she'd said to think of her doing her spring cleaning while I painted bluebirds. I barely saw her leave, clutching the radio to myself. Listening to Wilf Carter yodel for all he was worth, feeling the throb of his voice against my breastbone, I thought my heart would burst with joy.

But for two or three years now, not a peep could be summoned from the small bluish box. Same as with Carnation milk, Ev said batteries hardly grew on trees. They reminded me of Life Savers, neat little rolls of candy wrapped up tight. I wished we could have kept their juice from drying out. But as with Life Savers, there was no way of keeping them fresh. For over time, Kay's husband tired of sending batteries, or maybe he simply forgot. But I sure did miss the music's company. How I'd loved tuning in to pass the hours, once it got too dark to work. Especially when they played the Hanks, Snow and Williams, the Carter Family, and Patsy Cline and all of them from the Grand Ole Opry. It had near ripped a hole in my heart when I heard through the grapevine—from the keeper's wife over at the almshouse, Olive—that Hank Snow had come all the way from Liverpool to Digby to play his guitar one night.

I'd have given the world to see him! I suppose he's up here somewheres, if I had the eyes to see, the ears to pick out his tunes from others. If I'd had one inkling when I was growing up about where I would land on the road that runs past Marshalltown, who knows, I might have taken the ferry to New Brunswick, then the train to West Virginia or Nashville, Tennessee!

But it is probably best not to know too much of what lies ahead of you. Just say it's like roadkill at the next bend ahead, what then? If, like a skunk, the future pledges to be black and white, and not exactly as you would choose.

Enough hankering for things that weren't. Cozying up to the lamp, I treated myself to a whole cigarette. But then that Twohig woman's words came back, about me lacking a ring, like Ev didn't care enough to give me one. I wished I'd had the gumption earlier to dig my ring out of the basket and flash it for her. Butting out, I grabbed the basket, shook out the box inside. There on its little bed of cotton batting my wedding band gleamed, pure gold, only a little worn and tarnished in spots. One winter when the snow had got too deep for Ev to trap much more than squirrels and, against my will at first, we'd taken Olive up on her invitations to dinner at the almshouse, he had held the ring up to the lamplight, said his mama had talked to him in a dream: *You fool son, you cannot eat a ring. For land's sake, pawn it.*

"Well," I had said, real quiet, "a mother would roll in her grave, seeing her boy starve."

The very next dawn the snow had melted enough that Ev could set some snares. Before you could say "uncle," he had us a rabbit for our supper. So, he decided. "I reckon that ring ain't mine to pawn off, not really. Though you should consider it like assurance." Insurance, he meant. "Now put it back safe and sound, hear? Since you can't wear it. Though your finger's as good as a safety apposite box. A thief would have to chop it off to get at it."

So you see, Carmelita Twohig was full of raccoon scat; Ev did so care. He cared about me smoking as many cigarettes as I did. Ev didn't like my habit; he'd told the television people when they came. They'd visited one day in late summer the year before, 1965, which is the year things started going to hell in a handbasket, with me falling behind filling orders.

I dare say, like the Yanks walking on the moon, there's hardly a place where men with cameras won't go.

"She ain't very strong. She smokes quite a lot. Them cigarettes is full of poison," Ev had told our guests, the TV folks. "I don't say nothing to her, though."

If I had been smarter I might have chewed my tobacco like Ev did, like he said I ought to. Or given it up completely, like the hospital folks said, quite a while before I croaked and wound up here. The smokes are hard on your lungs, they said. No harder than chimney vapours, I wagered, enjoying every pull off every last fag I smoked. Even when I smoked rollies, a minor complaint, for before I switched to Players, I liked the tins Black Cat tobacco came in, with their pictures of felines with yellow eyes like Fluffy.

The only downside to cats is their delight in hunting birds. I still remember Fluffy skulking through the garden in Yarmouth, arse wiggling as he fixed to pounce on an unsuspecting robin. And how I had to chase him away when that rare and beautiful blue bird came to perch one day on Mama's rose bush. That bird's feathers were the colour of the south seas, someone said. Unlike Matilda, where he came from was a mystery. Father guessed he had been blown north in a gale. I believed he flew off a schooner unloading molasses from the Caribbean, took himself for an adventure winging up from Baker's Wharf just down the hill. The bird liked it so well in Mama's garden he decided to stick around for a spell, kind of foolish since where he came from would be warmer in wintertime, we imagined. Or maybe he didn't want to sail on to Saint John, the schooner's next port of call.

There was truth to what I'd told my secretary, how I hankered to paint crows. Not just any old crows, mind, certainly not flat black ones to be traced with Ev's help, but crows as they were and are. The way I saw Matilda—I sure would have liked to paint her, have her picture as a keepsake.

By now it was pitch dark outside. Nothing stirred beyond the house. The crows had gone to bed. In my mind's eye, I guessed Matilda up: all the blues, greens, oranges, reds, and purples in her feathers' sheen, if you looked close enough when the sun caught the rainbow there—its glistening matched by her glossy beak, her wise brown eyes.

Eyes that had such a glimmer you figured she knew things people didn't.

I tucked the ring in its box back inside the basket, the safest place I could think of for it. I chuckled to myself, thinking how Willard would've liked to get his beak on that ring, and imagined him giving it to Matilda.

It's thirsty work securing a treasure, making a treasure safe. I took a sip of water using the dipper by the range. There wasn't much water left in the bucket, only an inch or two. After Secretary skedaddled with the orders I'd thought of venturing out to the well, figuring it might be some time before Ev returned from his trip to the bank. But then I reasoned that it paid to be careful when it came to drinking; the last thing you wanted was needing to get up in the night. Once Ev carried me up the stairs, it took a lot for me to get down them again.

Ageing. There's not much to recommend it, as Ev used to say.

My thirst quenched, I dug out a clean board, laid it on my table-tray. Stared at it in the gloom. Thought if I could paint Matilda as she was, my life would be complete, I could stow my brushes in the firebox and die happy. But as I picked up a brush, gripped it between my fists, and smeared on a swath of green, I knew my hands weren't up to the task, nor was my sardine-can palette.

There were folks who would say neither me nor my palette ever were up to the task of making art, real art, that what I did was grown-up child's play. No matter how Mama used to tell people who looked down their noses at me, *"Think what you want of her, my Maud can turn out a beau-tee-ful set of cards,"* I wondered if those snooty folks were right. It did no good to dwell on it, of course. There always will be those who think the Earth is flat and that crows are just plain black. But as I stared at that green I didn't see how I could do Matilda justice. Part of me reckoned I had thought too late of painting her. The other part wished it could be enough just to guess up her picture and carry it with me in my head.

Now I am not just up here in the otherworld talking crow, badmouthing naysayers. But unlike humans, birds, all birds, come into your world knowing full well the Earth is curved. I always figured birds had it made in the shade, crows, jays, chickadees, robins, and indigo buntings alike, ranging over this county and the next, the land a ginormous patchwork quilt. A crazy quilt, seeing as how you seldom get two lines running straight out in the country, not like in the widow's walk– and steeple-studded town I was raised in. The fancy, fogbound town I once called home, with its Grand Hotel, parades, movie house, and ships coming and going. My old home. Though it pained me a little, stirring up a long-lost homesickness, I went there now, in my memory.

That fall, the fall of 1927, the weather stayed foggy through to Hallowe'en, winter more than willing to take its good old time arriving. At five o'clock each evening I helped Mama put supper on while Father washed up after work. It was finicky work he did, measuring and fitting out horses and oxen, cutting leather, stitching and hammering straps together, decorating the finished pieces with polished brass studs. My father's harnesses were things of beauty, people said, but in a kind of wilted, pussy-footing way as business ebbed. Surely things would pick up once the snow came and people started sleighing instead of driving cars? And as long as Bill Phillips's Moving Company just down the way from us kept using horses, we'd be all right.

Father took his place at the head of the table. "So, what trouble did you two get into today?" He liked teasing me and Mama, how we whiled away the hours tickling the ivories and painting pictures. This wasn't all we did; in summer we grew flowers. In the centre of the table was the green vase that in spring would spill over with tulips. The pink carnival glass vase on the mantelpiece held a big bouquet of dried Japanese lanterns, but in summer Mama would fill it with peonies the dark red I imagined Mary Pickford's lips would be. The one thing missing in the movies was colour, though half the fun was guessing up the colours things would be in real life if I could have seen them. The yellow of Mary Pickford's hair, the blue of her eyes. A swamp's green, quicksand's brown. The movies' black and white made me crave colour. It made me hungry to paint everything as bright as it looked in my mind's eye.

This evening Father wasn't in the best of moods polishing off his supper. He hardly spoke, but when he did he sounded tired. "It would help, you know, if you two brought in some extra with your painting—maybe get a move on this year with your cards?" Rising from the table, he put on his suit jacket. He had to be at the Majestic before the doorman, Ernest Hatfield, got there for the early show. Mama and I would mosey up later on for the late show. I'd decided I wouldn't mind seeing *Sparrows* again before it left town.

I hoped Emery Allen might have the same idea.

I thought then of the first time I ever laid eyes on the man. It had been a week earlier at the Majestic Theatre—my brother was managing it then. Every other night Mama and I went to the movies; we could because we had passes. Father helped Charlie take tickets, making a little extra dough when the harness-making business no longer kept Mama in quite the style she liked.

Even pushing sixty, Mama would dress to the nines in the very best from Peter Nichol's Clothing Store. That evening, a thick fog off the harbour frizzed the curls that escaped from under her fancy hat—it was one of those late autumn but mild-ish nights when the sea salts the air and people can barely see two feet in front of them, which suited me all right. I was as dolled up as could be, wearing a beaded headband with a flower on it—all the rage, Mama said, which was good and bad. Pretty as I felt wearing the headband, it wasn't like I hoped to draw attention, holding onto her arm.

Sitting in our special seats before the house lights dimmed, I felt like Mama's sidekick, hardly soothed by the bag of penny candy in my lap and certainly not by the gossip being whispered in the seats below and behind us. About who was sick, who was dead, who had run off or got run out of town for bad behaviour. Folks were used to seeing Mama and me together selling our cards door to door. I was relieved when the pianist came out and sat at the piano, and the curtains parted and white script filled the blackened screen. We had waited a good while for *Sparrows* to come to town, though in Yarmouth new features came and went three times each week. The music was Mama's favourite part. I liked music too but not as much as I loved Mary Pickford.

I'll never forget that movie. Mary's beautiful little face soon filled the screen. She was playing a girl named Molly tending a flock of kidnapped kids, fighting off the evildoer Ambrose Grimes. He was some bully, even for the movies, leaving poor Molly scared and sad, cradling a sick baby after saving herself from being chucked in a swamp. A tear slid down Mama's face when the baby died and Molly dreamt Jesus took the baby to heaven, and later on I would understand why. But all I could think of, watching Molly pray, eyes raised up so sorrowful, was Aunt teaching me that prayer "Now I lay me down to sleep, I pray the Lord my soul to keep, If I should die before I wake, I pray the Lord my soul to take." I wanted no such thing.

Mama and I let out a belly laugh when Molly head-butted Grimes into the quicksand. When she turned around and saved him, Mama gasped: "No! Wha' did she do that for?" I didn't answer, I knew it was too soon for the bully to die and that things would have to get worse before they got better and Molly and the kids could live happily ever after. The whole audience cheered when they got rescued. The man just ahead of us laughed out loud when the rescuer asked Molly about a husband and she said, "Ain't never got married, it's just me and the kids," like that herd of youngsters had simply hatched. At the end, when Molly played the piano and sang "Shall We Gather at the River" with the kids joining in, Mama hummed along. She was still humming as everyone poured out onto the sidewalk, where she got swept ahead of me.

Trying to catch up, I stepped on someone's heel. "If you'd pick your chin up off the ground and watch where you're going, maybe you wouldn't walk like you got two left feet!" I had to crick my neck up to see who spoke, a girl who'd been ahead of me in school. I'd lost track of her when I quit. All at once a nice-looking gent came up to us, the one who had been sitting in front of me and Mama. "What seems to be the problem, gals?" He wasn't an awful lot taller than me, and even with fog swirling through the street lamp's yellow light, as he bent closer I saw he had a face that would stop a clock. He had friendly eyes, and as I gazed up at him he smiled. I held out my candy bag, its paper already damp from the fog, nothing but a Chicken Bone, a humbug, and a licorice baby left to pick from. "Help yourself," I said.

The mean gal gave me a disgusted look and slithered off. All I could see of Mama was the paleness of her hat drifting towards Forest Street. Our house on Hawthorne was but a hop, skip, and a jump down the hill—that's how close we lived to the Majestic, that's how lucky we Dowleys were. One street below us was Water Street and Baker's Wharf where ships from all over docked and departed from. Never a dull moment, living there. But until *that* moment, nothing in my life had been half as exciting as looking up into this fella's eyes as he opened the bag, picked out my last three candies, and popped them all into his pocket. "For the road, eh." The fingers that had dipped into my candy bag smoothed his hair's sleekness. As he smiled I caught a whiff of pomade sharpened by the salty air. It had got colder. Any minute now rain would slice through the fog. How big and white his hand looked, his face, too, once we moved out of the yellow light.

"Yarmouth gal, are you?"

I don't suppose he noticed that Mama had vanished. She often raced me home; there was nothing for either of us to be scared of walking alone that short distance after dark, and I could manage it just fine.

"Who's asking?" Without too much trouble, I raised my eyes to meet his, batted my eyelids like Mary-Molly. "The Prisoner's Song" came into my head, the hit song about someone wishing they had someone to love them, someone to call them their own.

"Emery Gordon Allen." He reached out his hand and shook mine. I tried not to flinch when he squeezed it. "You must be—?" He spoke like he knew who I was but wanted to play around a bit, draw out this pleasant little interlude.

"Miss Maud Kathleen Dowley. That's M-a-u-d, no 'e.'"

"Okay, I get it. What's the deal going to the movies by your lonesome? Or was that old lady you were sitting with your ma?"

"Might be."

"Looks like she forgot about you. Guess I should walk you home—don't live far, do you?"

Just then Charlie came outside for a smoke with Joe Bent, the electrician who moonlighted as the projectionist, before they closed up for the night. Father had gone home when the show started, to get ready for work next morning and put on the tea Mama liked having before bed. My brother stood there talking to Joe; if he saw us, he didn't let on. By then Charlie had his own apartment across Main Street, where he lived with his first wife. A good thing, because I wouldn't want to sit at breakfast next morning with him asking who "the fella" was.

He had to have seen Emery talking to me, the two of us heading down Forest Street.

A fella fixing to save me from my life as a shrinking violet, a crippled one at that, I imagined Charlie teasing. Truth be told, I was neither a shrinking violet nor a cripple, not quite. Just because my chin was tucked and I kept to myself, maybe folks took me to be scared of my own shadow? Maybe you know how people can be, thinking they know better than you what makes the person inside the body they're gawking at, tick.

Emery didn't walk me all the way home, but came close. At the corner of Hawthorne he said "Adios!" Then he darted across Forest, hurrying in the direction of the Belvue Hotel next to Sweeney's store. I stood there and waved. He turned around once and waved back.

When I let myself in, Mama was at the piano picking out the tune for "His Eye Is On the Sparrow." "Where'd you get to, my girl? Out there in the damp, you'll get a chill." She gave me a mysterious smile as she went upstairs to bed.

If I'd known then what I know now, I would have said, "Mama, there's a lot worse you can get than chilled." It wasn't till I lived in Marshalltown that I knew what chilled meant. How could I have known my meeting Emery Allen would be part of what happened to send me, signed, sealed, and delivered, into that chill and into Everett Lewis's stringy arms?

That night a full week later, after we washed up, Mama set out the paints. We only had a couple of hours to spare but two hours was better than none, she said. "Seems your father figures painting ought to be more than a hobby. We'll see, I guess, though Christmas is a long ways off. But it wouldn't hurt to get a batch of cards made before folks buy elsewhere. Those Currier and Ives sell like hotcakes at Stirrett's. We could do some scenes like theirs. Though some people do favour store-bought." If we got busy now, we'd have plenty to peddle by December. Her voice was half wistful.

Those two hours dragged as we dipped our brushes until it was time to head out.

There was no sign of Emery Allen before or after the show. The night would've been more fruitful if I had stayed home and painted sleighs and silver bells, though I did love seeing Mary play Molly.

In warmer weather I painted on the little balcony at the back of the house, just above the cellar door. Perched over the back-yard's drop onto Water Street, it had a good view of boats and trains, people and horses, and teams of oxen coming and going. But now that the weather had turned colder with autumn, I painted in the little room above it. Filled with grey-blue light, the room looked out onto the wharfs and low treeless islands in the harbour, almost clear to the horizon. Best of all, it had a bird's eye view of the Belvue Hotel just past the Thibeaus' yard next door and across Forest Street. When it wasn't too foggy, I watched the comings and goings of men, all kinds of men—sailors from the seven seas, cargo being loaded and unloaded off of sailing ships, boilermen shovelling coal into the holds of steamships, and fishermen from fleets of schooners visiting Sweeney's store, just up from the piers, to buy supplies.

I kept my eyes peeled for Emery. I couldn't help thinking about Molly in the movie, how in the end all she had to do was care for ten kids she didn't have to birth, living it up in the fancy home of the rich man who'd saved them. All a gal needed was one good fella.

There was one good-sized piece of wood in the woodbox, and I banked the fire with it. I slid that board ruined with green in behind some rags where Ev wouldn't see it, rags crammed there to block the corner draft. No sooner had I hidden it than I heard him outside, the wobble of his bike bumping and being leaned against the shingles, his uneven gait on the doorstep. When he came inside, surprise surprise, I could tell he was in his cups. Stumbling over to me he didn't speak, just bent and, all wobbly, got me into his arms and hefted me up the stairs. It seemed to take forever. A thread of heat followed us as he fed me through the hatch into the attic and then, without a word, thumped back downstairs on his knees and went out again.

Alone, I peeled off, down to the nightgown that worked like an extra skin under my clothes, then tugged my sweater on over top of it. The bed swayed as I crawled underneath the blankets. A stretch of canvas slung between two poles, it hugged me good-night. All I could think of was that lullaby, *Rock-a-bye baby on the treetop, when the wind blows the cradle will rock.* I imagined Matilda sitting on a nice big clutch of eight or nine eggs, blue-green at the small pointy end, two-toned with grey-brown at the larger, rounded end. I imagined them all hatching, the hatchlings getting dizzy the first time they looked down at the ground. *When the bough breaks the cradle will fall and down will come baby, cradle and all.*

In nature all is fair game, I thought, though the baby mightn't approve. I imagined all of Matilda's hatchlings learning to fly, how thrilled they would be by the view.

Little did I know then how vast that view would be. Blues, browns, velvet greens, rust reds, snowy white, and the greys of wharfs, roofs, shingles, stilts, and pilings that shops and houses rested upon on riverbanks where the tide ebbs and flows like no one's business. The tide pays no mind to people's doings, only to funnelling Fundy Bay's waters in and out, day after day. As far as the eye can see, the bay is the same silver-blue shimmer as a run of smelts where the sun hits it, pretty as the aluminum paint Ev used to spruce up the range and the ceiling. Both range and ceiling started out shiny as the foil from a pack of Cameos when I wasn't pressed to roll my own Players or Black Cats, before daily living covered range and ceiling and everything else with the finest coating of soot.

But can I just say even all the colours of land and sea can't match the wondrous hue of that little bird in our yard in Yarmouth. When the weather cooled, Father had bought a pretty cage to keep him in and for half a season he'd lived in our parlour. Like in my dream, that bird became my friend and confidante. I imagined his deep blue-green carrying within it all the colours of the rainbow. I imagined him talking: "Maud! Maud!" I imagined he would trill. In my mind's ear, he had a gift of gab for all the world to marvel at. And so, in a way, he *did*, and his gift was a marvel to me.

Until I met Ev, that is.

That night in bed I let the March wind's whistling between the shims and joists sing me to sleep, a sweet, gentle chorus. The house sang lullabies all its own without Ev there. Who knew where he had gone, leaving me again? The fact is, I missed him on nights he wasn't there. Off on a bender somewhere—no doubt this is what a do-gooder like Carmelita Twohig would be only too happy to broadcast. Stories about my poor man passed out in somebody's barn or field or under the railway overpass up towards town.

As if I would be crazy to worry about him.

Of course I worried about him, he was my husband. As with deciding your cup is half-full rather than half-empty, you work around a marriage's ebbs and flows.

But that night I was well and truly beat, what with work and visits from troublesome customers—well, in the case of that couple and their annoying kids, the closest thing to tire-kickers we'd seen in a while. So I never heard Ev come back or get into bed, only felt the quake and jostle of him rising in the wee hours, like I told you about early on. The next thing I knew, I was hiding in the moonlight, watching him dig a grave for Secretary's pickle jar. I suppose he'd scarfed down the contents for a midnight snack.

Where I am now, I venture to say birds don't much mess with people, nor do cats mess with birds. They're both a presence here, one you can feel but not see, happy to live and let live. If Matilda's here I expect she is the same, with no call to be vengeful. In life, no one but an owl or the odd kid with a pellet gun ever posed a threat to that bird. But she knew how to be my lookout. I miss that. Because to every rule about living and letting live is an exception, and if it applies here, maybe I ought to watch my back?

I miss watching that crow, I can tell you. Every so often I spy one of her youngsters below, up to no good. But even having wings of my own, wings of a sort, I'm in no rush to swoop or touch down, not for a second, not even on a lazy riverbank or daisy field. Up in the air is where I belong, where most folks belong, truth be told, where they can do no harm—so I like to think. In the pure salt air I'm right at home—high above the smoke curling from stovepipes and chimneys, the smell of fish plants, diesel buses, and trucks bound for the Saint John ferry, and, rare nowadays, the whiff of turpentine and kerosene, spirits that brought light to my nights below.

Now all is light, no shadows are cast by the swoosh of weightless wings.

Nope, I would not trade this weightless state for all the tea in New Brunswick. It's why I was made in the first place, to float above beauty, take it all in. Marshlands, beaches, islands, and the sea are a rolling rug of greens and blues, every hue you can imagine is hooked into it, it's the prettiest hooking made by the happiest hooker. If there's a God in charge of all this, that's what she is, a hooker of borderless rugs. I hanker to see her. Just as, once upon a time, a long time ago, I hankered without knowing it to paint such a view. If a board big enough had existed, if paints could have been had in endless colours.

But it's best not to linger on regrets, just as it's best not to hover over sights you would rather not see. Clear-cut hills, dead stubble on the ridge, thorny fields full of wild asters that tell of oncoming frost, of winter's cold.

Every September, those asters were the first hint of these.

"For now I see as through a glass, darkly, but then face to face," my aunt used to read from her old Bible, eons ago. Whoever's face they meant I hardly gave a hoot, back then. Except, the word *darkly* gave me pause, because people who laughed at my pictures said I'd forgot to put the shadows in. Like the moon's dark side, the shadows were there all right, folks just didn't look close enough to see them. My paintings had all the shadows a person needed: blue on white snow, brown on blue water. The rest of the shadows were ones any fool could guess up on their own. Why spell out something anyone with a brain knows in their heart is there?

Pretty as the view from up here is, it fetches me back to where I set off from on this otherworldly flight. Looking down, I see the cemetery up in North Range, with its border of old apple trees setting it apart from the spruce woods. There's the plot with its polished black headstone. That stone is the nicest thing,

I have to say, that Ev ever spent our money on. My money, I mean, though he acted like it was his. *Wife* is carved at the bottom alongside my name, Maud Dowley, not *The Wife* as some fellas call their women, like they are a broom or a pot. Why, if that Nosy Parker Twohig woman had her way she would tell the world Ev was too mean to credit me as *His Wife*. That's my maiden name carved underneath his name and his parents'. Ev's pa I never laid eyes on, he was long gone to this other side by the time Ev and me wed. I'll wager Ev's father was a rougher, tougher nut to crack than Father, who lies in a bigger, finer graveyard full of worldlier folk than most of us buried on the ridge. Your world's notions of rich and poor, of worthy and unworthy, have a power all their own that would clip anyone's wings and sink them faster than a bellyful of lead shot would.

Now I admit at times Ev's notions got under my skin. "The man is the boss of his wife," he told those television folks who came to interview us a good five years before I was laid to rest. Ev was happy having some ears to bend besides mine. He was outside my window when he said it—or maybe it was a little bird out there shooting the breeze? "Oh, go on, git," I'd have said and given him a good hard nudge if he'd made his remark in the house with me sitting there. Then I'd have laughed to show those TV fellas it was best to go along with what Ev said, give him the benefit of the doubt, seeing how he liked talking through his hat.

They might want to be kind to Ev's memory knowing what befell him, something nobody on either side of any veil deserves. That was a dark time, Ev's passing, even darker than that business of him burying things that weren't his to bury. I can barely entertain such darkness, let alone recount it. It's an awful helplessness that takes over when your hands are tied—or you've got no hands a-tall to intervene with, not even swolled-up, half-useless ones.

Like the shadows you know are in a picture though they're

hidden, life has its moments you wish never happened. And the urge to keep the peace lasts past the grave, I know, with Ev's bones laying cheek by jowl with mine up on the ridge. Now, if I were vengeful, I might say as quick as he would, *Move over, you, quit hogging the dirt. It was me who paid for this plot of ground, not you.* The sound of worms and sowbugs burrowing deep would be the sound of his voice. *There you go, hogging the attention, like always. Always were a layabout, not like yours truly keeping you and the house, seeing as you weren't fit to mind a wood bug let alone a kid let alone yourself.* Such teasing might get to a person if she let it. *That's how it always was, Maud. You're the one you took care of, ain't it true.*

A more vengeful type would step on those bugs and squish them.

If a more vengeful person had feet.

Now here's a confession. When my parents died, those Bible words after *glass* and *darkly,* "but then face to face," made me tremble with hope that I would see them again. But after being married to Ev the same words would fill me with dread, like I would have to do more time with him just as things were. Even yet, gazing down at the road that winds from Digby to Yarmouth—the road that traces my travel from the grave to the womb—what I see isn't all bliss. I can't help glimpsing the scrubby woods where the almshouse stood, and the cage-like monument where our house used to be, handy the crossroads where the road to the ridge meets the highway. Though nothing looks the same as it did in our day.

I guess no one missed the almshouse after it got shut down and when, sixteen or seventeen years after Ev left Marshalltown, a bunch of hooligans set it afire. Good riddance, folks would say, though Ev might've had mixed feelings had he lived to see the place burn to the ground, seeing how he was raised there, and his father and maybe a sister or a brother or two had died there.

It's odd to look down upon the land of the living and think

of any of us belonging to it. With its spruce-wood hills and over-grown fields, this rolling, ragged-edged county stretches down to meet the county I came from. It's a quilt with all the world's colours, and not the kind of quilt that gets raffled at fairs, but stitched of oddments as random as the pickings Ev found on his rounds. No tidy patches, but scraps with selvages as frayed as life gets, though each patch means something to somebody somewhere, living or dead. But this quilt has no neat rickrack borders. Its borders are the ones folks put up in their minds. There are patches for "the coloureds," as Ev called the people in Jordantown, patches for the Frenchies in Saulnierville, as he called the Acadians, patches for the Indians in Bear River, as he called the Mi'kmaq, and patches for the plain white folks in Digby with its churches, courthouse, hospital, banks, and school and nice houses.

Some think God's in her heaven looking down at this quilt, like there's a rightness to it. I would say, Think dirt for embroidery, worn out goods for shacks and privies. Just so you know, on Rag Days at Frenchys I'm a hawk hitched to a downdraft, sighting ladies buying rags by the pound to insulate trailers while their men tinker with cars and cut firewood, like Ev used to, and like Ev on brown-envelope day might blow an entire cheque at the liquor commission, and kids glued to video games scarf down whatever their mamas might rustle up from a can, the way Ev did for me. Sure, now they have Digby Scallop Days and Frenchys springing up all over; the world has changed since I left it. But being country poor hasn't, not so much. Ev and I weren't so special. If things had gone a bit different for me, I might have hoed the same row these mothers hoe, or worse. Though part of me—a small part, mind—might have envied these women, once.

But, like I told those TV folks, so long as I had a paintbrush in my hand I was content. So long as I could paint, I got through what the world dished out.

How well I got through it, you be the judge of that.

I don't aim to candy-coat my time below. What I am saying is, it wasn't ever so bad I couldn't stand it. The way I look at it, I was lucky. Which leads me to wonder, though, if a reckoning lies ahead. All your life you're told you will pay for your fun, I learned it the hard way. I don't suppose the same goes beyond the grave, in the sweet by-and-by.

Now, where was I?

5.

I WILL
LIFT UP
MY EYES

fter Ev caught me out back that cold March night, after he'd put away the shovel and disappeared into the house, I made another quick stop at the privy. Then I paused outside the house to catch my breath and take another whiff of spruce gum. It was tonic for my lungs, as good as a belt of Buckley's cough syrup. I could have asked Ev to pick some up in town at the Riteway but didn't like to. It was just as easy to pick some gum off a spruce's bark and chew on it. It was best not to be fussy, best not to give Ev cause to fret.

It was still dark out as I stood there. Dawn's streaks hadn't yet lit the treeline across the road. The cold through my slippers near turned my toes to iron, but I hesitated before going inside, wasn't sure what kind of mood I'd find him in.

Ev had the fire stoked when I crept in. Sometime between coming home for good, devouring the pickles, and burying the jar, he'd fetched wood from the pile. In the glow of an open burner I glimpsed his face. Oh yes, he had been drinking. In the closeness of the house I smelt it off him. He had the same hangdog look as Joe got when Ev yelled at him to sit. Joe was sweet as a lamb when he knew you had a bone to throw and could curb his urge to take your hand off, lunging for it.

All I could think of was my ring. But I didn't dare ask about it, lest he think I was accusing him of something.

"Here. Have a cuppa tea." Ev poured out the stone-cold dregs from yesterday's pot, which I'd left sitting in favour of fresh-brewed. It was six of one, half-dozen of another, whether you chose hot tea from a used bag or cold tea that had steeped all day. He shook the empty milk tin.

"Next time you go to Shortliffe's you might pick up some more." I modelled my tone after Lamb-Joe, not wishing to sound bossy.

"You might go and pick some up yourself."

Dawn hadn't begun to light the room, nor had the crows begun to stir. But I didn't mind the dark. Like a cat, I was so used to seeing in the dark I took comfort in it. Ev watched me bring the cold tea to my lips, and nodded.

"You got your work cut out for you. When's your friend coming back for more orders? I suppose you had yourselves a big old chinwag yesterday, made no headway a-tall on them boards awaiting." He sucked his gums as he spoke, studying me. I hoped the rag pile didn't look any different with that ruined board, the beginnings of Matilda's portrait, stowed behind it. His cheeks looked rosy in the small circle of light from the fire. "Getting up like you did, coming outside in the dead of night— fuck knows what you were thinkin'. Whyn't you go back up and get some shuteye?" His eyes flicked upwards at the ceiling. His voice seemed to crack, with patience you could say. He rubbed his hands together, warming them, and sucked on the matchstick he'd put in his mouth. The matchstick's paleness bobbed up and down. His eyes had a watery look like they got when he worked at being gentle.

"I'll carry you up any time."

But it was warmer down here, and once I got up in that attic it would be like shaking a tooth loose getting myself downstairs again, especially if he decided to take himself off somewheres. I was already making myself comfy on the daybed.

Ev rooted behind the range and pulled out a board. In the dimness it looked like a half-done picture of oxen, a regular team, a Lion and Bright. I couldn't remember starting it let alone abandoning it. I hoped, come daylight, what was already there could be finished enough to look decent. Ev picked up on this.

"That's a good board, you best not waste it. Like I told you, I'll he'p all I can with them orders. Don't want you getting low."

Low in spirits or low in sales? I didn't dare ask.

It was too soon to start the day's work but I had no more urge to sleep than to venture out into the cold again. Ev lit the lamp like he'd only just remembered it was there. He stooped to run his hand over the daybed where I lay. Despite the draft coming through the wall it was shoved against, it was cozy being close to the fire.

"Next I s'pose you'll want breakfast."

By now the range threw a nice heat, warming the velvet upholstery under my cheek. In no time the air grew toasty, a little wisp of smoke curling from where the stovepipe cut through the ceiling. Ev sat on his chair, hung his head between his knees to sober up. Kicked off his boots. As dawn broke through my window it lit squiggles of dried mud on the mat from their treads. The toes of both his socks showed off his handiness with a darning needle. The poor man had no choice but to be handy that way, seeing how useless I was at such chores.

By and by he rose and dug around for the oatmeal in its paper bag. Someone had brought it over, a lady from across the road, maybe. She and I had been pals ever so briefly, before Ev pointed out how she got in the way, eating up whole afternoons with her visits when I should have been working, making me smoke twice as much while shooting the breeze and drinking us out of tea. He'd have said the exact same about Secretary if Secretary hadn't proven so useful. Ev had soured on the neighbour lady and her husband a long while back, when Ev still worked selling fish. "Two fucking peas in a pod, those two—take take take, that's him, think they can get something for nothing, like I should give my wares away. Him and his missus are just alike, believe you me." It was awkward when gifts of food appeared on the doorstep, no note, no nothing to identify their givers, the same as with the radio. If Secretary or, back when she was still over there, Olive from the almshouse hadn't brought them, I figured they came from across the road. Of course, my Ev had nothing against accepting presents.

The thought of my ring burned in my head.

The oatmeal bag had got gnawed on a bit, by another kind of visitor. Oats spilled onto the floor. Ev used his hand to sweep them into my pretty dustpan and from there into the white enamel pot. He poured in water from the water bucket, put everything on to boil. I laid still and let the warmth from the fire tend to my joints and ease their stiffness.

When the porridge was ready, he ladled a speck of it into a bowl and set it at my end of the table. A wad of *Couriers* made a placemat but set the bowl too high for me to eat from comfortably. I hesitated, holding my spoon aloft.

"What?" Ev's eyes were like Willard's. "Ain't it enough to get waited on? You want I should spoon-feed you too?" He shook his head and laughed. It was his after-drinking laugh, a bit sour. Perhaps he was feeling poorly. He made no move to get a bowl for himself.

It struck me as odd, he generally had a big appetite. "Not having any?" He acted like I had not spoke. "Something wrong, Ev?" I didn't usually ask when he was in one of his moods, figuring whatever was bothering him would eventually come out in the wash. But I couldn't help thinking about that family that had come the day before and how Carmelita Twohig had badmouthed Ev right to my face, him not there to defend himself—what was that about?

Without speaking, he stepped into his boots, pulled on his jacket. Its red and black blurred together like blood mixed with India ink in the weak sunlight just coming in. Without saying where he was headed, he took off again.

I was damned hungry, my belly's growl louder just then than concern for my ring. It could keep for a minute. The porridge could have used milk and a sprinkle of brown sugar. But it was thick and warm, and as I tried to lick the bowl, the sun grew bolder and shyly filled my window. Its peachy glow was only a little dimmed by the dust on the panes.

Ev had brought in wood but forgot to fill the water bucket. If he had remembered, I'd have done my best to wash the dishes. There was enough porridge for a second helping, which I scraped into Ev's bowl and set inside the breadbox atop the other breadbox with the rabbit. That rabbit needed to be cooked yesterday and had started to smell. If it were summer, the flies would've been thick. Short of laying it out of doors, breadbox and all, hoping it froze up a bit, I didn't see how it would keep much longer. Waste not want not: it was a cold day in hell Ev would willingly waste food. *"Are you joking, woman? You never know where your next feed'll come from, it's a fact."*

What a fine feast a rabbit would make for the crows. But I had something a lot bigger on my mind than birds. Listening for the sound of Ev puttering outside and hearing only the wind, I crept to the windowsill, dug inside my basket.

I felt a cold twinge in the pit of my stomach. Sure enough, the ring and the box I had put it in were gone.

So Ev had buried it. Along with some money, for safekeeping? You could never be too careful protecting yourself from thieves, he was always saying. I should have felt grateful for Ev looking out for us and our valuables. Instead, the notion that he'd buried my ring filled me with a naked, restless feeling. The Twohig woman's questions about why I had no ring on my finger itched like ringworm under my skin. They itched almost as bad as did Ev's worries that friend or foe could bust in any old time and rob us blind. If it happened while he was out, what could I do to defend myself? I counted myself lucky to have a man who looked out for our well-being as much as he did. Don't know what I would have done without a sharp businessman like him handling the money. It wasn't like I could walk or hitch a ride to the bank, or stop a thief from nabbing what was mine. Though I figured it would take a real conniver to think of looking inside a dusty old basket for a golden ring.

It was best, with Ev going off on his jaunts, that I wasn't left alone with jars of cold hard cash in the house, with strangers stopping in at all hours, strangers off the road, not to mention nose-minding acquaintances. Pests.

The way I see it, looking back, there was a veil strung up in my life too, not just the veil separating you from me, your world from mine. Call it a curtain with Before I Got Famous on the one side and After I Got Famous on the other. And imagine that curtain made of pictures—photographs, not just of my paintings but of me painting them in the house, every inch of the place gussied up with flowers, birds, and butterflies, and Ev hamming it up for the camera.

If he and I had stayed on the dim side of that curtain, I imagine our money worries would have been different. The same but different. And who knows, if that had been the case, but my ring would have stayed where I'd put it, in the basket. Or that he would have sold it instead?

When after a good long while I'd heard no peep of Ev being about, I put on my shoes, put the rabbit in the dishpan, and flung it out on the ground outside my window, where Willard and them would be sure to see it.

They say murders stick together, that crows have ways of warning each other of danger and spreading news of prey and man-made tidbits to feed on. Maybe their system worked like the party line folks had in the country, or so Secretary said they did, anyways, though I never had occasion to join in on such a line myself.

I had barely got back inside the house when the cawing started—such frenzied delight, I hurried as best I could to the window so as not to miss the show. Willard and one of his sons were having a standoff, peck-peck-pecking at the carcass on the ground and at each other, squawking and tearing the rabbit this way and that till it was nothing but fur and mince-meat. When Willard flapped upwards with what looked like a paw in his beak, the young 'un had the nerve to drag the rest out onto the road—fair game for his brothers and sisters, cousins, aunts and uncles, not to mention coyotes and other hangers-on. I hoped Willard had done right by Matilda and brought her the choicest bit. I cannot imagine being stuck in a nest high in a treetop for days on end, even in the finest weather.

Nor could I imagine Matilda liking interfering visitors dropping by any more than I did.

Much as I felt tickled having folks from all over creation come to see my paintings, even the nicest strangers stopping by unannounced made me nervous. Of course, as we had no phone, the only way they could warn us they were coming was by dropping us a line in the mail. Some folks I was not too keen on seeing or hearing from a-tall, truth be told. When the worldly side of that curtain brightens for you, suddenly a lot more people want to be your friend. They want a bite of the very piece of pie you were hoping to have to yourself.

Even before I got famous, strangers had come knocking.

The worst was when a blue car pulled up out of the blue one fine summer's day, years before the man from Yarmouth came with his camera or those TV folks appeared. At least, the day was fine beforehand. I peeked through the curtains. A lady got out of the car. I only caught a glimpse of the man who was driving, he stayed put. She knocked and I had to get up and get the door, as Ev was out back. Good thing he was, too, busy chopping wood so the ring of the axe kept him from hearing the car and coming up to the house to investigate.

Well, you think that Nosy Parker Carmelita Twohig going on about wedding rings was bad, this one made Carmelita look sweet. When I opened the door, the visitor stepped back and gaped at me. If Ev had been there he'd have said straight off, *You here to buy? If not, we can't help you. Can't you see the missus is busy?*

"Can I help you?" I said, as a person does. Standing there taking me in, this one gave me the queerest look. Her eyes gleamed wet and dark as stones in a fast brook.

"I guess you can," she said, this lady I had never laid eyes on before, swear to God. Her eyes seemed stuck on me, like they might draw me, body and soul, down inside of her. Her voice was sharp, sharp as a pair of scissors, and how I wished a truck had roared by just then to spare me hearing what came out of her mouth: "Hello, Mother." As if that wasn't foolish enough, she said, "It's Catherine. Dowley. I was a Dowley before I got married, just like you. Catherine Dowley, from Yarmouth," she repeated, like this should be meaningful.

I spoke right up. "Lots of Dowleys down Yarmouth way." Cousins and that, I meant, distant relations on my father's side, folks I'd barely met let alone remembered. Why one of them would come calling now, all the way up here in Marshalltown and after all this time, I had no idea. People can be strange, they have their notions. But before I could shut the door on her, this one invited herself in. Stepping inside, she barely gave the place the time of day, I mean as far as taking a gander at the prettiness I had lavished on everything.

Instead, she peered down at me, long and awkward, like a hug was owing.

"Please lift your eyes, look at me," she said, almost begging.

Like I should on-the-spot recognize and throw my arms around her. Perhaps she had heard about me being from Yarmouth and about the cards me and Mama used to sell door to door. Folks remember things like that, they think if their mother or sister or old spinster aunt remembered you, you should remember them too. This gal was too young to remember Mama or me, at least firsthand.

"I'm the one you gave birth to," she said, her words snipping the silence as if it were nothing more than a slip of paper. "I don't know what else to tell you. I am your daughter."

Ev had warned me about people like this. Shit disturbers. Nutbars. The type who get under your skin and take advantage, even when they are full of baloney and you know it. The world is full of 'em, he said.

I'd had people drop in and say, *"Oh my brother knew your*

brother," or, "*Oh my father had work done by your father*," or, "*I remember you coming into the doctor's office, my mother was the receptionist*," or someone else who worked in such-and-such a place and remembered us selling paintings and asking more than so-and-so figured our paintings were worth.

Still, this one's words were a kick to the stomach. I kept my head down, my eyes fixed on a doe I had painted on the wall. There is no depth of foolishness some people won't sink to, not to mention gall. "*Rudeness is the first fruit of a vengeful spirit*," Aunt Ida would say, not that I paid a great deal of heed to her words, but still—

I wasn't a bit shy telling this one off. "You are off your head. G'way. You are no such thing."

I thought of what Ev would say and let it bolster me: "*The first thing I am learning you, Maud, is you don't take shit off crazy people.*" Ev's old advice could have been a sharp-shinned hawk circling round and round in my head.

"I never had any daughter; don't have one now, I never did, and I never will." I laughed out loud at the very notion, a woman my age having a child! "I do not know what you're talking about. You are talking through your hat." I looked as straight as I could into her strange, cold peepers. They looked glittery-wet, and I heard her breath snag. "Now I think you had best *git*."

That quick, I sent her packing.

"You are no such thing," I mouthed from behind my curtains, watching her get back in the car. The roses printed on the curtains' plastic were faded to the palest pink. The woman was slumped over, sort of, leaning into the man in the driver's seat, acting like somebody had died, and it struck me, Oh my, you have got the wrong house, girlie, that's it, you must be looking for someone at the almshouse. Check over there, ask Olive, I should have told her, there are umpteen women who could be your mother and proud to know you, for land's sake. Talk about someone throwing a dart and missing the target by an eighth of a mile. Less, if you aimed to be particular. The poor thing.

See, I did feel pity for her. Enough that I had a hard time settling on my chair again, a harder time holding the match steady to light a cigarette. *Lord have mercy,* Aunt might have said, and, in spite of her churchiness, *Pull that smoke into your lungs, Maud, lickety-split, let it work its magic.* Calm yourself, for Christ's sake, I told myself. There is nothing you can do for that woman or others like her. You cannot let strangers upset your applecart; what right has anybody got to upset someone's applecart, especially someone busy as you are minding her own beeswax, not hurting a flea?

For I knew what it was like to be wanting: why would I inflict want on another person?

Because I had a small secret, shared only with Matilda, about something Matilda knew. Matilda knew about losing young 'uns, after the time an osprey had raided her nest, before her hatchlings were ready to fly. For I had had a baby once, a boy, a long long time ago. He had died at birth. In a flicker, I had thought of him before giving that strange woman the boot. I think I'd even blurted this out, crying "Git!" the way Ev would've.

Why I'd felt I owed her that much of an explanation I do not know. As I'd said the words I had pictured a featherless creature falling from the sky, its wings barely formed. I'd just wanted the woman gone. I did not need a troublemaker nosing around, upsetting Ev. Upsetting us.

And thank heavens I *had* given her the boot. Ev came in minutes later with an armload of fresh split wood. "Sufferin' God! You look like a frigging ghost. It's them cigarettes, I'm telling you, full of poison—that old smoke thins your blood. If you would chew your tobacco like I said, you wouldn't have the same troubles. If you had a lick of sense, you would listen and quit being so goddamn pigheaded."

"You're right." I let him think what he wanted. "Now, if you'd help me outside and bring that chair I'll sit for a spell and watch the birds and clear my lungs."

"About time you learnt the man knows best."

Not an awful lot later a letter had come in the mail. I didn't recognize the handwriting on the envelope, though that didn't mean much. But its look gave me a sick feeling. I just knew, even before opening it, the letter would be about something bad.

Sure enough, it was from that same one who had come by for no reason but to upset me. As though she hadn't left me shaken enough already. She was the one Ev could've called pigheaded.

She was on a mission to shake me like an apple from a tree.

The letter said she knew who I was, that I should know she had grown up in Yarmouth, raised by people that knew my father. They were a good family, a nice family, she said. They had taken her in when I gave her up. She was just a tiny baby at the time, and they had raised her up till she went off to get married, when she'd wanted a life of her own, and blah blah blah.

We all wanted a life of our own, I said to the page with its spineless handwriting. I balled up the letter and threw it in the fire, but not quick enough, for Ev caught me going at it with the poker. "You are acting some queer—what's that, a love letter from a boyfriend?" I caught his funny leer but didn't laugh. "The hell is eatin' you? Christ knows what you get up to when I ain't here. So where is it, the money? If there was cash in with that you'd best have took it out."

As if I would burn up cash money! "You think I'm that stunned?" I laughed in spite of everything. Yet, not quite trusting me, he grabbed the poker and thrust it in to turn and prod the envelope. As he did so it curled under a flame, return address and all. I forced another laugh and sighed, wondering to myself, What if I *had* forgot and accidentally tossed in a dollar bill, would you stick your hand in, Ev, to save it?

"It wasn't about an order, don't worry," I said. Which he wouldn't have found too surprising, as acquaintances from here and there often wrote, keeping in touch with news of the weather and whatnot.

Like I said, this happened back when Ev and me still dwelt on fame's dim side, the days on the far side of the curtain that marked where life turned suddenly shiny and bright.

Things weren't the same after the photographer came from Yarmouth to take my picture, and he and his writer friend had it and my story splashed across the *Star Weekly*.

If I had been famous when that woman came knocking, who knows the trouble she'd have brought, no doubt demanding a share of our money. Ev was right: people can be like that, opportunists figuring you owed them, just because. So I learned to beware, for the pictures that man took of Ev and me turned our life inside out—even if it was in a good way. Those pictures showed the world my smiling mug as I posed with my paintings for all to see while Ev played housekeeper. Ev posed by the range making my dinner, so the man and, later, his friend who asked us questions and wrote stuff down in a notebook could see how we lived, how our routines fit together neat as two halves of a walnut.

It was a good thing I had sent that one packing before she could become a thorn in our sides. Of course, living on fame's sunny side, Ev never outgrew his suspicions about the letters I got, letters that came from far and wide. They were all Greek to him. So I understood why they might rile him up—wouldn't you get riled up, too, fearing people were saying stuff behind your back, especially when you could see them talking but not hear them? It would be like that, being hardly able to read; the same, maybe, as being unable to look straight up into a person's face while hearing their every guffaw and sigh. The way the both of us would have felt, sure, if Ev and me had landed in Saulnierville, say, where they only speak French. I would be suspicious of people too.

Still, I tried to help him learn. Tried to pass on to him things I'd learned at Mama's knee. *"Have a seat and I will read you this. Here, set for bit and I will learn you to read it yourself, it ain't so hard, Ev. If I learned, you can too."*

So I would tell him, in the brightness of many a noon hour, that day's mail before us. I meant to encourage him, as a wife encourages her husband, that reading opened doors that otherwise stayed shut. Reading was something that never gave me trouble—well, except for that letter I burnt. But maybe there are two kinds of people: those who take to reading as easy as downing a cool glass of water, and those who choke and splutter and cannot seem to swallow it, no matter how they thirst.

But when that one's letter came that day I counted my blessings Ev could not read. Else I'd have dug the ashes out of the range and scattered them out the door. Lies, she was full of lies, that one. The worst of it was realizing all over again that you couldn't always trust a man to do right by you.

This was a bitter pill to swallow, so bitter I had no choice but to tell myself, as a person does: Put it behind you, it never happened, sticks and stones only hurt if you let them hit you, etcetera. If I was good at one thing besides painting, I reckon it was ducking.

Duck, and before you know it the ones throwing stones get tired and bored and go away. The fact that eventually they make themselves scarce tells you all you need to know about them.

One afternoon that fall, mild for the first of November, I helped Mama put the garden to bed. It took up our whole backyard, plus she had plots out front between the veranda and the fence. In summer these were a burst of peonies, iris, foxglove, and phlox pushing out between the fence pickets, greedy for whatever sun wasn't blocked by the Thompsons' big barn right across the street. My job was cutting and gathering dead stalks before Mama raked leaves from the maples onto her beds. She happened to go inside to get a drink of water. Stooping behind the fence, I worked the shears. Fluffy the Third stalked a blue jay. He ducked past the snowball bush then darted under the hydrangea, and the next I knew he had the bird in his mouth. I dropped the shears to chase him out of there just as someone ambled by on the sidewalk. I peered up through the hydrangea's dried, lacy blooms in time to catch a glimpse of the fella. I was close enough to see his blue eyes. He paused to light a cigarette. It was *him*. My heart near pitter-pattered out of my chest.

Emery Allen was just as much of a looker in full daylight, as handsome as I remembered. I wiped dirt from my hands on my skirt, tried to speak but nothing would come out. I watched him disappear around the corner past Thibeau's. I hurried down to the very back of our yard, in time to see him stop outside Sweeney's store. Then he turned and headed next door to the Belvue. I watched him go inside.

Mama came around back waving the rake. She had found the jay. Its neck was broken, its gizzard left spilling out. "Fluffy's been at it again." She was upset, like I ought to have been. Any other time I would have given Fluffy a talking to—though it was, and always will be, a waste of breath chastising a cat. "I don't know a thing about it," I told Mama, watching her dig a hole under the viburnum deep enough that Fluffy wouldn't come back for seconds.

I had fallen for Emery Allen, oh yes, hook, line, and sinker. He was a man I could look up to without having to look up too painfully far.

I spotted him a day later up by Main Street. He was standing on the sidewalk kitty-corner to Stirrett's store, where I had gone to buy tapioca flour for the dessert Mama was making. Somehow he did not see me, even when I followed him down the hill towards home. Halfway down Forest he lit a cigarette, passed the Belvue, and went into Sweeney's. I knew from going in there once with Father buying hardware that Sweeney's was dim as a cavern inside. It smelled of tar and hemp rope, was crammed to its tin ceiling with bright-coloured buoys, bobs, gaff hooks, sinkers, nets, lines, and pulleys. It was no Peter Nichol's store, no place where ladies shopped. But I had half a mind to go in and pretend to look for something amongst its mess of hooks and blocks and tackles.

I stood outside instead and peered at the window display of foghorns, anchors, and buoys. There was a big sewing machine for stitching sails. Through a drapery of fishing nets, I spied the bottom half of Emery at the counter paying for something. Funny, from what I saw he didn't look a bit like a fisherman, being slight and short of stature.

Scurrying home, afraid he'd catch me spying on him, I did wonder, how *ought* a fisherman to look?

The next night *Don Juan* opened at the Majestic. Mama and I had earned an evening out, having spent the livelong day painting cards. She wanted to go early and keep Father company while he took tickets at the seven o'clock show.

"You go on ahead," I said. "I'll wait for the nine o'clock."

Mama looked hurt, eyeing Father. Who knew what her look meant? I was tired of us two acting like the Bobbsey Twins. Couldn't I have a life of my own? I wasn't a kid, I was twenty-five years old!

Father shrugged, fixing his tie. "Well sure, no harm in you minding the fort, is there, sweet pea. Got your pass for later? Charlie gave you one, didn't he?" The Majestic Dowleys, that was us, always a Dowley either working or seeing a show. With a few minutes to spare, Mama went upstairs to primp.

Before she and Father left, I modelled my dress. Brand new from the Eaton's catalogue, it was cozy brown wool with green and yellow flowers embroidered on it.

"Now where will you be going in a dress like that? Unless you and your mother take up church." Father winked, but his gaze fell on Mama, his eyebrow lifted. "What did that cost?"

"A decent new dress each season is a *must*, Jack."

"And money grows on trees, does it, my darling?" Father's smile was jolly but his voice was not.

"No reason our girl shouldn't be dressed as pretty as any other."

Girl, girl, girl. Would I never grow out of being a girl, their girl? I would be twenty-six next March but felt doomed to be a permanent child. This is what got under my skin; if I felt gloomy all of a sudden it wasn't due to a fooforaw over a dress.

"I'll send it back, then. Got no real call for it anyways." Swallowing my disappointment, I bit back a pout.

But neither Mama nor Father was listening.

"Now look what you've done."

"It's just a dress, Agnes."

"You ought to know it's more than that, Jack Dowley."

"A *dress*."

"If you have worries over finances, tell *me*. Don't be taking it out on your daughter."

"Taking it out? You know I'd give our girl the moon. Eh, sweet pea, you know that, don't you." But Father forgot to wink as he said it, he didn't seem himself. "You should know things aren't the best at the shop. You can count on one hand the folks in town who still go by horse and buggy."

Mama went silent. She checked the tilt of her hat in the hall mirror. "Well then you ought to be glad you've got a wife and daughter bringing in extra. You should be proud of us 'hobbyists.'" The sharpness of her voice made me a little nervous.

"You two are something. I'm proud, all right." Except he didn't sound like he was.

Mama laughed and grinned at me. "Charlie'll have my new pass waiting, won't he, Jack? A penny saved is a penny earned, that's what they say. Though we're hardly in the poorhouse, are we. Not yet."

Father kissed my cheek goodbye. "Keep the dress, Maudie. Don't let me hear another word about returning it." And off he and Mama went.

Pretty as it was, the dress felt a bit tainted now. I started up the stairs to change out of it when the doorbell rang. I didn't want to answer it, as I had planned to spend the time to myself playing piano. Hoping whoever it was would go away, I slunk into the parlour, sat before the keys. By now, my hands were no piano player's hands but I could still pick out tunes. The bell rang again, then came a knock too loud to ignore. I rose and peeked out from behind the lacy parlour curtains.

Of all people, who was out there on the veranda? My land. I nearly fell backwards.

To think I mightn't have let him in, might have let him get away!

Emery Allen filled the doorway with his smile. "So I got the right place, then."

He peeled off his jacket as he stepped into the hall. His gaze flitted about. Pinch me, I thought, I must be dreaming! But I wasn't. It was him and he was standing there looking at me with those blue, blue eyes.

"Nice place you've got here. Your folks do all right, do they?"

I barely heard a word he said, I was so busy devouring all of him that I could with my eyes, breathing in his smell: hair tonic, tobacco, a hint of tar. As I watched his lips move I caught a whiff of Juicy Fruit gum.

After a while my own lips came unstuck from themselves enough to ask, "Cuppa tea?"

"Something stronger, maybe?" He sat himself down on the horsehair sofa by the piano. He squinted at Mama's sheet music propped there. "'Danny Boy.' You play?" He sounded surprised.

"When I'm not butchering whatever the piece is." I was careful not to boast, though I wanted to. My fingers sometimes had a mind of their own. What if he asked me to play? I remembered Aunt's advice: *"Don't hide your light under a bushel barrel."*

"'Twinkle Twinkle Little Star'?" I thought out loud of the nursery tune composed by that famous man, Mozart. Unsure of what else to do, I went over and picked out the notes.

Emery Allen held up his hand, grinning. "It's okay, you don't have to. How about that tea?"

He made himself right at home, with his legs stretched out, his feet in their polished boots on Mama's turkey rug. In the kitchen I fumbled with tea leaves, nearly broke one of Mama's bone china cups. I threw some coconut cookies onto a plate, brought it, the teapot, cups, saucers, and Mama's silver teaspoons on a silver tray into the parlour. As I set it down on the whatnot table, I realized I'd forgot milk and sugar. Emery's hand closed round my wrist.

"No trouble, I'll take it plain."

A sweeter fella I could not imagine. A man who didn't expect the least of what other fellas expected, fellas like my brother, I mean. You could teach Charlie a thing or two, I wanted to say.

Emery Allen patted the place beside him. "Come and sit. Take a load off." It was something Father would say. So I sat, happy as all get-out, taking care not to crowd him. A man like this must be as rare as a cuckoo, I told myself. You don't want to get too close too soon and scare him off. Never mind I practically wanted to paint myself to him. Like Mary Pickford painted onto Douglas Fairbanks. Feel our arms press together side by side, the warmth of our skin mingling through our sleeves. He didn't touch the tea I poured for him.

I could not think of a thing to say; it was like Fluffy had got my tongue and Emery Allen's tongue too. But it was enough just sitting together in the lamplight, watching our shadows barely moving on the rose-patterned wallpaper. If Mama and Father had been there we might have played shadow show, guess the animal, our hands for puppets, or charades.

By and by Emery spoke. "Don't talk much, do you. Not like some women."

When I didn't answer right away he elbowed me, playful enough to loosen my tongue.

"Reckon a person can speak without talking." I took a sip of tea.

"Is that right? I like a woman who doesn't say a lot. Not the type always flapping their lips." He poked his finger into my ribs. It tickled and made me jump. Now he really was like Father, teasing me.

I looked down into my teacup. "There's them that think I don't talk at all."

"Never met *any* woman like that." Then Emery Allen leaned closer. Before I could say boo, he put his lips to my ear. "I know how to make you jump. I could make you talk, how about that?"

My heart pounded. The warm, funny throb that felt so good *and* bad, sweet yet alarming, stirred low in my belly. "How? How would you do that?" I did not need to ask, for he moved closer, slid his arm around me, pulled me to him. It felt like being doused by an ocean wave that was warm instead of cold, that odd. He kissed me on the mouth. His lips were parted. After a bit, I parted my lips too. The tips of our tongues played tag. The parlour faded to near-black. Somewhere the mantel clock chimed, chimed again. The seven o'clock show would just be letting out, Mama would be home soon. She would have a conniption fit if she found a strange man in the house with me. Emery Allen must have guessed something was amiss when I stiffened and sat up. He seemed in a bit of a stir, not quite agitated or fretful, but eager, wanting. His arm tightened round my shoulder.

"Whoa, pardon me, ma'am, see what you went and made me do? Kissing on you like that. You have this effect on all the fellas?"

"What fellas?" I let out a jittery laugh, terrified of Mama coming in and finding us like this. But I could not tear myself away.

"Oh, someone as pretty as you? Must have fellas beating down that front door." He clasped my hand in his, moved it to the front of his pants. Oh my land, it felt like he had a tree root there, a hardness like wood.

"Wish that were true." The second these words popped out I wished I could stuff them back. My face felt pink as my teacup. I edged my hand away. "I mean, oh yes. Sure do. A beau on every block." I asked if he knew my brother, who had lots of friends, handsome fellas who played in a band with him after hours.

"Plays sax, does he? Don't know him."

Mama would be home any second. I knew how upset she would be, and I can't say I would have blamed her. I got to my feet, gathered up the tea things. Here's how sweet Emery was: he was good at taking the hint. He threw on his jacket. He kissed my cheek and, oddly enough, only in the closeness of the hall did I notice the faintest whiff of fish.

"Will I see you again?" I called out after him.

"Sure will, you'll see me real soon."

The instant he was down the front steps, I raced to tidy the kitchen. I was busy practising scales in the parlour when Mama came in.

I was in my corner working away one afternoon that April, waiting for my secretary to pick up more orders, when another car pulled in. As Ev wasn't around, I'd dug out Matilda's painting, thinking I'd give it another shot. Peeking out between the curtains, I glimpsed a black-and-white vehicle with a cherry-red light atop its roof. It looked awfully new and shiny for a Digby police car—but back then they only had one or two officers, so the town could afford to have its cops ride in style. "What now?" I said to myself, like our place had become Saint John's Union Station!

I slid Matilda's board beneath my table-tray, turned it to face the wall. I had no idea where Ev was, he'd gone off on his bike after the mail truck passed without making its usual stop. The way the truck just kept going had left Ev flummoxed. "What gives there? I'll bet that postman's up to no good, those mail folks are up to no good, they're onto us now, momm-itoring the mail for cash, I would not be surprised. He'ping themselves to ours." He had crossed the road twice to check and re-check the box, his fretting had all but devoured the morning's cheer. Before setting out he had thrown me a funny look, like I might have beat him to the post. Or Matilda had, I'd put her up to it—as if she would abandon a nest of eggs just to irk him.

Either way, I sincerely wished Ev were home to field this visit. I watched the officer unfold himself from the car, which had what looked like chicken wire separating the front seat from the back. I'd heard from Secretary that the town police did double duty driving the mayor around. Well, there was no mayor in tow; this husky young man in blue was by his lonesome—oh, one quick glimpse of him and I could see he was one tall, cool drink of water. Yet when he knocked on the door I jumped, nearly overturned paint tins rising to answer it.

I knew better than to yell "Come in" to any old stranger, even if he was the law.

As I pushed the inside door open, he stuck his head in, nodded hello, and touched his cap. Aside from his height and the way it made him stoop, what I noticed most were the sharp creases in his pant legs. As he stepped inside I knocked my hip against Ev's chair and lurched towards the woodbox, all but landed in it. I could already feel the bruising. The officer helped steady me, then he stayed bent over. Even so, I suspect his cap brushed the ceiling. His eyes flitted to and fro, finally lit on me, peering down. They had a bemused look. Was this a kid who had forgot his manners, agog at my home improvements?

"Good God." His voice seemed to crack. He whistled under his breath, and only then did he remember proper behaviour. "I should've told you not to get up, Missus Lewis—you are Missus Lewis, correct? Jesus Murphy, did you paint all this yourself?"

Who else would have? I stifled a little snort, it wouldn't be good to mock a man of the law. "Pleased to meet you—I guess."

The visitor half straightened up, removed his cap. Though I couldn't look up that far, I fancied his bristly hair grazing the silver ceiling paint. I thought of Ev applying the paint not just for prettification but to reflect and keep the fire's heat from rising too fast to the attic and out through the roof. "A science experience," as Ev said.

"Does Everett Lewis live here?"

The cop's voice was friendly enough, never mind its raw edge and the fact this was an awful dumb question. Do crows like shiny things? I almost said, smiling though I was shaking inside. Why does the sight of a policeman strike fear into an innocent heart? Mine did a flip-flop, the tightness in my lungs made it hard to catch my breath. "Who's asking, again?"

He cleared his throat and gave me his name, said he was from the town police and not to worry, he was just out doing some patrolling. That's a first, I thought. I thought of the jar and other things Ev had put in the ground—who knew how many jars of money he had buried?—and things he'd left in plain sight, like two old pocket watches. Every item he brought home was free for the taking, or the asking, that's what he said, nothing was gained by wrongful means—as God was my witness, Aunt would have said. Then an icy chill ran through me.

"Has something happened to Ev? Is something wrong?"

"Ah, no, nothing serious. Just hoping to have a word with him, is all. Issue a little warning. He's been hanging around the NSLC—not quite vagrancy. Loitering, you could call it. Mischief."

Despite his height, from what I saw of his face the man barely looked old enough to drive that car. His cheeks were pink. The badge on his jacket reminded me of the silver dollar I had received a few days back, inside a piece of mail Ev had forgot to open. Payment for an ashtray.

I spoke to the badge. "Didn't know visiting the liquor store was a crime."

But the officer did not seem to hear, stepping closer to admire the board I'd laid aside in order to work on Matilda's. A picture like all the others I had done of Fluffy times three, a row of small medium and large angora cats sitting pretty. Except black, not white as Fluffy really was. Black as crows.

"Cute. Any idea where your husband might be now, Missus Lewis? Or when you expect him back?" His breathing sounded like he had a cold.

I sucked my teeth, let it be known I was thinking on his question. "He keeps his own time, Ev does. Marches to his own drum. Comes and goes." Then it occurred to me, it was on the tip of my tongue to say, It's Carmelita Twohig who sent you, isn't it, telling bad lies about my husband. "The last I heard," I said, "it ain't against the law to take a drink."

He sniffed and swallowed. "When did you last see him?"

I coughed. "You oughtn't to believe a word that Twohig woman says." I breathed in a plug of soft air, smothered another cough. "Few hours ago. This morning."

"Approximately what time?"

I threw a glance at the cuckoo clock above the daybed, its cuckoo bird permanently stuck outside its hidey-hole. "Don't reckon I was watching the time, officer. Time kind of gets away on me, see." Through the corner of my eye, I saw his gaze slide from my table-tray to the empty cans taking up my windowsill to the stack of paintings ready for Secretary to mail, then back to the basket by the sill, where my ring should have been. I had accidentally smeared some green paint on its ash-wood, checking for the ring, which only added to my grief. The cop coughed into his hand, gazed at the basket like it held a secret treasure. Don't worry yourself, I wanted to say, it doesn't. Not anymore. But he had me that rattled I could hardly speak.

If Ev is in some kind of trouble, I thought, I will make it right. I can smooth things over, whatever the trouble is. I would give the cop a picture, get him to forget about whatever he figured Ev had done. Whatever Carmelita Twohig had said he'd done. "Take your pick." Without looking at him, I pointed to the finished boards, just hoped he didn't choose the one meant for a customer who had written all the way from Washington, DC, a man who wanted it for his summer cottage down the shore—when I'd read the man's order out to Ev, Ev had said, "Goddamn, maybe he lives in that White House?"

The officer went quiet, maybe he was puzzled. I cleared my throat, fought my sudden, desperate urge for a smoke. "As you can see, there's no trouble here." I lifted my gaze the best I could to meet his. "Go ahead, take a painting—it'll take your mind off your troubles."

"That's not how the law works, ma'am."

"Oh yes, the law." And I thought of men in suits, lawyers, taking people's money for services rendered or not, and how when Mama died the lawyer told my brother there was nothing left after paying debts. Though he was a good lawyer, an honest one, as far as I knew, not the swindling kind that picks clients' pockets—you heard about such swindlers. No wonder Ev was wary of people.

Then I had the terrible thought that this visit had nothing to do with Ev and liquor, or Carmelita Twohig's idle gossip. Instead, the cop, or someone, had seen Ev carting off boards cut for us at the hardware store and had jumped the gun, figuring the boards were stolen property, not given to us out of the owner's goodness. Donated, in other words. But before I could explain this, the officer let out a sigh and asked if I had heard the rumours.

"You are aware of them, maybe? A complaint came in from a lady who stopped by here."

Oh, here we go, I thought. But before I could fill him in about that Twohig woman, he got ahead of me.

"It was a family, actually—a woman with her husband and kids. You remember them?" His voice sounded tired for a fella his age.

Well, I was tired too—we're all tired, dear, I wanted to say. "Officer. Folks stopping by come a dime a dozen, if you will pardon me saying. Nice as most of 'em are. Whatever you need to talk to Ev about, I can't help you. I am sorry for your trouble coming all the way out here. Wish I could offer you a cup of tea, but—" Something made me blurt it out, even as I waved at the bone-dry bucket with its empty dipper. I didn't suppose I could ask him to run down to the well and fill it. With any luck Ev would soon return—but not too soon, I hoped, not until our visitor shoved off. *What has that fool woman done now?* I imagined Ev thinking out loud, pedalling up to see the black-and-white car parked there.

"Don't worry yourself." The officer's smile came to rest on the tea bags hanging to dry. A tin of corned beef sat open on the range top, the meat inside pink as Joe's tongue. The first fly of the season hummed nearby. I suppose I could have offered him a sliver of meat, to be hospitable. But I caught the movement of him tipping his cap as he stood over me, then he handed me a card. "You get in touch now, if there's anything you would like to talk to me about. If anything comes to mind."

Holding it up close, I saw the card had his name and some numbers on it.

"I sure will." I made it sound like a promise. Of course, he could not have known that even if I had wanted to call on him, short of making it across the road and up the hill to get a spot on the neighbours' party line, I couldn't—it was either that or send him a note. I thought, what would Secretary think of yours truly writing a letter to the Digby police and her being asked to mail it, with no explanation? I would sooner lance a boil or write a crooked lawyer a love letter than write to a cop.

"So long," I said, anxious to have him gone. "Nice meeting you."

He breathed in, the kind of breath you might take with a sore throat. I don't know if he was looking at me or not when he said, "And you too, Missus Lewis. You take care now. Call any time."

I watched him drive off. Poor fella hadn't a clue. Aside from sounding slightly under the weather, it was like he had only just crawled out of his mama's hoo-hoo. Still, his visit left me feeling queasy, thinking maybe I'd best have a talk with Ev, let him know he was the subject of some foolish rumours going around.

6.

WHERE
WE'LL NEVER
GROW OLD

"*For now we see as through a glass darkly, but then face to face.*" That's the full line Aunt would quote from her Good Book. Notice it never said "ear to ear." In Bible days no one thought of phones. Maybe me and Ev should've lived back then? Regardless, the *now* and *then* in that line remind me that you're no doubt wondering how I came to be here, in glory's otherworld. The way many do, it was through a slow dispatching. Ev's dispatching was more sudden, the nature of it, I mean, though his heart had been giving him trouble for a while. There are folks down your way, like Carmelita Twohig, who believe he had it coming, what happened. I would hate to think they were right. Everyone deserves their comeuppance, sure, but no one deserves to get here the way Ev did.

What those same folks don't know, or what they forget, is how when Ev was in a good mood his smile had a twinkle. How, when he wasn't drinking or burying things or being tight with a penny, he could be downright playful, a little kid in a grown man's body. Some would call his scraping together a life "resourceful." I would. I did. More's the pity, then, that he could turn on a person and act like a son of a bitch, that mean. But, like you and me and most of us, he had a side to him few if any folks knew or cared to know.

I suppose, like Fundy's tides, a person can push and pull— it's water under the bridge now.

Or is it?

My path to glory was a different kind of slog from Ev's, the passage from my mama's womb to our plot in the ridge's stony soil. It involved a couple of small meanders, like bends in a brook, before taking a route as straight, and rough, as Hardscratch Road in my hometown. Rough and straight, smooth and winding, every path eventually leads you-know-where. Looking back on mine means gazing in both directions down upon the highway that hugs sixty-odd miles of coast, from the crossroads below me right now—near where that odd monument stands, with a chimney inside that glows red at night like some kind of coronary vessel, as Ev's doctor would say—to back to where I started from. The closer you get to Marshalltown, the more that potholed road appears to be swallowed by woods.

Be careful what you wish for, both Mama and Aunt used to say. Turning famous brought true the wish I'd always had, to do nothing but paint—painting being the very thing that ended up wearing me out and hastening my arrival in this candy- and tobacco-less zone. Dying frees you from misery and all fleshly desires: I'll bet you've heard this before, even if you aren't a believer like Aunt was. I'll leave you to decide for yourself once you get here if it's true.

I left your world for good one whole year and ten days after the Yanks landed on the moon. A Thursday evening at the tail end of July 1970. Your world is a hard thing to leave in summer, wouldn't be half as hard to leave it, say, during a New Year's blizzard or on a March day painted with Sheila's brush. I got planted the Monday next. You might know that I had withered and shrunk so small by then that Ev had the people from the funeral home bury me, ring-less, in a casket you would bury a youngster in. Like a virgin bride, my dowry buried elsewhere in a pickle jar? Ev would have been mindful of the money saved, choosing that little coffin.

Between the hospital and the graveyard I barely recall a thing—a flickering, that's all, like the flame of a kerosene lamp in a draft. A feeling of hovering, like I was an invisible bee buzzing just close enough to people's heads to make them prickle a little. Feel the tingle of a presence that was neither here nor there. A chill, maybe.

The calendar on the undertaker's wall was from Shortliffe's Riteway and had a picture of kittens frolicking in a basket of yarn. It was a lot newer than the ones Ev and I had pinned up on the walls at home. Beside himself with grief, Ev was being a bit of an arse. "No goddamn way I'm waking her in a church," he told the undertaker at the viewing. I knew Ev was upset, but I wished he would mind his tongue. He had been on a bit of a bender since I'd landed in hospital for good—what husband wouldn't be?

The undertaker bit his tongue. "Now, think what your loved one would want. Nothing wrong with a nice little service, nice little country church like one in Maud's pictures. The Baptist church in Barton, how about there?"

This still makes me chuckle. I had not darkened the door of any church since Mama's funeral. Despite what you hear about churchgoing being a ticket to heaven, here I am.

Ev dug his heels in, hard. "They charge for that, don't they? Churches and hoity-toity churchy stuck-ups—fuck 'em."

His cussing mussed up the air in that stuffy room where my body lay. The steady glow of electric lamps warmed its dusty rose carpet and wallpaper. The fronds of a big lacy fern riffled ever so gently in my hovering wake. It was far from the first time I had felt on display, you might say. People whispered sweet nothings next to my dead ears. Constable Bradley Colpitts, Carmelita Twohig, and that nameless couple with the three kids could have been there, for all I knew. I had a hard time picking out faces, had no urge to seek out any particular ones. The best part of me, this airy part, hovered in the wings whistling, "Jimmy crack corn and I don't care."

"There's a lady minister out your way might do it as a favour, if you ask nicely," the undertaker told Ev.

That's when the flickers went from grey to black, and everything before me blew apart and scattered like dandelion seeds. It was a bit like having a song's yodelling cut out when the radio died.

Everything went silent and still and dark as your arse until the following Monday afternoon on the ridge. All at once, sound and light came rushing back. It started with the wind shuffling leaves. Soon the sun and clouds were dancing do-si-do, and I was no more a body jammed inside that narrow pine box than I was my old self sitting pretty in my corner painting cats. Before a person could cry "uncle" I was shimmying and shifting, sprouting leaves then feathers—feathers you couldn't see, mind you, but I could feel—and floating above people's heads, looking down at fancy hairdos, and bald spots turning pink in the sun. It was quite a scene. Men and women, most of them old, peered down over the lip of a fresh-dug hole in the earth. Worms wiggled free of the sunlight. I spotted Secretary. She and a few other women I had not seen in a dog's age wept into crumpled tissues. Gazing closer, I perused the rest of the crowd. From this height, it was hard to tell friend from foe. Then I spotted Carmelita Twohig, the purse over her arm like a lunchbox. My memory flew right back to the very first time Carmelita had come by the house and introduced herself.

It was March 1963. She didn't come to buy anything, just to snoop around and leave me some bad news.

"Awful sad about Patsy Cline and Hawkshaw Hawkins," she'd said. "What, you didn't hear? It's all over the radio. They're dead. Died in a plane crash. Flying home to Nashville, their plane went down."

Of course, Ev and I had the radio but no batteries. He was worried about money because the almshouse had shut, and with it, Olive's free dinners. Even when money started coming in he said we couldn't afford to buy anything that wasn't a life-and-death necessity. I was fit to give him a scolding until he said, "What do you want to hear the old news for anyways, it's always bad." It was true. I was so sad about Hawkshaw and Patsy dying that I quickly saw Ev's point.

I still wonder if I'll see those two floating around up here, too. Hear the sweet strains of them crooning "Crazy" together, or Hawkshaw by his lonesome singing "Lonesome 7-7203."

But gazing down at the folks gathered for my funeral, I looked for a certain someone in the flesh—not Olive, who had been so kind to me over the years and for all I knew had beaten me to glory, and none of the kind, caring customers from here and there who had kept in touch with letters—but the visitor who had caused me more upset, more grief than a hundred Carmelita Twohigs ever could.

The visitor who had come calling before I turned famous, the one who called herself my daughter.

She wasn't there, thank the sun, moon, and stars. Neither was her father, the man who had known *my* father, I mean—good enough. Of course, it had been ten or fifteen years since that gal had come knocking, and I'd seen her only the once—maybe she was in the crowd, I just didn't recognize her? Now that I was up here out of harm's way, to tell the truth I wouldn't have minded having another gander at her. Out of curiosity, I mean. But then I had the eerie feeling that she might've gotten here ahead of me.

There *was* a lady who could have been my old hairdresser friend from Yarmouth, Mae. I had not seen her in years and years, not since Mama died—so long ago I couldn't be certain the lady was her. If it was, she looked darned good for her age. So she'd stayed in the beauty business? I longed to reach down and pat her blue-rinsed hair. I'd have liked to introduce her and Secretary, they could have made friends. I admit it disappointed me some not seeing my nurse from the hospital, Darlene, or Constable Colpitts.

Chit-chatting softly, my mourners looked out upon the apple trees backing the cemetery, the thick spruce woods behind them. I wondered if Matilda or one of her kids might be hiding there. If so, I hoped a goshawk or osprey wasn't perched nearby.

From the roadside at people's backs a caterwauling rose from the ditch, not a bird squawking but a man. Ev. I suppose he hadn't come up for air all weekend, drinking through a span of days that was but an inky gap for me—a gap the Cat'licks down where you are might call purgatory.

The day was hot but not so hot as to make me fear I'd landed in that place even lower down. A perfect midsummer day, I'll bet it had most of these people longing to take a dip, feel the bay's cooling breezes on their skin. A day I would have near sweltered to death in my corner, the sun beating in thick with road dust. The kind of heat that turns flies stupid but not so bad the birds quit twittering. For blue jays yammered from the spruces. A crow couple swooped in to watch the festivities, then perched atop a big old maple. My spirits leapt up. Matilda and Willard, could it be? I hoped it was. Sun flickered through the apple trees' branches; the fruit was only just coming in. An unexpected breeze stirred the leaves so gently only the birds and me noticed. Out on the bay, miles away, whitecaps looked like gulls surfing its blue. Cape islanders dotted its expanse, crews hauled nets and lines. Closer at hand, the smell of fresh cut grass wafted up. They had groomed the cemetery for my send-off?

Voices quavered. "Abide with Me," that gloomiest of hymns, drifted upwards. "'*The darkness deepens.... Help of the helpless...*'" The loudest voice belonged to a woman in a navy blue dress, the minister. Balancing an opened book on her arm, she belted out the words so as to drown out Ev's wailing. "'*Through cloud and sunshine...Earth's vain shadows flee....*'"

I wish I could have put in a request. There was the hymn Mama used to play on the piano, the one that reminded me of us watching Mary Pickford cradle the dying baby. Then, next thing I knew, the crowd was singing it, I recognized it straight off. "'*Yes, we'll gather at the river, the beauteeful, the beauteeful river....*'" And for one long sweet moment I pictured Mama tickling the ivories, the sheet music before her, me turning the pages when I could still keep up. "Shall We Gather at the River," that was it.

"'*Gather with the saints at the river, that flows by the throne of God.*'"

On that note, poor Ev staggered up from the ditch. He waved a bottle, blaspheming the Lord and anyone else who might be listening. I felt sad for him, almost as sad as I had in life. He was a sorry sight in his ragged shirt, the knees out of his pants, the brim of his cap slipping down. He could barely stand. The reverend broke off singing. She held up her hand, as if to halt that river's "crystal tide." The reproach she fired at Ev was a lot harsher than her warbling about "silver spray" would have you expect.

"Everett Lewis. Shame! Bad enough you denied your wife

the dignity of a proper church service, you hear me? Least you can do is remember why we are gathered, to love and honour our sister." The word *we* rang out, not *you*. Folks said plenty of things about Ev behind his back but no one ever spoke like that to his face.

"Not *my* sister," someone slurred. It was Ev.

With the words of that hymn as armour, the minister refused to shine the "poor you" light Ev's way. A spotlight Ev enjoyed now and then, I guess, for he always did like attention. And he wasn't about to let an opportunity for attention pass without seizing it. For better or for worse.

"Who are you, talkin' about 'my wife'? I don't got a wife. Nor did I ever have one, not the decent kind of wife a fella has every right to expect."

For a moment the breeze stood still. People gawped at their shoes, dumbstruck.

I imagined Mama playing on, no matter what happened, bravely singing even when I fell behind, messing up the sheet music. "'*At the smiling of the river, mirror of the saviour's face....*'" What else could a person do but carry on?

If there's one thing I'd learned in all our years of wedded bliss, it was to pick my spots with Ev. There is a time to love and a time to hate, as the minister read now from her book.

Even if it was the liquor, the old TNT juice talking, what Ev had said was damned hurtful. But the reverend's sass was no less wounding as she broke off reading: "Everett Lewis. You will shut your mouth, or I shall have you removed."

At that, I could have hummed away happily into nothingness, less angry at Ev for being himself than at the minister for calling him up short. Without meaning to she had called me up short too: Oh, I could see the questions on people's faces. How had I put up with my husband's shenanigans, all his tippling? What was wrong with me that I had? I could see a few of the ladies wondering the same about themselves and their men, as if they hadn't occasionally tolerated behaviour they might not or should not have. Only the virgin spinster Carmelita Twohig wore a smug grin.

Ev let out a gurgling sound and slumped down in the grass. He was no more than a little baby sucking from the bottle. The reverend bowed her head and prayed, "'For thine is the kingdom, the power, and the glory.'" People prayed along, "forever and ever, amen." Then everyone launched into "The Old Rugged Cross." Twittering voices wavered in and out of the breeze, "'*The emblem of suffering and shame…where the dearest and best, for a world of lost sinners was slain.*'"

Just as I fancied myself being a bird, each word became a weight chained to my talons, airy as these talons were. Like a fledgling, I all but lost my hovering skills so newly learned. "'*To the old rugged Cross I will ever be true, Its shame and reproach gladly bear.*'" Eyes lifted skyward, the minister pitched the rest of the hymn my way: "'*Then He'll call me someday to my home far away, Where His glory forever I'll share.*'"

At that moment, someone pointed to some clouds gathered over the bay. The sun beamed through a far-off sheet of rain. Lo and behold, a rainbow arced! "Somebody's happy, crossing the rainbow bridge," Carmelita Twohig murmured into a glove worn so tight she could barely wiggle her fingers. Long, spidery fingers that would thread a needle or pluck a hair from paint faster than I could've blinked. Fingers that, despite their owner, reminded me of Mama's piano-playing ones.

"She was *so* shy." I do believe it was Mae the hairdresser who uttered this, speaking of yours truly. Her voice was soft with regret. By now the rainbow had vanished. I wanted to holler down, Forget those sweet fibs about a rainbow bridge and pearly gates. There's no such thing, or if there is, I haven't seen either yet. Though it was early days up here, I admit. Then someone threw a pink carnation at the coffin. The reverend tossed down a handful of stony dirt. Scattering over the lid, the pebbles sounded like a plague of June bugs hitting the wood. Before I knew it, people turned and started strolling over the lumpy grass to cars parked at the roadside. If I could've called out to Mae I would have, though I wouldn't have wanted to startle her as she picked her way in her fancy shoes, taking pains not to twist an ankle. The one person from my early life who thought enough of me to come all the way from Yarmouth, the friend I hadn't seen since she'd curled my hair to cheer me up. Thinking of Yarmouth opened up such a longing that I was almost sorry I had remembered it. But a person mustn't let the present spoil the past, or the past spoil the present. And at present the sunlit breeze was sheer bliss as it riffled skirts, neckties, hairdos. Imagine that breeze as me following close behind as folks got into their cars; it was me listening in, at times shaking my head.

"She was some sweet person. Didn't deserve the likes of that bastard—"

Not always, I wasn't, no sirree, I whispered. For I had my faults like anybody.

"Ev? A goddamn sin how he treated her. And her so *cute*."

Glad you think so, I breathed into the speaker's shiny 'do. You don't know the half of it, I longed to say.

"Sweet!? Shit would've melted in her mouth. Or wouldn't've. However that saying goes."

Now there's one sad excuse for a compliment. I looked around for the Twohig woman, who might've shushed the gal who had said it. Carmelita Twohig might have been many things but one thing she wasn't was vulgar. Where *was* Carmelita when she was needed? I looked in vain for her cotton-candy hair. I found myself pining for Mama's genteel manner, Aunt's upright tongue. I looked all around, before, behind, and even above me. Neither hide nor hair of Aunt or Mama was anywhere to be seen. But like I mentioned, it was early days yet—and I say *days* loosely. I reckoned we had forever—eternity like one big timely whirlpool—to find each other up here.

The "compliment" was one I could imagine Ev paying himself, no crudeness intended. Meanwhile, after his carrying on, suddenly he was nowhere in sight.

People rolled down car windows. Men loosened ties, women peered into mirrors, wiping their eyes. Voices wafted up.

"You know the President of the United States has one of her pitchers."

"Go on! Nixon? A painting of hers? Is that right!"

That voice startled me a little, I recognized it. Carmelita's. What her friend had said wasn't exactly true either, some distant helper to the President had bought the picture—maybe some acquaintance of that cottage-owner in Liverpool? I was in no position to argue or, just now, to care. Not while Ev was a worry. Where had he got to, had he slipped into the woods to sleep off a stupor? Or maybe he had straightened himself out enough to hitch a ride with someone headed for the highway. Stone cold sober, it would have taken him ages to walk those six or seven or eight miles. Even if he'd had his rusty old bike he was too gooned up to ride it, though it would've been an easy pedal downhill from the ridge to the house. *His* house, as he still liked reminding people.

I don't know why everyone was in such a rush to skedaddle. I'd have been happy to see the odd one stick around.

And I am not just talking about the folks below. Never mind Patsy and Hawkshaw, hadn't Aunt promised we would meet up here? Her words exactly when Mama passed. *"That's what the sweet by-and-by is for, dear. The promise of meeting on that heavenly shore consoles us in our grief."* Eager to ease my grief she had meant well, I guess. People say lots of things to lighten others' loads. Aunt had left the world quite a while before I did, and if anyone was bound for a heavenly shore it was her. So it was more than a bit discombobulating not to find her waiting, lounging at the top of the airy stairway to the stars I took to get here. I kept thinking of voices singing that song "If I Knew You Were Coming I'd've Baked a Cake." Already I was sorely missing the sweet taste of sugar. Unlike yours truly, Aunt wasn't one to fib.

Maybe she'd up and got tired of waiting?

You've got all day now, I told myself, don't you be so quick to give up.

When, down below, had I ever given up? I wasn't about to start.

Watching people drive away, dust devils swirling after tailgates, already I missed the mourners and their lifted voices. I knew as well as anybody about forgetfulness, how easily some memories turn like Crosby's molasses warmed in a pot: sticky-sweet but too smooth and runny to give a lot of comfort. Of course, memories stick with us. But folks remember what they want to, sure. At that moment, I was glad they could remember me by my pictures. Cheery, happy scenes that let on there's no such thing as trials and tribulations. For every single one of us has something we would sooner forget.

It should have done me a world of good—when I was down below it would have—hang-gliding over the land of the living and beyond, up to where the sun burns off heart- *and* headaches. Now there are two haitch-words naming things I knew well but used to chain-smoke to forget. Up here, where there's no hunger, sickness, or hurt, you could half believe paradise was one big hitch-less travel trailer, a dwelling you could stay parked inside while the rest of creation rolled merrily along—forget Aunt's old talk of a father's house with many mansions.

Up here, you would think I'd feel nothing but joy.

But joy is a slippery thing.

Life is like that patchwork below I told you about. Not all summer greens and blues, in equal measure it's a grey rack and ruin. Cobwebs, broken glass, shingles that won't hold paint. Yet the prettiness stands. Fundy's pink-red mud, black rocks and cliffs pocked with the nests of swifts. These colours crackle and pop like a bonfire. All this beauty hollers out that the world goes on even if people don't. Our ways are not the bay's or the hills' or the forests' or the birds' and beasts' ways. Show me a cat named Fluffy that'll take another cat named Fluffy by the throat and kill it, or a dog named Joe that'll do the same to another dog named Joe—though I suppose it could happen. But show me a crow named Matilda that will eat her own, and I will eat my hat. (If I could lay hands on my red one.)

But maybe I keep looking down at things through sunrise-tinted glasses, that's my trouble?

Down in your world, if I could have sewed a quilt (seagulls like flocked stitches, scraps of cloth dyed all the colours of nature), there is no telling what I might have guessed up for it. If I'd had paint at hand in each and every one of those hues and a board as big as Nova Scotia, I surely would have tried painting such a view as I enjoy now. But not even here, where everything flows ever onwards in sweetness and light, can you lay your hands on such colours or their shameless, burbling glow.

7.

STANDING
ON THE
PROMISES

I*guessed early on in marriage that I mightn't lay my hands on such* a canvas. So I turned my mind right away to the canvas at hand: the house. Ev's house. And forget a rainbow's array of colours. I started small, using up stray bits of boat paint Ev had in the shed, the dregs of cans he scavenged from the wharf soon after I arrived.

Standing on the promises of matrimony, each day I looked at the ring on my finger a hundred times if I looked at it once, and thanked my lucky stars that I had been saved.

But arriving in Marshalltown was not like arriving *here*, I had to do *something* to keep from going loony. It wasn't the happiest task trying to put Ev's dwelling in order—though this was why he took me in. The first few months I spruced up the place simply by shifting one mountain of his stuff to another mountain of his stuff. There wasn't a great deal of room to manoeuvre. Cupboards were scarcer in that house than tourists are in January, which is to say there weren't any. I do not know what I'd have done if there'd been space to hide things, or what poor Ev would have done to keep track of things then.

"Where'd you put my razor, woman? Where the hell did you hide my jackknife? And the can opener, what the jeezus did you do with that? You trying to drive a fella nuts, hiding everything?"

Making Ev's house into a home for two of us meant things got lost, in the way that trees get lost in the forest. More often than not my new husband would find the missing item inside his boot, or in his pocket, or resting in the rafters where he had laid it. More often than not he would laugh and shake his head, a crackle of regret in his bright blue eyes, and hustle outside to do chores.

The day I am thinking of was a month or so after the wedding—you could say ours was a shotgun wedding, but not for the usual reasons. A February blizzard reached under the door and around the windows, and covered the panes in patterns like the ferns that would unfurl by the brook if spring ever came. Wearing all the clothes that had come with me, save the dress I got married in, I freed up enough tabletop for us to dine off of, busied myself scrubbing at the soot ground into its wood. All that livelong day I sorted, tidied, folded, tucked, swept, and scoured, the white at the windows a guiding light. I had even got down on hands and knees to swirl a wet rag over the floor. Promised myself that when the snow let up I would haul the mat outdoors, hang it from a branch, stand on a chair, and beat it with a stick.

One step at a time was how I tackled the job: you put one foot ahead of the other and kept going. While I worked, I whistled along to tunes in my head. Tunes spurned the nattering in there that was like Aunt's, as if her voice came from just beyond the snow-covered sash: Take one step forward, girlie, set yourself two steps back.

That afternoon I had just finished sweeping crumbs from a breadbox when my man hustled in. He hardly spoke, just stoked the fire, then bustled about measuring flour and sugar like they were powdered gold, and behold, he mixed up a cake—land, yes, a cake, baked from scratch. It and the pot of tea he set out made a lovely supper.

"Notice anything different?" I ventured once we'd finished our meal. I peered at the tea leaves floating in my cup. If I could have read them, what would they have said? The way to a husband's heart lies through a feed of beef stew and dumplings? The feel of clean underwear against his rump? Of Old Dutch under his fingertips checking for grease? A newlywed woman, I could have used advice.

"What? Am I supposed to?" At that, Ev flicked his eyes around the room quicker than a blink. "Don't look any different a-tall. But you'd best not have lost the goddamn hammer like you did last time—or I'll have half a mind to hammer you. Crazier than a bag full of hammers, that's you. No, I don't see no difference, only that you best not have burnt up them *Couriers*—Christ knows when I might get more. I need them papers handy, don't forget, to wrap my wares in. Let customers think they're fresh-caught if you wrap 'em before you go to the door—not to mention keep the fish blood off the car seats."

Maybe it wasn't unnatural for a husband not to notice a wife's household efforts.

"Guess you care more for your car than you do the house, then." And the car and the house more than you care for me, I might have teased.

"See? Wha'd I say about crazy? Fuck's sake, you ought to know you can live in a car if need be but you can't drive a house."

Wiser words were never spoken; Ev's car was a blessing. Later, on our honeymoon, he used it to bring home a wedding present. The only present I had for him was a pocket watch of my father's, the one thing I had to remember him by. It was more an ornament than anything, since, like the cuckoo clock Ev and I found a while later, it didn't work. Its hands were permanently stuck on nine twenty-two—morning or night, your choice, I told Ev. Using the charred end of a stick I wrote his initials on a scrap of paper, which he scratched onto the back of the watch using an old nail. The present Ev gave me let me enjoy my inheritance from Mama, the last record she bought before things went bad, "Sitting on Top of the World." I wished there'd been the money before Father died to buy a machine that played discs. Our second favourite song, "Stairway to the Stars," came out too late to be recorded on a cylinder. Even on her sickbed Mama would try to sing along with me when it came on the radio, pretty words about sailing away and riding a thrill as high as the heavens.

Rising from the table, I sang the first little bit under my breath, about silvery moonlight leading through a velvet lullaby. I decided suddenly that not even the best lines from "Sitting on Top of the World" could match it, and wished there was a way to hear what Mama thought.

"Might be nice to have a radio," I ventured to say after a while. "But doing without is okay," I added. "A gal can get along fine so long as she's got a fella."

"And a fella can get along fine without a wife, except for one thing." He raised his eyes to the hole in the ceiling, the stepladder he had leaning under it at first, then nudged me, bored his finger into my sunken chin. "You got a kiss for me or what?" Leaning over me, he was so tall and lanky and loose I felt like I was wrapped in a big warm flapping shirt. His fingertip felt rough but smooth, cold but warm. Some flour was crusted under his fingernail when he brought it to his teeth to pick away a bit of cake. He let out a sigh. "Well, it'll be a long cold evening but I reckon you will have to do, keeping a fella warm. Christ knows—" At last he cast a decent glance round the room. "You ain't good for much else. Not like my ma—she could scrub a floor, do a wash, and put up enough bread to last a week in the time it takes you to wash a dish. I ought to send you down to her for lessons." The twinkle in his eye said he was joking. But he didn't let it go at that. His voice had a twinge of regret. "I guess it's fair to say you tricked me, didn't you. You were talking through your hat when you said you had experience. Experience, my eye—only thing you're good for is a decoration on a fella's arm, a poorly one at that." He paused and I stared at the ring and let lines from those songs fill me. "But I guess you can stay," Ev said after a minute. "I guess a fella makes his bed, he lies in it."

He topped up my teacup, tipped in some milk, helped himself to another slab of cake. I still had a good-sized morsel on my plate, was saving it for later.

"Not eating that?" Before I could move my fork, he took my leftover cake and popped it in his gob. "Oh she's gonna be a long night, I can tell," he said, crumbs falling from his mouth. "Them lunatics are gonna be shivering in their beds and wanting to git downstairs by the fire—I'll have my work cut out keeping them in line, I just know it. That warden and his wife are too frigging nice, never seen the likes. Who's running the show over there anyway, the lunatics or Olive? In my day—" Then he fell silent. I was just as glad because I had heard about when he was small and he and his mother and who knows what other relatives lived at the poor farm what became the almshouse, and I did not want to be reminded of things it was better not knowing.

"What is done is done. Telling me again is not going to change it."

He gawked at me, shook his head. "Have more cake, why don'tcha Ev," he said to himself, joking, or maybe pretending to be a lunatic, too, as if I was not anywhere near, let alone keeping him company at the table. Not for the first time, I reckoned teaching a bachelor how to act like a husband was like teaching an old dog a new trick—like teaching the mix dog Ev had out in the pen the day I first appeared at his door not to snap at strangers, it was probably futile. And yet, Ev said himself, the very first time I came calling on him, unannounced, that dog, Joe the First, had barely let out a peep.

So I rested my case about bachelors and husbands.

By the time Ev pulled on his boots to go to work for midnight, the blizzard had died down. But the drifts came up past the windowsill, so that in the lamplight the downstairs was like being inside a cozy little igloo. Throwing on his coat, he bent and pinched my cheek good night. In the scrap of mirror next to where I'd hung the dustpan, I glimpsed the tiny dent his thumbnail made. I guessed every gal would be so lucky as to have a fella think enough of her to leave a mark of his affection.

Especially a gal who had passed herself off as a housekeeper to a fella who fell for it hook, line, and sinker and married a dud if ever there was one.

After Emery's surprise visit that evening, I started spending a good deal more time primping, dressing nicer even though the rest of the time all I did was paint. Didn't matter that, except for my near-nightly trips to the Majestic, hardly anyone saw me. But it was like Aunt said, how the Lord could come as sudden as a thief in the night, you never knew when, you just had to be ready—in other words, you must look your best at all times. Emery Allen was no thief, but he was the closest thing I could imagine to the Second Coming Aunt talked about. I did not breathe a word of this to Mama. She had no inkling of the spell Emery had cast over my life, only the change in me it caused. A change she approved of.

"It's nice to see you go the extra mile fixing yourself up, you're a pretty girl. Never mind your chin. No girl ever suffered tending to her appearance. You're only young once, my darling."

If there's one thing painting taught me, it was patience. Love is patient, love is kind, I told myself, cribbing Aunt's biblical words as I waited for Emery Allen to call. Part of a week crawled by, I watched the last of the maples carpet the ground with yellow leaves, and still he didn't appear.

Then that Saturday night Mama and I were playing a duet—well, I was fumbling through the bass notes—passing the time before the late show, when we heard a car pull up outside. Peeking through the curtains, she looked puzzled then a little annoyed, not wanting us to be held up. "Who's this, now?"

Could it be? My heart leapt as I rose and peeked out too. It was him, it was Emery, come to take me on a date? I flew ahead of Mama. At the door he handed me a bouquet of wild asters he said he'd picked by the shore. I kept my eyes on them, and my hand on the little scarf covering my chin. He shook Mama's hand. He had left the car's engine running. I grabbed my coat and skedaddled outside before Mama could ask questions. Thank my lucky stars I was dressed up for the movies. If I had been thinking clearly I'd have run upstairs and grabbed my beaded shawl.

He helped me up into the car, tried to guide me into the back behind the front seat. "You might find it cozier in there."

"Reckon it's plenty cozy up front."

"More room back there."

See and be seen, I told myself.

"That passenger seat's a mite dirty. Never had time to dust it off." He sounded apologetic—as if I minded! He clicked his tongue as I climbed into the seat beside his anyways. "Might mess up your coat." A friend from the country had loaned him the car, he said, a fella in Woods Harbour. He himself was from down that way, it turned out. "Nothing like Woods Harbour for scenery—better than here, well, except maybe for Forchu, out there by the lighthouse. Not much going on down there besides fishin' though. How about you and I take a spin then go for drinks—the Grand Hotel maybe?"

His voice alone set my mind and heart a-swirl.

He was the cat's meow, he was the finest thing since sliced bread, he was sweet butter, custard cream, and jam. Thank my lucky stars ten times over I was dressed for the occasion if not for the weather, wearing the shimmery dress Mama had bought for me at Nichol's. It reminded me of a mermaid's tail, a lovely glittery, greeny blue. Along with my coat I had managed to grab the little sequined hat that matched it, which made up for the missing shawl. Mama's voice seemed to whisper to me as I squashed the hat down on my head: *"A girl can never be too finely dressed."*

Emery glanced sideward, winked in the rear-view mirror. "Look at you. All gussied up."

I could hardly believe my ears, the first time a fella besides Father paid me this much attention. Can I just say I was over the moon as we drove up Parade Street, past all the sea captains' mansions, the finest houses in town. We kept going past Central School and Mountain Cemetery till we reached Hardscratch Road. It was a chilly but clear evening, dusk had fallen early, but right before that the sun had laid a fine strip of orange light along the rooftops. I snuck a glance at Emery every chance I could. Let this not be a dream! If it is, don't let me wake up!

I kept thinking. Every now and then I caught a whiff of him, not the slightest bit fishy but fresh with the smell of shaving soap. Shaving soap and engine grease.

"Nice car," I said, after a while, to let him know I hadn't died of happiness. Emery nodded. I should have complimented his clothes, too, but thought it better to keep mum. His overcoat looked ever so slightly worn. Underneath, his suit was a jacket and pants two different shades of blue. If you don't have anything good to say, don't say anything, Father always taught me.

We drove past trees, fields, and a farmhouse with a solitary light burning in the window. In the headlamps' beams the roadside's wild asters and dying goldenrod flew by, lining ditches bordering woods. I wondered if this might be a road Father had taken us on on a family outing once. Except for those Sunday jaunts in the country with him, Mama, and Charlie when I was small, I hadn't spent much time out in the sticks. A town girl, I was used to paved streets, fine buildings, shops, sidewalks, street lamps, and picket-fenced yards.

Though still early evening, it soon grew dark as midnight. I saw for myself what people said: there's no darkness like country darkness.

It's dark as your arse, as Ev would say, later.

Stars beamed through the windshield. Bright spits of light, their beauty was out of this world! Emery said that up ahead was a clearing with the best view of the sky. I couldn't see for the darkness but Emery knew where to find it, a grassy gap in the woods where some old house or barn once stood. He pulled over, turned off the engine, got out and came around, put both hands on my waist, and lifted me down. The ground's damp came through the soles of my patent leather shoes. The smell of spruce reminded me of Christmas, though it was still too early for snow. A blessing it was way too chilly for midges, blackflies, and mosquitoes—in summer they would be fierce out here, I imagined; they'd have bitten through my dress and under its hem. If it had been summer, the bugs would have found Emery a tasty treat.

He put his hand on the nape of my neck, moved it slowly down my back. Even through my coat his touch made me tingle. I would have swooned straight away if I hadn't been so bundled up. With his strong arm at the flat of my back, he tipped me backwards like a plank till my chin pointed at the sky. "Look, look up—look at that!" Leaning behind me, half on his knees, he was so close I could hear his every breath. Together we peered up at the purple sky studded with diamonds.

"Hey, make a wish, you." With that, he set me on my feet again.

By now I had a wish perfectly formed: To marry Emery Allen and be his wife till death did us part. Even if it might mean leaving Yarmouth to live somewhere I had never stepped foot. Even a small place, which I thought would be fine so long as it had a movie house.

"Reckon I wouldn't mind seeing Woods Harbour. That's one wish."

Emery laughed. "Blink and you'd miss it. What would you give me if I took you there?"

I remembered something my brother had said while laughing with his friends. Something about women luring fellas with promises that were all talk, no action. I wasn't precisely sure what action Charlie meant, but figured I oughtn't get too far ahead of myself promising something I mightn't be able to deliver. I kept my bigger wish to myself, asked Emery what he wished for.

"How 'bout this?" Leaning over, he kissed me deep deep deep with his tongue. His mouth tasted like tobacco.

"Not a bad start. Why stop?" I shivered with the cold, but with the warmth of his arms around me, hardly cared.

We could see our breath. I guess the cold didn't bother him either. He loosened his tie as we stood there. I watched the starlight mark the trees as his hands roved under my coat. He whispered how strange it was to think the exact same stars had shone down on France when he fought in the War. They looked the same from the bottom of a trench, he said. Not only was Emery Allen the handsomest man in Nova Scotia, maybe all of Canada, I thought, but he was a war hero to boot! My, he was full of surprises. Craning back as far as I could without toppling backwards, I glimpsed his face, so open and sweet. It was turned up to meet the starlight like a flower that bloomed at night. An evening primrose.

Land's sake, the man's not a flower, I told myself. He's a porchlight, I'm a moth. This is what I thought as we got into the car and he spread his coat over the back seat. I guess he mustn't have felt the cold for the same reason I didn't. He moved on top of me so I was half-sitting, half-lying down. "I'll warm you up, don't worry." His chin felt sandpapery rubbing against my cheek. Somewhere far off, a dog barked. Close by, the only sound was our breathing. Emery leaned back to look at me, it was like he was listening for something. It was awfully cramped, it couldn't have been too comfy for him given how he was taller than me. I hoped he wasn't having the same thought. I didn't want him to stop. A smidge of pain for a lifetime gain, I told myself. You couldn't have one without the other—

"Don't stop. Please. Don't. Stop."

"Aren't you something else."

He breathed and pressed and pushed inside, and it hurt.

But what was a little sting but a reminder that I was young, young enough, and head over heels in love?

When it was over we laid there scooched together, Emery with his hand on my belly. I pictured Mama at the Majestic, eyes darting from the screen to the piano player's hands if she'd been lucky enough to get a front-row seat. With me as her date, we always had to sit way back, on account of my neck. I felt what I am sure Mary Pickford must have felt spooning with Douglas Fairbanks. What Mama surely felt once upon a time lying with Father.

All too soon, Emery straightened up, rubbed his neck. "You're one wicked little charmer." He clicked his tongue against his teeth, tugged his coat out from under me. "You know how long I've waited to meet a woman like you?" He lit two cigarettes, gave me one. I hardly knew what to do with it, though I had smoked before, with Charlie behind the box office. Inhaling set off a coughing fit but it soon passed.

A woman, he'd said. Not a girl. My head against the armrest, I tugged up my little scarf which had slid away, and looked up at him, dreamy-eyed, the way Mary would've.

"You won't tell, will you? About what we just did."

He laughed, and in the starlight his features looked smooth as a boy's. I thought how in bright sunshine his brown hair might be the colour of molasses toffee. He swore a little bit, stretching his neck. And I told myself that, even if you took away the love between us, what Emery and I had done—what I had caused Emery to do—was no more improper than having the doctor poke and prod me. I was used to *that.* Any pain Emery may have caused, briefly, was different; it was sweet and it was proof that he loved me, for surely what we had got up to must have hurt him, too, at least a little.

"How come you weren't already snapped up, a gal so eager and willing?"

"Was waiting for you. Now I'm snapped up good!"

Emery answered with an ear-to-ear smile.

How come, I wondered, the ride back from a place is always quicker than the ride going there? "Next stop, the Grand Hotel!" I trilled like a bird, I was so happy. The evening wasn't done yet.

Emery didn't say anything, keeping his eyes fixed on the road.

Soon enough we pulled into town. Traffic crawled down Main past the Majestic. The nine o'clock was just getting out. I looked for Mama, didn't see her.

It was five or six blocks to the Grand. Parked outside it, I straightened my dress and scarf and coat, fished my hat from between the seats. Emery's overcoat looked a little the worse for wear. Glimpsing it made me bashful. I giggled. Nerves, I guess. We sat there for the longest time not moving, watching people going inside. You could see the lobby through the big brass-fitted doors, it was all marble and potted palms, ladies and gents milling about. The men had moustaches like Clark Gable's, the ladies wore jewels in their hair and shimmery dresses. I imagined them waltzing into the ballroom, and I guessed up how that ballroom would look. Finally, Emery opened his door and got out, following behind as I got out and made for the entrance. A man wearing white gloves and tails held the door for me. Jazz music drifted out. A saxophone's bleat gave me a thrill. I hoped it would be Charlie and his band onstage; sometimes he had Joe close up shop by himself so he could sneak off early to play. I couldn't wait to see him dipping and swaying, blowing into his horn. But as I stepped inside, the man in gloves stopped Emery. "Formal attire only," the fella said.

"But I promised the gal—"

"Sorry, bud."

Emery snorted, disappointed. He gave me a funny look which I caught through the corner of my eye. I wasn't about to go in alone without my date, the date of my dreams. I won't lie, I felt disappointed too. Crestfallen, like they said in books. But, as we got back into the car, what mattered was our being at each other's side. Though his silence worried me. He needed cheering up.

"So what's it like in Woods Harbour, anyways?"

Emery didn't answer right away. As he wheeled out of the parking lot, he glanced over at me, shook his head. "You are a case and a half, aren't you."

"You could tell me how it looks."

"Woods Harbour? It's Upper Woods Harbour I come from, to be exact." A smile played across his jaw and I figured he was guessing up scenery in his head as we drove past Frost Park. The park's chestnut trees were bare and gloomy in the dark. "Well, since you asked. It's low and marshy and has lots of islands and more seals, probably, than people."

Now we were talking! His words were all I needed to guess up the rest: green and gold marshland, seagulls, mist, a big old white homestead, a captain's house, overlooking the sea.

"Satisfied?" With his word-picture of Upper Woods Harbour, I figured he meant. He swerved to make the turn onto Jenkins Street, the less-travelled route to Hawthorne. We passed the harness shop.

"Oh yes. Thanks."

On Hawthorne, our front porch light was on, the parlour light blazing. When he pulled in by the curb, I turned and leaned over and gave him a big smooch on the cheek. "That was grand tonight, Emery. Except for the Grand." He gave a belly laugh then. He *is* like Father, sloughing off a misfortune, I thought, waving to him as he drove off. Like Father, letting a disappointment roll off him like water off a duck's back, I could tell.

Mama was waiting up. Her eyes went straight to my dress. A thread had pulled at the hem, a sequin dangled loose. "So, my darling, where'd you go? Did you enjoy yourself? Have a good time?" Her anxious smile made me spill over with joy.

"Oh, Mama. The best."

In the dark of those nights Ev worked next door I learned to miss him, the lean, bony warmth of his body against mine up in the attic loft. Never mind that makeshift bed was only ever meant for one person. In the mornings after he returned long-faced with fatigue from his watchman's shift, his snores would filter downstairs while I puttered around as quiet as could be. Oh, I had no trouble scrambling down a ladder back then. I would sit still as a toad in my corner until he was rested enough to come down and fix breakfast.

Not only was I poor at heavy lifting and cleaning, I had hardly learned to cook—that is what happens when people care for you. When they believe they are better at doing things than you are. After a while—call me lazy—you say, Go ahead then, suit yourself. My lack of housekeeping abilities freed me up to do as I pleased.

One such morning I looked at the dustpan and thought, land, wouldn't a bit of paint be just the ticket to spruce that thing up? Its metal was rusty, a sight for sore eyes. By the time Ev came down to light the fire, I had done that dustpan up real nice with bright red poppies and hung it from a nail between the calendars and the clock. I figured those flowers might give that cuckoo a reason for staying popped out.

When I told Ev so, he clicked his tongue. "You're some cracked. But that's one way of looking at it. That bird's gonna be happier with flowers by it than without." He spent the afternoon trying to get the clock to work, with no luck. He just wasn't so sure about the dustpan's usefulness after I'd got my hands on it: the paint took forever to dry. "Try and sweep up a mess and watch what *don't* stick to that paint. Forget sweeping, you might's well give up on it." He grumbled but promised to keep an eye out for another dustpan on his next trip to town. I knew where he would go to find it, the spot where people—you know what some folks are like—disposed of stuff that was still perfectly good. Even Aunt once said so, living all her life cheek by jowl with the town dump.

"Waste not, want not."

"You got that right, woman."

In those honeymoon days, sure, the town dump proved as good if not better than Shortliffe's for yielding what we needed. Housekeeping items became the objects of my desire. Having the right tools can make you look like something you're not. More important, cookie sheets, cake pans, tea trays, and muffin tins cried to have pictures painted on them, just like scraps of linoleum begged to become pot holders. You name it, Ev found it. He brought such items home by the week, seeing what-all I could do with them. Didn't matter a whit if these things were rusty or worn in ways regular folks would turn their noses up at.

Regular folks like Mama's people and Father's.

You could say Ev took to testing me, aiming to see if there was one item he could find that I could not beautify. The flowers, birds, and butterflies I painted on his offerings brightened the place up. They brought sunshine inside on gloomy days.

Ev would act miffed. "Goddamn. You don't quit, there won't be an inch of bare wall to stare at." But he didn't try to stop me. He only brought home more old stuff for me to spruce up. Like it was a test of some sort. If there was bitterness in his words, I preferred to consider it a kind of wonder at what I'd get up to next.

"Ah, g'wan—I'm just teasing you," he said. "Do what you want. Though you act like the goddamn place is yours to do with whatever you please, like it's your place too. Don't know what give you that idea. Only reason I let you move in was I pitied you. Now look where it's got me."

I guess I fancied myself a Rumpelstiltskin or whoever that one was that spun ratty wool into skeins of gold. The more I stuck on the walls, the more padding we had against the cold pushing in between the shims.

"That's right," he said. "More padding—installation, you mean."

I suppose some might say it could be a bit of a tight squeeze at times in that house.

Now and then Ev would look at me and say, "Don't you have someplace to go?"

The answer was no.

"Find me more paint and I'll keep out of your hair." It was as much a dare as it was a promise. A veiled if idle threat that I could walk out of his life as easily as I had walked into it. I like to think it kept Ev on his toes. For marriage to succeed, Mama used to say, it helps for husband and wife to have interests of their own. Touring the dump occupied my man by day while six nights out of seven he kept watch over the ladies and gents next door, making sure none of them escaped or acted up, seeing that each stayed in their own wing and in their own bed. Not that Ev didn't have plenty of work around our place to occupy him. And mining the dump for treasures was more than a hobby; for Ev it was a job *and* a calling, the way prettying-up old stuff was for me. You could say his devotion fed mine.

Truly, if I had been able to hop, pick, and peck like a crow through the dump's piles of plenty the way Ev could, I would have accompanied him. I'd have been Ev's shadow.

By the time we had spent our first winter together, the pride I wore from childhood had dissolved like tarnish stripped from silver with hot water, tinfoil, and a bit of baking soda. Of course, Ev was a little territorial, a bit like Joe that way: the dump was his for first pickings. The same as in summer when he staked out berry patches, flapped his arms to chase the robins away, a living scarecrow. Don't imagine he made many friends among the gulls that hung around the dump, either.

What's yours is mine and what's mine is yours. That's what marriage is all about, talk-wise anyhow. But show me the perfect marriage and I will show you a bare mudflat at high tide. What was mine was Ev's, of that you can be sure. But what was Ev's did not always have to be mine.

And let me tell you about the date we went on while we were still what I like to call newlyweds. April 1938. We had to wait for winter to let up before Ev could take the car out—oh yes, a horse and buggy or sleigh would've been ideal. "Time we went on a date, I guess," Ev had said. I imagined us walking into a movie house and watching Mary Pickford and Douglas Fairbanks smooch onscreen.

Snow still lay in patches on the ground. I was wrapped up in a blanket to fend off the chill as we motored to town. Setting there in the passenger seat, a proper missus, I imagined *I* was Mary Pickford and that Ev's mother's gold wedding band had a diamond in it, and the faded kerchief on my head was daffodil-coloured chiffon. Behind the steering wheel, Ev was Douglas Fairbanks—well, maybe not quite so dashing as that, so I will say Buddy Rogers. The real star of the day was the scenery. I kept my eyes on the bay's hard glint as we got closer to town.

My belly knotted as we pulled up the street near Aunt's tidy white house. I had not seen her since the dead of January, when she slipped me some money in an envelope. I had half expected her to say, "Here, I am paying you to think twice about marrying him." But no. It was a tidy sum to pay the preacher with.

Ev drew in alongside the dump and hopped out. Hopped was the word for how Ev moved, him being like a big tall bird in my eyes—maybe some sort of crane. I could see Aunt's kitchen window just across the way, on the far side of some trees bordering the trash piles. The sunshine blazed off it like copper.

"The fuck you waitin' for? Go to it, girl. You wanted a

wedding present? Better late than never. Fill your boots!"

Oh, and nimble! Watching him leap past a smoking pile of rubbish I thought how he would make a graceful bird look ungainly. He stooped and rousted up a white enamelled pail with only part of the bottom rusted out, then a pair of gloves, then a doll, and a bicycle seat, and, oh my land! A phonograph record, a 78. It wasn't till I got close up that I saw the doll had no legs, the gloves no thumbs. Ev tossed the disc. It spun towards my waiting hands like a flying saucer. Only when I caught it did I notice the crack through it. I could have cried. "*Stairway to the Stars*" read the purple label, *by Glenn Miller, lyrics by Mitchell Parish sung by Paul Whiteman.*

What a terrible, terrible shame.

I spied a rat with its eyes pecked out. Alongside it was a clock with no hands, part of a birdcage, and a lone boot with the toe out of it. The waste! But none of it came anywhere near the waste of that beautiful broken record.

"Well, don't just stand there. Start digging—what are you waiting for? Christmas?"

I guess Ev thought I was slacking off. Already he had laid his hands on what must be a gem. Whatever it was was wrapped in newspaper and stuffed inside a string bag. He tore away the paper and, oh my, there was the sweetest little bowl. Blue china with pink china roses and the word *Baby* on it.

"What's it even mean? 'B' is for—? You got any use for it?"

"Nope." The sight of it set me shivering. Of course, I was already cold, having left the blanket in the car. I watched Ev turn the bowl in his hands before he chucked it down. Bits of china flew up as it hit the burnt edge of a brick.

I summoned up the stairway song's thrilling words in my head, let them stick there.

What I said about pride being a tarnish that rubbed off is a bit of a lie. Buffeted by the wind off the bay, I wondered if

Aunt might peek out her kitchen window and see us.

"Time's a-wasting—here!" Ev tossed the thumbless gloves at me. "Might get some use out of these, if you are scared of getting your hands dirty. I ain't leaving till we have given 'er a good going-over. Think I burnt half a tank of gas to take you for a spin, you got another think coming."

He was right, we should make the most of our outing, though I worried about Aunt up to her elbows in a sink full of dishes, spying the car and me searching for treasures. I have no idea what she would have thought. Well, actually, I do.

"I'm cold," I said and looked towards the car. I kept thinking about what the song said about climbing to the stars with your love beside you. I stooped and picked up a scrap of brown linoleum, just the right size for a pretty little decoration, and shoved it in my pocket.

"Whoa, now—did I say we could leave?" Ev's voice grabbed at me the way the wind did, sharp around its edges. So I stayed put, darting my eyes over the ground from trash pile to trash pile as he kept digging. A bottle sailed past me, and some cans. Then he was tugging on my sleeve. "Oh my jeezus, what have we got here?" He had unearthed what looked like a cabinet, nice wood under its patina of slime. "Is this what I think it is? Whoa, shit—we hit the mother's load, woman." He dredged the thing up, got it standing on its feet. He was right, it was a find, all right. A windup Edison like the one we'd had in Yarmouth. It even had the handle you cranked. When he lifted the lid, sure enough, it was the old kind of phonograph that played cylinders, the same as Mama's.

"Slim fucking pickings today, that'd be your fault," he teased, wrestling the phonograph into the car. "What are you standing there for? Git in, woman, before you freeze your arse off. That is a goddamn sin about that record, though. Ain't no way you could patch it?"

"Doesn't matter, it wouldn't work anyways." I was gleeful. I couldn't wait to try out our find. "Take me home and warm me up." I cast a clever, tilted gaze at him.

Now, maybe you people down there are wondering, just a little, why I chose to marry Ev. Truth be told, I wondered sometimes myself. But my reasons weren't worth dwelling on. The fact was, I was his very own Mary Pickford, and he was my own true Buddy Rogers. Which would make everything easier and harder as we strolled through life. Driving home with our booty, that's how I felt.

With a pang of missing Mama, I put on her record, the one record I owned, cranked the machine's handle till it would crank no more, the spring inside wound tight as could be. As Al Jolson's voice leapt out and filled the house, Ev got a pained look. I saw how it wasn't easy for him, giving up his bachelorhood and adapting to a shared life. And maybe he liked how I could lose myself in painting, as it kept me out of his hair.

One day he came home with a set of real artists' oil paints and a set of brushes, and a magazine he'd found with all kinds of coloured pictures in it. There was one with a gal in a red bathing suit about to step into a lake surrounded by snowy mountain peaks that weren't like anything you'd see in our neck of the woods. I listened to "Sitting on Top of the World" as I did my best to copy that scene on a board.

I could not get enough of the way Jolson wrapped *world* round his tongue so it sounded like *woild*. If those paints and brushes weren't a ticket to heaven, that record was my comfort and joy. It was my lifeline to the things I had left behind.

8.

WHISPERING HOPE

Now, on the subject of the dump, let me jump ahead some twenty-eight years to the first time that young police officer came sniffing around. After the constable drove off, I wondered if the complaints he'd raised had roots in other lies, lies meant to scapegoat Ev. Had someone spread falsehoods about Ev's visits to the dump? Say there'd been a robbery, the last place most people would look for their missing goods became the first place? Maybe some Nosy Parker had reported Ev treasure-hunting and the least likely of thieves had got blamed for another's thieving. All it took was one false accusation, and the next you knew a whole shit storm could brew up.

One thing I could vouch for: Ev was no thief. Tell me what kind of thief is as honest as the day is long. I should've said so to the cop. I should've told him what Olive Hayden said once, about her husband offering Ev more than a dollar a night and Ev turning it down, saying he didn't do much of anything, nights at the almshouse, to deserve a raise. Too bad the right words never strike till it's too late.

Ev came home unexpectedly early that evening after the cop's visit. He caught me working on my crow painting. I tried too late to cover it with a rag. He threw the rag aside. He'd been drinking, I could smell the dynamite juice off him—whatever they sold at the liquor store that had replaced his former concoctions.

"That don't look like a cat picture to me. Who ordered the queer-looking bird?"

"It's Matilda," I tried to explain. "I just took a notion to—"

"You fool woman. That don't look like any crow I know of."

"Oh, but Ev, I got it in my head to try, it's just for myself—"

"You mean no one ordered it? You got that pile of orders and you're here wasting good paint, and a good board, and fucking hell, who's gonna buy a pitcher of a crow that don't look like a crow, anyway? You're off your fuckin head." He'd grabbed the board and peered at it closer. An ugly look spread over his mouth. "Wasting time, always wasting time. And me busting my arse to feed you."

I don't know why, I guess the constable's visit was fresh in my mind and the queasiness the visit had caused made me speak up. "Ev," I said, "did something happen with them two little girls? Those two that came that day with their folks and their brother, remember, that little boy."

"What two little girls are you talking about? I don't have the foggiest notion what you are on about. Not you too—crazy as all the other bitches and sons-of-bitches out there in the world. Oh they're out there, crazy as all hell. Don't take nothing to set 'em off like a pack of curs, does it. You should know, you're one of them." He glared, pointing his finger at me.

I wanted to ask about my ring, too, but knew better.

I knew he was right. I knew it didn't take anything for folks to lie and set themselves against someone. But the minute he turned his back, I slid Matilda's portrait in behind a bunch of finished boards. I wasn't ready to give up on it quite yet.

Before I knew it, Easter came. It fell on the second week of April that year, '66. Matilda's brood had hatched; even before I glimpsed the chicks' heads peeping from the nest I heard them clamouring to be fed. Matilda and Willard ferried food to them, flying back and forth on missions that often took them out of my sight. I reckoned they couldn't feed those babies often enough. Sleet pelted my window pane fit to scrub the tulips off. I worried about those poor fledglings. To take my mind off them I day-dreamed, training my gaze on the raw, muddy ground outside. Imagined bunnies frolicking, snowdrops poking their heads up, deer leaving the woods with their tiny spotted fawns to drink from barnyard ponds. Resting my hands, I thought of the little cards I had painted in bygone days, the rhymes I'd penned inside. *Loads of Easter wishes are hurrying your way/Hope they're in time to bring you/Much joy on Easter Day.* Land, if I could have painted anything now it would have been cards. Cards would have helped me practice the fine details I wanted for Matilda's picture. But cards were much too small and finicky, I had lost the touch. Even if I had kept it, who would I send cards to? Any kith and kin I had left were as good as dead to me; poor Aunt had left your world years ago. I could have sent them to customers but Ev would have had words about that: "What, now you're sending them freebies? Give 'em the cow, they ain't gonna pay for milk!"

Ev had a point, of course. He always did.

I was setting there mulling over that Easter verse—so much pleasanter nowadays to let verses dance in my head than having to put them down with a pen and ink—when the car pulled in. It was late afternoon. Ev was off somewhere, perhaps combing the shore for whatever the tide had drug in.

Rap rap rap. Guess who it was. I opened the door to that sweet-faced policeman. It struck me, maybe I'm foolish, but I thought, here's a fella needs to be needed. What other reason would a man that age have for coming way out here to call on two old birds like Ev and me? Especially since I had the idea the man didn't care much for art. In any case, I knew he was barking up the wrong tree. Unless visiting the dump was a criminal act, no crime that I could think of had been committed, by Ev or yours truly.

Stepping inside the officer gave his name again, as I'd forgotten it: Constable Somebody. He had told me before but, just like the other time, I let it go in one ear and out the other. Same as last time, he asked, "Is your husband home?"

"Nope."

"Can I ask where he is?"

I did not hesitate for a second. "At work." Of course, this was five years after the almshouse shut, it was that long since Ev had had a regular job. But he worked plenty hard scouring the countryside for what we needed (though after twenty-eight years of wedded bliss, like any other couple, we had more than enough stuff, we had stuff spilling from every corner). The gods' truth, my words to the officer were hardly a lie, not even a small white one. Yet he persisted.

"Look. I hate to bother you, Missus—" He sounded healthier this time.

I jumped right in: "You can just call me Maud."

He nodded then launched in. "We've had complaints. Again. Mr. Lewis loitering, bothering the girls—a clerk at Shortliffe's, a teller at the bank. Unfortunately, the same general complaint as that couple reported."

"Couple?"

"The couple with the kids, a while back—I think you know who I mean."

I suppose I did, how could I forget? I remembered Ev's playfulness, inviting those little girls to see Fred the trout and his squirrel that day, the squirrel that would sit atop the dog-house and torment Joe something fierce. I remembered the candies they'd refused to take. The only hurtful thing Ev had done was pass Matilda off as his crow instead of mine.

"What would they have to complain about? That was more'n a month ago. I'm afraid they are talking through their hat. Making things up. Ev wouldn't hurt a flea."

"Well, maybe not intentionally." The constable took the liberty of sitting down on Ev's chair, so I could see more of his face as he spoke. The lower part of his cheeks were flushed pink, the shoulders of his coat shone wet. His mouth looked kind of disappointed. "Maybe not." Repeating it, his voice sounded stiff. "But how do *you* get along with him, Missus?" He cleared his throat. "Has he ever—?"

I felt suddenly hot, my shoulders prickled with the insult of it. For suddenly I could see what he was insinuating: had Ev ever hurt me? "Of course not." Though I wasn't fully clear what *precisely* he was asking. As if me and Ev got into it, scrapping with each other.

"He's never caused harm. Are you sure?"

I tilted my head back as far as I could, twisted my gaze up to meet his. At the same time an angry spark fired through me. Oh yes, the Twohig woman had been spreading lies about Ev. Hurling slings and arrows against Ev was the same as hurling slings and arrows against me. If anything happened to Ev, I would be in a bad way. It felt like my eyes were weighted with lead as my gaze sank to the mat. Then I thought even Carmelita Twohig wasn't so awful as to incite a perfect stranger's wrath against Ev, against us. I nodded. My smiling face felt as pink as the officer's. "I expect I would be pretty sure about something like that."

He leaned forward to meet my eye. He looked ashamed for a young fella, for a cop. The two kinds of people who, from what I gathered, would feel or show little shame. "That's good," he said. Not that I had experience with cops. I could imagine this one in his mama's kitchen drinking milk. Their chit-chat as sweet as this day was long—now that spring was here, at least according to the calendar.

"Others don't know Ev like I do."

"Well, sure. I'm sure you're right but—"

"Ev wouldn't hurt a soul." I raised my voice so there would be no misunderstanding. "He would not lay a harmful finger on nobody. Willful or not." Belting this out sapped my breath, left me feeling dizzy.

"Now, calm yourself, Missus. I'm not suggesting—" The constable's voice was gruff but quiet, chastened, Aunt Ida would have said. Perhaps he figured he had better straighten up and fly right, that is, not poke his nose into other peoples' business, or be too hard *or* too soft on folks in what, for all he knew, might be a delicate situation. "It's my duty, that's all, to investigate complaints. Other people's complaints, I mean. We get complaints all the time, we have to look into them. Even if a lot of the time they're just rumours." I fancied he turned pinker, if that was possible.

"Who's complaining, exactly? Do they have a name?"

"Well, now, I'm sorry, ma'am. We can't name names unless charges are pressed."

"Charges?"

"Should any of the complainants decide to proceed—"

By now I was mightily offended, not just miffed. Carmelita Twohig's powdered face loomed again in my mind. "Now why would they do that?" To slight an innocent man, the one person in the whole world who has stuck by me through thick and thin? I wanted to say. Who has kept me all these years, even when I wasn't the woman I'd let on I was. The one who, in spite of this, kept on keeping me. Like our wedding vows said, for better and for worse. In sickness and in health, and that.

I smiled sideways at the constable, kept a stony silence.

"Well, that's good, that Ev doesn't...that you're getting along okay, Missus. No need to be upset. Look, I shouldn't have suggested—I'm just responding...doing my job." He shrugged inside his stiff, shiny coat; I heard its rustle. Oh yes, I could picture him sitting in a big sunny kitchen, an older woman like Secretary doting on him. He handed me a card with his name on it. I held it up to the window and read it out. *"Constable Bradley Colpitts."*

"If I can ever be of assistance, Missus. Call. Don't suffer in silence."

I tipped my head back and forced my eyes to wander up to meet his once more and linger there, though it hurt my spine something fierce. "Why would someone like me need your help?"

His gaze raked over the range and the stairs and the daybed, taking them in in one eye-gulp. "A woman of your, ah, stature. You mightn't want to speak up, perhaps." He made a rough sound clearing his throat, so his cold was back or he too was a smoker? "Where others might be less afraid to. Afraid, I mean, of people knowing their affairs."

Affairs? Stature? Fame, I guess he meant. I stood four foot tall in bare feet if I was lucky, though some of you have me pegged at five two. Five foot nothing!

Fame, as if I were a proper mucky-muck! I couldn't help but blush.

"Afraid?"

I figured the constable must've seen me in the *Star Weekly* magazine the year or two before—or on the television. Heaven only knows how Ev and me appeared to folks in the pictures the nice man from Yarmouth had taken of us. The man and his friend, another fella, a writer, had arrived after another man and a lady from Halifax came all the way to Marshalltown to see me and buy some paintings. I guess word of Ev and me got around, one thing led to another. These two from the city must have tipped off Mr. Brooks who came all the way from Yarmouth with his camera—or maybe Mr. Brooks tipped off those two buyers. As with the chicken and the egg, it's hard to know what begot what. This is how things happened once word of my paintings got out: word spreads like a grassfire if the wind is right. What I hadn't reckoned on was how tickled pink these folks were by Ev and me. I admit I was tickled pink by their attention, gobsmacked by it, you could say. Land knows if that sweet Mr. Brooks had not taken our pictures, Ev and me and my work mightn't ever have got known beyond the lobster-arsed end of Nova Scotia.

Mr. Brooks had dropped by one dull February day—right out of the blue he appeared, asking if he could come in and take our photographs. Given no warning a-tall, I had no chance to spruce myself up first. Luckily I had my hair up in my best hairnet, one with a rhinestone band keeping it off my forehead, and I was wearing my best apron with pink flowers and touches of green edged in pink grosgrain ribbon, a decent sweater, and jewellery. Not only my gold brooch with its orange, red, and green stones, but my silver cat as well, with its tiny red stone for a nose.

Mr. Brooks kept aiming his camera at me while I worked on a painting of a man in a jacket and cap like Ev's, with a team of oxen hauling logs. Do you know, he got down on his knees, right there on the linoleum, like I was the Queen of Sheba and he was my subject, saying he wanted pictures of my face not the top of my head. Then he had me stand outdoors in my coat, hat, and mitts to get a picture of me holding my sleigh painting. We went back inside and Ev chewed the fat with him as he snapped pictures of this and that around the house. He got Ev to stand at the range dishing out my dinner, and had me seated like a Royal Highness before my table-tray with a square of pink material over it for my linen. Dinner was a rabbit stew Ev had made. I admit it made me blush with pride, untarnished pride, having this admiring set of eyeballs take everything in. Once upon a time, in my earliest married days, I might have fretted like Aunt Ida, only for all of thirty seconds, that unfamiliar eyes would linger overlong on where my scrub brush fell woefully short. But this visitor cared only about the beauty wrought by my paintbrush. He never mentioned my hands but I knew he was looking at them. He was too polite to say anything, obviously better brought up than some who came along before and since. I could tell by the way he smiled at me what he was thinking. It wasn't exactly pity in his eyes so much as wonder, a guilty kind of wonder as in "there go I but by the grace of God," like Aunt used to say. I reckoned Ev saw it too, the look in his eyes. After a while Ev got him to leave me to my work while he toured him around his rabbit snares and sheds. I wondered if he might be offering our guest a swig of the cocktail he'd got up to brewing down there.

Little did he know, the attention Mr. Brooks brought us would soon let Ev buy his liquor already made from the liquor commission. Before our visitor left, he came in to thank me for my time and to say goodbye.

I should be the one thanking you, I almost said.

It turned out Mr. Brooks had a friend, a scribe of some sort named Mr. Barnard who had just moved to Halifax, a city I could only half imagine, from a metropolis I could not begin to: Toronto, Ontario. The day Mr. Barnard came calling was a sunny one in June, warm but not too hot in the house. Ev was cooking up some fish. Mr. Barnard asked Ev and me a whole raft of questions, about how long I'd been painting and how Ev managed all the housework while I was on Cloud Nine doing what I did, painting and bringing in the bacon, like someone said.

"Always a pleasure meeting an artist," Mr. Barnard said.

This well and truly made me blush—nearly as pink as

during that chat I was telling you about, between me and Constable Colpitts a full year later. "Well I ain't no real artist, I just like to paint," I told our kind visitor.

"Listen at her," Ev piped up. "She don't like to brag or nothing. My Maudie is like that, see." He was blushing too, with pride and something else—I hate to say it, maybe a teeny trace of envy—that his little wife was the reason these fine men in suits had called in, Mr. Brooks and then his friend, not just to buy a painting or two, which they did, or to hear Ev's stories, which they also did, but to see me doing what I did. And not just see me for themselves, but each promising as he left to tell people who couldn't get to Marshalltown all about me.

Mr. Barnard was no sooner gone than Ev went on a talking jag, which happened if he'd been sipping. "He liked what I done with the garden. Said, too, he never smelt a tastier dinner— hinting to have some, I bet. I hope you're happy. Another slick, fast talker seeing you got a man in your pocket doing all a wife ought to do for her husband. You could've said how good I am at fetching water and hauling wood, holding up the business end and keeping you in smokes. All the stuff I do, to keep you happy. You could've let 'im know—"

Talk talk talk talk talk. At times, I had to admit, the sound of his voice was a bit like the sound of a rusty saw cutting a wet log.

"Uh-huh," I said, to let him know I was listening. "You are. You do."

Mulling over both men's visits, I was happy, oh yes. I hung onto the feeling. It was like having a sunflower bloom inside me and its big nodding head ripen with seeds for the birds. For happiness is like this, you soak it up like summer sun to remember during the cold, dark days of the winter ahead. Though, truth be told, during each of their visits, stealing glances at those men, I kept wanting to laugh. Not unkindly, but like a trickster sure the joke was on others. Nerves, probably. The risk of being tickled so pink I was scared I'd wet my pants?

No way I was going to let Ev pick that sunflower of happiness until it seeded the ground and withered of its own volition. The joy it spread was a lingering glow. I was beside myself with glee when that summer the magazine came in the mail. Instead of stuffing it in the box, the postman brought it to the door. There we were, Ev and me, our pictures splashed across several of its pages. I dare say I hardly looked happier before or since, the light from my window catching a warm, fiery twinkle in my eyes. Do you know, seeing those pictures I felt something I had not felt since I was a girl dressed in finery chosen by Mama: I mightn't have made a Queen of the Apple Blossom Festival, but I was almost pretty.

Pretty is as pretty does. This is what a smile does to your face.

A smile is God's facelift, my hairdresser friend Mae used to say, unless you are a movie star.

Ev raked his eyes over Mr. Brooks's photos like he couldn't quite believe what he saw. "What were you grinning about, anyways? Grinning like the fucking cat that caught a cannery. That you got me wrapped round your pinkie finger?" Of course, Ev came around soon enough after I read out what Mr. Barnard wrote. He wanted me to read the whole article out loud, so I read the parts he would like real slow and skipped the parts I knew he would not. A big smile spread, tugged at his mouth, at hearing himself called "a hauler of water and hewer of wood," as I put it, making up and adding parts here and there to flatter him.

I'd learnt a lot from those visits. They helped prepare me for what came next. I was good and careful to wear a different getup when the television people came to see us—a clean blouse with a different pin, the palette brooch with its dots of different coloured paints that a lady gave me. I needn't have fussed about the state of my skirt, seeing as how I sat behind my table-tray the whole time, let Ev do almost all the talking. Like Mr. Barnard had done, the television fellas asked a load of questions. They kept calling me an artist. "I ain't an artist," I had to tell them too, "I just like to paint." The fella that talked the most asked how much I charged for my paintings, would I take more if someone offered it?

"Oh yes." I smiled, thinking, what kind of question is that? Does a clam squirt water? Does a cat dig a hole to poop in? Then one of them asked what I would like to have more than anything in the entire world. I needed all of two seconds to think of it.

"A trailer," I shot back, then laughed. Worried I'd been too brazen, I let my eyes sink to the board in front of me and covered my chin with my hand. "Couldn't afford that."

"There's dreaming in Technicolor," I heard another of them say under his breath, whatever that was supposed to mean.

I sure would have liked to see Ev and me on TV, like they said we would be, these men who said they were from the Canadian Broadcasting Corporation. They told us when the show would "air" so we could tune in and watch it.

All we needed was a television set. After they left, Ev wondered what the chances might be of a set turning up at the dump. A working one, he meant. "Wouldn't have a jeezly clue how to jerry-rig a busted one, would you."

The chances of finding either kind of set would be slim to none, I figured, and gave a shrug.

Just as well, said Ev. "TVs are for lazy-arsed folks with nutting better to do. Besides, you don't want any more attention swelling your head. Already got swolled-up hands, don't want a swolled head too." He laughed, but then sounded a little worried. "You were some smiley around those Cee Bee Cee fellas, weren't you. Like you couldn't get enough of 'em. Yup," he gulped the word in one sharp inhale, "like you'd of run off with any one of them strangers if they asked you. Flirting, I seen you. An old woman like you. Your husband setting right here. Shame. You could learn some of that, a dose or two of shame. Couldn't you."

I remembered all this as Constable Bradley Colpitts stood before me, hoping to weasel some unkindness out of me regarding Ev. I listened to the officer's spiel about people being fearful, how fear kept some people from admitting the truth when the truth was unpleasant. Like fear was something I needed explained. It was the very thing that prevented some people from following their dreams, heck, he said, from getting out of bed in the morning.

I waited for him to finish before I spoke.

"Constable, you are barking up the wrong tree. Reckon if I was a scaredy-cat I never would've raised my prices." I laughed. "Don't suppose feeling one way or the other about fear has any bearing on painting." Which was all I wanted to do and which was all I did, I told him.

Constable Colpitts held his cap in both hands crossed in front of him. His knuckles seemed to tighten on it. He let out a little whistle of amusement, or maybe confusion. When he coughed, it stirred some soot and a little shower of grey sifted down between us. He pulled in a deep breath, squared what I glimpsed of his smooth pink jaw. "What's it like, anyway, being on TV, Missus? I guess everyone all across Canada knows who you are, not just Digby County. How'd you like seeing yourself on the screen?" I couldn't tell if he was making fun or not. I glanced at his shiny black boots, then I wondered if he had a holster under his jacket or a billy club or nightstick or whatever those things are called. He ducked down low, angling his boyish face towards me. It looked washed with regret. "Oh boys. Put my foot in my mouth there, didn't I. Watching TV might be a bit tricky for you and Everett, I guess?"

Ev-ert, was how he said Ev's name.

I chose to play along. "I guess." What was the point in acting miffed or offended? Ev's wisdom sprang to mind, naturally it bore repeating. "Seeing as we have nothing to plug a television into—a television set don't run on water, does it, Constable."

He laughed then, rubbing the brim of his cap, realizing the extent of his gaff? "Right." A more uppity soul, a Carmelita Twohig, would have taken umbrage to my remark. But Colpitts was a decent enough fella, I could see. Well-mannered, maybe even well-meaning. To spare his feelings I bit my tongue, held back what I was thinking: Lord love a duck, if we owned a television set, wouldn't you see it, even if we used it to stack stuff on? Wouldn't I have it turned on for company? Just the picture, maybe, and no sound: people talking, just a steady rush of silence pouring out their mouths? I do confess, a television was the one thing that might've made better company than the radio with juiced-up batteries or the Edison, which had died so long ago it felt like part of someone else's life, someone else's dream.

Way back in our newlywed days, not a month after our date at the dump, putting on Mama's record I'd cranked the handle a little too hard. Something inside the phonograph had let go. A rumbling had set the whole thing dancing in its corner, it shook so. Poor Ev, it gave him a bit of a fright! "Jumpin' jeezus, wha'd you do to it?" Then he saw my face. "For Pete's sake, don't cry. It ain't the end of the world."

Ev had lugged the Edison outside and opened it up like a carcass. Its innards, yards and yards of twisted black spring, spilled over the ground. The spring had snapped clean in two. "That's what you get for windin' 'er too tight. Never mind." He'd disappeared down to his big shed where he'd kept the Ford that first winter, and the fixings for his cocktails, came back with a spool of black tape—the kind Joe Bent the electrician wrapped things with, I remembered from Yarmouth. Laid out, the two pieces of spring stretched from the road all the way down to the potato patch. Ev spliced them together, wrapped every inch of the tape around the joint. The worst was trying to wrestle the whole thing back into the cabinet, worse than forcing a gigantic jack-in-the-box back into place. Finally, cursing, he crossed the road and went up the hill, and I watched him knock on a neighbour's door to ask for help. The man came back down the hill with him and they worked like buggers stuffing that spring back where it belonged. I thought how nice it would be to have the fella's wife come for tea sometime and listen to Jolson.

But at the first crank of the handle, the spring busted again.

"Fuckin' waste of time. Spend all your time listening to that music, you got nutting done anyways. Good fuckin' riddance, I say."

I was sad, but felt worse for Ev wasting his effort and I let him know. "Better it went this way than in the middle of playing music—it might've ruined Mama's record." Of course, having a cylinder and no machine to spin it on was the same as having a radio and no batteries. But nothing lasts forever, does it. And I imagined the loud *thwump* the patch would have made each time the spring passed through its housing, causing Al Jolson to hiccup. Kind of like when, in the midst of tickling the ivories, gazing at the sheet music, Mama blurted, "Turn!" Still, it grieved me that the Edison was a goner. Ev sold it for its wood, I don't suppose he got much. Perhaps it went towards my smokes.

And then the silence had descended, except for Ev's talking. The silence around his voice had filled my ears, until the radio appeared, that is.

But so much for enjoying an evening's entertainment now, music music music was no more than a happy thought without batteries. I didn't suppose they had music shows on television? I thought of asking Constable Colpitts this very question. But

I didn't want to hold him up, this young fella who I guessed would have been more at home in someone's big tidy kitchen, eating pie. So I let my silence speak for me, silence softened by the wind's whistling outdoors until a loud cawing broke it up. At last the constable put on his cap, as if to leave.

"Well. I appreciate your time, Missus—Maud. Like I said, if you think of anything I should know, you have my number"—he cleared his throat again—"you know how to reach me."

I waved his card like it was a dollar bill. But then he made no move to go, glancing at the stairs. They hadn't always been there, of course. Ev had found them somewhere and nailed them in place, kit and caboodle, sometime after we were married, to replace the stepladder that was there first.

"You paint those yourself?" From where I sat I could feel his eyes latch onto the open hatch above them. I suppose he could see part of the old bureau Ev had recently found and stuck up here. A place to keep the money, he said.

Regarding the stairs, I could not hold back a beam of pride, and felt it warm my cheeks. "Oh yes."

The constable bent low to get a better look, eyeing the stairs like he'd never seen stairs before.

"Can't be easy for you, going up and down."

I shrugged. "My stairway to the stars," I uttered under my breath, "like in the song. Ev carries me up them." Land knows why I felt the need to say it, especially if it gave the constable fresh cause to linger. I only know I wanted him gone before Ev got home. I guess he read my thoughts. Slouching to the door, all at once he gave me a curt nod then left in a hurry.

"Don't suffer in silence." Those words of his roared back to me the way his car roared when he started it. The words goaded me as I watched him hit the road.

Suffer in silence: when had I done anything but? Me and most of the world. *"Remember, my darling. There's always someone a thousand times worse off than you are,"* Mama used to tell me, even when gals wearing hats and dresses a thousand times nicer than ours passed us by.

I rubbed the constable's card between my thumb and fingers, enjoyed the smooth feel of it though it pained my whole hand gripping it. Under his name, *Constable Bradley Colpitts*, was the phone number for the Digby station. *"You call me, you hear, if you need help,"* these words lingered too as his car disappeared in the rain.

"Sure, I'll call," I told the window, "same as I'll see myself on TV." I slipped the card into the fire. I suppose I could have ripped it up first, but Ev wasn't about to read it, though he would have recognized Town Hall pictured on it, where the police had their office next to the mayor's. "Well aren't you a long, cool drink of water, Constable Bradley Colpitts, sharing that fancy building with the mayor," I told the range. A long, cool drink of water, he was, just like a handsome fella I knew in my younger days. For the constable reminded me, if not in looks then in manner, of this man I had loved once. Whom I had fallen for, yes, and would have married if I'd had my druthers. Of course, then I might never have met Ev Lewis, or married him, or done my paintings the way I did, or had my name travel beyond Yarmouth, likely not even as far as the French shore between there and Marshalltown.

And what a foolish thing, anyways, to compare that fella to a fella like Constable Colpitts, who was young enough for me to be his granny.

9.

WILDWOOD
'FLOWER

I *guess Emery had fishing to do. A week passed, then another* week, yet he didn't come by. I imagined him rising before dawn to go dory-fishing from one of the schooners that docked at Baker's. I imagined him lowering and hauling nets, coming ashore to land his catch, then heading straight back out to sea again. It's not like they had telephones out there.

"You going to see that fella of yours again?" Mama had a hopeful sparkle in her eye. That sparkle made me blush. Just because her and I were close didn't mean I'd share *all* my beeswax with her.

"Oh yes. Sure as shootin'." It was what Charlie would say.

By now the weather had turned cold for good. I tried not to worry about Emery fishing, riding the waves in a dory, tossing in and hauling up nets. All it took was one rope tangling round an ankle and, just like that, over the side a man would go. But I refused to think such a thought. The best way not to worry was by sitting up in that room at the back of the house and painting. From there I would be the first to see the fishing vessels sail in.

Mama and I got a good head start on our Christmas cards. Then one Saturday afternoon, while she and Father were off visiting neighbours, who appeared at the door but Emery? I'd been so fixed on watching the docks that I'd forgot to keep watch out the front.

Pulling him to me, I smothered him with kisses. Drew him into the hall, into the parlour.

"I thought you'd never come back."

"Your folks aren't here? Thought I seen your ma walking down Water Street, was that your father? Expect them back any time soon?"

Not if Mama had a cup of tea in her hand and Father had someone to chew the fat with for a couple of hours. "Expect they'll be gone a while." I gazed at his mouth, beaming all the love I had in my heart. Rolled my eyes up to take in his whole face. "What have you got in mind, Emery Allen?"

The smile on his lips put the boots to any tiny, niggling worry I might've had during those weeks that he would not come back. That look drove away any fears that would cloud my happiness.

"Oh, I think you know what I'd like to do."

"Did you miss me? While you were fishing and that?"

"'Course I did. Reckon your bed is more comfy, isn't it, than this old couch?"

Emery was right, it was. And what we did didn't hurt as much this time. The worry that Mama and Father would come home and find us together dulled some of the sweetness, but not all. Emery was good at reading my mind; he rose and pulled up and buttoned his pants right after. Then he said he had best skedaddle before my folks arrived and got the wrong impression.

Of him, of us. He would see me again real soon, wouldn't leave me waiting again.

"You promise?"

"What a foolish thing, you. Why wouldn't I?"

So I painted and painted till Mama and I had a whole raft of cards to sell by the second week of December. Painting got me through waiting for Emery to call. When he hadn't called by the third week, I figured he was extra busy at sea, or he had gone to see folks back home ahead of the holidays.

By Christmas Eve Mama and I had sold all the cards, going door to door. Customers invited us in for hot cocoa, fruitcake, and carols. I hung back, on account of not feeling so hot—even the smell of shortbread made me queasy. "It'll pass," I said, and left Mama to her socializing.

"Good gracious, I hope you don't have the flu. Or worse, my darling." Mama had fear in her eyes, thinking the illness in my joints had maybe spread to a new place, in my stomach.

Later, as she and Father and I decorated the tree in the parlour, I kept hoping Emery would appear with a gift to put under it. When he didn't come, I figured like everyone he was spending the holidays with his people. You couldn't fault a man for that. But Christmas and Boxing Day came and went, then New Year's, and not a peep.

I wondered what besides family was in a place like Woods Harbour to keep someone like Emery there. It had no Grand Hotel, no Majestic Theatre, I was pretty sure. I worried sick that he had been lost at sea. My worry was so raw it staved off my monthly visitor. Then mid-January came and still no sign of Emery, or of my monthly. I needed to talk to him—needed badly to talk to him, to feel his arms around me. I needed my wish to come true sooner than later, my wish to marry and live happily ever after with him in Woods Harbour, Upper Woods Harbour, Lower Woods Harbour, or what have you.

Until that January, I had understood why Mama called it "the curse"; monthlies were a curse when you had to put up with them, and they sure would be one day, living in Marshalltown and making do without conveniences. But when my monthly visitor didn't arrive and still Emery hadn't come calling, I thought what Mama called a curse would have been a mighty blessing

It couldn't be, it just could not be, that I had something like a baby growing inside of me.

Then one snowy day at the tail end of January, watching from my upstairs room, I spied Emery on Forest Street, walking up the hill towards Main. Barely stopping to tie my bootlaces, I hustled outdoors after him. He was going into Stirrett's by the time I reached the corner. Cars stopped as I tried to dart across the street, hurrying the best I could, though I thought both ankles would give out before I reached the store.

I was in luck. There Emery sat at the soda fountain having a cup of coffee and a hot turkey sandwich. I smelled the food almost before I spotted him sitting at the counter all by his lonesome. His hair looked stringy from the cold wet wind that blew so hard it swept into the harbour any snow that fell. My fella was dressed for it, head to toe in oilskins.

"Emery! So you're just back now!" I clambered up onto the stool beside his. The gal behind the counter plunked down a menu for me. My stomach was in knots; it hardly knew if it was coming or going, starved half the time then turning on a dime at the very whiff of food.

He ordered me a soft drink, kept on eating. I figured it was now or never. If I did not speak my mind no one would speak it for me. Out it all came in one big rush.

"I got something to tell you. About Upper Woods Harbour,

remember you said make a wish? Well, maybe you and me put the horse before the cart, just a little. We'll be bringing along a young one, I mean. When you take me. As your legal married wife."

When he didn't speak, I grabbed his free hand and held it. His other hand clutched his fork tighter, paused in midair as if all he could think of was how he wanted to pile it with more food. "I'm having a baby, Emery. Your baby. Isn't it something? I couldn't wait to tell you."

Looking back, I reckon this was the most Emery Allen heard me say in all the hours we spent together. It's kind of funny to think of now.

"I just had to tell you. I saw you going by, hadn't seen you in so long, land, I thought you drowned! Guess I'd best not waste a second planning our wedding. Mama will be tickled pink."

Emery set down his fork, wiped his mouth on his sleeve. He shook off my hand and nudged my glass closer to me. "You gonna drink that? If not I will. Thought you wanted it."

"Not like I want you. Just think, you and me and little baby. We'll get a place by the marsh, all green and gold like you said it was. You can fish and I can—"

"That's right. You can have this brat of yours and I can foot the bill for it and for you and life will be grand, just grand."

"I love you, Emery. I do. I always will."

"Hope so. Hope you've told your other fellas the same. Do they know about your little problem? I'd suggest you tell 'em, each and every one. See who steps up to home plate, eh?" He slapped a dollar on the counter and stood up. I reached for his hand again.

"No one needs to know we did it, put the cart before the horse. We can tie the knot quick as can be. It'll all come out in the wash, you'll see. A fella and a gal in love! There's not a minister or judge wouldn't marry us."

Emery bent down and kissed me on the cheek. "In love,

that's us." Then he said he was leaving for the Grand Banks but would be back before Valentine's Day, we'd have the wedding I wanted. "The wedding of your dreams," he promised me.

"Don't suffer in silence. And don't be a stranger," Aunt said when I married Ev—though she was the one who became a stranger, at least to me, keeping her distance though she only lived up the road in town. "We all have our crosses to bear, Maud," she would say from the time I was small. Mama said it too, though not in those words. *She* was always, "Be grateful for what you have, not ugly about what you lack—we're all better off looking at things in that light." Though Mama's words did not always match her behaviour, she was right, without fully knowing it, perhaps. The older I got, the more I learned just how right Mama was. When did bellyaching ever make things better? Unless you have something good to say, zip your lip, my brother used to say. He was a good one for spouting clever sayings while elbowing me in front of Mama.

I wished he was around to give Carmelita Twohig what-for.

For his part, Ev had even sounder wisdom: "Whatever you hear bandered about, consider first who said it. The source, I mean, who it come from." The character of the gossiper was a yardstick for measuring the truth. "That one's got an axe to grind bigger and different from the next one, and the next. Mark my words. Everyone around here's got some bee or other up their arse."

Aside from his choice of words, it was hard to find fault with what Ev said, considering the Miss Twohigs and Constable Colpitts of the world and how they liked to pry.

"In their *bonnet*, you mean, don't you, Ev?"

"That too. Nah, up their arse. Don't argue."

So I didn't. I had learned a long time ago not to argue with Ev or anybody. In this spirit I knew it was best to keep the constable's visits under my hat, and not give another thought to the complaints he had mentioned. Because of course Ev was in the right, just as I am sure Bradley Colpitts was in the right about other things, things not having to do with us. Of course, in their own mind everyone thinks they're right. Look at Carmelita Twohig.

Up here looking down, there's not a whole lot in the world to make me see different.

I know what it's like to tell a fib now and then, when you're not sure what the next person wants or expects to hear. I mulled all of this over after the constable left.

I don't doubt that those gals who complained about Ev felt some need to tell their fibs, maybe even had reason to. People lie all the time, often without even knowing it. Sure, they had mistaken Ev for another fella. I am not saying men who do bad things to women don't exist, they do. But every one of us bends the truth from time to time, through no fault of our own. That's just being human. What good was it to fret over other people's lies I could do nothing about?

Their lying would blow over. Just like a spell of dirty weather, wait five minutes and it would pass. As long as I lost myself in my painting I would get along all right, Ev and me would get along all right.

Telling myself this, I got out my crow painting, such as it was, and surveyed its smudges of green and the black and blue lines I'd added the last time Ev had made himself scarce. It was all I could do to dab on one round brown eye, an eye that seemed to watch me. Then I must've dozed off because next I was dreaming of June. The backyard was a cathedral of blossoms. Lilac, apple, mountain ash. The ground was decorated with lady's slippers, starflowers, and tiny, bristly white flowers that looked like dolls' hairbrushes. Such beauty. When I came to, Matilda's painting sat unchanged—how I wished my dream could've painted itself upon the board and filled her in, too. But I harkened back in my memory to my first summer morning in Marshalltown, the longest day of the year 1938.

I had followed Ev out back while he turned the ground to plant seed potatoes. I'd ducked under the trees' fresh-green umbrella, longed to get down on all fours to smell the carpet of starflowers under the spruce, figured if I did I mightn't get up again, not without help. I didn't like asking Ev for help; even back then he did enough for me already. It was up to me to hold my own, bad enough he'd married a woman about as useful as tits on a bull.

Ev had finished his planting, then he'd come over and helped me get onto my knees. Kneeling beside me in the grass, he'd picked a tiny white starflower, twirled it between his fingers before he flicked it away.

Batting my eyelids, I'd made my Mary Pickford eyes at him. "Don't suppose you'd pick your wife a bouquet."

His forehead was smudged with dirt. He'd wiped it with the back of his hand, tugged his cap down, swatted the black flies brewing around us.

"Pick it yourself. What, you can't even do that?"

And I realized then that I had no call to expect Ev to be anything other than himself. Himself, and not like Mama picking a big bunch of peonies to make me smile, or like Father bringing Mama a bouquet of mums for her birthday. I figured the only bouquet Ev's mother had ever received, and that Ev had ever picked, was a handful of coltsfoot from the poor farm's yard.

Sometimes I fancy myself a wildwood flower poking up from the dirt somewhere.

You can't fault a person for being wanting—for failing—at something about which they haven't two clues to rub together.

"'*The Lord is my shepherd,*'" Aunt had prayed along with the preacher at Mama's funeral. "'*I shall not want....Thy rod and thy staff comfort me.*'" Make my rod a brush and my staff a can of paint, and work was my lord, shepherd, and personal saviour, I had decided to myself. Aunt would have withered in her sturdy, low-heeled shoes at such blasphemy.

If she's anywhere handy I expect she still would, wither, that is.

Meanwhile, I have to laugh, thinking of the constable asking after my staircase.

Funny, in my early days up here I would hear a song down your way about a "Stairway to Heaven" blaring everywhere. Snatches of it drifted up from radios, cars barrelling up and down the highway, and from kids sitting on beds picking out its tune on guitar. The melody had a nice lilt until the singer's keening ruined it. That singer was no Hank Snow, I can tell you. But for a while it was like that song aimed to outdo the wind, in these parts anyway.

Now—depending on where I park myself, like a seed on the ground or hovering at the mercy of the wind—silence rules. A whole darn orchestra of quiet. The air, the earth underground, rocks, tree roots, the tiniest grubs—treats for Matilda's great-great-grandchildren—each and every one of them sings out to me loud and strong. *You are dead a long time*, goes their song.

But, speaking of longevity, they say a crow can live four-teen, fifteen, twenty years. The murder I've seen flitting from the trees up on the ridge and down around where the house stood must be three and a half generations removed from Matilda. I wager they're Matilda's stock, how they've gone forth and multiplied! Steadfast and quiet—by quiet I mean keeping to themselves, the way I did. The quiet of birds, flowers, grass, and trees consoled me after Mama passed, these things became my best friends. So how could the quiet of the grave not be my reward?

From what I've seen, humans are awfully noisy beings; for all their sweetness, children might be the worst. Take that crowd that called in that cold March day, those parents and their three troublesome kids. Squalling to shatter the peace. Don't try and tell me they didn't take delight in gawking at Ev and me. Those wee gals might have been dressed like chickadees but they had hawks' eyes. Truth be told, I was happy that morning when Ev stepped in and got them out of my hair, taking them out back—their mother, too, with her uppity look.

If only I'd told Constable Colpitts about this when he brought it up. But it's hard to think straight when you're put on the spot. When someone casts a cloud over you.

Certainly, the day of my funeral in North Range cemetery was not the first time clouds gathered over Ev and me. Storm clouds fit to darken the sunniest days the same way noise dims silence. Though, granted, down where you're at, calling silence *quiet* sometimes sugar-coats it.

A person has got to be plenty careful what she pays attention to, more careful what she heeds, and even more careful what she says. Like the saying goes, See no evil, hear no evil, speak no evil.

"The man is the boss," Ev had told those CBC folks. They had a good laugh over Ev's talk. Oh, Ev liked joking around, liked it even better when people listened to him. He liked having their full attention. I figure those men were just as happy hearing him put into words what a lot of men thought back then but didn't say.

Now Ev's silence is deeper than the worms' tunnelling. It's the sound of bones turning to dust, of birds and raccoons scratching at the grass above for insects. Sharing the ground as man and wife, our bodies are more as one than when we lived day by day, cheek by jowl. Jawbone to jawbone, rib to rib. If Ev has a voice, it might be the very dirt he sprang from, thin dirt that's on the stony side. Meager as his means always were—who can fault a man for what he is born to?

I do hope he saved himself some cash choosing that little coffin for me. Any sensible person knows it's a waste of good wood burying it in the ground. Though, looking to find fault, Carmelita Twohig and even Constable Colpitts might have something snarky to say about Ev putting me in a small box: *Figures, doesn't it, after the way he kept you in that tiny house?* Why, I would tell them if I could, Ev just wanted me to feel cozy. And by the way, I am on the lookout for the constable; he might be up here too for all I know, as they say cops don't live the longest lives. Anyways, I wager it cost Ev more to bury me and have *Maud Dowley* cut into the headstone—my name before he made an honest woman of me—than he spent on my thirty years' worth of cigarettes. And that is saying a lot!

My name before he saved me from myself, Ev liked to say.

10.

BRIGHTEN THE CORNER WHERE YOU ARE

"*N*othing *is new under the sun,*" Aunt used to read out, in love with her old Bible. "*The rivers keep running into the sea, the sea never gets full.*" That about describes this otherworld, where time means nothing and the wind never blows itself out. Time doesn't stand still nor does it crawl like it used to sometimes in my corner where flies buzzed and swarmed, and the summer heat and smell of turpentine and old piss made my head ache. The only cure then was a slow, sweet drag on a menthol cigarette, the smoke filling my lungs as cooling as a dip in the sea or holding a wrist under cold water. In your world, I had given myself over to time's crawl, what choice was there? If there had been a choice I wouldn't mind hearing about it.

Before I wound up planted in North Range's rocky soil, there was the hospital. I guess I should tell you about that. I laid for what seemed a dog's age, running out of breath in a bed with sheets like fresh snow. Lying idle afforded time to mull over the long and short of my life, including the looming prospect of winding up in a box for all eternity. Weaving in and out of sleep, I dreamt of being wrapped up like a painting and carted off to the post office.

I dreamt of walking with my secretary in the woods on a snowy evening, like in a poem I heard recited on the radio. In the dream, snowflakes were stars sifting down from a purple sky. We walked arm in arm, singing. Secretary knew all the words to "Stairway to the Stars."

I woke to the stink of cleanliness, a vexation after the smells I was used to, the smells of home. It was like waking up in a snowdrift. There were women in the room, some lying in beds and two on their feet dressed all in white. Ghosts, I thought at first. Angels, Aunt would've said. Nurses.

"Where'd you say I am, again?"

Their hands smelled of white ointment. They rolled me from my one side onto the other. Pain clamped down. Their voices racketed above me like blue jays'.

"Jesus Murphy, she's no bigger than a minute, the poor thing. Nothing to her, is there, besides skin and bones. Look at the bruises."

"From falling into things? Eats like a bird—don't you, Missus?"

"I'd say she's near starved. Do you suppose keeping her light made her easier to lift?"

They shifted me like a little piece of driftwood. One gal was named Darlene, the other was named Carla. Darlene's laugh was like the tinkle of icicles falling from the eaves in a March thaw. Except this was in summer, four years after that March I was telling you about, with the dirty rumours and the chickadee girls. The ceiling was white with dots more plentiful than stars on the clearest night—more dots than the sky had stars viewed from beyond Hardscratch Road, the way I fancied the stars would appear if you lay in a meadow with the man of your dreams, and looked up, way up.

Or the way the stars would shine through a car's windshield on a cold, clear autumn night, driving past Frost Park with that same man, your beau.

All of *that* was more than a horse's age ago.

You want to see stars, you have to get away from Yarmouth town with all its bright lights, this man told me. Get away from the coast where fog makes everything grey. Riding the crest of a thrill, I would have gone star-gazing any place that fella would've taken me, anywhere he asked me to go. Yet, if not for him, I most certainly would not have ended up living in Marshalltown or buried in North Range cemetery. I mightn't have kept on painting, and I most certainly would never have taken up with Ev Lewis.

Valentine's Day came and went without any word from Emery Allen. By then I was three, nearly four months gone. Even the curse had abandoned me. Mornings, I took to laying in bed till the queasiness eased—it was an empty feeling like I needed to eat more, or was coming down with the flu. Please, not the flu, I kept telling myself. I didn't want to think of all the people who had died from it after the war, like Emery had mentioned that night under the stars, that night that seemed like ages ago but was only a season past: *"If the war didn't kill you the flu would."* I had thanked those very stars that night that he had dodged death by both means.

I marvelled at how easily my body had tricked me. Then again, it had let me down before. The same way the aches in my joints did, the flutter in my belly followed me everywhere. It was a ghost, and to think such a fluttery, invisible thing was to blame for Emery's disappearing, which it must be—though I still could not convince myself that he had disappeared on purpose, that he had chosen to. He'd been lost on the Grand Banks, had fallen overboard. He had drowned and was buried at the bottom of the deep dark sea. Or, a schooner's boom had swung about and struck his head, knocked all sense from it. He was wandering lost around some strange port town, not knowing who or where he was. Or, he had somehow found his way home to Upper Woods Harbour where an illness worse than flu claimed him, or some invisible injury from the war.

It's possible he had injuries I didn't know about. I'd never really gotten a good look at his body, not all of it.

Desperate, I wrote a note—*To Emery Allen. Meet me at Frost Park, the bench under the biggest chestnut tree, this Friday, 2pm*—and slipped it through the slot in the Belvue's door.

The next day a blizzard hit. The light through the kitchen window whitewashed Mama's face as she eyed me. I'd just devoured two slabs of porridge bread slathered with butter, was slicing a third when she cleared her throat. Her look passed from amusement to horror, the same as when she saw someone fall into quicksand in the movies. Her mouth opened but nothing came out. Then she said, "I would say your eyes are bigger than your belly. But that's not the trouble, is it." Her voice was hard; it had the same bitterness as when she had caught Charlie hiding liquor in the cellar, lugging bottles back and forth right under my sunroom perch. "There's something ailing you. It best not be what I think it is."

The anger in her voice sucked the air out of me.

"Why, Mama...what are you getting at?"

"I know that look, when someone's expecting." Looking away, she dropped the teapot lid, it broke in pieces, she started to cry.

Sleet pinged the windowpanes.

Until that moment, the jam I was in hadn't fully sunk in.

"When, Maud?"

"When what?"

"Your last—your monthly, when was it?" Not looking at me, she dried her tears, she didn't care to hear my answer. Suddenly she was all business, the way she acted with people who balked at paying full price for cards. *Five for a quarter. You don't know quality when you see it?* "Don't even try lying to me, missy. What in Job's name were you thinking, getting yourself up the stump!?"

That's a funny way of putting it, I wanted to say. Like a she-bear had gone and climbed a tree that was about to be chopped down. The bitterness in Mama's voice stopped me.

"Wait till your father hears. You have ruined your life, my girl. No man will want you now. No man buys the cow if he can get his milk for free! No man wants second-hand goods, let alone damaged ones. Now you really won't be able to show your face outside this house."

Ru-inned, she said, not "roont" the way she usually said it. She turned her back, scrubbed tea stains from the lidless pot so furiously I thought its spout would snap off.

"And where is your fella, hmm? That weasel of a man who did this to you? I suppose he's left you high and dry, hasn't he."

"No, Mama. It isn't like that."

But oh, it was. I saw now, oh my land, it was.

Mama latched onto my silence as if I'd hoped to defend Emery Allen with it.

"Not so fast, letting him off the hook. Not so easy either, letting yourself off it."

Sick as I felt, hungry-sick for more bread and butter, I suppose I smirked, as a person does when at a loss. For Mama's words summoned a picture in my mind of a gaff hook like they sold at Sweeney's, Emery dangling from it. But then I pictured a bigger, longer hook, and me hanging from it by the scruff of my neck.

Pleading for myself, I let the words come out in one big rush. "You're a mother. I can be one too, like you." Having a little baby would give me someone to love, something besides painting to fill my time, I thought. It would make me a truly grown-up woman the way Mama never let me be.

Then Mama put her arms around me, she held me tight. "How will you tell your father? How ever will we live this down? I never dreamed a girl of mine would turn bad."

Well, crippled and bad, I thought, leastways I'm not poor. That would have made three strikes against me.

And Father? Mama made me tell him my news. The misbehaved child, I couldn't look at him, fixing my eyes on the window instead.

"And no man to make it right?" His voice was as hard as the harbour's glint as the storm blowing in from sea lifted. I turned just long enough to glimpse his eyes, the same frozen blue. "What bastard takes advantage of a girl like you? Or maybe you aren't the girl your mother and I raised." He waited for my answer. I had none. "Don't tell me—one of Charlie's buddies, was it? Not that the bugger will admit to it, I bet. Whoever he is."

So there I was, going on twenty-six years old: If my life wasn't completely ruined, it had just tightened around me, a sweater that shrank with me wearing it, the both of us doused in boiling water. A sweater that had fit okay before, it was too tight to get out of. There I was stuck inside, a growing belly underneath it.

"What's that, darlin'?" Nurse Darlene bent low. Her breath warmed my ear, it smelt of butterscotch—Life Savers maybe? "Can you speak up, honey?"

Had I spoken? "You're hearing things, is all." The words bobbled out like pearls bursting from a string. The pearls Mama wore with her laciest dress, like the blooms on the popcorn bush in her garden. Nurse Darlene laughed her laugh. Alas, its sound made me think of dirt thawing, a nest being raided, baby birds falling from the sky. I imagined staring up at a ceiling of mud. But the thought of popcorn brought back happiness, the happiness of going to the movies like we did in Yarmouth.

But then this happiness turned to a fear of the worst kind— a fear not so much of the dark but of too much light, like just before the Majestic's house lights dimmed so the movie could start. Like the last time Mama and me went to the movies before she took to her sickbed, not long after Father passed away. Heads turned. There were whispers. People pretended not to look at us, and Mama and me pretended not to see them looking. There are scarier things to fret about than the dark, I told myself then and later on, when I was first married, adjusting to Marshalltown's country darkness.

Though Aunt wasn't wrong, cribbing words from the Bible to say only those up to no good wait for darkness's cover to do their deeds.

Brisk young fingers drew the sheet to my chin. Their touch was pussy-willow soft. Yet I flinched remembering a nurse gripping my ankle a long time ago, cold hands yanking my knees apart before I went out cold. Now *that* was a time I would rather erase from my memory entirely.

Another nurse spoke now. "Are you comfy, hon? We can give you extra for the pain."

Words trembled inside me but my poorly lungs and wet breathing made it hard to talk. "Don't...fret over...me." I aimed to save my breath for those I half hoped, half expected to see over yonder: Mama, Father, Aunt. Their faces crowded my head as my dream of Secretary faded.

"Don't be worrying about *us*, now." Nurse Darlene laughed. "You know how to buzz us? If you want to get up. Of course, we don't want you getting up by yourself and taking off on us."

As if I would run away. My laugh struck up a coughing fit. Pain shot the length of me, bolts of pain were screws turning. Nurse Carla pulled up the bed's shiny rails. As if I would *want* to leave this bed, warm and safe as a baby's crib. "This way you can't fall out." She sounded sorry for fencing me in. Oh but I am used to being corralled! I laughed again. And what wasn't to love about a bed with a mattress, sheets, and pillows—even if their crispness brought back memories of living under Aunt's roof, under Aunt's holy thumb? I stroked the blanket with my fist. Its blue border against white was the sky and clouds.

Nurse Darlene spoke real low. "She's agitated."

My ears still worked fine, they seemed to forget, talking about me like I was no longer there.

"Don't worry. He hasn't come around, no doubt busy makinganuisanceofhimselfelsewhere.I'mguessinghewon'tbein."

Talking about Ev, aren't you, missy? I rested my gaze on the other nurse, Carla.

"I think she's waiting for his visit. She has got denial down to an art, hasn't she just."

If I was fussy, agitated like Nurse Darlene said, blame it on their lame ears and thinking they knew what I was feeling.

Darlene stroked my fist, looked into my eyes. "It's the pneumonia, dear." The weight she gave those words! The glance she gave Carla was an eyeful. "Hubby just wants you to get a good rest, I bet. Doesn't want to come in and disturb you—that's all."

I waited for Darlene's tinkly laugh but Nurse Carla piped up instead. "Maybe she's missing him? Your hubby?" Carla half hollered. "You're worried about him, is that it? Well I'm sure if we have to we can find someone to go check on him, see that he's all right. Tell him his sweetie wouldn't mind a visitor."

More than any visitor, I wanted a smoke. I'd wound up in here before, knew how they harped about smokes being bad on the lungs. I pictured the Cameos on my table-tray, one blessed drag was all I asked. I imagined Secretary stopping by to get them, Ev refusing to let her in. I imagined Carmelita Twohig appearing and Ev chasing her off with the broomstick he used to prop open the storm door. I imagined Constable Colpitts knocking, Ev pressed up against the inner door's flower-painted wood. Like most folks, Ev would be none too pleased to see that vehicle of Colpitts's outside. Short of scurrying up into the loft, there was nowhere in the house he could escape an intruder's prying eyes and lay low. I shook my head, rubbing it back and forth against the pillow as easy as I could without sparking pain: No. Don't bother Ev, I meant. He's best left to his own devices, what good would it do him seeing me like this?

"No? It's quieter here without him? I'm sure he's fending for himself." Nurse Darlene shot Nurse Carla a glance. I nodded. Carla shook her head and cringed, don't think I did not see it.

For I had heard her whispering during my last hospital stay, about Ev bringing the nurses a pretty heart-shaped box of Ganong's chocolates, some of the pieces with bites out of them. The same box he tried to give the gals at the Royal Bank, I'd overheard. Sure, I had heard the nurses snickering, then talking through their stiff white caps about Ev peeking in at a patient getting undressed. "An old perve" someone called him. "Shh. You shouldn't spread stories like that," someone else said. "If it's true, how come you never phoned the cops?"

"Well, I never saw it myself."

"I imagine that officer has better things to do than chase down some lonely old lush."

"Oooh, the young guy? He's some cute."

I guessed they'd been talking about Colpitts, as back then the town only had two policemen. The other one was old and grey and set to retire, I'd read in the *Courier.*

The hospital was nearly as good as a radio for hearing the news, true and false alike. Mostly I remembered Darlene's voice of reason cutting their gabfest short. "Say what you want. But 'There go I but by the grace of God,' right? What good does idle gossip do anyone, especially someone in her condition?" By *her* they meant me. God or no God, Darlene had it right: it was luck of the draw who got the shitty end of the stick and who didn't.

And I'd decided right then if I could have had myself a daughter, I'd have picked a Darlene. Pure and uncomplicated, she knew enough to keep troubles to herself and in so doing could help make troubles disappear. She was the opposite of the Carmelita Twohigs of the world and these gals I kept hearing about, who had nothing better to do than gossip in the streets and on party lines, piquing the suspicions of otherwise well-meaning folks who should know better. Folks like Constable Colpitts. Gals bending the truth to win his attention, fighting over it, no doubt. I knew what girls were like. I'd been one once, after all.

Oh yes, the competition to snag and bag a steady young man like him would be fierce.

Gently, Nurse Darlene peeled back the covers, stuck a pillow between my knees. I took in her cap, its ribbon as velvety black as a winter sky. My eyes grazed the little gold watch pinned to her blouse. It and the ribbon were the only parts of her garb that weren't white. Yet, for all her wintry getup, her smile was apple-blossom sweet. I tried smiling back, raising my head a smidge until pain forced it back against the pillow.

"Now, easy. Don't be overdoing it." She went to touch my hand but stopped short, afraid of causing more pain? This is why I liked her, she thought before she acted. Like Secretary did.

My voice lifted itself up, its strength startled me: "When do I go home?"

Now Nurse Carla hovered near. "Home?" Lying on my side, I had a pretty good view of things. She and Darlene exchanged glances.

"You know, I got work to do—" A sky-high pile of orders to fill, I thought with a sinking heart, but I lacked the breath to say it.

Darlene nodded. Her eyes were dark as an otter's. The lady in the next bed woke up then. Acting like a regular Rip Van Winkle, she pointed at me. "Is that the famous one?" Her voice was like Matilda's, no offence to the crow.

But talk about the pot calling the kettle black, me calling her Rip Van Winkle: I had no more mind of what day or time it was than my roommate did. The door swung inwards. A girl wheeled in a cart with trays on it. Each tray had a plate under a silver cover, like dinners at the Grand Hotel when I was a young thing. Van Winkle groaned. Darlene turned me onto my back, swung the tray over to me on a movable table, wound up the bed so I was almost sitting. The handle she cranked to raise it reminded me of the Edison's. A fuzzy pain settled in my backside. Carla lifted the silver cover and made a face. Oh, but the aroma of hot, delicious food near brought me to tears, such a feed as I had not seen since my previous stay. Sliced meat that might have been turkey, mashed potato, turnip, carrots, all slathered with gravy, a feast such as I hadn't enjoyed since our last Christmas next door, thanks to Olive.

Might I just say, such feasts are another thing, besides smokes, that I miss up here?

I managed to hold the fork between both fists long enough to spear some meat, but try as I might I could not raise it to my lips. The meat and the fork got away from me. Gravy smeared the sheet where they landed.

"Don't you worry about a thing. Let me help."

Laying back, I let Darlene spoon mouthfuls of heaven into my trap.

"Great you've still got an appetite." Potato plugged my gullet as she spoke. "Good heavens, didn't he feed you?"

Suddenly I had no more stomach nor the heart for food.

"Have a little rest, then try to take some more. You need nourishment. Maud." Nurse Darlene addressed me the way Secretary would. Up to now I had been their "Missus Lewis."

I felt Missus Van Winkle staring. "Why, I seen you on TV a while back! Is it true your man does all the women's work while you have all the fun? My land, where'd you find a fella like that? I'll take three!"

Then someone buzzed for Darlene. I shut my eyes and went to sleep.

One night while Ev was working next door at the almshouse, he came home seeking my help. Creeping up the stairs in the wee hours, he wakened me, jingling his big set of keys. "There's something needs done," he said. "I reckoned you might keep me company. It's only right a woman should be there, not that there's nothing you or anyone can do—but I wouldn't mind having you handy."

It was odd. The only reason Ev woke me at night was for one thing and one thing only. I would roll over and lay still and let him have his way. But on this occasion, he seemed shook up.

Peering at me through the hatch, his face looked weak. Ev was the type hardly got phased by a lot of stuff, I suppose growing up he had got used to things not going as happily as some folks believed things should. This was why he took those candies to Olive's kids, figuring no child should grow up surrounded by lunatics the way he had.

When I didn't hop right to it, he got a bit peeved.

"Get your arse in gear. Would you come out back, for frig's sake. That's all I'm asking."

It was a warm night, right before the start of summer. We'd only been married a year and a half. I crawled down the ladder after him as fast as I could, slipped outdoors in my nightie and bare feet. The mossy grass felt cool and wet, and sent shivers through my heels—but nothing like the shivers that went down my spine when I spied what Ev had left on the grass by the shed. A bundle wrapped in a blanket. He picked it up and held it in his arms. I thought first it was an animal, maybe a puppy or a cat that got hit on the road. When I looked closer, I thought it was a doll.

He bent and picked up his lantern in his other hand. He swung it to light the way as I followed down the path from the end of our yard to the field before Seeley's Brook, past the woods behind the almshouse. His old shovel lay there in the weeds.

I held the lantern as he laid the bundle down on the ground and dug the hole.

"It's like the runt of a litter that don't make it. That's what I tell myself. The runt of a bad litter, the mother no good for nothing let alone making a kid. Can't even keep it alive."

"Oh, no, Ev." I had no other words, nothing but a cold, hard pity in my heart.

A dull gibbous moon slipped through streaky clouds. My hand shook so bad the lantern's flame near blew out.

"Come on, you, it don't do a lick of good being sentimental.

Now pass me that bundle and we'll get this done quick. Out of sight, out of mine, the warden says. The gal whose spawn it is don't know her arse from her eyeballs, it's a fact. So it's no skin off anyone's neck. Not mine, not yours. Pass it here, would you. Hurry the hell up, I gotta get back, got lunatics to tend to."

The bundle, when I picked it up, was no heavier than a couple sticks of butter, no bigger than a loaf of bread. Like bread out of the oven, it was still warm. No, I'm lying—it was as cold as clay and that hard. When I glimpsed the face where the cloth slipped away, I almost dropped it. It was the tiniest, sweetest face you could imagine, with all its features perfect, like you would expect a normal baby to look. For a second, I don't know why, I held it to my chest. The feeling inside me was like my heart had also turned to clay.

"Give it here."

Ev took it and put it in the hole and I wanted to spin around and hustle straight back to the house. But that clay feeling moved through my ankles and weighted my feet to the ground, and I could not stop watching as he shovelled dirt on top of it. Maybe I choked, maybe I made a queer sound like I was crying. But I was too chilled to cry.

"What the frig you going on for? It ain't yours."

I turned my back, moved like a windup toy through the trees back to our yard. I didn't know if Ev was behind me or not. By and by I looked and he wasn't there. But his voice called out from a distance, "You never seen nothing, got it?"

When I awoke it was dark. I fancied the bed was melting. My neighbour was gone—maybe they'd sent her home because she didn't like their food? Paintings I had guessed up in dreamland played in my head. Snowy scenes, teams of horses pulling sleighs, harnesses decked with jingle bells like in the Christmas song.

Until a warm breeze rippled in, I forgot about needing to pee. Darlene said they had rigged a bag for that. I felt for the button clipped to the pillow, pressed my knuckle to it. Pain flashed bright as smelts running in Seeley's Brook, slicing through the current.

A different nurse, the night nurse, came and snapped on a little light. Put a pill on my tongue, held a straw to my lips. Drinking that water was like swallowing a lake. I coughed, she rub-thumped my back.

"I've got stuff needing done, I need to go home," I explained. I could see their faces: Aunt's and Father's in the corner, Mama's by the door. They were there waiting. I didn't suppose they would mind being held up a bit if I asked for the paintbox and paper I knew were here somewhere and got started on some work. The nurse was a large white bird opening a drawer and bringing out colours. Markers that Secretary had brought, and a box of watercolour paints.

The paints—purple, pink, blue, and cream—reminded me of Ev's sweet peas. The sweet peas he grew every summer and once, just once, picked and brought into the house for me. He'd dipped water into a mustard jar, aces, spades, clubs, and diamonds on its glass, and set the flowers in it. "For you, missus. The scent of those things is out of this world, ain't it?"

Then I remembered, before my breathing had got so bad I'd done a painting just for Secretary, of moonlight at midnight. So she had visited me here in the hospital, once to bring the paints and paper, again to bring the markers. The last time she visited I'd given her the painting: "For you. Not for the post."

There were flowers by the bedside. Bluebells and cornflowers. I'd thanked her for those, too.

"Don't thank me. Carmelita Twohig brought them."

Maybe I had been hearing things?

Then I'd asked Secretary if she had seen Ev.

"Not hide nor hair."

So now, surrounded by darkness, there was a writing tablet, a piece of white card. Night Nurse—Nurse Nightingale?—propped the card on a magazine, bit off the markers' lids, laid them atop the tablet tucked in the sheet.

"You're supposed to be asleep, like the rest of the ward."

Nurse Nightingale's footsteps whisked off, retreating. In her place I saw an apparition of Ev. I spoke not to it but to the circle of light on my lap:

"Remember when we had no money for pencils and you touched a stick to the fire, handed it over. You always did keep me in smoking sticks."

A spill of weak laughter, my own.

Quit bellyaching. You never did 'preciate me. The apparition's voice went round and round in my head, like Joe chasing his tail.

One by one, Secretary's markers rolled out of reach. There wasn't enough light to draw by. The apparition vanished, replaced by the faces of the dead, Mama, Father, and Aunt watching from their corners.

It was hopeless. To finish the work I had waiting at home, I needed a special pen. A quill pen made from one of Matilda's feathers, this would help me finish her picture. I needed to fashion such a pen. I needed to finish her portrait. I needed to get home.

Stubbornness is a hard habit to break, especially when you lack the will and maybe the sense to give in and quit. I spent enough time in your world to know a lack of weakness is what normal folks revere and cling to. Maybe it makes them feel immune to trouble and better, less guilty about having things others have no hope of having. Maybe supposing "there is *us*, and there is *them*" makes the world easier for them to judge on their terms. People love the sound of *She don't have much but she keeps on keeping on.* I don't suppose anyone, normal or not, finds enjoyment in hauling themselves out of bed in the night and outdoors to an outhouse in the middle of a blizzard to do their business, all in the name of dignity. Plenty of country folks did just that in my time.

But I am here to testify that sunny thoughts can get you through that hardship, even in the dead of winter. No one prospered by sunny thoughts more than I did, too bad *they* aren't contagious. Though, truth be told, some nights in Marshalltown the only way I knew I hadn't croaked was by seeing my breath or my shadow. The moon was a big old eyeball peering down, watching over me. For years it lit my path from the house to the privy and back. You could say it saved me making the misstep that would've ended my life sooner.

But then everyone's end comes sooner or later.

Though I could barely grip a marker, in that summer-stuffy hospital with the dead cheering me on, I got a second wind. Secretary's markers were a rainbow array of colours. I guessed up and filled in shapes—brown for horses, blue for moonlight edging white for snow, green and orange for trees, black for a sleigh, red for the coats and caps two newlyweds wore. I added a church, bells in the belfry. To the snowy road I added streaks of blue. The light I saw was the moon on the crest of the new fallen snow, like in "The Night Before Christmas."

It was good practice for when I would start back in on Matilda's portrait. But it took all I had in me, bracing one fist with the other, pushing the marker's tip over that little piece of card. The sun was just coming up as I coloured in the red bits.

I could hear seagulls waking, there was one that hung around the window. I overheard Ev say, later on, that it liked me—I wonder if Darlene told him so, or Secretary? It hurt my heart not being able to pen a verse like the ones Mama and I had writ on our cards. *Best Christmas wishes. Folks never get too far away, For friends to wish them joy to-day.* Never mind, I told myself. And then I heard the crows. Was it too much to hope that Matilda and her kin had leap-frogged from pine to pine and from telephone pole to telephone pole all the way here from Marshalltown, looking for me?

They were coming to take me home; I had a pretty good idea I wouldn't be hanging around in hospital much longer. The jays and robins struck up their morning hootenanny. I remembered Xmas was a long way off but I wanted to be sure Secretary got my card, the best way I knew of thanking her again for everything. But I wanted Darlene to have a card too, in case Ev didn't think to bring her candy, if he ever thought to come in that is. I'd just close my eyes first, take a moment's rest.

When I woke, the markers were gone. Nurse Carla was rubbing at some blue on the sheet. I fought to get my breath. "Hope...that...spot...won't...get you...into trouble."

She clucked at me like a little hen—"You're quite the card, aren't you?"—and she tugged away the sheet. My back-to-the-front shirt had ridden up but I was past caring. "Don't worry, hon. Yours isn't the first I've seen, won't be the last." She held up my handiwork. "Is this for me? You sure are jumping the season. Ah, you'll be back in the saddle by then, surely." Her voice was so cheery I think she believed it, trundling off with the sheet.

Then a voice whispered to me: "Maud? What's keeping you?" A voice as kind as Secretary's but older if not wiser.

"Aunt Ida?" I called out, "Ida, is it you? Are you there?"

Matilda answered back. Her answer was a clicking sound.

"'*In darkness you were made, fashioned from the depths of the earth.*'" Oh, back in life Aunt was full of such foreboding. Comfort or caution, I took it as a veiled warning to behave myself. A reminder of what we learn soon enough, that we come from dust and, in the blink of an eye, return to it.

The sunshine filling the room should have kept me alert, made me listen harder for the crows. I knew their warning system, clicking and chattering when they'd found food but foe was near. Was death my foe? Only if you consider it an enemy. It was near impossible to breathe. A menthol cigarette would have fixed me up. I wanted Secretary—Get my secretary, I tried to say. She would bring me one. But Secretary had said goodbye. I remembered her leaning over me, tears in her eyes. I wanted Darlene; maybe she would bring me a cigarette if I said I wouldn't set the bed afire. All the times I had drifted off with a smoke in my hand and nothing had happened. Poor Aunt—living in her house, I had put more than a vacant fear of hellfire into her. Hellfire burning her place down for my sins. I would have sold my soul for a smoke: "*Sell your soul and Gehenna will be your reward, that's a fancy name for hell,*" she'd said. I would go to Gehenna and back for the heavenly reward of a smoke.

One to see me through, wherever I was headed.

I dozed in and out of myself. The snarl of my breathing was a coyote. On a winter night. Closing in. "Darlene," it cried out, "Darlene!"

"Dar's on nights." Hands drew the sheet tight, bound me as tight as the mummy I was once but not even for a day. Bandages wound round and round and round my chest to keep the milk from coming in. A mummy swaddled like a stillborn baby boy, a baby son born dead.

"Would she want the minister, you think?" The voice was

mustard-pickle sweet. It was honey from a spoon. It was green as fresh-cut grass.

My *no* was a bee buzzing in a jar.

"When's Dar in? She might want to come in a bit early."

Ev never once mentioned that night, afterwards. I never brought it up, though months later, out of the blue before heading off to work, he said he figured he would dig more graves before summer was through. "And you best button your lip about it. Ain't nobody's business what goes on next door. Nature's way, putting the poor little bastards out of their misery is how I see it. Putting them out of it before misery gets ahold of them. Nature takin' care of business, proper thing. Can't argue with that."

No, I couldn't, could I.

I am not sure what all Ev got up to over there next door at night, other than burying babies that ought never to have been born, and keeping wayward women and girls, indolent men, and lunatics in line. Some mornings he came in smelling of women, my imaginings of which brought but a very cold comfort. Once, down by Seeley's Brook, I found a locket in the grass. A locket with a picture of a man in it. The man looked nothing like Emery Allen, but seeing that stranger's picture made me pine for him suddenly. Never mind what-all Emery had done, leaving me in the lurch the way he did.

Then all I could think of was Aunt's saying about "Suffer the little children."

Babies died all the time. Not just human babies, bird babies too.

Like the time later on when I was helping Ev dig potatoes— that is, he was digging; I was tossing fresh-dug spuds into the bucket—when I should have been up the house, painting. A ruckus of squawking burst from the trees, and I spotted the crows. It could've been Matilda's mother and father, they were raiding a nest of robins. The last I'd seen of the baby robins was their pink, hinged beaks straining up from the nest, opening and closing, not long after they'd hatched.

Then there they were, four or five of those babies lying on the grass, still too young to have proper feathers. Their wings were so thin you could see the bones through the reddish feather-flesh.

Dead, those babies were beautiful and ugly both.

"So much beauty in the world, Ev, even so." I dropped a potato into the bucket, let the sound it made mark my words.

Way too late, I flapped my sleeves to scare off the crows watching us.

Ev just shook his head like I was half cracked. "Don't bother. If it ain't crows that gets those babies it'll be cats. Either way someone gets a good feed. Babies die all the time, ain't a thing you can do to stop them."

Going from the fat into the fire might be one way of putting it, the way things happened. Yes sirree, babies died all the time, I longed to offer my agreement.

When my time came, to go to the Yarmouth Baby Hospital, I mean, Mama took me. How she must have worked to swallow her pride. Father kept his distance. The months leading up to this, he and I might've been two stray dories passing before the eye of a storm. It was a hot night in August 1928. Mama and I got there in the dark, I can't remember how. Mama comforted me, by now she plainly pitied me. "We reap what we sow, I suppose, like 'bringing in the sheaves.' You'll forget the pain when it's over."

(To that I still say, as Ev might, if he had half an inkling of the pain that surrounds birthing: Horse. Shit.)

They gave me something to put me into "twilight sleep." All I remember is lying on my back, a nurse forcing my knees apart. Another nurse grabbing onto both ankles to help her.

It was a twilight with no stars, even darker than the night Ev buried that baby.

When I came to, I asked could I see it? The creature that had taken so much room inside me and in doing so had snuffed out any joy in our house. There was a nurse on the far side of the room, and Mama.

"He's gone, Maud. They've taken him."

"Where?"

"Buried him, of course."

"*Where?*"

The nurse left us alone. Mama had tears in her eyes. "I don't suppose I told you, you had two baby brothers who died. One was George, he came three years before you, and one was Victor, he came a couple of years after—you were too little to remember, I suppose. I should've said, I guess." It was like the sky opening up, the torrent that spilled from her. "I know how it feels, a bit, to go through all *that* and end up with empty arms. Cruel, I know. No other word for it. But there it is. We don't know what's in store for us. I suppose, like Ida says, we have to trust that Someone Up There knows better than we do. That everything happens for a reason."

I thought of Mary-Molly cooing over that dying girl-baby in *Sparrows*, Jesus coming in a soft, gauzy cloud to take her up in his arms. There wasn't much conviction in Mama's voice, just weariness.

"You're hurting now," she said. "But you'll see it's for the best that your baby is in heaven and isn't here to worry about. Think of it, what people would say. 'There goes that Dowley girl with her...offspring.'" The word swung like a bat between us. "This doesn't *touch* the fact that he would be yours and yours alone to feed, clothe, and school—and on what? The money cards bring in?" Mama reached out then, smoothed the hair pasted to my brow. "Oh, my darling girl, it's hard all around. Hard enough rearing kids in a home with a mother *and* a father. Too hard a row to hoe for a woman on her own." Her voice was as starched as the sheet pulled up to my chin. "Now, we will put this behind us. I won't have you moping. The sooner you're up and about, the better. We'll put this whole sorry episode to rest, like it never happened. You have the rest of your life ahead of you still. Well, to some degree anyways."

When Mama left, the nurse came and wound gauze round and round my chest till I looked like a boy, titties flat as fried eggs. This would stop my milk from coming in, she said.

A few days later Father came to the hospital to visit. He acted real shy, like Fluffy had got *his* tongue—or I was a vague, distant acquaintance he was used to seeing around town but hadn't passed by in a while. Except, he had a little bunch of lilies for me from the flower shop. When I cried, he got up and left. I heard him ask the nurse to put the flowers in a vase.

Well. I imagined my dead baby boy as a dead bird buried in the ground, like the jay Mama buried that time under the viburnum bush. Except with no bush, no flowers, nothing, to mark his grave, wherever it was. I didn't ask. I didn't want to know.

And I went home, and I painted, and you could say I became invisible, a ghost living under house arrest on Hawthorne Street. Better Hawthorne Street, I thought, than the Arcadia Poor House as punishment for my wickedness. Father was never the same towards me, though he did not stop loving me, Mama said. I could describe for you how I passed the rest of my days in Yarmouth. But it would be the same as describing how paint dries, and how, like a weed that comes up from the soil but doesn't flower, sorrow becomes something you hold inside of your body.

"Out of darkness comes release," Matilda and them croaked through the curtains. Light flickered, dark shapes fluttered past the window.

I saw Matilda fly overhead three times, land, and perch on the roof—the hospital roof or Ev's roof, it doesn't matter, roofs were all the same now. Not a feather stirred. Then a crowd of Matilda's babies lifted me and carried me up above, where the wind is.

What I can tell you from up here is, it's a healthy wind that draws dampness from the fields in spring and spreads a cool warmth over the woods in summer.

Before my very eyes, the world became a mist-covered vista teeming with every tiny living thing that was imaginable but invisible to you.

And this is the vista, the view, folks shrink from their whole lives?

For land's sake, I died. There's worse things than dying.

Pretty much the next thing I knew, I found myself here.

11.

ABIDE
WITH
ME

*A*irborne, *I reeled and spun willy-nilly—it took a little while to latch* onto the wind's direction. Across the bay a fogbank loomed. At the water's edge four crows played tug-o'-war with a starfish. *One crow sorrow, two crows joy, three crows a wedding, four crows a boy.* Hovering over the town, looking straight down, who did I see but Nurse Darlene and Constable Colpitts—together. They were sitting in the window of a diner on Water Street sharing a plate of fish 'n' chips. Darlene was wearing a bright pink top and drinking orange soda through a straw. Bradley Colpitts was in uniform but appeared relaxed and right at home, being in a place with ample headroom. Darlene looked so happy I couldn't help feeling glad for her. Tall, sincere, and rosy-cheeked, Bradley Colpitts was the kind of fella you would be happy to have your daughter date, or even be a daddy to her children. I guess he rarely got a day off, being on call and that. But the way he was laughing and grinning, he didn't seem at all harried or tired. Then I spied the jewel on Darlene's finger; it sparkled sharp as the sun shining on Digby Gut. I should have been surprised but somehow I wasn't.

I thought sorrowfully of my gold wedding band, lost to the world.

But it warmed me to see the lovebirds together, though I would be lying to say it tweaked only a fledgling regret. The pair could have been me and my beau forty years back, sharing an ice cream soda and hot turkey sandwich at a Yarmouth lunch counter. Except I could tell the way Darlene and Bradley Colpitts carried on, they had a ways to go before knowing each other as intimately as me and my beau had. Of course, with her job and all, Darlene didn't have time for smooching and spooning like I did back then, especially with the constable working all hours. At least Colpitts's work kept him on dry land and not out at sea where fishing had kept my Emery. So that was promising. For them, being sweethearts. Getting together on regular dates and that.

Truth be told, in spite of his nosiness, I had grown kind of fond of Bradley Colpitts, from a distance. He was the sort of fella who would make a good brother, I guessed from the visits he had paid me. His suspicions about Ev notwithstanding.

Catching an eyeful of him and Darlene, I nearly missed seeing who was at the next table. Land, if it wasn't Carmelita Twohig sawing into a Salisbury steak. I admit the sight and smell of that meat made me long to be back in your world, if only to eat up a dinner like the one Carmelita was enjoying. Bradley Colpitts only had eyes for Darlene, so I couldn't tell if he'd noticed Carmelita sitting there before Darlene smiled over and called out, "How's the steak?" Carmelita looked up as Bradley turned and glanced her way.

"Miss Twohig," he said stiffly, sounding displeased. The last thing he wanted, I suppose, was lunch with Darlene being interrupted. Carmelita put down her fork and said, "That's some sad about Maud Lewis. I heard she didn't last the night."

The smile wiped itself from Darlene's face. "The poor thing. Well, she's in a better place now."

"If you believe in that stuff." Carmelita wiped her mouth on her serviette. "Now that you're in front of me, officer, I've got a bone to pick with you. Remember that man I phoned you about? The one who I told you beats on his wife, getting drunk and disorderly, out by my place in Guinea—the one you said, Oh, so a little bird told you about this? Well, I saw him just this morning lying on his porch passed out drunk."

"Ma'am," Bradley said. "There is not much we can do to stop a fellow doing what he wants in the privacy of his home. Unless the victim reports the assault herself, if you read me."

"Well that's just stupid," Carmelita said.

Darlene laid her hand on Colpitts's arm. He patted then squeezed it and gently brushed it off.

"I agree, it is. But we just can't go arresting someone on the basis of hearsay."

Carmelita scowled, pushing her plate away. Her Salisbury steak was only half-eaten. If either of the lovebirds could've scooped it up and saved it for Matilda, I'd have been happy. But they turned to each other then stood up, and Bradley gestured to the waitress for the check. Carmelita didn't look up as they left.

After the early visits I've told you about, Constable Colpitts paid me a couple more later on, right before my *first* stay in hospital and just after I went home, to Marshalltown I mean, to recuperate. By then two years had passed since the constable had first come by looking for Ev, back when he was new on the job.

One summer's day, round about 1968, he had appeared out of the blue once again. To my relief, it turned out he was interested not in Ev but in the stairs of all things, my fancy stairway to the stars. He wanted to know how I had managed to paint all but two of their risers. Bradley Colpitts was just that kind of person, I guess, inquisitive about stuff others wouldn't think to ask about. Some would call this the mark of a first-class Carmelita Twohig nose-minder. I'd call it the mark of a natural-born detective. I found it sweet that he showed an interest—and to think I almost missed this visit!

Do you remember when those TV people had come around three whole years before, one of their questions was, If you could have anything you wanted, anything in the world, what would it be? Saying I wouldn't mind a trailer, I knew I was whistling Dixie, this was asking for the moon. But here is the magic of television: little did I know, little could I have guessed, that fairy godfathers watched what was on it.

Yet, one day, lo and behold, a man appeared with a trailer he told Ev was up for grabs. I could barely believe my eyes looking out and seeing the truck with this wondrous abode like a tin can on wheels hitched to it. "Pinch me, am I dreaming or what?" I watched the man park it on level ground beside the house. Ev shushed me in short order. "Don't be looking a gift horse in the mouth." For the trailer was real all right. It was like I'd died and gone straight to heaven (well, heaven as I thought of heaven back then).

A gift from above, it seemed, free for the taking.

Well, the trailer had windows that wound open and shut, with screens to keep out bugs and let in fresh summer air and cooling breezes. It had a fold-down table, a cushioned bench for a body to bunk down on. It had a little gas stove if ever I took a notion to cooking (which I did not). It even had a tiny washroom with a throne for doing your business but with no pipes attached. And here's the best part. The fairy godfather had the Nova Scotia Light & Power hook it up to the wires where Matilda liked to sit when she wasn't brooding. "Let there be light," I said, and oh my land, so there was! Of course, a part of me wished the trailer came with a television set—but there is human greed for you, no different from having a big slab of cake and even before you've finished it, craving seconds. You want to tell your bellyaching self, Git out! Be content with what you've got, you don't know hardship when there are folks living deeper in the woods than you, out in Mayflower or Guinea, say, making do with less than you can imagine. I was not going to jinx my good fortune with a lack of gratitude!

The trailer had barely got parked before Carmelita Twohig came along in her little blue car. She came to the door with a grocery bag. Ev grunted when he saw her and wouldn't let her in, just took the bag and waited till she drove off before he looked inside it. "What the hell—it must be for you. Unless that one thinks I play with dolls." Handing it over, he shook his head in a mix of disgust and bafflement. Inside was a doll with shiny yellow hair and a big full skirt knitted out of orange Phentex yarn. Instead of legs there was a roll of toilet tissue under the skirt. It was kind of cute. In spite of my feelings about Carmelita, I was gobsmacked that she had brought a present. A peace offering, or a token of apology?

I was setting up shop in the trailer when the constable came to call. He nearly sent me out of my skin rapping on the screen door, the sound was so new to me. He had gone to the house first and, finding neither me or Ev there, had the sense to come around to the side. He'd crept up so quiet through the grass he found me in a reverie enjoying a fag. I'd been thinking how nice it would be to have Secretary stop by for a leisurely chinwag.

The breeze stirred the smoke's bluish wreath round my head. Call it a halo if you want.

Constable Colpitts's smile filled the doorway. A hornet buzzed close. He flicked it away.

"Well well well, Missus Lewis. Isn't this something? So Everett's come through, buying you a bit of breathing space, this place."

"You forget, or what? You can call me Maud. And it weren't all Ev's doing, he had help."

The constable's smile became a shy grin. He stuck his head a little deeper inside the door, keeping his body parked outside. "So your friends at the CBC came through, did they? Didn't know Fletcher Markle was Santa Claus." It was a funny time to mention Christmassy stuff. The day was hot; the man must have been cooking in his serge jacket. When he lifted up his cap and pushed it back on his head, sweat gleamed on his brow. "Well, this is an improvement. You deserve it. It suits you, Missus Maud, a place of your own." He squinted up at the ceiling, it had a round white light in the middle of it. At night when it was turned on, if I laid on the bench for a rest I could see flies inside the glass shade. Better they were in there dead than swarming round a person's head like they did in the house. "Don't tell me Ev's let you have electricity too."

My smile said all he needed to know. I guess it emboldened him to continue.

"All righty then, forget what I might've said in the past. People say things, I guess. Seems Everett's done right by you, finally—more or less. Springing for a place that's at least a bit more comfy for you. Better late than never. I hope no one took unfair advantage—wheelers and dealers, they're out there. And, you know, at the Royal in town the manager's always wondering why Ev Lewis won't spend any of that money he's piling up. What's he saving for, a trip to Las Vegas? He's quite the saver, I guess? They seem to think he's got more over at the Bank of Nova Scotia. But you would know. Like I say, people love to talk, don't they. I'm glad he's finally spending some of it on you." He peered around, and I wondered if a trailer was something he coveted.

I should have invited the constable in out of the sun. But, truth be told, I liked being a foot higher than the ground he was standing on, so I was slightly less obliged to bend over backwards to look at him. This way we weren't so very far off meeting eye to eye, and there was no need for him to fold himself in two venturing inside. Pleasant as he was, he was still the law. You didn't really want the law entering your abode, not if you could help it.

"A place of your own. It's about time." The way he took *his* time gazing about, I wondered if he was looking for the washroom. It was the size of a closet and had a bucket that worked. The door was ajar. Atop the empty toilet tank sat Carmelita's toilet tissue doll. "No offence," he said.

"None taken."

"I guess you've got your work cut out, haven't you, with decorating and that? Place is kind of plain, if you don't mind me saying." He sounded like he was teasing, maybe having spied Carmelita's gift, which was no match for tulips, swans, or bumblebees. But he quickly turned earnest. "Must feel like a blank slate. After the house, I mean."

This was how we got on to the subject of the stairs. He said ever since the first time he'd dropped by, he had been wondering how on earth I tackled them, especially if I relied on Ev to carry me to the top.

"You don't want to know." I laughed, though I was seized by a stray, sudden notion that Ev might try selling Carmelita's bathroom doll if he thought he could get something for it. Chances were Carmelita might see it someplace and think I was ungrateful.

Constable Colpitts asked how long the stairs had taken me

to do. "The paint must have stunk up the place pretty bad? I suppose it kept the upstairs off limits sometimes. You sleep up there all the time, do you? Hope the paint dried before night-time." He flicked another hornet away and I almost said, Come in and shut that door before half the neighbourhood buzzes in.

"Some fellas get owly missing their bed," he declared. I figured he was speaking for himself about working long hours, going without sleep. Then I thought of Carmelita Twohig and him. In all likelihood, even back then, before I spied them in the diner, they must have been acquainted.

"What did Ev think of your project? Must've inconvenienced him a bit."

What a question. "The stairs?" His curiosity walked the line between Carmelita's Nosy Parkerdom and police routine, it seemed to me. I probably blushed, more than a little confused. But I was happy enough to give him the benefit of the doubt. "Oh, Ev's bark is worse than his bite. I reckon the two of us made do, staying off 'em. Like we'd do now if we had to. No big hardship." Really, I was thinking how hot it got in the loft, how these nights it would be no great mischief, my sleeping on the daybed, even if Ev wanted me upstairs.

How I didn't like thinking about what went on between Ev and me up there—between Ev and a part of me, I mean, a part I don't want to talk about—and how, for years, in my bravest imag-ination, while he lay on top of me the stairs would keep going up through the attic and the roof and all the way up through the black velvet sky to the North Star and the Big Dipper.

But I kept this to myself, it was nothing an officer of the law needed to hear.

"That's good," Constable Colpitts said. "Some fellows would growl about the inconvenience. You know, plenty of fellows like to be king of their castle, that line of thinking." The con-stable smiled with his eyes, eyes that were green but not like a cat's—eyes I could imagine washing over a pretty young woman, taking all of her in. Bending over, he leaned his head in further, the rest of him staying put. "It's quite the wonder you've worked next door, Missus Lewis. What I would like to know is how you managed to reach the top few steps especially, then getting all the flowers to match, and—well, I'm asking for a friend." He looked embarrassed. I guessed why. This was women's work he had delved into, the work of prettying things up. I could be wrong, but I guessed Carmelita Twohig had passed on some of her observations about Ev cooking and that. Perhaps Colpitts was too good a listener, just the type Carmelita would happily draw into her web of suspicions.

"How did I? Oh I just stuck with it." This was getting silly, I'd had enough. I gave a little laugh, stubbed out my smoke, and picked up my brush, my hint that our visit was over. I hoped he would take it. The paint on the bristles had started to harden in the little time I'd stopped for a break. The officer craned forward to take a gander at the board lying atop the newspaper spread over the table. It was kind of comical, him being almost at my level. The painting was half done, a picture I could've almost done in my sleep, of three black cats under sprays of apple blossoms.

"That's pretty nice. Guess I ought to leave you to it, then." Except he made no move to straighten up and go, even when I sighed—he was right about me having my work cut out. It would take years and years to do up the trailer in style, like I had done up the house. Plus I still had Matilda's portrait squirrelled away, crying to be worked on. Even if I started now—just between you and me, I'd turned sixty-six that March—who knew if I'd live long enough to gussy up the inside of the trailer. How the heck would I manage? By tackling it one bird, one butterfly, one cat, one blossom at a time, I decided, eyeing the constable. One riser after another was how I had done the stairs, well, the top four, before my back and whatnot gave out attempting the bottom two. Day by day, one minute after another, the same way you handle life.

I gave Colpitts the stink-eye, a polite version of it, wondering if he would ever hit the road. Colpitts eyed me right back. "You know, while I'm here, I might kill two birds with one stone. I'd like to have a look at your stairs again, if I could. And I wouldn't mind having a word with Ev."

Not this again. Just because I found Bradley Colpitts pleasant enough didn't mean he wasn't getting under my skin. "Well, he ain't here."

"Good enough. But I'm in no huge rush, I can wait. You can tell me more about your paintings."

Laying aside his interest in Ev, in spite of myself I felt more tickled pink than annoyed. After all, here was a man with a lot bigger fish to fry thinking enough of me to pay a visit. For one fleeting moment, though, the fool notion dawned that maybe he had caught wind of the trailer on Ev Lewis's property and worried it might've been stolen. Pretty hard to steal something this big, wouldn't it be? Don't be foolish, I told myself, Bradley Colpitts is too smart to think such a foolish thing, and since when did anyone prosper by assuming the worst and acting on it? Colpitts was so clean-cut, so straight-talking, it was hard to peg him as a person always bent on finding, no, borrowing trouble.

If only Emery Allen had been so clean-cut, so straight-talking, all those years back.

"Oh all right, what harm, I guess." I stared down at the cement block the trailer had for a step, gripped the doorframe with both fists. Before I could work up the gumption to ask for help stepping downwards, Colpitts had his big strong arm around me, lifting me up and over the block, setting me square onto the grass. What a gentleman.

"Sorry." More than sounding embarrassed, he sounded

like he meant it. I do believe he figured he'd done something amiss, or perhaps the sun had got to him, as he flushed and sweat stood out on his face.

"What for?"

But he didn't say nothing, just followed real slow behind me over to the house. He held the door for me, stood patiently as I climbed over the threshold. It was hot as blazes inside—the leftover heat from the range hit us as we stepped in. "There, you can see for yourself, Ev ain't home. He cooked my dinner then skedaddled, don't know where he's at. You might be waiting all afternoon."

Stooped over, Constable Colpitts took off his cap, fanned himself with it. He edged over to the stairs, bent low to peruse them. Of course I'd been more agile when I'd done them. Why, way back when, if a handsome fella like this had come round to find me perched on Ev's chair reaching with my brush for the top riser, I'd have fallen off at the sight of him, busted myself up good. Sure, even in my better days it had taken all I had, painting the orange-and-yellow hearts of those blue forget-me-nots in the middle of that top riser to match all the hearts of all the forget-me-nots on all the risers leading up to it. I watched the constable run his big square hand over the board Ev had nailed up to hold the railing in place. His left hand, no ring on his finger. What was wrong with the gals in these parts, I wondered then, that no one had snared him yet? Why, if I was young and pretty and single, I'd have been all over a fella like that, over him like a wet shirt—in my head I would have been, anyways.

"Have you been to Yarmouth?" It just popped out; I was thinking how Yarmouth was where all the fine folks lived, sweet young gals especially.

"Excuse me?"

What had gotten into me, asking? There likely wasn't a soul nowadays who had not travelled there and perhaps farther.

"Nothing," I said.

The constable ran his hand over the stairs' yellow paint. "Can't be easy for you, relying on Ev. He carries you up, but how do you get down?" I just shrugged. I had to laugh, all these years later, remembering how Ev had come home to find me standing on his chair, painting, and near had a fit. *"For chrissake, woman, take a tumble off that and you'd be done for—me too, what about me? I'd be done for too. You think a fella don't care what happens to his woman? I'd be the one hafta get the ambublance to come. I don't know why it ain't enough that them stairs are yellow, yellow is good enough for me, like I done them. Ought to be good enough for you. Come to think of it, did I say you could paint flowers on them? You'd think you owned the goddamn place. What are folks gonna think, what kind of man lives in a place painted up like this, seeing how you've taken over? 'That Lewis fella, he needs to get that wife of his in line. Next she'll have him sleeping out there in the dog house, her acting the queen bee.'"*

The officer gave me a funny look. "What is it? You were going to tell me something about Ev?"

"Nothing at all." Oh put a sock in your mouth, I remembered thinking, looking Ev in the eye that time, all the while smiling sweetly at him. For in spite of his haranguing I had known Ev's heart was like a sparrow with a broken wing. A bird that you wanted to keep someplace where no bigger, stronger birds could harm it, at least until the wing had a chance to heal so it could fly right. Even after thirty years together, it felt like waiting for Ev's heart to heal from the life he had as a kid—his crowd, his mother, his father, his sister, and his brother all living at the poor farm—was like waiting to see a robin in December.

The constable moved away from the stairs to peer at the big red poppies I'd painted on the range's front and on its warming oven's door. They were cheery and bright as clean, fresh blood. He shook his head like he could not believe the effort I had put into prettifying a stove of all things—effort better put towards cooking?

His back was turned when something darkened the window in a flash of shade too big to be a crow, too quick to be a passing cloud. I swear, the constable must've had eyes in the back of his head. He spun around, was out the door faster than you could say "uncle."

I heard him yell out Ev's name, heard the shed door slam. Joe was barking up a storm. Honest to God, I thought, what now? Oh my nerves—all I could do was sit down at the table and wait. I don't know why, but it was like waiting for the sky to fall or a tree to come crashing down. Joe calmed down and then, by and by, Ev came inside, Constable Colpitts right behind him.

Ev scowled, keeping silent as if the constable had cut out his tongue, and went upstairs. I caught a glimpse of Colpitts smiling at the sight of him crawling up through the hatch. I did not say a word, just watched Colpitts eyeing the ceiling. Don't know what Ev was doing up there. We heard stuff being tossed about and something being scraped across the floor. All I could think of was the cardboard suitcase I had brought with me years ago, with my beautiful blue wedding dress inside it—it had been a dog's age and a half since I had taken that dress out and looked at it; it was likely nothing but dust.

Soon enough, Ev must have found what he wanted—was it something I'd misplaced on him? I hated to think—for he came down the stairs, backwards like always on account of his height, then stood before the constable. He had a jam jar in his hand and he shook it in front of Colpitts's nose. It had a bit of silver in it—not much, maybe a few nickels and dimes.

"There! Satisfied? This is all the cash money I've got in the world, officer. Them folks at the bank are full of baloney, telling you I been hoardin' it. They are full of shit. You think if I had money I would give it to them? No sirree. I would sooner have it go up the chimbley in smoke than trust my money to them birds. Lyin' and thievin'—that's what them bankers do."

Colpitts's voice was calm. "I'm not interested in your money, Mr. Lewis. I think we have got some wires crossed, I think you are mistaken about why—"

"Only wires crossed are the ones them bastards from the Light and the Power have set up draining the juice from *us*, goddammit. How do I know I ain't paying to light up the whole county? Them streetlights in town, how about those? And that fella and his woman up across the way, how do I know I ain't paying for them? Since the stuff runs off them wires like water from a brook. That's how it works, i'n't it?"

"It's not your money and it's not how you pay for your power that concerns me, Mr.—Everett. What worries me is things I have heard about you liking the girls, maybe a bit too much for their liking."

Ev's eyes narrowed. "What girls? Who is it you are jawing about?" Then he half smiled. "Oh, I see. You been talking to that Stick woman, what's her name. One of my wife's—"

"Twohig," I put in. Sure, the way we said Carmelita's name made her sound like a Stick.

Ev glowered, gaping at me. "Excuse me, officer, I don't mean no disrespect. But you have got the wrong fella, you have no fucking business coming here disturbing the peace. Upsetting my wife with your lies." Ev looked at me and his eyes were like Willard's, and I saw how it wasn't exactly a picnic—never had been, never would be—his having to go back and forth to town, over hither and yon, getting cigarettes for me, paint, boards, and tinned goods, and ferrying them home on his bike—and on hot, sultry days like this, to boot. Just like it couldn't have been a picnic for Willard keeping Matilda fed while she brooded.

"And you—" Ev took a plug of tobacco and worked it between his jaws, then went to the open door and spat it out onto the ground. Turning, fiddling with a pot on the range, he wouldn't look at me. I knew what was in his mind: "What are you thinking, entertaining the law in my house?" He peered into the constable's face, and I swear Ev grew a few inches taller rolling up onto his toes, the two of them with their heads bent over. That posture will give you a pain later on, I wanted to say. "I don't suppose you got a warr'nt."

The constable looked flustered. His face was ruddy and his smile had soured to an unhappy smirk. "A warrant. Hmm. No, as a matter of fact—you're right. And my being here is my doing not the missus's. I wanted to have a look at all she's done here. I was just calling in to see how she's doing, see that she's all right."

"Why the fuck wouldn't she be?"

"Well, I suppose you are the one who might answer that." Colpitts glanced over at me. His whole face was a smooth pink apology.

"Well I suppose you oughta git your arse out of here before I call your boss-man. Mr. Mayor, that's who you work for, ain't it?"

"Ev." I used my mouse-voice. It was the best thing I had to calm him down.

"Shut up."

Constable Colpitts reached inside his jacket. "Now, Ev—" I held my breath, half expecting him to bring out a gun. His big hand came away empty.

"You don't know me, you got no call—it's Mr. Lewis to you, don't you forget it."

"Good. Good then." The officer lifted his eyebrows and gave me a questioning look. He nodded, bit his lip so his jaw looked firmer, and then he strode out the door, not another word about my paintings, and the next thing we heard the roooom-rooom-rooom of his black-and-white Barracuda car and a little squeal of rubber as its tires gripped the pavement.

"Now, he was just paying a visit, just being—"

"Did I say you could talk? 'Just bein' neighhhbourly,' that's what you're gonna say, isn't it. Only someone as stupid as you would call a cop neighbourly. Now git your arse outta here, leave me alone. Go sit in your goddamn treeelor till you get some sense back into your head. You stupid bitch."

Truth be told, Ev had a point; though the way he made it left something to be desired. I should question Constable Colpitts's interest in me, and so I did question it. Yet it seemed a waste of time to fret over whatever darkness clouded the officer's friendliness. I figured it was better to dwell on the goodness in a person's heart, otherwise you would spend your whole life sad and worried.

As I hoved myself back to the trailer, wondering how I would get back into it, I thought of my fairy godfather, the kind man who had delivered it. Imagine someone giving away a trailer, like trailers grew on trees! Of course I had been bashful, for all of thirty seconds, about accepting his gift. But somehow sidling up to, clawing, and shimmying myself aboard my heavenly little abode, I reminded myself how Ev had his sheds, his drinking shed in particular. On days like this the house was not just sweltering but buzzing with flies and mosquitoes, never mind the heat from cooking should have been fierce enough to stun them. Instead the bugs seemed to like it. But there were other reasons for loving the trailer. Keeping my paints out of the house spared Ev breathing their fumes, no matter the weather. I knew those fumes could be trouble. When they weren't turning your thoughts to mush they set up such a pounding in your head it was like someone from the Department of Highways was in there working a jackhammer.

Inside the trailer a sweet little breeze poured through the screens. It carried the scent of grass and a hint of the marsh's rotten-egg smell, enough that these smells, mixed with the smells of paint and sun-warmed metal and plastic, concocted the fragrance I'll call *eau de trailer*. By and by, as I took up my brush, some gentle cawing from the trees outside reminded me that I was not alone, that Matilda and Willard and them were nearby, always nearby. They were friends who would not fail me. Not that Constable Colpitts failed me—but he had no idea how being on the wrong side of Ev had its repercussions. I chose not to think about these, or about Ev next door stewing, ruminating, I mean. I set down my brush and looked all about me, admired each nook and cranny in my mansion-on-wheels. When I started back at the board I'd been working on—a picture of three black Fluffies—I daydreamed about my mansion being hitched to a truck, rolling along the highway all the way to the dock in Digby. But instead of my mansion riding the ferry across the big, vast Bay of Fundy, I had it perched on a steep, wild cliff on this side of the bay. I pictured myself there in all kinds of weather, painting up a storm.

'Course, I did not need to leave Marshalltown to paint up a storm. By and by I started humming the "Stairway to the Stars" song. And as I painted I got to remembering back when I was a kid and how Mama taught me piano, and how, if things had worked out a little different, if my hands had worked better by the time that song came out and if Mama hadn't died right after it did, I might have played it for her.

But nothing in life works out perfect, I thought, and I stopped to have another cigarette.

To pass the hours after losing my baby, I took up serious smoking. Mama looked the other way. To get me out of the house she would send me up to Rozee's Beauty Parlour, where Mae had our cards for sale. Once Mae gave me a permanent wave, after saying how pretty I would look with the right 'do. I liked Mae, she talked so much I hardly needed to speak. I loved the feeling of her washing my hair, her strong fingers massaging my scalp as the soapy water sluiced from my forehead into the sink. If not for her talking I would have drifted right off to sleep, staring at the drain. "Look who's in the moon," she teased once.

Afterwards, as she worked away, tugging and twisting what she called my lovely locks around the curlers, I daydreamed, even guessed up a kind of a movie, one that starred Emery Allen. A talkie in real-world colour, it began like this: Emery stepping out onto the porch of a big old house, squinting at Woods Harbour shining through a maze of spruce-covered islands, then going inside, locking the door behind him. A sea captain's house, it was filled with treasures from the seven seas, dressers stuffed with fine linens, a silver tea service on a grand mahogany dining table, needlepoint upholstered chairs to seat a whole crowd of company, just waiting for rear ends to sit on them. Except none did. There was no wife, there were no children, no friends or relatives, just Emery himself rattling around the big, square, tall-ceilinged rooms, pining for what was no longer his but could have been, once, and should have been.

Of course, Emery was no sea captain, that I knew.

Mae liked how I kept still with my head down. After she finished doing my hair she smoked a cigarette with me, waiting for her next customer. She talked, I listened. There was no need to be ashamed, not around her, she said.

"You're not the first to have a baby and give it up."

"I don't know what you are talking about," I told her, blushing all the same. What she had said just went to show how people talked, and how badly the truth got twisted in the telling.

"The Crosbys are nice," Mae said. "Mrs. Crosby's a sweetheart."

"I reckon they are?" I butted out my smoke. Her next customer had come in and Mae was already holding out the cape to wrap around the lady's shoulders before her shampoo. To my mind, Mae saying someone was nice meant they were a good tipper. Her comment about this Mrs. Crosby made me feel a bit bad, for Mama had a strict arrangement with Mae, who did my hair in exchange for cards. Dis-for-dat: the barber system, Mae called it.

The next time I went to see Mae, half a year later, she said as she usually did what a nice head of hair I had. "If you like frizz," I said and came out of my shell enough to laugh. She waved her comb like a magic wand and said "Frizz-be-gone!" And I wished it *was* a magic wand and this could have been the old days, before Emery Allen, before the baby hospital, before.... I knew she was looking at my hands but instead of acting like she wasn't, she came right out and said, "You poor dear—I'm afraid to ask, but have they gotten worse?" Then she asked if I had any paintings she could put up, because customers liked having things to look at while waiting for their perms to take.

That day I paid for my haircut with the money Mama gave me. Mae said nothing more, just slipped the money into the drawer. "Book you now or later for your next cut?" Her voice was warm but rushed. Her next customer was already waiting in the chair, Mae asking her how the family was, the kids and that. I guessed if you didn't have a family to talk about, you didn't have much.

While I was smoking, Ev came and peeked in through the screen at me. He looked sorry for getting mad, said he wanted to make sure I was okay.

"There you are, smoking again. Jayzus. You think them store-boughts go for nothing? You know they ain't good for you, chock full of tar and that. You're gonna give yourself the emphasizema, you don't watch out. Christ." Then he opened the door, climbed inside with me, and craned over the table, taking in my progress. "Not bad, not too bad a-tall, for a cripple." He nudged my arm, made me laugh, pulled a face that showed his gums—his toothless baby smile. "Don't be slacking off. And I got a reward for you, over the house—you know them Rosebuds you like?" The chocolate ones, he meant, and yes, I would do anything, well almost anything, to feel and taste the sweetness of a chocolate Rosebud melting on my tongue. "You be good, and I might bring you a couple. Save you hobbling over." It was like we were two people who hadn't ever shared a place, were good pals, a fella and a gal taking a shine to each another, and him saving me the trouble of leaving the house to go on a date. After thirty years wed! How many couples you reckon could say that?

He stepped back down to the grass and disappeared, and came right back with a little box of Rosebuds. Some had been eaten, but the ones that were left were nice and soft and half melted. "Here you go—these'll keep you going till supper. Or breakfast, if you ain't fussy about eating in this heat. Heat like this, a body don't have much appetite."

Then off he went to chop wood, or dig clams, or catch a mackerel. If he did catch one, it would keep till morning, I supposed.

So I painted through supper hour and into the evening, and when it got real dark I snapped on the round white light above the table and painted some more. Ev did not like the trailer having electricity, as you may have guessed. He had his reasons laid out plain and simple: folks in our shoes could pay for grub *or* pay for power, it was a choice. Only the rich could afford both. As far as Ev was concerned, a person could live without light but not without grub. He was mostly right; our lives were proof in the pudding, like they say. I knew different, though. Light was as important as food, just look at plants, how they croak without it. Still I took pains to burn the trailer's light sparingly, waiting till I could barely see before turning it on. Then I leaned into the brightness it shed upon the table. I reckoned this light could not cost more than what a week's worth of sardines cost, or what I brought in with a few paintings. Plus the blueberries out back were coming in, and if the sunshine held and the patch gave Ev a good yield, this would bring in more money. Never underestimate the power of light!

I listened to Joe out there barking at a passing car. When I finished the painting, I set it by the window to dry, then I turned out the light and set there in the quiet polishing off Ev's Rosebuds. With their sweetness in my mouth I took a tour in my imagination, of all the coves, hills, and valleys I had guessed up for my pictures. What a nice trip. Then I imagined staying in the trailer all the rest of my days and never leaving it, not even to splash my face in the cold water from the well. One day Secretary would come to pick up that week's work and find me asleep, and try as she might to wake me, she would not be able to.

Land, I thought back then, if that were to happen, what would become of Ev?

I could just see him sniffing at the air for a whiff of me in the paints drying in their cans. The only other sign I had been there a handful of butts laying in a scallop shell.

A whiff of turpentine or sardines mixed with the smell of tobacco smoke: that would be the extent of the earthly spirit I would leave behind to console and comfort him. Truth be told, I worried how he would get along without me.

12.

EV'RY
PRECIOUS
MOMENT

With *Ev on the go so much, you could say I was lonesome—but* never lonely, no sir. I was never bored, not with how I travelled in my head. While Ev went off on his bike, when I didn't have a paintbrush in my hand, I read letters people sent, from all over creation—from famous folks and regular folks alike who had seen us on TV. Some of them sent me presents, magazines, little tubes of real artists' oil paint and real artists' canvases, and trinkets, oddments like that brooch I told you about, the little palette set with tiny coloured jewels. Some of them wrote to thank me for paintings they had come all the way to Marshalltown to buy.

As you know, not everyone who dropped by was a buyer. Quite a few were just tire-kickers, like Ev called them. Some just wanted to take my picture, some wanted to talk. I confess it made me want to lock the trailer's door and pretend I wasn't there, even when they rattled the latch and stood there, thinking if they waited long enough I might appear.

That was just the cost of being famous, Ev said. "Yup, and being famous ought to let you pick the wheat from the chaff, oughtn't it? You find out who your real friends are. Take that police whatsisname. Now there's a tire-kicker. If he was a real friend like you think, wouldn't he be here buying something? The gall, coming here and pestering you when you got work to do! Christ knows what shit he's filled your head with. And you stunned enough to listen."

That summer the berries were loaded down back. Ev set up a scarecrow to frighten off the birds—sure, by then Matilda's latest brood had flown the nest but only so far, and the whole crowd of them would sit up in the trees watching him pick. One morning before I could ask Ev to help me into the trailer, he took off down to the patch. I took the foolish notion to go down there too and see if I could pick a handful—as if I were one of the birds of the field, craving the berries' sweetness in my craw. Of course blueberries were best baked in a pie with loads of sugar, the sugar brightened up their shoe-polish taste. But it took a lot of berries to make a pie, berries Ev could hawk in town.

Before I could get my shoes on, from my window I spied a pack of children from up the road cross over and sneak towards the backyard, some girls and maybe a boy or two. Ev didn't like trespassers of any age, didn't like sharing what was his by rights of the blueberry bushes growing right behind his property. I didn't much like being stared at either, and kids, as we all know, like to gawk, especially with no adults to stop them. So I bided my time in the house before going out back, thinking I should be in the trailer mixing a bit of paint—not that I did much mixing, the way the colour went from the paint can into a sardine tin was pretty much how I used it.

By the time I got down there, those kids had been and gone. Ev was setting on the ground with his pail half full. He had his pants half undone. "Look at that, I popped the goddamn buttons off my fly," he said. He had a funny look in his eyes, kind of weary but satisfied—the look he'd had sometimes coming home from his night shift next door.

"You had best do yourself up," was all I said, "before something falls out." I meant nothing by it but he took umbrage to my wisecrack: "What, a fella's not allowed to take a piss?" I turned my back and somehow got down on all fours and picked and popped a few berries into my mouth. But the berries were disappointing with no sugar to help the flavour. They were best left for the birds, I figured. So I let Ev help me to my feet without saying another word, and got him to boost me up into the trailer, then shut myself inside.

Well, it wasn't long before the car pulled up—the black-and-white Barracuda car—and my friend the constable was rapping at the screen door. Long time no see, I wished I could have said. But I did not want to let him in, and turned away from his shadowy face in the window. When he called out I answered, like Ev would, "What can I do you for?"

"I'm here to buy a painting," he called out. "For my mother." And he explained how his mother lived down Barrington way, how she had heard about me from a friend of hers in Woods Harbour. Then he started talking about Woods Harbour, Upper, Lower, and Middle, and about Shag Harbour being nearby, how just the previous fall, the same year our country had turned one hundred, people had seen a UFO fly overhead then fall into the sea just offshore.

"A You Eff Oh?" I peeked out at him then and opened up.

"You must have heard about it?" Constable Colpitts smiled like he could not believe I hadn't. "You live just a hundred miles up the coast and you didn't know about this?" He shook his head and he laughed—and in spite of everything, his laugh felt the way a cough drop would on a sore throat, it was a relief.

I could not have cared less about a flying saucer. For all I could think of was Emery Allen, who, as you know, had come from down that way and who, as far as I knew, might even be buried there—in one of those Woods Harbours, Upper, Lower, or Middle.

"So—" The constable practically doubled over to step up inside. "—Ev's behaving, then?" He stood jackknifed over the table, hands behind his back, and admired the seventh painting of three black Fluffies I had done that week—with Ev's help, of course, him tracing their shapes on the boards. "Seven times lucky," Colpitts said when I mentioned this. "How much?"

"Fi' dollars." I spoke without a second's hesitation, for I had that Fletcher Markle's question firm in my head: *"If someone offered more than four, would you take it?"*

Friend or foe, you bet I would. Tell me one good reason why not.

"Sold." The constable pulled his wallet out of his pocket and I glimpsed the holster on his belt. It had no gun in it, and I thought, what is the use of that? He handed me a ten-dollar bill.

"You got nothing smaller? I don't have change."

"Keep the other five—a tip. For your trouble."

I thought of him visiting his mother and giving her my painting. Maybe the way I had imagined him sitting in a lady's kitchen having pie was not so far off the mark.

"Oh, I couldn't." I had good reason to be polite but it stuck in my craw. I sure could have taken the extra money, what was to stop me? But I thought of Ev saying how kindness could be turned against you, how you needed to keep on the good side of the law. Plus, you didn't want to drive up the price of your work too high in case it put buyers off. "Here. Have two." I shoved another painting at Colpitts, a poorly one of Lion and Bright that had not come out so good as the rest.

"Well. If you're sure." There was that manly blush again that I had come to watch for. "Don't want to shortchange you. But I know someone who would like that one quite a lot."

I wondered then, just for a second, if he meant himself. Or his boss, the mayor.

"I just like to see them go to a good home, officer."

He looked at me a little askance, as if I was talking about kittens, real ones. I breathed in, wanting a smoke. "My paint-ings—I like to think they'll bring someone a bit of enjoyment."

And that was it for his visit. Taking up his purchases, he left without saying anything or asking further about Ev, who I am pretty sure would have stayed hid in the blueberry patch if he had seen the car. Only I hope if he had come up from out back he'd have had his pants done up decent.

By and by, seven years after my trouble, the birth of my dead son in the baby hospital, Father died. Seeing Mama going around the house in her widow's weeds stirred up in me a bitter mourn-ing, not just for Father but for the way death carried off people's dreams, put the kibosh on things they held dear, their ties with other people. His passing away did something to my head: it filled it with such longing it made me look at things no longer as they were at all, but as I wished they could be.

This raised up feelings I thought I'd laid to rest a while ago, about Emery Allen. Oh yes, I blamed that dead baby boy for driving us apart. In my heart I forgave Emery, though I would not forget the way he had ditched me. The summer after Father died I drew a picture of Emery and me together kissing on each other. Emery's face was next to mine, his eyes were full of love for me. I knew it wasn't true, was just a made-up scene. But it warmed my heart as I dipped the pen in the ink, moved the nib over the paper, and by the time I put my John Henry on it—*M. Dowley, Yarmouth, July 1935*—you could almost say I had forgotten the trouble Emery Allen had caused me. For drawing us as lovebirds fixed in my mind forever the notion of us being this way, just as an old photograph fixes forever the idea of what it shows. Otherwise my idea of love would have flickered and died, love being no different from a candle whose wick runs out. I figure it's better to keep happy dreams alive in your head than harbour the sorrows life doles out.

But then, not two years later, Mama followed Father to the grave. Before Father passed, the harness shop had gone belly up. By the time Mama got sick, there was little money left. The house was cold, more often than not the larder almost bare. Yet Mama and I soldiered on, as some might say. She more or less took care of things. Those ten years between my birthing a dead baby and losing Mama I barely showed my mug in public, except for those visits to Mae's salon just up around the corner. I didn't dare go to the movies lest I disgrace Charlie, my ruined reputation as contagious as my illness was in some folk's eyes. But when Mama got bad, things changed. I had no choice but to venture out. Mama's taking to her bed for good left me to do whatever shopping we could afford.

The first time I went, Mama made shopping sound like a happy adventure, a hunt for buried treasure. "Go on up to Stirrett's, see what you can find for our supper." Like I was searching for a rare and special treat when her list said cabbage and the smallest joint of beef they sold, to do us all week.

After being mostly housebound for so long, I felt timid as a mole shying from daylight, venturing uptown past Mae's. It was a foggy day, thank the stars *and* the moon. Walking along Main Street was like stepping foot on another planet, but somehow a familiar one. Inside Stirrett's I gave the soda fountain, where I had last seen Emery, a wide berth, also the goods counter where

Mama had once bought lace and silk and satin ribbon, all a vanity now. I made my way to the groceries, ducking people's stares the way you duck rain showers. I crept up and down the aisles of tinned goods. At the meat counter, I pointed to some gristly meat and, saying little, Mr. Stirrett wrapped it in paper for me. I pointed to the vegetable bins and he came around from behind the chopping block and placed a cabbage in my arms. I cradled its roundness against my chest.

Behind me there was a little scuffle. "Catherine Dowley!" I heard. "You put that back—what did I say about candy?" It was funny to hear an oddly familiar-sounding name. Though I guess we had relatives scattered here and there, after Granny Dowley died our family were the only Dowleys in town that I knew of. But it was the first name that stopped me, so like my middle one, Kathleen. When I went to pay, Mrs. Stirrett was behind the cash. A lady and a little girl were in front of me. Maybe the girl wasn't quite so little, was maybe eight or nine years old, by the looks of her. Mrs. Stirrett gave me an odd look but that was nothing unusual. The woman with the child turned and stared at me, then grabbed the girl by the hand. "Come along, Kaye—*Catherine*! Quickly!" Like I might up and bite her, for pity's sake. Gazing back at me, taking me in, the girl had a funny look about her. She was a pretty thing with brown hair and dark eyes. I had a shivery feeling I had seen her someplace—impossible, as I had barely strayed from Hawthorne Street for about as long as she'd likely been alive.

"I said, come along." The mother stared at me with the strangest pained expression, not annoyed so much as panicked. Make a picture of me, why don't you, missus? It might last longer, I wanted to say. But speaking would've drawn more attention. Bad enough being gawked at by a child let alone its mother like I had cooties, and if the mother didn't put some distance between us, she and her precious daughter would catch them.

That little girl would need her ringlets dipped in kerosene—shame, shame—and that would just be the start of a life gone wrong: next she would be running with men and doing what I had done with Emery, causing her mama more heartache than a house on fire!

As the mama dragged the child out the door and onto the street, the little girl turned and gave me one long, puzzled look. She started to wave to me, until the mother grabbed that hand too and held onto it.

When I arrived home, Mama called out from the parlour where she had set herself up on the old sofa, a quilt covering her. Her voice was chipper, the way it sounded when she was too sick to get up but pretended not to be. "Who'd you see on your adventure?" she wanted to know.

"No one."

"You must've seen someone. Don't tell me the store was closed? You got what we needed?"

"'Course it wasn't closed. And yes, I did. Got what you asked me to." I set the things down on the piano bench, long enough to take off my coat. Then it came to me, where I had seen that mother before, the mother who'd been in Stirrett's. Her husband had done business with Father, I remembered. I reckoned I had seen her and him at the harness shop once or twice. It felt good having something to report to Mama. "Seen the wife of one of Father's old customers, don't know her name."

"Guess if she was anyone important you'd remember it, wouldn't you. Did she speak?"

"Heck no."

"Was she by herself? Who else did you see? I don't imagine she was the only one in the store? How were the Stirretts?" Even when she was sick, Mama was as sociable as I was shy. She needed to be in the know.

"Had a wee girl with her."

"Oh? How old?" Mama tried to reach for the water glass on the table. This movement alone spurred a spell of weakness. She closed her eyes, waited till it passed. In case I hadn't heard the first time, she repeated her question: "How old was the child?" Mama's face didn't look too good, though I had got used to her being pale. Her voice dipped low, "Wasn't Mrs. Crosby, was it, and...and her daughter?" She breathed in deep and held onto her throat, waved at me to pass her the water.

"How would I know? What difference, if it was or wasn't?"

"You didn't catch her name, did you—the child's, I mean? It wasn't 'Catherine'?" Mama closed her eyes. I held the glass to her lips.

"Might've been. Her mama didn't like her having a sweet tooth, seemed like. Nah, she wasn't a Crosby, you must be thinking of someone else. She had our name—funny, isn't it, having our name, not being related. Didn't know 'Dowley' was so popular, did you?"

"Oh, you know—Moods, Stirretts, Bakers, Dowleys, common as can be. Like MacDonalds up in Cape Breton." Mama laughed, and took a coughing jag. She looked so bad I ended up calling Charlie and asked him to get the doctor. So much for that woman and her daughter, whoever they were.

If Digby County was close to heaven, the trailer was a piece of paradise on earth. But nothing on your side of the veil comes without cost, even if it's free. It was true what Ev said: having the Light & Power meant I needed to sell more paintings to earn more dough—that is, to work even faster. "You seen those paint-by-number jobs—they sell kits for those in town. Folks won't want to buy your pitchers if they can pick and choose and paint their own, have 'em come out just as good if not better."

Even when he was in his cups, Ev was a smart cookie, don't let a soul tell you different. As I've mentioned, he had his way to help me work faster, copying my bestselling subjects—oxen, cats, boats, horses and buggies—as a real artist would call them. It was especially helpful when my hands pained too bad to draw things by my lonesome. He would ask where we should start tracing almost before I picked up the pencil. "You knows best where stuff goes. You done this a hun'red times."

Or a thousand, ten thousand. Of course, only I knew where the lines and shapes fit nicest, lines and shapes and colours placed just so to catch a buyer's roving eye, make it fix on a flower here, a bird there. Then get that eye to dipsy-doodle a bit, wander, then stop and look closer. "That's how you put a smile on a stranger's face," I explained one chilly evening. The two of us were sitting in the trailer. The blueberries were finished for the season, with only huckleberries left to pick, and these were so few and far between even Ev said it was best just to leave them for the deer.

I aimed to enjoy this time together under the trailer's warm white light.

"It's the way you get people to look at a picture. Know what I mean, Ev?"

"Nope. But who gives a shit so long as they hand over their dough." He rose and fiddled with the switch, turned out the light, and left us in darkness. The dark and its chill were a foretaste of the months looming ahead. "If I wanted a lesson, reckon I would ask." As he slouched across the table, his eyes had a pale gleam, not so much the twinkle I sought. I could smell liquor off him, not as strong-smelling as the stuff he concocted himself, but sweeter, a bit like apples. I kept my mouth shut about it, of course. It wasn't worth riling him up over it.

But, to me, the way a person looks at a picture *was* a matter worth discussing. Looking at pictures was different for everyone, I figured then and still do: beauty lies in the beholder's eye. Just say, for instance, what grabbed their eye first were the matching snouts of a pair of oxen. The dangling hook chained to their yoke pulled that eye closer. The chain helped whoever was looking guess up the rest: the weight of the burden those beasts were hauling, the shouts of the driver behind them cracking his whip. The warmth of the oxen's brawn, the smell of manure. You didn't need to see the whip striking to know it would hurt.

Sitting there with Ev in the trailer made me wonder how it would feel to speak face to face with a person who called themselves an artist. In the dark or in the light. Someone to say, Yup, that's how it feels. Someone who wouldn't think I was full of baloney, flapping my gums just to hear myself talk. There was that John Kinnear in Ontario who sent me stuff and wrote me letters. I had written back to thank him for his kindness, but I'd never talked to him. I don't know what I'd have said! I figured Ev understood me as best he could, as much as I had a right to expect him to. I felt for him. Though he had started painting pictures of his own, more or less copying mine, for his own amusement, he said, or in case something happened to keep me from filling orders. But painting didn't mean to him what it meant to me. It wasn't his friend like it was mine. It hit me, not for the first time, that Ev was the loneliest person I knew. So even when he'd been drinking I could hardly give up on him now, could I?

"Now, Ev. Do you ever suppose what makes a picture look pretty might be the parts of it you can't see? The hardship behind it, I mean." Ev might have been lonely, but he was smarter than folks like Constable Colpitts and Carmelita Twohig could know, or, for that matter, claim to be. Practical and canny as could be when it came to money, he was playing with the full deck of cards that I lacked. I couldn't blame him for acting impatient.

"Oh g'wan, quit talking bullshit. All talk, no action—that's you." He laughed, and there was that twinkle. As he sank into the bench, I caught it in the moonlight that came creeping in. Who wouldn't get impatient, depending on strangers the way he did, people buying things they didn't need. Pure luxuries, that's what paintings were, he said. "Spending cold cash on something just to look at, something that won't fill an empty belly for love or money." He had a point, so it wasn't hard to give Ev the benefit of the doubt, like they say. But now I'd started talking I wasn't ready to quit.

"Listen." My voice cut through the pocket of silence we'd slipped into. Its strength startled me. "You don't need to show ox keeled over dead to make someone 'magine their strength hauling logs five, ten times their weight."

Ev barked out a laugh. "The hell you know about lumbering and hauling, or anyt'ing else? Wouldn't know work if it snuck up and bit your arse. Living the life of Riley, you are. Always have, always will. Not like me."

Once Ev got an idea, shaking it loose was like freeing the very last drop of molasses from its all but empty carton.

"What I mean is, why tell folks what they can guess up for themselves, if they have half a brain? You show them too much, they'll think you're calling them stupid."

This got Ev's back up in a way I never expected. "Who're you calling stupid? Folks *are* stupid, seeing what they come and spend their money on. If I wanted your stupid opinion, the fuck I'd ask for it."

"Good enough." I folded my hands together as best I could. Suit yourself, I thought. "Didn't mean to argue." I pulled my sweater tighter around me. Fall was here all right. The trailer had a little oil heater but no way could we afford to run it. Now Ev was jawing about the price of tea, how Red Rose was owned by crooks. I did not make a peep, didn't need to, for I had begun carrying on a chinwag with myself as I often did. This time the chit-chat in my head was about colours, how you could get a charge out of folks who liked their hills and maples in winter to be white by painting these things green or, heaven forbid, orange. It was no great mischief that Ev preferred not to hear about this. It would be a strange marriage, wouldn't it, if man and wife were complete copycats, their every thought and deed a round of Simon Says. Fancy that, like seeing nobody but yourself in the mirror for thirty years!

I had my own ideas, like Ev had his and Secretary had hers and, I'm sure, the Hanks, Snow and Williams, had theirs. As far as I could tell, pictures were not a lot different from songs, songs not a lot different from pictures. They all had their riddles and rhymes, though these might sink into you differently. Like when you first heard a song on the radio, you might forget the words but the tune would worm itself into you and stay long after the song quit playing. I learned this as a tyke sitting on Mama's lap while she played piano, and later on when she had me pick out tunes for myself on the keys.

Oh, the melodies! What a grand time we had, the two of us tickling the ivories in the parlour while Father was at work and Charles was at school. "When You and I were Young, Maggie," "Shall We Gather at the River," that tune we loved so much from *Sparrows*. When Mama got going, fingers thumping the keys, dishes rattled on the sideboard. The pictures atop the piano jumped in their silver frames, photos of me, Brother, Mama, and Father, displayed so nice. I'm not sure what Mama would have thought of Hank Snow, Hank Williams, Hankshaw Hawkins, or Buck Owens. Maybe not much.

Or maybe she would have loved them all, who knows? When I get to see her, I will ask. I figure they're all up here somewhere, Hank Williams especially. There ought to be a special place for him, you'd think.

But all of this is a roundabout way of saying how each picture has a melody of its own that's hard to copy. No tune sounds quite the same played twice on the piano, at least no tune did when I played it, not the way Al Jolson's sounded the same on that wax cylinder played over and over. My point? When Ev helped with his stencils to trace the same old lines time and time again, I felt a bit like a machine, not an Edison but a spirit duplicator like at the hospital—the Ditto machine that printed the day's menu in mauve, with boxes to tick for this or that food, the choices of which I hadn't seen in a dog's age, until my *first* time in there. Now there's a story and a half....

I'll bet by this time I had painted Fluffy a thousand times and Lion and Bright a thousand times on top of that. The truth was, I needed Ev's help making those lines on the boards. I often thought how in cutting out his cardboard stencils and tracing my lines and my shapes, he was getting a free lesson in learning to make pictures of his own.

As I later saw from up here, he had a lot to learn about scaling things to size. Why, just the other day I happened to see a painting of Ev's for sale. It had oxen like mine and two tiny horses with tiny people riding them, one horse on either side of a rabbit big enough to swallow them all in one bite. What, I wonder, was he thinking?

Slaving away in the trailer, God forbid, I could have used Ev's hands guiding mine as I filled in all the shapes with colours. It took everything I had to stay inside the lines. You could say, like Aunt would've, that while my spirit stayed willing, day by day my flesh weakened. One could hardly save the other.

As for salvation, poor old Aunt had saved me once, of course, which you shall hear about in due course. But she could not save me twice, let alone thrice. By the third time I needed saving, she wasn't alive to try.

Can I just say it was my own fault for not bunking down in the trailer that night like I could have? But after that chinwag with Ev about painting and whatnot, the last thing I wanted was him thinking I felt uppity or miffed at him. He hadn't been so wrong about tea being pricey and folks being stunned. (Take the Twohig woman: even when she acted nice, what kind of brains lay under that bird's nest hair of hers, the blue chiffon scarf she tied over it?) Truth be told, it is cozier lying snugged up to someone than lying by your lonesome, in a house or in a trailer. I did not like to lie alone out there, you can take this however you want. So after our chat I let Ev lift me down from the trailer, help me back into the house, and carry me upstairs. With the two of us slung together in bed, I made like the trailer hadn't entered my life. Now don't you get the wrong idea. I was sixty-six years old, Ev was a good nine years older. Despite what Olive said once about us being so sweet together and in love, him and I weren't ever what you could call lovey-dovey. But age didn't stop him from rubbing against me, exercising his married rights. No rest for the wicked, I guess. Like always, I laid there wishing I was asleep. In minutes, I was.

You can blame my bladder for what happened—like Aunt said, fleshly weakness will trip you up every time. In the night I got up to take a pee, made it on hands and knees to the hatch. Ev was out cold, on account of his imbibing, I suppose. Going down shouldn't be a problem, I thought—figured once I got downstairs I'd use the bucket, then finish the night on the day-bed. But one foot must've caught on something, the bottom of the bureau? Through the hatch I went. Instead of leading me to a blaze of stars overhead, my stairway sent me on a cartwheeling tumble where the only stars were the ones sparking in my head.

As I flew and skidded downwards, my flowers came to life. Stems reached up and wound themselves round my ankles trying to catch me. Their hold only meant I felt the bump and scrape of each riser as I fell. I thought for sure I was a goner, that the blooming staircase the constable had been so taken with had done me in.

Looking back, was this a practice flight? Like Matilda's babies being pushed from the nest to find their wings. But in my dazed brain, Bradley Colpitts crooned about the six steps Ev had put in once I was more than a glint in my husband's eye.

A grassy meadow of daisies would not have softened my landing. Yet the sparks I saw were no longer stars but fireflies flitting through me.

Hadn't Ev said my posies were a frill? I let them distract me, fixed on them and not on my bladder, hips, and spine. It wasn't Ev's fault the stairs sagged and quaked with wear, wasn't his fault I'd had to *go*. Or that he was in dreamland as I came to, arse over teakettle at the bottom, wedged between the range and the stairs. Somehow I wormed into the cubby under them where warmth from the fire's embers was trapped.

Gazing up, not a star to be seen, I thought, You have landed in a cellar! The cellar of the house in Yarmouth where Mama, Father, me, and Charlie lived, one happy family. But no, I had fallen through a hole in the sky? My hip throbbed to the in-and-out of Ev's snore overhead. His snore throbbed me back to Earth. I would have fallen off the planet otherwise.

Why wouldn't he waken? It did no good to think hard thoughts, did it. Hard thoughts never helped anyone. But my mind couldn't be stopped in that moment from dreaming up the last time I'd been trapped in a place so dark.

When Mama died it was like someone threw me down a well without a rope, a deep dark hole I hardly knew how to see inside of, let alone climb out of. Nothing hurts worse than losing your mother. Do you know, I would wake up and the feeling of being down that Mama-less hole would be in my *bones*, grief as deep as marrow. I figure you can get used to pretty near anything. But the hurt at losing Mama and the longing to see her again would never leave me. Charlie had married and divorced and taken up with a new wife, of course. He was busy pleasing her. I didn't want to ruin their lives too. Making up for lost time after his old wife gave up on him, the last thing Charles needed was a cripple on his hands. A cripple with a ruined reputation.

After paying doctors' and lawyers' fees, there wasn't much left over from the sale of the house. What remained went to Charlie—the sole male heir, the lawyer called him—save Father's watch.

"It's not how I wanted it to be," my brother said in the fella's office. He wouldn't look at me as he spoke. "You could have the piano—we don't have room for it in the apartment." Same as we don't have room for you, Maud, he meant without saying it.

"Fine and dandy," I said, choking back a big fat well of nothing. A homeless gal owning a piano she could no longer play: wasn't that just swell! "Guess you might as well sell that too, Charlie, if you don't want it."

"You can come live with me," Aunt Ida had said after Mama's funeral. It meant leaving Yarmouth for her place in Digby. But what choice did I have, hitch a ride to Arcadia and go knocking on the poorhouse door? Aunt liked to talk almost as much as Mae did. Except her talk wasn't about pretty stuff like curls and waves.

"You're safe with me, and with God," she told me when we got off the train. "He values every sparrow, why wouldn't

He count every hair on your head?" We were all special in His sight, she believed, though it might seem some got treated more special than others. The Lord loved those who helped themselves and in Glory all would be equal, she said, though here on Earth everyone suffered. What didn't kill you made you better equipped to resist temptation, was how Aunt put it. She said evil came in many guises. One guise was stubbornness. Another was giving in to despair. I missed Mama so bad it was all I could do not to.

"Rest assured, He sees what's best for us." This was Aunt's promise as she showed me my room. The dress she had sewn for me was laid out on the bed. Her having sewn it reminded me of Matthew Cuthbert buying that dress with puffed sleeves for Anne Shirley in that book Mama and I had read together once, *Anne of Green Gables*. Except this dress was as plain and simple as could be, made of navy blue gabardine. The sight of it made me light up—a smoke, I mean.

Aunt wasn't exactly pleased. "Would you put out that cigarette, for pity's sake. You don't want the bedclothes smelling of it, do you. And the curtains I just washed."

Digby was a pretty town but smaller than Yarmouth. It was hilly, with steep streets lined with big trees sloping down to the waterfront with its wharfs, fishing boats, and ferry dock. Like Yarmouth, it had plenty of nice houses, their sun-dappled yards filled with tumbling roses. Aunt Ida's house stood on a street up behind the prettier places, trees blocked our view of them and of the water. I missed seeing the water, missed watching the comings and goings of sailors, fishermen, and teamsters. Still, I hoped things would get better at Ida's. I'd brought all my worldly possessions with us on the train, which amounted to some clothes and paints and one of Mama's records, that old wax cylinder, and that keepsake of Father's, the old silver pocket watch that had long ago given up the ghost. Aunt had nothing to play Mama's record on. I whiled away the days in silence painting in her porch. But painting couldn't mask the fact that, kind as she was, Ida and I were like oil and water, not the best mix. She tried to be patient, but after a few weeks her patience wore thin.

"Tidy up, would you, dear? That turpentine stinks up the rest of the house. Anyone coming to call will think it's kerosene and we're infested with vermin. They'll be scared to sit by us in church." She laughed to couch this with humour, for she meant well. "Oh don't look at me like that, I'm kidding. We are *all* put on this Earth for some purpose—even lice must be, to humble us. Your purpose is seeing that the house doesn't reek of any bad habits. Am I clear?"

She barely heard me say yes, she was. Clear. Oh, ye-es. Mama always said it was living a spinster's life that made Aunt Ida gabby when she got the chance to be. I owed her for taking me in when no one else would. I supposed the least I could do was lend a willing ear.

"And might I suggest that you're a little old to be spending every waking moment on a hobby. It's high time you thought about earning some kind of a living. God rest her beautiful soul, Agnes was more than a bit indulgent with you. If you can hold a paintbrush you can hold a Fuller brush. You know, dear, cleanliness is next to...." Her lip quavered. "I could put you in touch with ladies who'd be glad to pay you to come in and clean. It's not what your mama and father intended for you. But we have all got to do things we mightn't want to."

There wasn't much I could say to argue with that.

Before bed, she and I would listen to the radio for an hour or two in her parlour. Four years earlier, the Carter Family had that big hit, an old song Mama and I knew from the movies, about a little girl asking the operator to put a call through to her mama in heaven. Sara and Maybelle Carter sure knew how to pull on your heartstrings with that line *"You can find her with the angels on the golden stair."* Every time the song came on, Aunt's eyes would glisten, with sadness I thought at first, until I realized it was a look of hopefulness. "There, you see?" she said, wiping tears away. "We'll all be together again someday."

Meanwhile, Digby soon proved that it was no Yarmouth, I can tell you. The rumble of an automobile passing, the toot of a train whistle, broke the silence if and when Aunt stopped conversing. These noises pulled me back to the world I knew existed somewhere, a world I had no part in. I would watch Ida take up her hymn book and flip through it, humming until she found her favourite song. Then she would sing, *"'Are you washed in the blood, in the soul-cleansing blood of the Lamb? Are your garments spotless? Are they white as snow? Are you washed in the blood of the lamb?'"*

Mama had loved her sister, had looked up to her, maybe even been a little afraid of her. Aunt wore her churchiness the way fishermen wore oilskins to protect them from the weather.

When I didn't sing along, she would get after me. "There's more to life than having fun, Maud."

"You might like a bit of fun yourself, Aunt Ida." Instead of singing hymns and burying your nose in the Good Book all the time, I wanted to say.

"Too much fun paves the way to hell, if you're not careful. You of all people should know." As she wagged her finger at me, she smiled. I wanted to believe that smile had a touch of deviltry. I wanted to think Aunt wasn't always so good and righteous. That underneath her goodness was someone who might just sneak a penny candy without paying if given the chance, and be glad, of course, to turn around and give the candy to you or the next person.

"As you said yourself, Aunt, every life's a 'work in progress.'"

"Exactly right. Like one of your paintings, I dare say. Oh, I never said they weren't nice, dear. There's things to like, how you can copy a picture. That one you did of Forchu with the lighthouse and the boats looks just like the postcard." But then she snapped back into her holier self. "No matter how hard we try to improve, no matter how willing the spirit is to better itself, the flesh is liable, you know." I trusted that she spoke more in sympathy than in judgement. But then, quoting her Bible again—"'*From darkness I knit you*'"—in her very next breath she grew prying: "Now why in creation would a girl like you seek comfort in darkness?"

What she meant was: What in creation is *wrong* with you, Maud?

The upshot of her question, what she was really saying, was, That fish man who comes around is no man for *any* self-respecting woman. That shifty fella who's got his eye on you.

I knew full well who she meant. The man's name was Everett Lewis.

Wedged there, if I could but stretch out one leg, then the other, somehow roll onto my hands and knees, could I get myself outdoors onto the dirt, crawl across the road's pale strip of moonlight to that other world, the world of neighbours? The road Ev didn't want me crossing. The neighbours Ev didn't want me visiting.

To call on anyone meant going against him. I couldn't move an inch anyway. I ground my teeth against the throb of cracked bones. Imagined dashing like a deer after windfall apples, skittering back into the woods. Bit down hard on my fist, keeping that quiet.

I didn't want to wake him, didn't dare wreck his sleep.

Moonlight barely reached in under the stairs. Instead of the cellar in Yarmouth, I guessed up the cellar at the almshouse

Olive had told me about, the room next to the laundry, where misbehavers got locked away. Ev used to have the key to it dangling from the big ring of keys he would take to work.

The pain was like that room. Don't go in there, use your head to make it disappear. I fixed my mind on better things, happier things. Like the first time I saw Olive, a stout, smiling lady going by with a rabble of yammering women and girls in tow. As they passed my window, this kind-faced lady who looked to be in charge waved to me. When I told Ev, he said, "Oh that's the warden's wife. She treats them lunatics like they are her own. Don't mind a bit giving them praise when praise is due." Next thing, he came home from his night watch, saying "Olive wants you to come over for dinner sometime."

"Oh yes, and like I would do that." My face had burned. I didn't even try to say it nicely. He couldn't see why I would object to going there for a nice big feed, saving us—him—from cooking. "Don't think I'd like the food," I said. "They probably don't let you smoke, either." Then a hymn had come on the radio, the one about being washed in the blood of the lamb. Speaking through it, Ev kept at me. "You ask Olive real nice, sure, and she might let you take a bath too." "Oh yes" was all I said. Over my dead body would I take a bath there, who cared how nice Olive was?

Now, years later, as I laid under my flowered stairs, a lot of things went through my mind. I remembered my short, happy visits next door, how eventually I had gone over there, a willing guest. The strange, airy relief I felt coming home afterwards, at being able to leave. For I was privileged, I was blessed. *There go I but by the grace of God*, Aunt would have said, oh yes. There is nothing like seeing people unluckier than yourself to make you grateful.

Are your garments spotless, are they white as snow? Are you washed in the blood of the...?

"You go ahead, you take her up on it, Olive's offer of a bath," I had told Ev. "Don't let me stop you." I would take meals there, though the thought of lying in the almshouse washroom in a big tub of water with God knows who peeking in through the keyhole was too much for me. But as I lay under the stairs waiting for dawn, and for Ev to come and the pain to go, I took myself back to the dinners he and I ate with the poor and the destitute in the big echoey dining room graced by Olive's kindness. At least we didn't have to eat with the lunatics, they ate on their own. The first time we went, then every time after, Ev brought humbug candies for Olive's own little boys, one for each child.

"Isn't that nice. You're some sweet, Ev. Say thanks now, young fella." That was Olive nudging her youngest son closer to put out his hand. She was always smiling. Even at dinner when one of the lunatics in the rooms above us took to cursing and Olive's husband, the warden, had to put him downstairs. I felt just plain cocky being there, like I was tempting fate. Tucking into a feed of boiled dinner alongside other gals who had got themselves in trouble but had their children and no place to go, no one to help them, nowhere else to hide or be hidden. I knew in my heart even that basement room would be kinder than the judgement of folks with no clue how life can be. Uppity folks who didn't mind heaping shame on those unlucky enough to wind up here. "You remember Everett's wife, Maud," Olive would tell the ladies every time, even the ones who weren't off their heads or indolent, the ones whose sufferings were healed by work.

At Christmas, Olive brought us gifts of fruitcake and chocolates, and had us over for turkey with all the trimmings.

I don't know how she slept in that place, living cheek by jowl with some of those sad cases.

Under the stairs, darkness tightened around me. Damned if I hadn't wet myself, the puddle under me going from warm to cold. *Are your garments spotless are they white as...are you washed in the....*

My head throbbed. I imagined strong fingers kneading my scalp, washing my hair—soap suds sluicing into a sink, swirling away... swirling down a deep drain somewhere as my gumption ebbed before me, and as dawn's pinkness slowly warmed the floor I thought of a lady's voice. The lady who had done my hair in Yarmouth. Washed and set and made it pretty. Mae.

I sucked on my fist to keep from yelping out as the tune from "The Darkest Hour is Just Before Dawn" played through my head, the Stanley Brothers ditty I'd always liked. A peeping accompanied it, a field mouse trapped somewhere handy? Realizing the peeping was coming from me, I whimpered, waiting, breath bated, for daylight. Yet, whimpering, I was still more scared of Ev waking up mad than of him sleeping in. Waking and yelling, "Where the hell are ya? Where'd you get to?" Finding me hiding. Hollering "goddamn this, goddamn that," how dare I give him such a fright? Like I had stole something of his and snuck off with it, a thief in the night.

Now, a Carmelita Twohig would say what goes around comes around. And that my lying there in the cold and the dark should have been a warning to Ev of what he had coming, the way he was to meet his maker later on. But just when I was ready to give up the ghost, a string of farts sounded overhead. The boards quaked. The stairs juddered under the weight of Ev's knees. The wall the stairs were nailed to trembled fit to shake free the linoleum basket of tulips I'd painted and hung there as a newlywed.

Reaching the bottom, he knelt there. He half looked like he was praying—now there's a notion. Then he loomed over me in the rosy light. "What the devil? You foolish...hiding on me, what the hell. Like a goddamn mouse. What, the loft weren't cozy enough? Get up out of there now, you silly—" But his face was pale. He grabbed the wooden spoon off the shelf, gave it to me to bite down on. The spit rattled between his gums as he breathed in. The fear in his eyes was wilder than the panic that rose up in me. His worst fear had come to pass: the housekeeper he had ordered and kept all these years was well and truly pulling a Hank Snow, leaving for good.

I saw this and more in Ev's eyes. I saw the boards waiting to be painted, orders drying up, customers abandoning us. In a crazy blur I remembered him burying the jar of money. I remembered the constable's talk of money in the bank. Even worse, worse for me, I remembered the trailer and my worry that the Light & Power people would cut us off. The Light & Power were my salvation. Now, I had somehow curled deeper under the stairs, eyes shut tight, and I felt a nudge. Ev's big toe poked at me through his sock. His boots stood before the range like a pair of those china dogs rich folks set before their fireplaces. The folks in Yarmouth who had kept Father in business, whom Mama aspired to know. Imitation being the highest form of praise, she said.

Now Ev was muttering, like he had come unglued. "What were you thinking, falling? What should I do? Run acrost the road, get someone to phone a hambublance?"

If not for the pain, his bungled word would have made me smile. I suppose I blacked out.

13.

HELLO, CENTRAL! GIVE ME HEAVEN

A few weeks after my arrival in Digby, Aunt caught me watching Everett Lewis through her parlour curtains. An Indian summer breeze twitched their lacy goods to and fro, but I was careful to keep myself hidden. I didn't want to cause her any trouble, seeing how kindly she had stepped in to save my sorry skin. If I can save a flibbertigibbet from herself, I can bring a middle-aged orphan to Jesus, she might have thought. The words of that gloomy old hymn "Abide with Me" that we'd sung at Mama's burial were words Ida took to heart. Why people like that hymn I have no idea, with its dark old valley and shadow of death. Darkness is old hat, everyone knows about it. But maybe Aunt Ida had seen it as a command from God to take me in. Of course, my abiding with her more or less meant being adopted at the ripe age of thirty-six, an age that didn't just teeter on being over the hill.

When Everett Lewis came to the door one breezy afternoon a while later selling mackerel, Aunt bought one, then practically shut the door in the man's face. She caught me peeking out at his shiny old car, a Model T Ford. She didn't say a word, just bustled to the kitchen sink, gutted the fish, dredged it in flour, and fried it up for our supper. She was saving her breath, I guess, for saying grace.

"Very tasty," she finally said when we were almost done eating. "Though to tell you the truth, I'm suspicious about where that fella gets his catch. Says he waits around the wharf to see what's been landed. Then I suppose he dickers with the fish'men till they can't take his arguing anymore and let their fish go cheap just to get rid of him."

As she spoke, that saying came to me, the nasty one, how company is like fish after two days, it starts to stink. I had been at Aunt Ida's place more than two months by this time.

Having got that suspicion about Mr. Lewis off her chest, Aunt kept talking. "He drives a fierce bargain, that one. Last time, his fish wasn't fresh. So I thought twice today before buying. Didn't want him lingering, though." She took a deep breath, eyed my cigarettes laying on the sideboard, and heaved a sigh. "But, there it is, Maud. We've got to make allowances for others. If the Lord condemned us on the basis of a single transgression, there'd be no room in hell for another sinner— would there, dear?"

"Suppose not. If you believe in that stuff."

Aunt Ida's powdered cheeks turned pinker at any hint of doubt. "Well. He's a queer duck, anyway." I guessed she meant the fish man, not the Lord. "I suppose it's not Lewis's fault. Considering where he came from. His people started out in Bear River,

I think, before the poor farm took them in. Unreliable, you could call them. But, you know, 'there go I but by the grace.... Far be it for us to question or judge His plan."

"Plan?"

Aunt Ida looked at me funny, gave a little laugh, and picked a tiny fish bone from her tongue. "Each and every one of us has a purpose, like I've said. Given to us before we were even a glint in our parents' eyes." She flicked the fish bone onto her plate. "Who knows what He had in mind for the Everett Lewises of the world. Beat and battered before they leave the womb, then causing more trouble than the rest of us should have to put up with. But there, you see?" A smile spread over her face. "It's His plan, that the poor and unwanted are here to teach us. That we're our brothers' keepers, so help me. Whether we like it or not. The more surly and ungrateful, the more they teach us patience. Like that conniving fish man." She got up, cut two pieces of pie for our dessert, and poured tea.

"Everett Lewis. A conniver, is he." I laughed, risked dribbling tea down the front of the stiff green blouse Ida had embroidered. She had a gift for needlework, she truly did. Like Mama, she liked clothes. Unlike Anne Shirley's Matthew, and more like Anne herself, or Matthew's sister, Marilla, Aunt Ida wasn't shy about speaking her mind. I got up and lit a cigarette. Aunt waved at the air, making no effort to hide her disgust. High in her cheeks were spots of white where their blush of pinkness ebbed.

"Laugh all you want. But watch yourself." Ida spoke into her napkin. "That Lewis has got quite the roving eye, I've heard all about him. Can't keep his hands to himself." She got up and cleared the table. Her silence said we had slipped onto shaky ground, raising things best left unsaid. About people keeping their hands to themselves, or not. People like me and Emery Allen. Sinning in ways that could never be undone.

The sin of smoking was just the icing I kept slathering on the cake.

Cigarettes were the devil's way of keeping me under his thumb, Aunt said. Next I would be playing cards, though probably not dancing. When I smoked upstairs in my bedroom, even with the window opened wide, the late autumn air blowing in, somehow the scent found its way to her nostrils. One day, not long after our mackerel supper, she lost her temper.

"I'm afraid, missy, if you want to stay on, it's my house, my rules."

I figure you might call this the last straw. I did, though winter was just around the corner. As you know, I had no one else to turn to, didn't know another soul in Digby. I couldn't hide my desperation, preferring the devil's thumb to Aunt Ida's. Yet, Aunt was so good. One afternoon she gave me money to buy myself some soap at Shortliffe's Riteway.

Guess what I spent it on? I remembered too late that she'd asked me to buy milk, too.

Suddenly, right there in the store, all the past years' hiding, penny-pinching, and doing without, all the looks people kept giving me—someone's whispers about "poor Ida what's-er-name" getting the shitty end of the stick, saddled with "that one from Yarmouth"—it all spilled over faster than potatoes on a hard boil. I could not see living out the rest of my days at Aunt's. I didn't have the fare to catch a train back to Yarmouth or even halfway there. And even if I'd had the fare, who would have taken me in? Mae? Nice as she was, I didn't think so. No, I had run plumb out of options. Maybe I'd never had options to begin with. It wasn't ever as if I could run away, with these ankles and knees. I'd be lucky if I could walk five miles.

I had seen the place out in Marshalltown from the train coming up from Yarmouth that day with Aunt. Marshalltown wasn't even a whistle stop. It had nothing more than the big, shabby building I had glimpsed as we flew by, the place Aunt called the county home. She said every county had such a home. I decided this one couldn't be worse than Yarmouth County's place in Arcadia—that forlorn-looking place my family had passed in the buggy the day of our picnic, when I was barely an adolescent. Lingering there in the Riteway, I thought to myself, if they were to give me a bed, a bit of scrap paper and a pencil, and leave me alone, I might get by all right, I might even get used to it. In time. Used to it in a way I would never get used to Aunt's well-meaning rules.

The shop girl eyeballed me. "Is there something else you wanted?" Her eyebrows arched when she spoke. Not much taller than me, she had on a soft-looking moss-green sweater. She should've guessed I was penniless the way I'd tucked away my purchase, then picked up a can of milk and held onto it for some time before setting it down again. I was thinking how I could follow the train tracks, though it might be smarter to find the road that must run nearby. The pale look of the girl's eyes helped me work up the gumption to speak.

"That poorhouse in Marshalltown, can you tell me how to get there?"

Her voice was as even as if I'd asked where to find the ferry or the fish plant, she sounded so ho-hum. "You aren't the first person to ask. Guess you won't be the last, long as they allow visitors. Just head out of town here and keep walking—you can follow the train tracks, then once you cross the bridge, get on the road and watch for Ev Lewis's shack, and go from there. It's the big white place next door to him. It's back off the road a ways, but you can't miss it."

She kept looking at my hands. I pulled my sleeves down over my fists. The cigarettes were safely tucked into my coat pocket. She stared so, I had a mind she would step out from behind the counter to take a gander at my ankles—they were swelled pretty bad, I figured I would be lucky if they got me to where I had to go.

"How far is it?"

"Fi' miles or so? You know Lewis, the fish pedlar? That's whose shack I meant—you can't miss it. Matter of fact—" and she pointed to something tacked on the wall near the door. "Have a gander at that—you might get yourself a job, you never know." Then she laughed and said, "Good luck, honey."

I set out walking the rail bed, stopping every so often to sit on a rock or a stump beside the tracks and have a smoke. It was a grey afternoon, early December, not a stick of snow, the trees stripped bare. Tried to pace myself, seeing as it might be the last pack of cigarettes I would ever buy. Did they provide smokes at the almshouse? Something told me they didn't. But they fed you there and gave you a place to sleep, I'd heard it said. And maybe I would just lie down on whatever bed they gave me and not get up again. In Aunt's absence, there would be no one to say I had sinned of despair.

I walked and walked till I could barely lift and set one foot ahead of the other. I had Everett Lewis's notice in my pocket, I had given it the once-over. He was advertising for a live-in housekeeper. When I came upon his little shanty I almost laughed out loud—what Ida would have thought! The house was the size of a shed. A housekeeper to keep a place that small? And a live-in housekeeper, no less, the same as a sea captain would hire to keep a mansion like the ones on Parade, Cliff, and Collins Streets back in Yarmouth. A big huge turreted pile with servants' quarters and a carriage house out back.

Then I thought, Everett Lewis must have a sense of humour, which I figured not every man did.

As I passed by, I heard a dog bark. Smoke curled from the pokey little chimney. The place was little more than a shack. I wondered where in tarnation a live-in anything was supposed to sleep. It gave me a laugh, anyways, as I limped and hobbled onwards, anxious though none too keen to reach my destination.

How much farther was it? How bad would it be? The answers to both questions came pretty quick as I rounded a tiny bend in the road, and there it was, the almshouse—a big wooden two-storey house with a steep pitched roof, four little peaked dormers set into it with one big pointy-roofed dormer in the middle of them, a two-storey wing at either end. The laneway led in a beeline to the front door. There was a rusty-looking ladder on the roof and a little cupola and a chimney that looked ready to fall down. And I stopped at the top of the lane and I looked and looked at it, and thought of the poorhouse in Arcadia and Charlie's words, *"That's where you'll end up."*

I wager things might have turned out different if Olive had been there back then and seen me and come outside. Or if I had knocked and someone like her had answered, taken my hand and brought me inside. Maybe even if I had gone close enough to peek in a window and get a handle on what it was like in there. If I had spied a smiling person like Olive tending the sick, the poor, the knocked-up, and the feeble-minded, it would have changed everything.

But nobody saw me, nobody came out to ask what I was after. I was but a crippled ghost passing through the world. Except I had that note in my pocket, real as could be, tucked in with my cigarettes. How hard could housekeeping be in a tiny, ramshackle place like that? At least it would pay, wouldn't it? Though probably not much, seeing as I had no experience besides baking the odd cookie, dusting, and helping Aunt do dishes.

At the same time, I got it into my mind that if I went up and knocked on the almshouse door and they took me in, that would be it. The end of my life, really. I might never paint another picture or step out under the sky again, might never get to pick a flower or feel salt fog on my face or pet a cat or smoke a cigarette or suck a humbug or piece of toffee.

What would be the good of living like that?

So I turned and shoved off and started walking back the way I had come. It didn't take any time to reach Ev Lewis's shack, weary as I was. When I got there, I told myself what the heck, and knocked on his door.

The devil you know is better than the devil you don't know, I thought, as a dog came up and nuzzled my skirt. He was a mid-sized dog, big to me, but he didn't bark. Though if I had had any treat besides cigarettes in my pocket I'd have been ready to bribe him if he acted up. Before I could change my mind and take off, the door cracked open and Ev Lewis peered out at me. What I saw first was his ragged shirt tucked into his pants.

"Yeah? What can I do you for?"

I held out the ad.

"Put it away." He cocked his head towards the mutt. "Guess you must be all right if Joe likes you. Some others, he'd bite the head off of." He stepped backwards, as if to allow each of us a more fulsome look at the other. From that bit of distance, the crooked smile on his lips was like a half-moon laying on its side.

No beating around the bush; talking to his shirt, I cut straight to the point. "How much do you pay? Where would I sleep?"

He held up one hand. It was bony and long-fingered, with thick yellow fingernails. "Hold your horses—settle down, we'll work out a deal, how's that?" He kept looking at me, suspicious now. Worried. "First things first. I got to know that whatever's wrong with them mitts of yours ain't catching."

"Swear on a stack of Bibles, no, it ain't, *isn't.*"

He clicked his tongue. "When didja say you can start?"

"What? Well. Any old time, I guess."

He waved his hand like as to sweep me into the house, the way that Grand Hotel doorman had done years ago before barring Emery Allen on account of his attire. And I could not help thinking, all those years later, what if I had gone in and left

Emery out there in the cold, all alone and lonesome in his suit.

"But, wait. What about my stuff, back at my aunt's? Quite a trek to Digby." For I had spied the car out back, the one he sold fish from. Figured this should be a strong enough hint that he would give me a lift.

But no way, no how. "I'll see ya when I sees ya, then," he barked before shutting the door.

So I walked all the way back to Aunt's, hobbled was more like it. It was well after dark by the time I got there. Aunt stood in the kitchen wringing a dishtowel, twisting her hands.

"I was worried sick. Waiting and waiting before I put on the tea. Where's the milk?" Her face fell as she caught a whiff of cigarettes off me. "I knew it!" Without another word, disgusted, she stumped up to bed.

After a bit, I worked up the nerve to go and rap on her bedroom door. "Got a job, I did."

No answer, nothing but the silence of a stone.

The next morning, I heard the sounds of breakfast being readied downstairs. Before I could greet Aunt, she looked up from setting the table. "The job isn't looking after that reprobate, I hope. I saw the ad at Shortliffe's. If Lewis wasn't so pitiful he'd be a laughingstock." She looked me in the eye, her eyes widened. "Oh my Dinah and all that's sacred—you *answered* it? Why?"

I think it was her reaction that washed away whatever misgivings I might've had. I waited for her to say something about honouring Mama's memory and behaving, holding up a shred of dignity for myself. But for once, Aunt Ida was speechless. So I chimed in.

"Because it is high time I acted like a grown lady."

"But, why on earth him of all men? The man barely owns a pot to do his business in. What fool would think he needs you—or anyone—to keep house. *What* house?"

If I'd had similar doubts before, now my mind was made

up. Everett Lewis was no Emery Allen, especially in the looks department, that's for sure. But he owned a car *and* a house, which was more than you could have said for Emery, as far as I knew. And we all know looks can be deceiving.

That very day I hiked back out to Marshalltown with everything I owned in the world in Mama's cardboard suitcase, including the wax cylinder and Father's watch.

Next there were voices. Fingers digging into my armpits—Ev's—someone trying to raise me to my feet. Someone else yelling, "Don't. You don't know what's broke." I remember a flashing light, red, the colour bleeding everywhere. Wood smoke in the air. Me being loaded into the back of somewhere, light flashing dark.

And then whiteness. Such a dazzle it hurt when I truly came to. I wasn't wearing my red sweater or nightie but a shirt tied on back to front, my bare back against the sheet. I was a child again, lying in a crib.

"You did a number on that hip." It was Nurse Darlene, this was the very first time we met. "Don't fret. You're in good hands." The last person who spoke that way had been Mama, when I quit school. But Mama had chased her words with a sigh. *"You get to stay home with me. Never mind, we'll have fun. You'll get used to it."*

Thinking of Mama confused me. "Am I home?" My voice was bumbling and stupid. The place was too big and bright and bare to be the place I shared with Ev.

"What?" Darlene's voice was so calm. "Oh no, darlin'. You're in Emerg. You had a fall, I hear. Hope you didn't wait *too* long for the ambulance."

"Ev?" My voice keened but surely it was someone else who called out, "Where's Ev?" I looked around as much as I could, pinned flat on my back. The pain was like I imagined fireworks might be, bright but distant. Ev was nowhere in sight, where had he got to? He'd hitched a ride home with the ambulance men? Or he was off having a chew of tobacco, biding his time before he lay into me about how stupid I'd been taking the stairs by myself. If I wasn't so stupid I would have made it down them all right, down to the bucket or even the outhouse, and back up to bed without a peep, and we would not be stuck cooling our heels in this place.

Darlene's face was like a doll's, I remember, with wide, painted eyes and long lashes. Her lips were a pale pink that reminded me of the odd forget-me-not that springs up amongst blue and white ones. She tucked the blanket over my hands.

"You're the artist, aren't you? A friend of mine—"

I imagined Ev's proud answer, if he'd been anywhere handy to give it: *Yeah, she is. Five bucks, and she'll paint you something real nice. She's good at flowers and that. But she will do whatever your heart desires.*

The pain made me think out loud, "Oh go on, shut your gob."

Darlene leaned in close. "What was that, honey? Is the pain real bad? Must be, with that hip. Doctor's on his way, he'll fix you up. Just be patient."

When wasn't I patient?

"A friend of mine knows you, really likes your work." Darlene peeled back the blanket, held my hands in hers, studying them. When I breathed in, the pain lit up my spine and cartwheeled. Then Nurse took a gander at my legs. I knew they weren't too pretty, with those big black bruises on my shins from banging into things. It was hard to avoid doing so in the house. "Best keep your eyes to yourself, miss," I said and laughed in spite of everything. Nurse Darlene yanked up the covers right quick. "That's better," I piped. "See? Nothing to get riled up about."

It is better for all concerned when no one looks too close at your ailments. Nurse gave me a needle for the pain. "Your friend, is she a Twohig?" I asked, but missed hearing her answer.

I woke from a dreamless sleep. The sheet was pulled away. The yellow shirt was flipped up, my lady parts there for the world to see. A young man with a black cord around his neck pressed a cold metal disc to my chest. Darlene tugged a bit of the sheet over me but not before the doctor got an eyeful. Then the two of them disappeared and I was alone.

I smelt Ev's presence before he stepped through the curtains around the bed and came close. I was woozy from the needle but not too far gone to know that Ev was a little tipsy. He took off his cap, waved it. His breath was sour sweet like old wet leaves. His voice hissed the way rain does through fog.

"Think I don't know what you were up to, sneaking off in the middle of the night? Goin' to meet 'a friend,' wouldn't put it past you. Aiming to meet up with that cop, maybe? I know what you're like. Think you can pull the wool over my eyes."

What is in that dynamite juice of yours? You know that's crazy talk! I wanted to say, but it hurt too much. When I didn't answer, he growled about the hospital people making him wait outside. "They don't know their arses from their eyeballs, telling a fella he can't see his own wife—"

Just then the doctor appeared. He shot Ev a look and cleared his throat. "Mrs. Lewis?" He spoke as if I could be someone else. "You have a bad fracture, compounded by your other issues." Suddenly Ev had the sense to keep quiet, though it wasn't like him. *Issues* was a word that I knew applied to offspring and magazines.

When Ev spoke it was to put this stranger at ease. "If you are scared of what ails her being catching, don't be. Been with her thirty-odd years and I ain't caught nothing off her yet."

The doctor glanced at Ev and shook his head. He looked about the same age as Constable Colpitts but wasn't near as handsome. When he smiled at me, he looked barely old enough to drive a car. "We can't do the surgery here. They might do it in Yarmouth or Kentville, but I'd rather send you to the city. Halifax." I didn't like the sound of this, had never in my life been to a city, let alone a city so far away—what, a hundred and fifty miles from here?

Luckily Ev piped up and I forgot all about him drinking and hinting in so many words that the fall was my just desserts. "Now what would that cost, doc? How much would a trip like that set me back?" Out of the corner of my eye I glimpsed something in Ev's hand. It was a fat roll of dollar bills that looked sullied with mud or dried blood. Banks didn't bury your money for safekeeping, did they?

"To see the specialist?" The doctor looked confused. "That's taken care of. But the ride there and back mightn't be—"

"How much, for the ambublance and that?"

Poor Ev! But it struck me that the pity I felt for him, that let me excuse him time and time again, could only go so far. For if Ev had learned to read like some of us, he would not have struggled so with his words. Yet, like my tumble downstairs wasn't my fault, his failing wasn't all his fault either. So he got hot under the collar, who could blame him? And he stuck by me, nudging those musty bills at the man. "Look here, doc. Money's no object. It's my wife we are talking about. I got an investiture here, see?" The devotion in Ev's voice would've swept me off my feet had I been up to standing.

But I understood. I was that *investment*, all Ev had in the world besides the house. What if I never walked again? Never painted again? If I didn't get proper treatment it might well be. It flew through my head—as if in one ear and out the other—that Ev's not springing for the trip meant our livelihood could dry up, just like that.

"If Maud was *my* wife," the youngster said, "I'd have her

looked at in the city. I'll let you think about it." But there was
no need, Ev's mind was made up.

"Quit jawing about it, let's git her to the affirmary or the
Vee Gee or wherever. They won't dick around, will they, not
like you fellas. They'll fix you right up, Maudie. Nothing but
the best for my gal. Best get us down there quick, down to
Half-an-axe."

Halifax, the capital city of Nova Scotia. I did not like
the sound of that big place any more than I liked the sound
of the Infirmary. *Hospital* sounded respectable, *Infirmary* like a
warmed-over word for almshouse, somewhere with cots and
locked rooms. But then I thought back to Olive and her kindness. Maybe wherever I went there would be three square
meals and nurses to put me in a warm tub bath, a step up
from the cold-water lick-and-a-promise sponge baths I gave
myself now and then at home. Maybe there'd even be someone
like Mae to wash my hair and comb it. I remembered how I'd
given her cards in exchange for a hairdo, and how, before the
almshouse closed and Olive and her husband and their boys
packed up and left, in exchange for Olive's kindness I'd given
her paintings for the dining room to cheer up her charges.
Who knows if the paintings helped or not? By the time the
place burnt those paintings were long gone, the man in the
moon knows where.

I'd have given anything to see Olive waltz into that hospital
room, but the best they had was Darlene. "Could I see that
nurse, please?" My voice was small and weak and must have
worried Ev and the doctor. They both peered down at me, then
the doctor pressed something pinned to my pillow, and he and
Ev left me by my lonesome.

That smiling Darlene appeared, back from emptying bed-
pans, dressing bedsores or what-have-you, all the things nurses do,
still as pleasant as could be. "Soon as the ambulance is available,

they're taking you." She patted my arm and straightened the pillow, she was that sweet! And I noticed the flush in her cheeks—I knew that look. It had been forty years since I had seen it, eyeing myself in Mama's gilded mirror. But I hadn't forgotten. It was the look of a woman in lust.

"That friend of mine just popped by." Her blush spread to her voice, made it rosy too. "He's wondering if you'd like a visitor—once you're shipshape again."

"Oh?"

She blushed even deeper, this wasn't just my imagination grasping for something to spurn pain. "Constable Colpitts. I think you know who I mean." She quickly changed the subject. "My gosh, how long did you lay there, after you fell? Must have been miserable, poor dear."

Do bears poop in the woods? I fastened my eyes to hers as she poked me with a needle and said the medicine would kick in soon.

"Oh yes. I know him. He's come by a few times. You tell him I said hi."

She pressed one hand to my wrist, used her other hand to hold up the watch pinned to her top. "Mr. Lewis has got quite the pile of cash on him, doesn't he? There's no problem covering the ambulance, anyways." She patted me. "Don't you worry about a thing."

Like I would worry. If there's one thing I was good at, it was not stewing over stuff I couldn't fix. I refused to ruminate over Ev having the money, though Constable Colpitts would likely want to know where it came from, and, I suppose, how it got so dirty. Even with the hospital smell all around, I'd caught a whiff of its moldering smell, like rotting leaves.

Then Nurse Darlene drew up the sheet and out I went like a light.

14.

KEEP ON

THE

SUNNY SIDE

I *wasn't completely stunned, if that's what you're thinking. If there's* one thing I had learned from Emery Allen, it was just as Mama had said and like Bob Wills sings on "Milk Cow Blues": no man will tie the knot if he can make whoopee for free. Lovin' didn't factor into the deal me and Ev Lewis brokered, an arrangement meant to benefit both parties. I got a place to lay my head, he got company. I reckon if anyone got the shitty end of the stick it was him, seeing how I couldn't skin or cook a rabbit to save my life, or build a fire or scrub a floor, never mind what Aunt had said about ladies in town hiring me.

I bunked down at night on his daybed. But it wasn't very long before Everett started acting like a man, overstepping the terms I had agreed to. Demanding more than just company, I mean—once he knew what ailed me wasn't contagious, that he wouldn't get "lobster claw hands" from touching me. At least I was canny enough that no fella was going to have his fun with me then pull a stunt like Emery had—pull a "Hank Snow" as I thought of it years later, when "I'm Movin' On" came out.

So Everett gave in to the one condition I set before him. "Okay okay okay, I'll marry you, for frig's sake—but under one condition of my own. It ain't gonna be in a church, I can garnishee, I mean guarantee you."

I suppose him and I didn't get off on too bad a foot with our bargaining.

"Fine by me, as long as I get to be your legal wedded wife."

No one can say I walked into my marriage to Ev blinkered or blindfolded. If Aunt had had her druthers, she'd have rescued me a second time. But then, she had no idea how close I had come to throwing in my lot at the almshouse. I didn't tell her because I knew how baffled and hurt she'd have been and what she would say: *What were you thinking, there? "If you can't beat them, join them." Was that your reasoning?*

Which would not have been so far off the mark. And I am still not sure how she'd have lived it down, having kin living off the county purse.

For my thoughts had run to something like this: The next best way to meet my fate head on, maybe even play a trick on it and have the last laugh, might just be hiding in plain sight, in the poor farm's shadow. Of course, by the time I came along there was no farm over there, just the building that passed for a home. You could say Ev Lewis saved me by the skin of my teeth. I would say he did. There was a lot to be said for getting married, still is. I figured being married would be for me what Aunt's churchiness was for her, a comfort and a shield against what the world could dish out. Nobody dared call a married lady a slut. Why, that would be like calling a preacher a crook! Which Ev would've done without hesitation, mind. But, being obtuse, he said there was no way he would stand before a justice of the peace, either.

His mother kept house for a man in North Range, Ev said, and we could have the wedding there. I sent Aunt an invitation. I believe the funds she sent were to pay a preacher, but she made herself scarce. Maybe under threat of his mother, Ev finally agreed to have a preacher if not a judge officiate, the lesser of what he saw as two evils? I wore my dark blue beaded dress bought from the Eaton's catalogue while Mama was still living. It wasn't meant for winter wear but served its purpose that freezing-cold day just past mid-January, when Ev and I tied the knot.

The day we wed was one of those perfect blue-and-white winter days, snow sparkling on the evergreens. Not a cloud was in the sky, the distant bay was one big, clear stretch of sapphire. Blue jays called from the trees back of Mrs. Lewis's employer's house, and I do believe the crow watching from the tree out front could have been Matilda's grandmother. Tiny snow flurries twirled down, sparkling pink as a show of petals blowing off apple trees in bloom—so it was as good as a May or June wedding. The preacher met us in the parlour. I don't know where the man who owned the place was. "While the cat's away the mice will play," Everett's mother said. She was tall and bony like Ev, with iron grey hair and the same grey-blue eyes, except without his twinkle. She moved like a stiff old bird, upright and cheerless, and I figured that her dress, never mind the small stain down the front, must be her best. Ev hardly looked at her when he introduced me: "This is her, what answered my ad."

Mrs. Lewis kind of smiled at me and nodded. I could feel her looking at my chin, waiting in vain for me to look up at her. There was a pot-bellied stove in the parlour, which threw a good heat. I parked myself as close by it as I could. Then, lickety-split, the preacher joined Ev and me in holy matrimony—though when it came time to slip a ring on my finger, there wasn't one. "Come with me," the old woman said, "I got something for you."

She took me into the kitchen where a big cookstove threw off an even lovelier heat. The sun coming through the windows made the wainscot's light blue look buttery soft enough to sink into. But I pulled my mind back into the room where I stood with Everett's mother. "I figure I ought to be grateful to you," she said, but didn't explain why. I only reckoned it was because mothers of sons liked to see their boys fixed up with a steady companion, even if their boys were old goats. "Better late than never, eh?"

I figured by this she meant Ev's giving up his bachelor-hood. "Oh yes." The same goes for me, I almost said, but remembered Father's advice about keeping your trap shut: better keep it shut than put your foot in it. I wasn't about to confess to being "damaged goods" or "bringing in the sheaves" of shame and grief. Not on my wedding day.

"You need a ring, though." As she spoke, she set about slicing the cake. It was on a plate painted with blue roses, and it had yellowy-pink icing with tiny lumps of butter in it. She took something from her apron pocket. She passed me a sliver of cake on a saucer, and slipped the ring into my other hand. Just then Ev came into the room, the preacher behind him, and she cut slices of cake for them too. "Go on, put it on," she told me. Ev butted in. "What?" But his mother pretended not to hear, busy straightening the cloth on the table, handing out cake to the two or three neighbours she had invited as our guests. "Your wife needs a wedding band; I'm giving her mine—reckon I don't need it, do I?"

And I wished I'd held off on giving the preacher all of Aunt's money and divvied it up instead, given him just a bit and Mrs. Lewis the rest to cover the flour, sugar, and milk for the cake, not to mention her ring. As Ev grabbed the ring and with no small amount of difficulty pushed it over my knuckle, I hoped her wedded life had been one of bliss, and that her ring would bless mine. Though from what little Ev had told me about his childhood, I imagined his folks hadn't enjoyed much snuggling and spooning. His dad sleeping in one dorm, his mama in another.

Before the wedding, I had made myself as comfy as a body could be sleeping on that daybed. Bit by bit I had got better at heating up beans and steeping tea for Ev's suppers. "I am giving you a week," he'd said at first. "You got to pay your way or you're out." At the end of that week he'd said, "I ought to pack you off next door and maybe they'd learn you how to cook!" Then I made him a stew with fish he brought home, had it bubbling away when he came in from chopping wood. He liked it well enough he ate the entire pot.

No matter how much Ev ate, he never lost his look, like a hawk hungry for whatever moved. He was always ready with a complaint: "Now I got two mouths instead of one to feed!" The same way he hadn't figured on any housekeeper worth her salt taking one look at the place he lived in and saying, "Forget it, buster," he hadn't figured on me getting out my paints or setting myself up in that sunny corner, as far from his chair as I could get. The house was so small, the only thing that separated his chair by the range from mine in the corner was that hooked mat. When he sneezed, I'd feel the spray. When he picked his nose and flicked whatever he dug out, it would land on me. I was wrong when I'd figured the size of the place would make up for my poor housekeeping skills. "What kind of crackpot you take me for? Hire you to cook and clean and you sit on your arse all day painting? I ought to turf you out."

But he didn't.

For there was and is more to marriage than keeping house; there's the part I would rather not think about, and would prefer to forget. After the wedding ceremony, with his mother's ring on my finger, I sat up beside him in the passenger seat of his old black Ford, and on the drive home, relieved as I was at being spared the almshouse, I thought, Well, you have made your bed, now you have got to lie in it. There's one duty you cannot get out of.

Everett Lewis did so have a pot to piss in, it was in the corner by the range, and in the beginning it had a lid, as did the pot he found later to replace the one he buried. But before I followed him up that ladder to bed, despite the cold, taking my sweet time, I crept out to the outhouse. I still had my airs about me, wanting to keep some privacy, didn't want my new husband to hear or get too close a whiff of my business. In the January dark the air snapped so I thought the pee would freeze as it trickled down the hole. Out in the woods a coyote howled, and in the stillness surrounding its cry I heard the faintest sound of wailing from next door—some poor creature lamenting land only knew what. But I wasn't scared. You are a married woman, you're safe now, I told myself. No one can blame you for what you have or haven't done; it's all behind you, in the past. You've got a man to stick up for you now, a tall, ornery man who doesn't give a hoot what people think, isn't one bit ashamed of himself, so why would he be ashamed of you? A hardworking man who thinks enough of you to have made you his wife.

This gave me the courage to scurry as fast as I was able through the snow and back into the house. It was pitch black inside, except for a skinny crescent of orange light where a lid on the range top was ajar. I went and stood at the bottom of the ladder. For all I knew, Ev might have Joe the hound under the covers for extra warmth.

But no, Ev was by his lonesome when I climbed up there. He was awake, waiting. Moonlight leaked in through the frost-covered gable window. The air in the loft was as still and cold as the air outdoors, but at least there weren't wild animals ready to come and tear me apart. Tear *us* apart. I heard the beat of wings nearby—an owl, maybe, warming itself under the eaves outside. Ev threw back the covers, scooched over to let me into the canvas sling he had rigged for a bed. Foolish, but one of Aunt's crazy old Bible verses came to me: *"Everything is naked and exposed to the eyes of him to whom we must render an account."* Not that these words were any comfort or consolation.

What passed for bedding was a far cry from the perfumed sheets I had lain in at Aunt Ida's.

My new husband was more than ready for me. The cold took my mind off his hands moving over me, his fingers with their crusty nails. I pushed away the thought of cleanliness, of Aunt's clawfoot bathtub with its turquoise-stained drain. Her songs about garments washed white by blood. Leave it, it's all behind you now, there is no going back, I said to myself.

While he did what he did I shut my eyes and lay as still as if I was dead. Maybe it wasn't all that different from being with Emery, from what I could remember. After a while I opened my eyes and stared at the rafters above Ev's head, and pretty soon the roof wasn't there and though my body laid there, I wasn't really inside it. I was out of my body. I was a puff of cold air longing to touch the nearest star, then reaching out to meet it.

Till death do us part.

Afterwards, he rolled over and yanked the blanket up over himself; he took most of it with him. As he started to snore, a stripe of moonlight crossed his face. Watching it through the fog of my breath helped me see him for what he was: a boy inside of an old coot and curmudgeon. A sad boy, a coot with more than one axe to grind.

I fixed my eye on the real rising star just visible through the ice-ferns on that single frozen pane of glass. Was it the same North Star Mama and I had looked for from the porch on Hawthorne Street, coming home from the movies? I guessed up a ladder unfolding down from the star that I could climb to reach up and grab onto it.

When the wind blowing in through the cracks finally lulled me to sleep, I dreamt of an orange. It was fresh from the hold of a sailing ship from the south seas, round and bright as the sun. As I sucked its juice its seeds stuck in my teeth. And in the dream Ev yelled at me for not saving him some. For he expected me to share it: what's mine is yours, what's yours is mine.

That orange was the colour I would've painted the entire house if I could have.

Now, Ida used to say when the Lord closed a door, He opened a window. This is what I thought the day I met Secretary, when she rescued me from the roadside where I had fallen. I let her think I'd stumbled while jumping out of the way of a speeder. I didn't tell her why I stumbled, that being unsteady on my pins was due to a weakness on top of my usual ailments. If I was poorly it was because of what had happened the very night before, a loss that happened only the once in all my married life. Now there's a cause for gratitude. Granted, I'd had no business being out by the road, like Ev said, and as he would point out once I started getting famous, "Take your life in your hands being out on that road. Only safe spot for you is on your chair."

Even up here in eternity, thinking of it brings it back like it only just happened, what happened one night after we'd only been married a couple of years.

"Ev? *Ev?*" I had hollered out, squatting over the piss-pot. What started as a cramp brought a flow worse than the curse. Pain was a fist low in my belly, grabbing onto my inner parts and twisting. I'd gone without the curse for three or four months, but who was counting? With no bathtub to soak in, going without was a blessing. My belly wasn't so sure of this, though. It knew how long the curse was overdue, was keeping count.

Oh, my belly had known just what to do. Once I was able to, I crawled aside, got on my knees, and raised myself up. I glimpsed *it* floating there in the pot.

Ev came running in. He'd been chopping wood, had bits of tree bark on his sleeve and in his hair. He took one look at me and turned almost white. "Goddamn. When were you planning to tell me? Or were you not gonna say nothing and pull a fast one?" He whistled through the teeth he had. "You know I seen this all the time. Gals losing babies. Well, come on, calm yourself. Here, lay down, I'll git you a cup of tea and take care of it." He shook his head, half prideful. "Jesus. What were you thinking, bringin' a kid into this world? I don't know. It's better off. We is better off." Then he laughed, sheepish. Frozen there, like he did not know what to say or do next.

Yack, yack, yackitty-yack, never quiet, a tongue that never stopped wagging so long as he'd been drinking: this was the Ev Lewis I had gotten to know, had by now grown used to. Yet, in silence he unfolded an old *Courier* and spread the "Wanted" section over the daybed. For the first time in the two years we'd been wed, he was lost for words. But only for a bit.

"Now you lay down and stay put. Maybe we oughta git a doctor to take a look at you. Though Christ knows what they charge for that, making a house call." For he had up and sold his car one day, had done so not long after our honeymoon jaunt to the dump. What was he going to do, carry me to town on his bike, me bundled up and riding crossbar? At least it wasn't freezing out. But he'd been into the sauce.

"Nah—I'm all right." I hauled myself up, leaned against the range, then doubled over with a cramp. I fought it enough to insist, "I'm all right, I said. I'll be okay."

The last thing I wanted was a doctor inspecting me, asking questions. The kind of questions that would lead to the kind of judgements people make whether they aim to make them or not. I imagined what Aunt might say, *"The Lord gives and the Lord takes, and makes His punishments equal to our sins. He does no more and no less than use the folly of our mistakes to turn us towards Him."* I had no idea what this meant. But I knew the worst punishment on earth would be Ev finding out about the mistake I had made with Emery Allen.

Shaking his head, Ev picked up the pot real gingerly, set it outside on the doorstep. It was already dusky out there. He came back in and lit the lamp for me.

"What are you gonna do with it?" I hated the thought of the contents being spilled down the outhouse hole or onto the ground, the tiny mess of it attracting animals.

"What do you think?" He clicked his tongue at me, like there was any question.

"Could you give it a decent—"

His grimace was the grimace of a horrified boy and a baffled, disgusted man.

By now the pain had begun to slacken off some. "Wait. Give me a minute, gimme time to straighten up and come with you."

"Reckon I can do that." He sighed long and loud but took a seat. He popped a plug of tobacco into his mouth and tongued it inside his cheek. In the lamp's jumpy light, from across the room I watched his jaw working. The rest of him sat as still as a deer. His eyes were hard, bright coals in the gloom. "Where would we have put a kid, anyways? Hung it from a rafter?" His voice was half tender, not all the way gruff. "And what if it took after you, got handed all your troubles? More trouble than its life woulda been worth."

I bit my tongue so hard I tasted blood. I almost told him then, I almost did, about that other baby, the boy I'd had in Yarmouth that died.

"Ev?" It was on the tip of my tongue. I did not want his sympathy any more than I wanted the punishment of his anger. I only wanted to tell him so things would be fair and square between us, with no secret separating us. Though land only knows what secrets he harboured and kept from me. I shuddered to think.

"Well, do you want I should bury it, or chuck it out with the rest?" With the rest of what was in the pot, he meant.

"Leave it be." I half expected him to gripe about how we would miss the pot and need a replacement.

"I reckon down by the brook might be a good resting place," was all he said. "There's more pots at the dump."

The moment had passed where I could say it, could tell him about my mistake, without him flying off the handle.

"That'd be real good, Ev, by the brook." The best of a bad situation, I almost said, recalling Mama's words twelve years earlier.

Ev helped me into my coat. His fingers were rough as they accidentally brushed my cheek. Picking my way, I followed him out back. He grabbed the shovel, carried it and the pot through the brambles guarding the path. Giving quiet, gentle yips, Joe followed along for a little while. He helped us make a kind of procession until he saw there was no treat and turned back. The ground was just thawed, it oozed mud. Branches snapped and grazed my face. I kept up the best I could. When Ev had a purpose he could be quick as a fox. The quick brown fox jumps over the lazy dog, I thought crazily, remembering penmanship lessons at school.

Beneath a slim crescent moon, ignoring the ooze of blood between my legs, I sat on a rock and watched Ev dig a shallow grave and set the lidded pot down into it. Right quick, he scraped and kicked loose dirt and grass over top of it. The thought dug at me, for pity's sake: if only I had known a prayer to say, any sort of prayer. Not so much for this beginning-of-a-baby as for the one I had felt move in my belly twelve years before. For, most hurtful of all, remembering it made me think of Mama and Father. A cramp seized me, but it was nothing like the ache those words of hers had caused: You had a boy, he was born dead.

Something stirred from the woods. A big horned owl alighted and peered down from a branch. Its head spun around as it watched us. I was glad Ev was not like that bird, all-seeing and wise. Goodness knows what-all birds would have to say about people's doings if they could talk. The same went for the moon, curved as an eyelid hanging sideways. My secret was its secret.

We picked our way back to the house, Ev just ahead, swinging the shovel. Never mind the sadness, I said how the field by Seeley's Brook was a nice, quiet place to end up.

It was that, he agreed. "And a good spot for poorhouse-spawn that no one in the world wants."

All at once, I knew that I could not keep my secret inside me anymore. I knew what I needed to say, what I was going to say. I didn't want to say it. But it was like a stranger leapt up inside me and took over my tongue. "I imagine somebody did, want their baby, I mean. Their own real baby, that is." I breathed in the shadows, real deep, then let the shadows out. "I know it. Because I did, once. Want it. Mine, I mean. When I was a girl."

Ev's face was bent close to mine. I could smell the moon-
shine. He looked confused. Then his eyes hardened, turned
like sharp stones in the brook. "You what? You telling me
this mess ain't your first?" His look burned through me as he
straightened up. "So you whored around, did you? Before? Who
was the fella?" He raised his hand and down his palm came,
grazing my cheek, just catching my nose and lip. He looked at
me, shocked, and I guessed he felt sorry. And then, "You shut
the fuck up about whatever you did, and I'll make like I never
heard you say it."

Later on, after the radio landed on our doorstep, it seemed
like every time I turned it on I heard the song "Blue Eyed
Darling" by Roy Acuff and his Smoky Mountain Boys. *"You'll
always be my blue-eyed darlin'."* Under that cold crescent moon, I
searched in my mind for the blue of Ev's eyes, their twinkle.

As I wiped blood from my nose, my voice was hardly more
than a squeak. "Deal," I said.

I chalked everything bad up to his drinking.

And on the ground at my feet I spied a tiny piece of pink
ribbon—a hair ribbon? I picked it up and put in my pocket. A
trace of some other woman likely, who'd run afoul of love and
lost part of herself by the mud of Seeley's Brook.

15.

OPEN UP
YOUR
HEART

So much for travelling. *Ev said I slept all the way to the city.* To think he paid all that dough for the ambulance and I did not see a bit of scenery. But they were nice at the hospital. The doctor there was a dapper man with silvery-blond hair. The nurses treated us kindly, though I'm not sure what they made of Ev. After he fixed my hip, the same doctor came to check on me laying up in bed. He took a pen from the pocket of his white coat and while he was writing on something clipped to a clipboard, Ev pulled out that musty money. He nudged it at the doctor, gave him the eye, tried to get him to take it. Ev's look was prideful, cocky.

"I want her to have the best. I want her back on her feet—can you do that for me?"

The doctor eyed Ev like he had never seen so much cash, but sounded put out.

"That's not how things work."

Now it was Ev's turn to act miffed. He pocketed the cash, it looked like a rolled-up sock in his pants. And suddenly I knew where he'd got all that dough, saved up from the mail and pulled from the tin we kept customer's money in, not to be put in any bank but buried out of sight and out of mind.

"Well, if this is how city life works, city life ain't for me."

Before I knew it, Ev left, disappearing without so much as a goodbye. Maybe he caught the Acadian Lines bus home, though the fare, seven or eight dollars, would've made him flip his lid! Maybe he thumbed his way back? I only know that I was a fish out of water laying up in that big hospital for weeks on end. The worst was not being allowed to smoke in bed. You were supposed to go all the way down the hall to a room with jigsaw puzzles and a television set. It was all I could do to haul my sorry arse to the washroom. I'd have liked to take a gander at the TV, thought I might get lucky and see myself and Ev on it. I missed seeing his face.

Finally, the ambulance took me back to Digby General. At least Darlene and them weren't such sticklers about smoking, except that they nagged about my lungs. Said if I didn't get back on my feet, I'd fill up with pneumonia. I laid around there for a good three months. By this time, you mightn't be surprised to hear, I had got used to regular hot cooked meals and other fineries we lacked in Marshalltown. The nurses took turns sponge-bathing me and washing my hair, which brought back memories of Mae giving me the royal treatment. It also brought back the words of that hymn about being washed that made me see red, a woolly lamb with its throat cut, except instead of being white I pictured it as a tiny black sheep. And as I enjoyed the nurses' pampering, another of Aunt's sayings came to me: *"Pride goes before the fall."* Maybe it was prideful of me to enjoy these creature comforts, as if I was *owed* them. Comforts, or feeling you deserve them, will soften up the toughest old bird. Maybe it wasn't pride pushing me so much as it was the flesh's weakness seeking its due. Maybe it was Aunt's ghost whispering in my ear.

Rest assured, the torture of getting back on my feet paid for any comforts I enjoyed.

One day Darlene came in with a newfangled thing called a walker, saying, "Use it or lose it. You can't go home till you can manage on your own." I wasn't used to her being a bossy-boots like I was used to Ev. She got me up off the chair she'd had me sitting up in. After lying so long in bed, my legs were like jelly and my chin was soldered to one shoulder. I guess someone had to make me do it, or I'd have never walked again. After some time Darlene had me moving down the hall like a snail, but almost on my own steam.

"Good," she said. "But there's no way around it, you're gonna have to do stairs."

She and the other girls would take turns day in and day out, helping me move towards the stairwell. It overlooked the entranceway to the parking lot. Through the big glass doors you could see people lounging outside, patients and visitors, nurses, orderlies, and gals from the kitchen and laundry taking smoke breaks and that. There was nary a bird, save the odd seagull circling.

One afternoon Darlene took the walker away, gave me a cane. Standing there at the top of the stairs, gripping onto it, I chickened out, refused to budge. "Them stairs aren't going nowhere. I'll try 'em tomorrow. Or next week. Or the week after." The truth was, I was scared skinny. All the weeks lying around had stolen my gumption.

Darlene was full of gab. "I'd have thought you'd be keen to get back to your painting and having hubby spoil you. He told me once how much you like his cakes. A nice white cake—or spice cake, is that your favourite? He never said—" Just like that, though, she quit talking. I guessed what she was thinking. Ev had made himself scarce as hen's teeth since he'd left me in the city. He hated hospitals, hated their smell—hospitals made him sick, he'd said. It made sense, I guess, if you'd never lain in a nice, fresh hospital bed or eaten hospital grub, three square meals a day that other people cooked.

Of course I stuck up for him. Someone had to. If a fella's own wife won't stick up for him, who will?

"Cakes aren't the half of it. Cigarettes, candies—he spoils me something fierce. The candies he buys me?" Hunched into myself, I gave a good strong laugh, which made my chest hurt. "All these years and I guess he still figures I am not sweet enough, need all the sweetening up he can give me." I gave another good strong laugh, which hurt my heart or maybe my conscience, just a bit, for telling Darlene this fib. Though nothing pained me nearly as much as her nudging me nearer the stairs did.

She kept one arm about my waist, held my hand in her other hand, squeezed my arm tight under her other arm, like we were skating partners. Of course, I had never skated in my life, nor had Ev, each of us for our own reasons. But I imagined us whirling around the frozen surface of a pond like the skaters in my paintings, never mind my feet would have slip-slided every which way. The notion made me smile like a fool. Peering down into my face, Darlene rightly took this to be a sign of nerves.

"Don't let go," I said. If I could have raised my head up, lifted my eyes and looked off into nothing, it mightn't have been so scary. But all I could see were my feet in my slippers on the edge of the hard, speckled riser.

"Come on now, I won't let you fall."

"You'd be in some pile of doo-doo if you did." I laughed
louder, muckling onto her for dear life. In my mind I begged,
Don't make me. Please please please, no more stairs for me in
this life. "Tomorrow," I said. But, like Ev going out of his way
to drum up orders, Darlene wasn't one to take tomorrow for an
answer. "What, don't you trust me?" She laughed, her warm
breath in my ear. "Who else lets you smoke?"

It was only three steps but it might as well have been thirty.
She made me grip the cane with my left hand, the railing with
my right—easier said than done with my fists balled up tighter
than ever. She had a saying that was supposed to help me
remember: "Left foot leads going down, right foot leads going
up. Because going down is hell, yes? Going up is h-e-a-v-e-n,
proper thing." Aunt would have approved.

I snorted, balking. "So lefties go to hell, eh?"

Darlene looked flummoxed, her face flushed against her
uniform's snowy white. "Hell? It's a manner of speaking. Hell
is just what you make it, surely."

I had to laugh yet again, thinking of Aunt, though every
part of me hurt like the bejeebus. I gripped the railing like my
life depended on it. Darlene stayed right behind me, her breath
warming the top of my head. With her arm around me, one step
at a time, I did it. I reckon I went to hell and back.

"A bit more practice and you'll be fit to go home."

Back in my room, who was waiting to see me but Secretary,
with a box of Peppermint Patties and a bouquet of pink carna-
tions. Now *that* was heaven.

A few weeks later, the day before I left hospital, I was
having a sit-down in the lobby when I saw the police car pull
up outside—it was hard to miss it—and who hopped out but
Darlene? She was wearing a yellow dress and a boxy pink jacket
and carrying a grocery bag, with her uniform in it, I suppose.

Smiling behind the wheel, Bradley Colpitts watched her come inside. Just before he pulled away from the curb, Darlene twirled around and blew him a kiss. I knew then that those two were more than just friends.

I recovered enough to get along in the house, going from the daybed to my table-tray and to the pot to do my business, a path like a triangle made of three yardsticks. It was all right. But my days of enjoying the trailer were done. In my absence, the Light & Power had been cut off. A family of chipmunks had moved in. I couldn't climb up inside it on my own and Ev wouldn't lift me, scared I'd bust something else. As wondrously as the trailer had landed in the yard, my ability to use it left me. So much for the delights of a house, a studio, on wheels.

"'The Lord giveth and the Lord taketh,'" Aunt used to say. Though I have yet to meet the Hoary-Bearded Man in White Robes whose mention made her tremble, I had to agree. He or Somebody or Something gave and took all right, though not always in equal measure, it seemed to me.

Ev set up my paints in my corner, like old times. My heart sank when I saw the boards that had gathered dust, the unanswered mail, the backed-up orders. "Better get at 'em and to 'em," he said in a no-nonsense, teasing way. Fixing on holding a brush steady in my hand, bracing that fist tight with my other fist, took my mind off losing the trailer, which I suppose Ev sold. It took my mind off most of what ailed me, almost like before. And Ev did his best to brighten things up. He picked a sprig of wild blue asters and stuck it in a jar of water. I had a hankering for the sweet peas he grew out back but they were long past their prime. A person makes do with what Nature provides. Though those wild blue asters weren't the most cheerful posies, foretelling as they do a hard frost and the end of fair weather.

I had expected things in Marshalltown to be pretty much unchanged, and they were, all but one thing. Matilda, Willard, and their flock seemed to have abandoned us, maybe seeking greener pastures. Secretary said she spotted a big murder up the road, though, which Ev confirmed was Matilda and them. I knew they never nested in the same tree twice, but this didn't mean they wouldn't be back. We had nothing but trees. I stayed hopeful.

Secretary got a travelling nurse to come when she could to sponge-bathe me and see that I was getting on okay—at least I thought Secretary arranged it until the nurse asked how I knew Miss Twohig. Turned out Carmelita Twohig was the one paying for her visits. I bit my tongue. Ev saw to it that I got toast with my tea, and beans or sardines with toast for supper, my choice. I had to laugh the time a stranger came to the door while Ev was off on one of his jaunts, a man wearing what looked to be pajamas, who announced that he was here to bathe me. I don't know why, but I thought of Olive rubbing a washcloth over someone's back, some poor feeble-minded girl-child, sudsy water lapping over her. The sound of someone else's breathing through the keyhole, and Olive chasing whoever it was away. Over my dead body, a stranger would wash me!

"Oh no you ain't!" I told the man in pajamas and shut my pretty door in his face.

"You didn't!" Secretary laughed into her glove when I told her. "Carmelita Twohig must've called him. Least she could have done was warn you first. I wonder how come she got a man? Guess the VON were hard up for help that day."

Well, as you might guess, I learned early on in our marriage it was best to keep my trap shut. If only Ev could have done the same—talk about a man with the gift of gab, talk talk talk.

When he was in his cups he could have talked a person under the table or into the roaring path of a truck. The same as later on, I mostly stayed hunkered in my corner. Like I've said, if I had a brush in my hand I was content and could handle pretty near anything. If I had been the praying type, my prayer would have gone like this: Lord, let me paint and I will take whatever you dish out.

But one morning he had started drinking early, right there in the house, and by eleven o'clock I'd had enough of an earful to do me two weeks. When I put my hands over my ears he got owly, fixing for an argument, I could tell.

It wasn't a bad day outside; I figured if I went out there and loitered by the road for a spell, he might simmer down or have nodded off by the time I took myself back inside. I had my coat on, and the painting I'd finished the day before tucked under my arm—aiming just to look at it, find some company in it, I guess. Thinking how when all else failed it cheered me up to look at what I wanted to see, things I had guessed up placed straight and square in front of me on the board, the way they looked in my mind. As I was standing there a car stopped and a man got out and said he was going to Yarmouth, he could give me a lift there if I wanted. Just then I heard something let loose inside the house, something hard hit the floor or the wall.

"All right," I said, and just like a fool, with no purse and no money and nothing but my painting, I got into the car. I didn't say two words the whole sixty miles, just kept my head down for most of it. I was scared to look up as we entered the town, scared it would pain me too bad to see what I was missing—all those places like the Grand Hotel and Frost Park. When the man asked how long it had been since I'd visited, I shrugged. He shut up and kept driving down Main Street. I looked up in time to see the top of Forest Street but didn't make a peep. He kept going, past Pearl Street and Emin's Lane and Moody's Lane, and it occurred to me that maybe I should be scared, that here I was being carried off by this stranger who for all I knew might take me down to the Chebogue River and throw me in, or worse, deliver me to that place in Arcadia. But he slowed down by the Lewis Fountain, a beautiful watering hole for people and horses alike. A present to the town, Father had said when his business was thriving, given by the wealthy Lewises, no relation to Ev as far as I knew, a family who owned a big shipping business.

Just past the fountain, the man turned down Lewis Lane and delivered me to someone's house. A woman named Mitchell came to the door and looked baffled, but she remembered Mama and our cards and invited me in. And she fed me then proceeded to call some ladies she knew who soon showed up with presents. A pound of this and a pound of that. Butter, flour, sugar. "For me?" I said, and they laughed, and not one of them would accept my painting in return. And when the tea and cookies she made were gone, she went to the phone and called the man back, I guess he was her son or her nephew or some such, and he came to drive me home. Imagine, driving one hundred and twenty miles in one day.

Slouched in his chair, Ev nearly cried when I stepped through the door and plunked down my presents. He was relieved, I guess, but beside himself and none too pleased that I had taken off and not even said where I was going. Once he'd had a lick of the butter, his relief gave way to anger. "Running off like that, who were you chasing after, huh? Going off with the first fella who strikes your fancy. What's all this stuff anyways, his payment for your whoring? Try that stunt again, don't bother coming back. I oughta turf you out now!"

But I climbed the ladder and went to bed, worn out from my long excursion. He was right, I figured. I had no business disappearing on him like that, even for a day, even when he was drinking. For better or for worse, our vows had said.

And back then, just when I figured Ev Lewis had every right to turf me out on my ear, if that's how he saw it, knowing my past and seeing as painting pictures was all I could do to make money, something happened that gave me a leg up.

We heard Joe the First bark before we saw the car pull in a few days, maybe a week after my jaunt to Yarmouth. A lady got out and came to the door. The day was warm for spring, and we had the inside door open to air the place out—of course, all that did was invite the bugs in. Ev was kneading dough for porridge bread to go with our butter and some beans. His fingers were stuck together with oatmeal and molasses goo. I'd just lit a smoke, was thinking on what to fill a board with: a snowy scene to cool my thoughts, or a scene from the docks, lobster boats riding the tide, gulls angling for bait?

The lady stuck her head in, not a bit shy. "Is this where I'd find the artist?"

She had a wavy hairdo, dark and glossy. Ev smacked his lips, looked her up and down. Acted like I was no more than a fly setting there. You have got the wrong place, missus, I thought. When the lady spied me behind a stack of magazines and whatnot, her eyes lit up. They moved to the picture propped between a breadbox and a tin of peas. She dug in her purse, took out a two-dollar bill. She laid the money down right in front of me, then reached for the painting. It was one I had slaved over, of a boy with a red rag on his head, kneeling before a lake in autumn, feeding nuts to a squirrel while its relatives looked on. I'd taken great pains with the reds and yellows and greens, using fine, careful brushwork to show the grasses and leaves and reflections and the look on the boy's face and on his squirrel buddies' faces.

Only then did I start to get up. "Sorry. That one i'n't quite dried yet—"

Ev scooted over and snatched the bill out from under my nose. He stuck it inside the empty Player's tin sitting atop the table. "Hold on. It's dried enough. You like this one, the wife's got plenty more where it come from." He dug under some papers and fished out another one I'd done, with yellow finches and bright blue delphiniums.

"Why, I'll take them both." The lady took out a change purse, laid down two fifty-cent pieces and a dollar bill.

"Sold!" Ev added this sum to the Player's tin and danced a little jig for her on the spot. "Whaddya say, Maud? Thank the nice lady for taking these off your hands."

The lady beamed. Even glimpsing it at a tilt, her smile looked as sweet to me as a cat's. "Oh—are there more?"

Ev grabbed a picture off the wall, the tulips I'd done on the piece of linoleum I'd found that day a good while back at the dump.

"That's okay," the lady said. But she asked if I took orders. A friend of hers was looking to have two pairs of shutters decorated for her cottage down the shore in Queen's County. Oh my sweet Dinah, I thought years later when Hank Snow went big, wondering if these folks might've known him since he was from that part of the world, Liverpool. At the time, though, Queen's County meant frig-all to me. Just as well, since Ev was the one doing the talking.

"Damn right she does, she loves taking orders. She'll paint anything your friend's heart de-sires. But she will need what you call a de-posit."

"Oh? Well. I suppose so." The woman opened her purse again, out came another couple of dollars.

Ev put them into the tin too—it was a pittance, I'm thinking now. But Ev was as pleased as I was, so pleased he drew a humbug out of his pocket and gave it to her. "A sweet for the sweet," he said. Never mind it was covered in pocket fuzz. The lady took out a tissue, wrapped the candy in it, and tucked it in her purse.

As for me, my mind was already dancing with the pictures I would do for her friend, one for each shutter. *Fountain and Birds*, a bird bath surrounded by tulips, two birds bathing, three birds soaring upwards. *Flowers with Candle Lantern*, pink roses and butterflies. *White Flowers with Bluebirds*, just like the words said. *Flowers with Yellow Bird*, blue, white, red, yellow spikes of blossoms like delphiniums or lupins standing tall, taking up the top two-thirds of the shutter, shorter, thicker ones filling the bottom third, and one fine feathered yellow friend bursting upwards above the tallest flower.

I had guessed up all four in my head by the time she arranged to drop off the bare shutters. And I made up my mind then and there that no matter what, no man would steal the happiness I felt, least of all my husband.

After the lady left, Ev took the money out of the tin and slipped it into his pocket. He patted his pocket, feeling the bills. Some bread dough from his hands clung to the front of his pants. "Well, I guess you are good for something after all, ain't you." And he came over and elbowed me, as playful as could be.

"*Blessed are the poor in spirit*,'" Aunt Ida used to recite, "'*they shall inherit the earth*.'" Well, I don't know about that. If you are rich in spirit, what then, die empty-handed? Maybe the world where you people are just wasn't for me—not to sound smug, or fudge the fact that the bodily part of me lies handily under its dirt, gone from ashes to ashes like everyone else who leaves the world as you know it.

Up on the ridge the wind rattles the trees. Clouds scoot by. Murders of crows rag at each other from the branches, each caw like one of Ev's tirades against folks he didn't trust. "If you are not for me, you're agin me," he used to say. To tell you the truth, the memory of his voice goads me. It plucks at my guilt. This might surprise you, or it might not, but, pontificating, he could sound a bit like the Bible Aunt sent for a present and I flipped through just the once. Maybe Ev thought he was the Lord bearing with me. Like he told those TV people who came that time, saying how I tied him down: "T'ain't like someone else. You can't go out all night with your friends. She can't get around like she used to. She can cook some. She does all right what she can do. I don't expect much of her."

Friends? Ev would have been friendless if not for me. But he filled those folks' ears with stuff about his own life, as if those men were his chums. "I got partway through grade one. When I went to school they made fun of me. I was only on the ABC book. I told the woman I was workin' for they teased me. I got the prize, writing on a slate. One cent. Didn't they cry! I bought me a big stick of candy. Went out to work when I was ten years old. Five cows to milk night and morning. All kids had to work. No pension in them days."

Don't know how or where I figured in this chatter. But he shored himself up against losing any way he could, and many a person will say he used me to feather his nest and pay his way. He had his reasons for taking charge—"It's a man's job to manage fi-nances"—making no bones about telling those strangers what he thought.

Maybe there was good reason women like Aunt Ida and Carmelita Twohig never got hitched?

Lo and behold, it wasn't long before Bradley Colpitts came to investigate, not the appearance of the would-be molester sent by the Twohig woman but the circumstances surrounding my fall, never mind my fall had happened many months ago. Once again it was autumn. I guess the constable had an exceptional memory of things pertaining to my stairs. Bradley Colpitts quickly laid to rest the mystery of the perve at the door, a male nurse Darlene had suggested Carmelita Twohig might contact to help me out. The constable gave the whole business short shrift. "I'd react the same way you did, assuming the guy had no ID."

Then his voice grew serious: "Darlene says you lay there a good long time before Ev got help."

All these months I had done my best to put this out of my mind. I saw no point in raising it, as long as I kept living under Ev's roof.

"Don't know. Don't remember." It wasn't against the law to sleep through an accident, was it?

"It's true, though, isn't it, Ev never visited all that time you were laid up. You must've wondered where he was, what was keeping him from coming to see you? Or didn't you miss him?" He gave a smart-arsed laugh that I did not much appreciate.

For Bradley Colpitts had me on my toes, so to speak. He made me wary. I thought of that muddy roll of bills Ev had used to pay the Digby hospital people with, for my medicine and stuff, I guess. If Colpitts had gotten a wind of Ev having all that cash, next he'd be asking about where it came from, knowing banks didn't bury your money for safekeeping. Why would Colpitts care if Ev visited me or not. What was it to him? If the constable had been harder to look at, rest assured, I'd have sent him packing. But he was handsome as ever, as handsome as all heck, bent over, looking down at me. And I couldn't forget his kind interest in my stairs.

"Officer. You would have to ask Ev about that. Talking to me, maybe you'd best mind your own beeswax." I chuckled into my chest so he wouldn't think I was being too forthright, though I surely was, as forthright as I dared without being rude. Rolling my eyes up as far as I could, the sideward look I gave him was sweet and coy. Never mind my eyes ached from being strained so. "You remind me of somebody."

"Not Miss Twohig." He smirked. At least the man had a sense of humour. Thanks to his looks, I was thinking of Emery Allen—until trouble of a more recent kind lit my memory.

"Officer. Can I ask you something?" He had his jacket open. I looked at his belt, its shiny buckle. "Did anything ever come of that family, you know, a couple years ago, that mother or whoever, complaining about Ev? Bothering her kids, I mean."

The constable sighed through his teeth. I knew from the times I'd caught a better look at him, for all their straightness, his two front ones were spaced with a generous spit-hole. Maybe it was that toothy sigh that made him sound boyish. "Like I told you before, if no one presses charges, these things tend to disappear."

It wasn't fully what I had hoped to hear, but it was good enough.

"So there, you see? Ev did nothing to merit that woman's badmouthing." I kept right on looking at his buckle, didn't let my gaze drift down. "Oughtn't you to consider the true source of trouble when you go seeking the culprit? When the trouble is hearsay and no more, I mean."

Bradley Colpitts squatted right down before me, fixed his unwavering hazel eyes the best he could on mine tilted there. They had a surly, dogged look I had not noticed before. "You didn't have help, did you, falling down those stairs?"

His question caught me short, it took me full aback. The brush I'd been gripping onto rolled from my fist onto my table-tray, knocking a can with black paint enough that some spilled over. My mouth went dry. All I could do was gawp at him. How dare he think such a thing, let alone say it?

For all your niceness, I wanted to cry out, how knuckle-brained are you? I wondered how Darlene stood his blind dog-gedness, this blindsiding refusal of his to let sleeping babies lie.

He hardly noticed the spill. I grabbed a rag, dabbed at it—paint blotted out Reddy Kilowatt in the *Courier* ad on the tray, the little cartoon man for the Light & Power. I swallowed hard, flailing around in my head for words.

Maybe realizing how bad he'd overstepped himself, Colpitts blurted out some fool question, about what had become of the crows.

"Crows?" Uttering it calmed me enough to murmur about them finding "greener pastures." Not the best explanation, I realized, stringing a better one together, picking the words real carefully. "While I was gone Ev had no scraps to throw 'em—" Considering Colpitts's nerve, my voice's steadiness surprised me. "You know, the extras off my plate I never had room for, that's what he usually fed them."

"Ah." The constable gave a breezy laugh, sounding relieved. Like he was off the hook for asking that hateful question!

Be wise, I told myself. Serpent wise. I had something to ask him, wanting only to move the talk along. Being canny meant being gentle, kindly, even when it wasn't deserved. And this was on my mind, albeit a minor botheration. "You and Darlene—don't suppose you two are thinking of tying the knot, are youse?" I glanced at my hand as I spoke. Smudged with paint, it was so swollen and balled up into itself, my fingers were nearly welded together. I could not have *held* my wedding band, even if Ev were to unearth that pickle jar, take out the ring, and give it to me. His mother's band of gold.

Constable Colpitts acted like his blunder hadn't happened. Still squatting there, he grinned to himself, brought one of his hands to the back of his neck and rubbed it. He put his hands on his thighs, rocked back on his heels, and stretched his head back. I imagined his neck's pink shaved skin folded over his collar, like a puppy's—I suppose he'd got a crick in it from hunching over. The stripe on the shin of his pant leg made me think of a line on a road, a line not so easily crossed.

"Darlene's a fine lady." His voice was full of pride and he flushed, easing himself forwards. His face was only inches from mine now, and I thought, Tit for tat. Get nosy with me, I'll get nosy with you. But, eyeballing me, he went right back to beating his same ugly old drum, trying to catch me out. Catch *us* out. "So Ev's looking after you, is he? There's nothing you need?"

I gave him my best slanted grin. "A roast chicken dinner would be nice, like they give you in the hospital. Just joking." The last thing the fella needed was ammunition, seeing how he had it in for Ev, was bent on showing Ev up any way he could. I knew this all too well now, there was no backpedalling, glossing over, or covering it up. "Can't complain."

Then he dealt a less sneaky blow. "Now you are sure Ev didn't have anything to do with your fall?"

This was as good as a swift, wild crack to the head. It made me mad, real mad, like all at once a swarm of bees had got under my hairnet, all buzzing, buzzing mad. I'd had it with his wheedling and digging, with having his two-faced mug in mine. I fastened my gaze to my chest. I tried to keep my voice even but still it came out in a thin, raspy huff. "It's my husband you are talking about. Ev may be bossy and he might like money, but he ain't vicious."

This sent Colpitts into a flap, for his voice was hot and

defensive. "I didn't say he was, I never meant—"

"But that is what you're getting at." I was at the end of my patience and I trusted he was at the end of his, too.

Then he came right out with this: "Okay, Missus Lewis. I'm asking if he pushed you."

I believe I sucked up what air was left in the room, pulling in my breath. When I spoke, my voice was sharp as a needle in my own ear, as the voice inside me counselled the folly of mixing up serpent smarts and being dove-gentle. "Officer Colpitts, I am saying Ev ain't that kind of man. I am telling you, he would never do that."

Yet Colpitts kept at me. I didn't need to look at his eyes to know they were those of a dog after a fat, whittled stick. "But it's true, isn't it, Ev's got money. Hasn't spent much, though, to make the place"—he looked around, I felt him give my pretty stairs a final once-over—"comfortable for you."

My sigh made a shrill, whistling sound as I let it out. "Well there's a big difference between a fella liking his money and trying to kill his wife."

Colpitts breathed in, an inhale so deep I saw his chest puff out like Willard's. I fixed my sideward gaze on his badge. We were close enough that I could read the numbers on it. He hesitated, but only for a bit. "And, yes, you'd be absolutely right."

A little bead of silence fell upon us then.

"Say hi to Darlene when you see her." Goodbye, git, and don't you come snooping round here again, was what I meant. When he still didn't straighten up, I said to myself, No more beating around this bush, you. And to him? "Now Constable Colpitts, unless you got something important to talk about, it'd be nice if you hit the road now and didn't come back."

It wasn't how you talked to the law. But I had thought of Bradley Colpitts as a friend, and now I knew different. A lot different. A friend would see, like Secretary did, that I was at

Ev's mercy, that if not for Ev I would be well and truly done for. What had always been true had only got truer. Colpitts reminded me of someone, all right. For this was not the first time I had been disappointed by a man masquerading as Prince Charming, making like I mattered to him, making like he cared. I hoped Darlene knew what she was getting herself into, I would have hated to see what had happened to me happen to her. Falling for someone who wasn't as he seemed.

16.

I SAW THE LIGHT

"*There's no remembrance of men of old nor of those to come will there be any remembrance among those who come after them,*" Aunt would recite. Horseshit! I remember men, all right: four in all if you count my brother and Father. From what I have seen of folks down where you are, men remember *me*, a few do, strangers. Helps when someone puts your picture in a magazine and the house you lived in tells your story: four walls as steeped with your presence as socks dried in air thick with wood smoke, the way the four walls I shared with Ev were.

If not for those walls, my paintings would be but tinder now, I dare say, my name no more than dust lifted by the breeze from the stone carver's chisel.

For all the paintings Ev had me do, after I left for good there wasn't a finished one in the house for him to admire or copy, though he had his stencils to work with. As for my work, there was just that half-done portrait of Matilda that I had abandoned. I don't suppose he thought of finishing it? It grieved me to leave it behind, never to see the light of day. Looking down one night, I caught the full view of him burning it in the fire, the smoke rising from the chimney. I guess that was the only thing a half-done picture of a crow was good for. I trust Matilda wasn't watching. Ev sold pretty much anything I'd put my hand to that wasn't nailed down like the stairs were.

To his credit, after that night out back when I confessed my "sin," he never raised his hand to me again. Perhaps I should have told Constable Colpitts about it, said it was in the long-ago past and had never happened again. But I didn't want to explain about Emery Allen and that—the more people who know your trouble, the bigger that trouble grows till there's no hiding it anymore. None of this was Colpitts's or anyone's business. When Ev heard about my baby boy, I don't know why he didn't kick me out right then. I suppose he was biding his time. My guess is it was that lady and her friend's willingness to pay good money for my paintings that saved my hide.

Otherwise, Ev would've shown me the door. A useless cripple-arsed mouth to feed: I could imagine these words on his lips as he gave me the boot.

But he didn't give me the boot. And I never brought up my past again. Although when that Catherine woman came knocking, claiming to be my daughter, well, you can imagine how scared I was of Ev getting riled up, of him believing her and going off the deep end, sure I had been lying to him from the day I had walked into his life, that my whole married life was a lie. If he had gone off the deep end so crazy with rage that he *had* kicked me out, I would have kicked the bucket then, plain and simple. No roof over my head, no food. I'd have starved before I would've gone next door seeking a bed, kind as Olive was to me. I had avoided the almshouse once; there would have been no going back there as an inmate, especially after having dined as an invited guest. I had my pride. I'd have rather lived in a hollow tree.

"*Love is patient, love is kind, love is slow to anger, love is quick to forgive.*" So I read in that Bible, cracking and skimming through it just the once. I reckon you could add to this, Love is jealous, love is greedy, love is taking what you need and making off with it, assuming you are lucky enough not to get caught. I don't doubt that such thoughts nursed Ev through to the end of his days. But you could say this about a few people, I imagine.

It was a Saturday afternoon at the tail end of December, eight and a half years after my arrival up here, when a visitor dropped by Ev's. Ev was warming his hands by the range, the jar on his lap. The jar with my wedding ring in it and a bit of change. He was having quite a time trying to open it. Before the ground froze that fall, he'd dug it up and hid it under the floor—I guess he thought if his heart got real bad and he needed money and had one last thing to pawn, it was best the ring stayed close at hand.

He had seen the doctor about the pains in his chest, had parted with a pretty penny buying the green and yellow pills the doctor wanted him to take. For the first time ever, Ev did what he was told. Why, he had enough pills in the house to stock a drugstore, I heard a cop, not Constable Colpitts but another one, say. So it was hard to say why he was so anxious to have my ring in his palm. The jar's lid was welded on with rust. Even with warmed hands, no amount of wrestling with it made it budge.

His visitor's knock came as Ev cursed, prying at the lid with a knife.

I had seen this man drive by Ev's countless times over that

Christmas. Had seen him almost stop then keep driving, like some unseen hand prevented him from pulling over and going in. The man didn't look like a preacher, for his lack of a pastor's collar. But all through the holidays I had seen him coming and going, opening and locking up the little white church up towards the Valley where he preached.

On this Saturday, the thirtieth of December, I saw him leave the church, get in his car, and head towards Marshalltown. He had the radio on. It was frosty, and I could see his breath as he sang along to that gospel song Hank Williams made famous. He tapped his fingers on the wheel, talking out loud to God, "Give me the strength to witness to your word, bring the Good News to the poor and downtrodden, and free those captive to sin." Instead of gunning the engine in front of Ev's, he slowed and turned in. Ev had the storm door propped open with the same old broomstick, never mind it was almost January. The preacher got out of his car, went up and knocked on my old door. You could still see the birds and flowers on it, though the paint was blistered and peeling. Still cursing, Ev set the jar down and cracked open the door.

The preacher invited himself in.

Now what is he up to? I wondered. I agreed with Ev that you couldn't trust someone who boldly called himself a man of God. What was a man of God, anyway? This one handed Ev a pamphlet, which Ev took from him and threw on the floor. It was late in the day, the sun was low in the window. Ev said through a squint, "You're looking for money in the wrong place."

The preacher wasn't a tall man like Bradley Colpitts. He didn't have to stoop, standing inside the doorway. He picked up the pamphlet, held onto it this time. "God loves you, like he loves every man, woman, and child." When the preacher spoke you could see his breath.

"Is that right." Ev laughed into his fist, then launched into a coughing fit and rubbed at his chest. He was a sight, the poor fella, bundled up in his ragged old checked jacket and pants that hadn't seen a washboard since well before I'd croaked, and they were crusty then!

"The Lord's not after your money. He wants you, he wants your heart, your soul."

I was sure Ev had been drinking—the good stuff, not his old cocktails—there were empty bottles of Hermit wine and Golden Glow piled round the room, along with six or more weeks' worth of garbage to be burnt or tossed outside. But when he lowered himself to the chair, still rubbing where his ticker might be, I knew from the way he sat that he was sober, just not feeling one hundred per cent. He had aged since I'd been gone. Not a tooth left in his head, and the rattling cough he'd always had was a lot worse. I could hear phlegm rattling inside him when he breathed.

"'No one comes to the Father except by me.' Those are the words of our Saviour, Everett."

Ev was sharp as a hawk. "How'd you know my name, you?" As he spoke he clutched at himself, as if safeguarding his heart. "So if you ain't looking for money, what does a fancy fella the likes of you want from me?"

"I don't want a thing, Mr. Lewis. I am just here to tell you the Good News."

"Now what makes you think your news is good and that I want to hear it?"

I expected Ev to raise his fist and tell the visitor to git. But he seemed too weary to, tuckered out by the effort of trying to open the jar. Instead, he said, "Take a load off, preacher man." The preacher pulled up my old chair and sat. It was so wobbly and the seat so worn I feared he'd go through it.

Ev rolled a smoke, all the while giving his guest the stink-eye, you might say. "Think you're gonna get me into a church, you got another think coming.'" Ev's eyes were rheumy and yellowed. But there was that twinkle, a glimmer of it. "I'd offer you a drink, preacher, but I'm off the sauce. Doctor's orders. Not that pills are any prostitute for liquor." The preacher smiled. That's not the best word for substitute, I suppose he was thinking. Ev smirked back. For the first time since I'd landed up here, he had a captive audience. Heck, he didn't even have a Joe for company, after the last Joe had got sick and he'd used his shotgun to put the dog out of its misery. I had heard the gunshot, saw Matilda's granddaughter or maybe her great-granddaughter and her flock flap from the trees at the sound, as alarmed as if a great horned owl had descended.

"I'd offer you a cuppa tea but I got none." Ev crossed his arms tight, swayed a little in the cold. Was he in pain, or what? If so, his visitor didn't notice. The preacher smiled and blew into his hands to warm them. "I am not here to take from you, sir, only to offer you—well, show you what the Lord is offering. His cup of everlasting life. The water of eternal—"

"I wouldn't mind a cup of everlasting TNT, Reverend." Ev's grin was sly and tough, and I realized that living without me hadn't changed the person inside. "Wouldn't mind a bite to eat neither, a slab of bread and a chop or a mess of stew."

"Ah." The preacher considered this. "But 'man does not live by bread alone,' you must've heard this at some point in time. About the special power of—"

"Can't say as I have." Ev scowled, his eyes on the preacher as he picked up the jar. He held it on his lap, hands wrapped around it. "Think your special power might get the lid off this bugger without smashin' it?" The setting sun tinted Ev's face orange. His look signalled that he'd had enough already and whoever tested him had best retreat from the line of fire. Talk-fire, that is. "What outfit you say you're from, preacher? Bothering a fella in his home at suppertime."

Instead of answering, the visitor reached into his coat and

pulled out a Pal-o-mine bar. The sight of its yellow-gold-and-red wrapper made me miss your world. He laid it on the table, the one spot free of empty cans filled with butts, dirty old papers, and junk. "You like sweets, Everett? You got a sweet tooth at all? Sorry I don't have something more substantial."

There was nothing about Ev that cried sweet or sour. But he eyed that candy bar like it was a turkey dinner such as Olive had fed us. "Now what about that water you're talking about? That 'everlasting' water." Ev's voice was a sneer.

"Drink of it and you shall not thirst."

At this Ev was seized by another coughing jag. As he crumpled over on his chair, I thought, Come on, man of God, leave the poor fella alone. For I had a stark feeling Ev's days were short and getting riled up might cut them shorter. "If you want to see another year, I'd quit drinking if I were you," the doctor had warned. If I'd had hands, I would have shown the preacher the door.

But then Ev's shoulders started shaking, shaking like a little poplar tree in a harsh wind, and he was making a noise the likes of which I'd never heard him or any man make before. Next, it was like all the sound had been sucked out of the room and out of Digby County and maybe all of Nova Scotia. Suddenly there was no wind. No crows calling from any trees, no cars racing past in the growing twilight, not even the hiss and spit of the dying fire. There was only the sound of Everett Lewis crying.

The preacher got up off my chair and laid his hand on Ev's shoulder, whispered something in Ev's ear as he kept his hand there. In the sun's dying glow, a tear streaked Ev's cheek. His one hand on Ev's shoulder, the preacher raised his other hand like I imagined either of the Hanks would do, Snow or Williams, saluting fans at the Grand Ole Opry. Eyes closed, the preacher mumbled softly, his voice slow and urgent. He said

Ev had a choice to make, which he could act on then and there. That he could accept the Lord as his saviour or spend the rest of his days in misery.

"You've got a choice here, Everett—you don't mind me calling you Everett."

Ev's nose was running. A mix of snot, tears, and spit sputtered out: "You tell me what I have to do, then if you bugger off, I'll think about it." The preacher moved his hand to the top of Ev's head and raised his eyes to the ceiling where smoke from the stovepipe made a veil.

"You don't have to do anything. The Lord knows you need His love and grace. You just have to say yes."

Hovering, I waited. Listened to the wind slowly come to life outdoors and start blowing round the house again, through the trees and over Seeley's Brook and out onto the bay. It got so gusty I almost missed Ev's reply.

"Reckon you can sign me up then, to whatever it is you're sellin'. Long as it don't cost." I could tell by Ev's sigh that he was relieved, sure that by being agreeable he could send the preacher packing.

"Now you've seen the light, brother—Mr. Lewis. The Lord won't forsake those who call on Him, those born anew unto Him. Feel the air in the room? Doesn't it feel different?"

"Oh yeah. I sure as fuck do. It sure as fuck does."

"You've got a place in heaven, Everett. Don't ever doubt it."

It was these words that rang out. Oh my, had the vow "till death do us part" been just a fancy hook, a lie to make marriage easier, shining a light at the end of a very long tunnel? As unlikely as it seemed, the thought of bumping into Ev up here was sobering—and when eternal peace had finally come knocking on my invisible door and found me oddly reconciled to its sugarless, quiet if windy state. For I had seen the light, oh yes, the light that's everywhere, though it struck me that perhaps I had always seen it, the light that reaches down even at night and didn't only shine through my window to fill my head when I was painting, but shone regardless of anything.

Who knows what the preacher was thinking, beaming ear to ear as he patted Ev's shoulder, or what Ev was thinking, glued to his chair? He looked like a deer that got hit by a car but had managed to lope off either to die or lick its wounds. Just because I can see folks on the outside never meant I could see them on the inside, too. You can't know the heart or mind of someone else, not even from here.

The preacher shook Ev's hand. "Well, I'll leave you be, Mr. Lewis. I thank you for inviting me into your home. The Lord helps those who help themselves, don't forget, and He listens to all who obey His call. You have a happy new year, now, you hear?"

"Don't mind if I do," said Ev, standing up, bolting the door in his visitor's wake.

The preacher hummed Hank Williams's tune getting into his car. "I Saw the Light" was so hurtin' and true it would make a believer of anyone, I figured, at least for as long as the song took to play through on the radio. When it came to hurtin', at last I understood the benefit of being here. It's *not* knowing what lurks in others' hearts and minds, the freedom from sharing their worries and woes.

I never did catch the preacher's name, I'm not sure Ev did either. By the time the Reverend So-and-So drove off, poor Ev had wolfed down the Pal-o-mine bar and tossed the wrapper into the fire's dregs. A single piddly flame devoured it.

"Happy frigging new year!" Ev yelled to the range and his righteous newly born self.

Then he picked up the jar and jingled the loot inside. No matter how he pried at its rusted lid, no special power would budge it. Oh yes, the only way to free that ring and those coins would be to take a piece of firewood, say, and give the jar a whack and bash it to pieces. But, having a good stash of pills and money upstairs, he wasn't anywhere near that desperate, and besides, the woodbox was empty. So he kicked aside the mat—the roses' red beaten right out of them, sunken into their black background—and pried up that loose board. Reaching down, he lowered the jar through the hole. It clinked as it landed, the ground underneath was froze so solid. At least the hole was ready to receive it.

By now the gloaming gave way to dark, and he was too winded and weary to traipse to the woodpile and back. Forget what I said about others' woes, if I'd had hands I would have gone and got wood and banked a toasty fire to last Ev through the night and longer—but regret is neither here nor there, nothing but a drafty enemy to peace and calm. Only, if the house had stayed warm, he might have fared better. At least he mightn't have suffered so.

Like I've said, time flies up here even as it stands still. Imagine standing on a bridge looking down on a river: just because you see the current doesn't mean there's a damned thing you can do to stop its flow, even if you wanted to.

If Ev did not deserve the way he entered the world, he surely did not deserve the way he exited it. Maybe, like most of us, he truly did not see the end coming. If I could have saved him I would have. See? Here lies the regret about lacking hands, any hands, even messed-up, fisted, lobster-claw hands, to work any sort of trick.

Without hands, what good is there to an all-seeing view? Too bad Constable Colpitts did not have this kind of view, though. If he had, he mightn't have stopped and gone in somewhere for a doughnut when he ought to have stayed in the cruiser, cruising around on patrol. Parked and sipping a coffee, maybe he was just waiting for his shift to end so he could go home to Darlene and the kids—oh, those two lovebirds had been married going on nine years, by now they had two kids. A girl and a boy that would make any parent proud. Plus Bradley Colpitts had more company at work. The RCMP had taken over the town police and brought in some new officers. Maybe Constable Colpitts's nose was a little out of joint at having to share a car? I suppose he saw no need to visit Ev now that Ev mostly stayed home and had grown too old and sick to cause trouble.

I had seen the young fella hitching rides now and then, travelling back and forth on the highway out by Deep Brook to Marshalltown. A few times I saw one of Colpitts's partners in crime pick him up and give him a ride this way. I heard the partner ask the young fella's name—can't fully put a finger on it now, except that it made me think of Emery Allen, not Emery himself but where Emery came from, one of them Woods Harbours. By this I mean the name the fella gave sounded like a buzz saw sawing wood. Once, the officer had dropped him off just past the almshouse, long abandoned though it'd be another fifteen, sixteen years before vandals torched it. Now I'm not suggesting this young fella had a hand in *that*, only that he spent a fair bit of time visiting the trailer that was handy, a trailer that was a lot bigger than my old one. I guess the young fella had a friend living there. Only one person I knew of—I still won't call her a friend in the way Matilda was a friend—had a trailer that big, as I had yet to find out.

That December afternoon the preacher called on Ev, Buzzy—I'll call him Buzzy—was just down the road watching his friend make a New Years' rappie pie, a task best undertaken, I guess, with company over drinks. That's how it looked through the trailer's kitchen window: a few young fellas and a gal or two swigging the old dynamite juice, watching water being squeezed from potatoes—it must've been like watching ten paintings dry. Maybe they were all promised a slab of the finished product slathered with molasses come New Year's Eve. Maybe this made Buzzy hungry, maybe he had a headache and wanted fresh air.

Next, I saw him stumbling along the road. His jacket looked like one Roy Rogers the Singing Cowboy would wear, fringes swaying as he went. He had something in his pocket. He was awful close to the pavement, hardly seemed to notice the cars whizzing past in the dark, not even after a driver or two laid on their horns. He looked too young to be hard of hearing but he must've been, or he was a bit of a stunned arse. It was a few hours since Ev's visit from the preacher and it was dark. But the sky was full of stars and it was too early for Buzzy to call it a night and thumb a ride home, where his mama would be wondering where he was and how drunk he would be stumbling in, interrupting her and her boyfriend watching TV. They might be having a few drinks, too, warming up for tomorrow night's party to ring in the new year.

Buzzy's father was dead. I'd seen his mother going into Frenchys and visiting the tavern in Digby, where it used to be only men were allowed. I'd also seen carloads of young fellas who'd had a few drinks slow to a crawl passing Ev's place, wondering, I suppose, if Ev was inside. I have no doubt it was Bradley Colpitts who spread the rumour that Ev had money hidden all through the house. And Carmelita Twohig or someone like her pretending to be helpful, who told anyone who would listen that any cash Ev had once kept in the bank was buried out back in jars.

There wasn't a thing I could do to warn Ev—if there had been, he wouldn't have listened anyhow. *You mind your beeswax and I'll mind mine. I can look after myself, always have, always will. For you were no help,* I imagined him saying, making no bones about it a-tall.

Yet folks wondered, as I did, where all the money we made off my paintings got to. The money Ev made off me. He sure as heck hadn't spent it all, not so anyone would notice, not before I died or since. But I remember Secretary getting after me: "You're bringing in the dough. Get Ev to spend some on *you.* Get him to buy you some batteries. Sure, they cost, but if you're not running the radio day and night, they'll last you. Have him hire a plumber to build you a loo. It's the least he could do, spend a bit to make your life easier." It was along the same drift that Constable Colpitts took up later. My friend and secretary had a point. So did I, saying, "I'm all right."

But I did worry that without me to do Ev's reading and writing for him, there were human coyotes just watching for the chance to close in and take advantage. I wondered whether that jar he had stowed under the floor with my wedding ring in it was safe, and how many other jars with cash inside might be stowed with it. I could flit over the rooftops of the Bank of Nova Scotia *and* the Royal Bank but I could not see inside their vaults, let alone inside the canvas bags they kept bills in. Forget what I said before about seeing *everything* from up here: seeing is as seeing does. There are things I won't watch and things I refuse to see.

Who knows but someone hadn't spied Ev that fall, digging that jar up out of the dirt? And who knows but that someone saw him roust up others stuffed with folded-up twos, fives, tens, and twenties. I always knew without letting on that Ev had more planted back there than flowers and root vegetables, more jars planted than you could shake a stick at. Ever since he'd hauled out that money at the hospital, the roll of bills steeped in mud.

Who knows but some young fella with darkness on his

mind hadn't peeked in through my old window to see Ev pushing back the mat, lifting the board, and feeding jar after jar
through the floor—Ev thinking they'd be safer where, if a thief
tried to get at them, it would be over his dead body—Ev rocking
back on his heels to nurse one last, self-satisfying drink. Who
knows but such a young fella hadn't heard how Ev talked when
he got drinking: "Just because I don't look like much doesn't
mean I ain't rich. I got twenty-two thousand dollars, and it ain't
just sitting in a bank." And who knows but the young fella didn't
just decide on a lark to go shoot the shit with him?

For the first time since leaving your world, I honestly
wished I was there with Ev that night before New Year's Eve.
The pair of us smoking cigarettes and chewing tobacco, and, if
there was juice in the radio's batteries, listening to Hank Snow
give the old year the boot, singing his song about moving on.
Ev might've banged on a pot for a drum and I could've sung
along....

I had a bad feeling watching that young Buzzy fella stump
up to Ev's in the dark. The headlights of a car cast a passing
glow over the dirty snow by the road. The young fella pulled a
pint of something from his pocket. Swinging it, he pounded on
our pretty door, which had gone a long time without its birds
and butterflies getting freshened up with paint. He pounded
fit to bust the lock.

"Old man! Open up! Got a drink for you. A fuckin new
year's drink a fuckin day early."

I wanted to cry out, I would've if I could have: Ev! No!
Make like you ain't home. But even if I could've warned him,
it was too late. Ev opened the door just wide enough to hiss,
"Git lost, I don't want no drink, don't want nothin from you." I
wondered if it was the preacher's words speaking to Ev's heart,
or the doctor's.

But young Buzzy wasn't taking no for an answer. Maybe

his mind was as feeble as his hearing, though his body sure wasn't feeble. As Ev tried to shut the door on him, Buzzy heaved it to with all the weight of his shoulder and sent Ev skittering backwards. Before you could say "uncle," Buzzy was inside, his voice buzzing mad as a hornet. "Don't say no to me, you fuckin old bastard."

The sound of Ev's screams flew straight up through the chimney to where I hovered above, helpless. I heard the crunch of something ploughing into something, the sickening thud of something hitting the floor. I made myself slip down through the stovepipe and look. There was Ev sprawled there, Buzzy standing over him. Ev had fallen so fast he might've clipped his head on the opened oven door—there was more trash heaped inside it, saved for one ginormous blaze? Maybe Ev had opened it hoping to throw a bit more heat? Or maybe it had been closed but got bumped and swung open as Ev fell. To this day, no one can say for sure.

Now Buzzy was crouched over Ev, hollering as he lay there on his back: "Where is it? Where'd you put it, you old fuck? Gimme the fuckin money and you won't get hurt." Then Buzzy wrestled his arm around Ev's neck and hauled him onto his side. He was holding on like as to strangle Ev and punching him in the face. Blood poured out of Ev's nose and mouth so bad he could barely breathe let alone yell for help. His voice was a terrible, tiny bleat: "You're gonna kill me."

On account of his heart, did he mean, or the blood pooling everywhere?

If I'd had a heart, hearing this would have stopped it cold.

"Get my pills. Getmypills." I could barely hear Ev's voice through the ugly welter of blood and Buzzy's flailing around. He was rooting like a mad dog through Ev's stuff like as to trash the place, if trashing trash was possible, searching for something—money?

"That cabinet—there—" Ev's voice gurgled, he was gargling blood. Buzzy was sweating bullets. He got his bloody hands on a pill bottle, popped the top off, and emptied the whole thing into Ev's open, gasping mouth as he laid there. The pills' yellowish green mixed with red spilled over the floor. Land only knows what was going through Ev's poor old mind. Now Buzzy was tossing stuff. He found Ev's pocket watch, that old one of Father's I had given him that hadn't worked in years, and another watch that looked like it, which Ev had got somewhere and also scratched his initials into. Buzzy shoved both watches in his other coat pocket, as he'd thought enough to keep his vodka pocketed. As he did this, I saw his wild eyes roll upwards, taking in the hatch to the attic.

I will never forget the sound of Buzzy's greasy, bloodied boots stumping up my yellow stairs. Their count of one-two-three-four-five-six to the count of Ev's breath jigging in and out around the pills. The blackish-red pool under his head spreading wider.

At the top of the stairs stood that bureau Ev had scrounged somewhere. Any fool could've seen the lonesome five-dollar bill sticking out of the top drawer. Who knows but it wasn't the proceeds from a Fluffy painting? When Buzzy opened the drawer to grab it, what did he find inside there but two old purses stuffed with money. Four hundred dollars. Buzzy stuffed the pockets of his dungarees with all that cash.

It's a good thing Ev had stuck the jar with my ring under the floor or Buzzy would have grabbed that too. By now the fire was well and truly dead and Buzzy could almost see his breath, skidding downstairs, stepping over Ev and fleeing as if Ev might up and stop him, Ev laying there like that. Didn't even have the courtesy to shut the door but left it flapping behind him. The storm door was still propped open with the broom.

His face bashed in, Ev could have been dead for all Buzzy cared. Somehow he was still breathing. The only trace of warmth was from the dark puddle spreading under his head. In no time a-tall, the puddle started to cool and thicken.

Outside, Buzzy took off like a scared raccoon. I suppose he'd got what he had been looking for? His boots left a pinkish trail on the snow by the roadside. He stopped long enough to pull the bottle from his jacket and take a soothing swig from it. Like I said, I am not too clear on Buzzy's name. Maybe a person who would do what he did has no name, just a pair of hands that happened to have blood on them. He's the one who has to live with what he did, as I guess his people have to, too. I tried and tried to think of the people he came from, especially his mother.

I'll bet five dollars Carmelita Twohig would have known something about them. If I had been the praying type, I'd have called on the sweet by-and-by itself, on all of its peaceful, airy nothingness, to send Carmelita tooling along in her car just then and have her stop. Carmelita would have noticed the door hanging open. She would have known what to do. Even if she'd had other plans, she would have gone for help, she'd have called the police and the ambulance and maybe, just maybe, the hospital could have saved Ev. I imagined Darlene washing away the blood, dressing Ev in a clean white garment, Ev lying in a spotless, snow-bright bed for the first time in his entire life. The police might have tracked down Buzzy, caught him right away with those watches on him, and the money. Ev's blood on it.

Being hand-less myself, as I've said, there was nothing I could do.

Close to town, I glimpsed Bradley Colpitts's cruiser climb

the hill below the police station. He pulled into the lot outside it and parked the car for the night. He was getting off early since he'd worked through Christmas, double time and a half. He went inside to wish his buddies a happy new year, since he would be taking the next two days off. They asked how he and the wife would ring in the new year and clapped him on the back, horsing around. Bang some pots and pans and be in bed by midnight? Wink, wink.

As Buzzy stumbled alongside the roadside, then into the woods, I thought the trees might be the only friends he had, never mind the ones in the trailer. I thought of Emery Allen being from that harbour named after Woods. I loved the woods myself but wondered all at once if I had stayed a town gal, would I have been spared the life I lived? Spared the backwoods evil I had just witnessed, a hungry kind of hopelessness having at it.

By and by, I watched Buzzy slip from the woods and stick out his thumb, and after a while a car came along and stopped for him. I watched him get in, and the car moving along the highway till it passed the road to Bear River and stopped, and I watched Buzzy get out and head up the dirt road towards home. Pretty soon his house came in view, the motley coloured rags from Frenchys poking here and there from the snow butted up against the foundation. I hoped this bit of insulation made the place cozier than it would've been otherwise. Buzzy's mama and her man were inside, passed out. Maybe they'd been quarrelling, how her man would have to move out if she hoped to keep getting her cheques.

As Buzzy fell into bed I thought how he and his mama weren't so different from Ev and his ma, maybe. Neither had much of a leg up living under the laws of the land or learning what a lot of folks call proper behaviour. Oh, it was horrible what Buzzy had done to Ev. But I realized, just like Ev's Ev-ness wasn't his fault, maybe Buzzy's buzziness wasn't really his fault either. The fault, I figured, was being dirt poor, the products of dirt-poorness being more than qualified to eat themselves alive.

"See no evil, hear no evil, speak no evil," Aunt used to say. Now I see why her lofty way of thinking was a wall built as protection from the low life creeping over the ground below it. I had overheard Carmelita Twohig telling people Ev got uglier and meaner once I was no longer in the picture. Before this terrible thing happened to Ev, I wager a lot of folks, some folks anyway, felt he had it coming to him. There's that weary old saying, What goes around comes around. Maybe it's true.

But a memory stirs in me, a pleasant one from when we were first married, of Ev training sweet peas to grow up a length of fishing net he'd strung behind the house, flotsam he'd drug from the shore. "Plenty of use left in that." He had sounded so pleased with himself, and no wonder. It was like everything cast off by somebody else was cast there specially for us. He had picked me a little bouquet when the first of the sweet peas bloomed, flowers so pretty it almost hurt to look at them—pale pink, purple, white, and a deep, deep rose. I'd have done anything to paint those flowers exactly as they were, but paints in such colours could not be had for love or money. I'll bet they still can't be.

But something about how tender, paper-thin, and fragile those blooms were made my heart sing for Ev, even as it made my heart cry for him, too.

Begging Buzzy for his life, he had sounded like the kid Buzzy must have been once also, raw-boned, scared, and delicate in a sad, doomed way. Doomed by a world that don't give two shits whether a kid prospers or not, or lets badness take root. Still, it grieved me how he left Ev laying there like that. Even when I remembered back to Ev raising his hand to me that once, and making me work so hard on orders, and scrimping on food sometimes, and other, little things he said and did which I have chosen to forget.

What I said about "seeing is as seeing does"? It means there are places this windy soul of mine will never go. The difference between what ailed Ev and what ailed me was that his trouble was buried too deep under his skin to be seen. The way a person is in life carries over to how they are remembered in death. What separated me from Ev was his hunger, the hunger that coils up inside a person and leaves them always wanting. I had learned a long time ago not to hunger for anything.

If I could have laid beside Ev on the floor, I would have. Held his hand and comforted him, poor Ev, laying there in the cold as his heart slowly, slowly gave out. I'd have banked the fire all through the next morning and afternoon and through the next night. I'd have drawn water from the well, helped him sit up, and tried to get him to drink and swallow one of those big pills, though his jaw was busted and his poor nose broken in three places. I'd have sung him to sleep, all the songs we used to hear on the radio, about precious moments, whispering hopes, and happy harvests, land rest Ev's ragged, hungry soul.

So I hung around for his sake, hovering close but not too close. Like his guardian angel, a Cat'lick from down the French shore might say. I hovered there pretty much steadily through the next day, New Year's Eve Sunday, and through that night and into the very dawn of the new year, nineteen hundred and seventy-nine, when Ev finally quit breathing. It was a mercy when he took his last breath. Yet, even after he was gone, part of me lingered until the afternoon of New Year's Day, when a boy passing by noticed the door banging open, and peeked in and saw the body.

It was a gruesome enough sight for a grown-up to behold, let alone a child.

But do you know what Buzzy did that Sunday, the day before Ev's body was found, while Ev had lain slowly, slowly dying? Well, I glimpsed him going up the road with his wallet full of Ev's money, then taking it out to buy a skidoo off a man who had it for sale in his yard. A New Year's present to himself, I guess—Happy New Year, Buzzy. A skidoo was something that sure would have made Ev's life easier by times. Better than biking through the snow, I'd imagine. Yet he never would have spent that kind of money on himself, especially not on a luxury. Maybe Buzzy was fixing on turning over a new leaf, figuring out a way of getting around besides hitchhiking.

Once Ev quit breathing, my loftiest self watched for his arrival up here. Best be on the lookout, I thought, you don't want to be caught off guard. He was bound to turn up any time. I was set to greet him singing Hank's song "I've Been Everywhere," which helps a newcomer see some benefits to being here.

If I knew you were coming I'd've baked a cake.

As soon as the boy found the body, he went running for help. Someone called a doctor named Black in Digby and he came out with the ambulance. The rest, I guess, worked like a party line. A head nurse at the hospital called the police and got them to come out to Marshalltown. Two officers arrived to inspect the murder scene, one of them the officer who knew Buzzy from giving him rides here and there. They got a police photographer to come all the way from Yarmouth to take pictures of Ev and the house. Isn't that something, not just once but twice having a man come all that way to take your picture. Ev was lying there a foot and a half from the range, those pills still in his mouth. The empty pill bottle was on the floor. Someone, I don't know who, thought to close the oven door before the man came with the camera—good thing, I didn't want him or anyone banging their shins on it, especially if Carmelita Twohig were to happen by and find someone sporting a major shiner.

You see? I'd have wanted to tell her, that's exactly how I got that big black bruise that time, and you thought it was Ev did it to me. You and Bradley Colpitts both.

It wasn't till suppertime, after the photographer finished taking all his pictures, that they finally put Ev in the ambulance and took him to the county morgue at the hospital. I wish Darlene had been at work; knowing she was there might have made it easier. But she and Bradley and the kids were at her mama's having New Year's dinner: ham and scalloped potatoes and pie. Her mama, formerly a Twohig, was Carmelita's sister, you see. Surprise surprise, there was Carmelita sitting at the head of the table holding court.

The police called in another doctor, one from up the Valley, to open Ev up to see just how he died.

This is my husband, I thought. I could not listen to the sound of a knife slitting skin.

I could not look when the doctor held something in his hands, then weighed it.

A heart. *This was my husband.* Heart failure was the *cause* of death, I heard the doctor say. Coronary something something something.

How much do you think the pain in someone's heart weighs? There is no way of measuring any of it.

This is when the air swam around me, its sorrows and its joys pooled together in a feeling that was cold and hot, that was hate as much as it was love. Each smoothed out the other so the nothingness was a stew simmered so long you could not tell one ingredient from another, potatoes from carrots, meat from gravy, only draw in its soft, tasteless flavour. It was a flavourless savouring of all who had lived and died and were never to show our faces again on this *or* your side of the veil but would be here waiting, and maybe even all those who had yet to come into your world as well. I saw at last that glory has no need of faces to kiss or arms to hold the weary or for the weary to be held by, or of feet to carry the weary to or from those arms, or any need of fleshly anticipation at all.

Yet I felt myself surrounded. My loved ones were themselves and not themselves, bearing no traces of the selves we had lost. None of us was as we had been, there would be no reunion in this or any by-and-by. Yet here we were. Even Ev was here, where there was all the air and sound and light a person could ever need.

As for Ev's heart, perhaps it had failed from the get-go, broken in ways no one could fathom, least of all him. As for Buzzy, I wonder if the almshouse next door hadn't shut he might have found a home there, what with his problems. How he had trouble telling right from wrong and saw things that weren't really there. Hallucinations, his head doctor called Buzzy's problem in court. But I am ahead of myself.

On New Year's Day I happened to see Buzzy give those two pocket watches of Ev's to his mama's man to bury behind her house. It struck me as a lot of trouble to go to for one timepiece that barely worked and another whose hands were still froze on the moment they'd been froze on when I'd pulled it from the lawyer's envelope in Yarmouth, my inheritance from Father. Neither watch was much good to Ev now. So it was no great mischief that for a few months the watches stayed buried, until Buzzy's wristwatch gave out and he needed something to tell him when he was supposed to be where. So his mama's boyfriend dug up both of Ev's watches and gave the one that sort of worked to Buzzy.

I figure this was the start of Buzzy's undoing, the beginning of the end for him. His mama's man took the other watch in to the police. I hope if Ev was watching, he gained some satisfaction when they saw his initials scratched on the back. For that matter, I hope Father gained some too.

I don't know where Constable Colpitts was the day the boyfriend brought the watch into the station and set the big black ball that would take out Buzzy rolling against him. The good constable might have been in Florida taking Darlene and the kids to some flashy theme park. I caught wind of a transfer being in the works; they were sending Colpitts to Yarmouth to work with the police there. I don't imagine Darlene was thrilled about uprooting the family, leaving her job and moving away from her mother and, well, her aunt.

I never felt the same about Bradley Colpitts after his last visit, and my feelings for him cooled further when Ev got attacked, though it wasn't Colpitts's fault the attack happened. Not his fault he was home having a beer and a snuggle with Darlene that Saturday night, a bit more than a snuggle. Quite a bit more, since I saw later on that she was expecting. Who knew Bradley had it in him to be such a family man? He's a good dad, I have to give him that. I just hope he watches his P's and Q's. Being a cop has its dangers and I would hate to see Darlene left to raise three kids by her lonesome. I would hate to run into her hubby up here, by that I mean feel his presence mixed up with the rest of us in all our boundless, shapeless form. Except for folks who wreck their own chances for peace and create one of their own making, I have decided there is no hell. There is more than enough badness down where you are to qualify as punishment, even for the worst of youse.

Show me someone with no stain upon them and I will show you the Bay of Fundy drained flat and entirely emptied of water. I figure you have to forgive people. What I mean is, never forget what they have done but bear no grudge. As he wolfed down his doughnut while Ev was being beaten, maybe Bradley was thinking about Darlene, wondering if she was happy. Maybe she had a late shift and he needed to be home to put the kids to bed. Maybe he just wanted to sleep. I hope he rested easy. I hope he and Darlene and even Carmelita Twohig rest easy.

Buzzy, though, has to get up each day knowing what he did.

One fine April morning, the cop who knew Buzzy from hitch-hiking took another cop out to the gas station in Deep Brook where Buzzy was known to hang around. He might have even worked there sometimes filling tires with air or pumping gas, I wouldn't know. The cops went in and invited Buzzy to go for a ride. They brought him into Digby for questioning. When Buzzy said he didn't know a single thing about how Everett Lewis died, they locked him up in the little jail for the night. The next day they got Buzzy's mama and his sister, a friend of the rappie-pie fella, to come in and talk to him. "You'd feel better with all this off your chest," they said. He seemed upset, maybe realizing those watches should've stayed where they belonged, not in the ground, I mean, but in Ev's house.

A few months after this, one fine Thursday in July—a full nine years almost to the day after I left your world—Buzzy appeared in court. It was just a preliminary inquiry, they told him, which meant they just wanted to hear what some people had to say. He wore a colourful shirt that his mama might've bought for him at Frenchys—like I said, I had seen her going in there the odd day. I would like to say his shirt was all the colours of the rainbow but it wasn't, not by any stretch. I had trouble looking at him, which is why to this day I wouldn't be able to tell him from Adam, as Aunt would say.

"You are charged with the second-degree murder of Everett Lewis in contravention of section two-eighteen-point-one of the criminal code," the judge said.

Buzzy might have cried but I can't say for certain. He let out a choked sound after the judge heard his statement read out and found him guilty. At least he didn't have to go through a trial, people said. They sent him some place up in the Valley, I believe it was, maybe to some county home, to serve out his sentence. Five years, I think he got, for summoning the Reaper to Ev's door sooner than the Reaper might've come without help. Ev was eighty-five or eighty-six, depending on what he told you. Buzzy was just nineteen, wouldn't turn twenty till that fall. I don't suppose they have birthday cakes in jail. Even back then, twenty was still a kid. The judge must've thought so, choosing not to send Buzzy to Dorchester or someplace really rough like that.

Now Buzzy has done his time, like we all do our time, I suppose, one way or the other. He is down there somewhere living his life, only he has to live with that picture in his head of Ev lying there, up until his own death, and for long after.

17.

I'M
MOVIN'
ON

I have pretty much laid to rest Aunt's sayings, even the one about seeing through "a glass darkly, then face to face." Face to face with whom? I always wondered. But the thought kept me going, that eventually I might roll in Emery Allen's arms again. Sing along once more to Mama's piano playing, laugh at Father's jokes, watch Mary Pickford with my brother—heck, eat dinner with Aunt after church. I hoped we'd all be together, hugging and eating pie. One big blueberry pie with more than enough pieces to go around three and four times, forget twice. I hoped things would look like they did in my pictures, that every wall in heaven would be filled with paintings as plentiful as stars. My paintings becoming what I came to see as my "children" seemed no big stretch of the imagination, seeing how they slithered from my brush, birthed by one fist bracing the other.

If on *this* side of the veil more than the wind's voices lingered. If the earthly side of it wasn't all practice at losing what you loved to defilement and hurry-up-and-waiting.

Now the crows' cawing on the ridge rattles me, would rattle my bones to dust if they weren't dust already. Even silenced, Ev's voice goads me at times, almost as bad as when we lived cheek by jowl, though I have more or less forgiven him. Imagine the two of us cooped up in that house! It could have been worse. Your world passes, this world goes on. Somewhere Mama, Father, Aunt, and those friends of mine, Mae and Olive and Secretary, whisper to me. Oh yes, their voices are in the trees, in the crackle of dry leaves under strangers' feet. Maybe my own voice is an airplane zipping across the sky, though I wasn't much for travel, content to stay *right here.*

But I'm restless now; maybe it's time to pull a Hank Snow, then shut up for good. Before I do, I'll give this a try, knowing even as I do, it's doomed to fail.

"Aunt Ida?" My voice wisps over the wooded hills. "Can you hear me? I still owe you money. Maybe I should've heeded your advice and not gone back to Marshalltown that day or ever. Hid myself away instead, reading the Bible like you. 'The Lord helps those who help themselves,' you said. That's just what I did, I helped myself."

Aunt doesn't answer, of course. There's only the slosh of waves against the shore, tossing up bits of rope and fishing gear and a shoe, always one lonesome shoe, as though in every cove, every bay, off every coast, some poor one-legged jack has gone overboard.

"You've got two hands, two feet, and a head on your shoulders. There is no reason to take up with that terrible fool," Aunt had said. In some ways she was right. But it's a little late to say so, isn't it.

I hope wherever he is now, Ev wasn't watching the day a crew came to Marshalltown with a fleet of trucks, including one hauling a flatbed. They unloaded hammers, saws, and pry bars. Why, after Ev left your world the house had fallen to such wrack and ruin I hate to tell you the state of it after the squirrels and raccoons moved in. The roof rotted, it rained inside, half the ceiling fell in, and the range rusted out. Eventually the critters abandoned the place. Only Matilda's grandkids could tell you what became of the warming oven decorated with my ruby red poppies—some human critter had made off with it? The wallpaper I had so long ago painted over with flowers and deer and whatnot hung in rags. All the scroungings, scrimpings-and-savings of our lifetimes lay in heaps laced with scat—every cookie tin, knick-knack, postcard, and note.

The only recognizable thing was my staircase, my stairway to the stars, a stairway to nowhere. I'm still surprised that after I left Ev didn't cut it up and sell each blue-flowered riser for whatever it would fetch. If he had done, Buzzy might not have made it to the attic and gotten his hands on Ev's four hundred dollars. Though I never saw this myself, I heard it said that after I passed, if a stranger came looking for a piece of my art painted on the wall, why, Ev would cut it right out of the wallpaper and sell it to them.

I reckoned this pack of strangers with their trucks meant no real harm as they set to clearing out the mess of rusty old junk, the rubble of our lives. They set about taking apart my stairs, working real gentle, riser by riser. They numbered and wrapped up each piece in some sort of cloth, like it was bone china, and loaded them all into one of the trucks. Fools, I thought. What good was a staircase in pieces with nowhere to climb to? I figured they'd sell each piece to the highest bidder. What remained of the range was so rusted out they didn't need to worry about it.

But, seeing what happened next, if I'd had a heart it would've felt like a knife was being plunged into it. They started sawing into the house like it was an empty cereal box. They cut off what was left of the roof, opened the attic to the sky, cut off each gable. Before my very eyes, they sliced the place up into ten big slabs. Mouldering gables, slabs of mouldering wall, both halves of mouldering roof. They took too much care with each slab to be hauling them off to the dump, I thought. Taking great pains, they loaded them onto the flatbed truck. By now the place was practically torn down to nothing. There was just the floor, the linoleum worn to black smudges on the punky boards—land only knows what had become of the mat, maybe moths had eaten it up. A man took a noisy round saw to the floor and cut it up, too, loaded what boards weren't too far gone on top of all those big pieces.

Taking a rest, they milled about admiring their handiwork. I guess they were too tired to notice what was lying in the sour old dirt the house had stood on top of. I guess they were in too big a rush to pack up their tools and tie down everything on the truck, to see some broken glass, a few nickels and dimes laying there waiting to be picked up, and something else, something gold. Pure gold, only a little the worse for wear, it looked like to me, after sitting under the house for going on five years, ever since that night Ev was visited by the preacher, then robbed by Buzzy and left for dead. I guess it was a lucky thing Buzzy hadn't stopped to look under the mat. Otherwise he'd have lifted that board, reached down, and felt the jar below, and I'm guessing he'd have taken it along with the four hundred dollars and those watches. Why would Buzzy have hesitated? He could have given the ring to his mama, or he could have pawned it—then who knows where it would have ended up?

It was a funny thing that Ev had kept the ring—who knows, maybe he'd forgotten about it till he went to see the doctor. Maybe he only remembered it being buried out back in the jar when his heart trouble and the cost of pills weighed heavy on him. Maybe he had wondered then how much it would fetch. Maybe having it close by gave him comfort.

It was a funnier thing that those folks so bent on cutting up and carting away the house as though its pieces were precious jewels never thought to look for anything small, shiny, and truly valuable. As the truck lurched off—where they were taking their treasures was anyone's guess—I had to laugh, even though it was sad. I couldn't help imagining some oversized child making believe the house was a puzzle, sitting on the floor with his tongue between his teeth as he tried to put it together.

Curious, I followed the flatbed's progress for a ways, watched it lumber over hill and dale, past Digby and the dump, and head past Deep Brook. There I let it disappear from view and took myself on a little side trip down the road towards Guinea. I recognized the trailer by the flowery wreath on the door. It was the kind of wreath a person who liked Phentex slippers and skirts for toilet paper dolls might favour. And sure enough, I spied her behind the picture window. The window had fancy-looking drapes and sheers hung for privacy. But I could see into the living room. Carmelita was sitting on a puffy blue chesterfield with a little girl beside her. She was showing the girl how to knit. The child had Carmelita's eyes and mouth, but, fortunately, not Carmelita's thinning bluish hair—thinning, I supposed, on account of all the teasing she had done to it over the years. The little girl was having trouble casting on stitches. When Carmelita bent to help her she kissed the child's hair, took the tangle of yarn and needles from her small hands and set them down. The child wriggled closer, buried her face in Carmelita's shallow bosom. Then she pointed to something on the wall and smiled. That child had a smile on her that would stop a clock, truly.

They had the TV on, a wrestling show or something with loud cheering, but listening closer, I could hear them talking.

"You like Nana's picture?" Carmelita was grinning from ear to ear. "Some sweet, isn't it? Some day it'll be yours, dear. Let me tell you about the lady who did it. A lot of stuff about her pictures didn't make sense. She was a corker, that one. A character. But you know, all these years and that picture still makes Nana smile. Every time I look at it, I smile inside. Though that lady's life, oh my, I wouldn't wish it on anyone. Now when's your mama supposed to come and pick you up? Guess we should pack up your knitting; we'll work on it next time." Then Carmelita hugged and pulled the child onto her lap, though the child might've been a bit big for this, and started singing "You Are My Sunshine," some old song like that.

Seeing this made me happy. Maybe I should have been happy, too, seeing the cut-up house get hauled away. The way some folks would be happy eleven years later seeing the almshouse burn. Little did I know that once Ev's house got to where it was going, my story would be chained to it, my life and my work like one big keepsake for strangers from all over to buy pieces of, wanting reminders of me. Some look at that house the way you look at a cage. Well, if it was a cage, I tried to make it like one you would put a beautiful pet bird in. An indigo bunting. Or a bird like Matilda, which would have been all right so long as the door stayed open.

This brings me to the part of my tale I expect you've been dreading. That day in the North Range cemetery with Carmelita Twohig and my other mourners gathered in song was the last time I saw Matilda alive. Oh yes, that was her cawing from a treetop all right, I'm sure now that it was, as the rainbow arced over the bay. Now don't be silly, that rainbow was just a happy coincidence, a sign of gladness, not a bridge or stepping stone to anywhere. Why would you need anything but forgiveness in your heart to get from there to here? Though folks are entitled to feel in their hearts whatever brings comfort, I do hope the daughter I turned away somehow found it in hers to forgive me.

I never heard Matilda's caw again after that day. I have heard it said crows can live as long as *forty* years—only five years fewer than Ev had to his age when we married. Matilda was getting up in years. I believe she was twenty-two or twenty-three years old when I left her world. I was ageless when she left mine.

Not too long after the funeral, I saw a big black bird laying by the roadside as you head toward town. It must have got hit playing chicken with a transport truck, its poor body was flattened to the pavement. Then I spotted Willard and them watching stock-still from the trees. They were standing guard over the body, hardly making a peep besides that somber nattering sound crows make when they're rattled but wary of bringing further doom upon themselves.

I knew then that the dead bird was Matilda. I guessed she never had a chance, stalking a piece of tinfoil tossed from a cigarette pack that had blown to the centre line. A shiny-feathered youngster, a teenage version of Matilda, hopped up to the carcass and chattered a string of mournful notes. "It'll be okay, don't worry, little buddy," I lied, whispering down to her. Matilda's daughter, she had to be. A bird after her mama's heart, a bird to make her mama proud, I mean. She flew off in search of safer shiny things to pad the family nest. Before this young one knew it, she would be brooding over her own clutch of eggs, bringing Matilda's grandkids into the world, your world. A consolation, it cheered me up some from the sorrow of Matilda's fate.

All things must pass. No one knows better than I do that it's true.

Now, picture my ring laying there by its lonesome on the barren ground fourteen years later, without the house to shelter it from wind, rain, sleet, snow, and thieving men. On the day they took the house away, *I* was a bird, a bluebird resting atop the telephone wire like Matilda used to, watching the crew's slicing, dicing, and loading unfold. After the truck disappeared from sight past Deep Brook, after I finished spying on Carmelita and her granddaughter, a cawing caught my ear. Rising above the wind's whistling, it spoke of an incoming storm. So I let the wind blow me straight back to Marshalltown.

The treetops swayed, the wires did too. But birds have an uncanny grip; it takes a lot to knock a bird off its perch. I stayed put, looking down on the bruised ground where the house should've been. As the wind howled, a crow swooped down out of nowhere and joined me. She was a beautiful young thing, as glossy and clever and quick as my old friend. I guessed by her call and the way she looked up and seemed able to see me that she must be kin. A few generations removed from Matilda, but kin all the same—Matilda's granddaughter? If that spinster woman Carmelita Twohig could have a granddaughter, why couldn't Matilda? Before I could do the arithmetic, this black beauty swooped down to where the house had stood and plucked something up in her beak. Something gold and shiny, exactly what a crow would covet. The object's glint caught my eye as she flew upwards with it. I wondered if Everett's old mother might have something to do with this. I dare say I near felt the old woman's presence above the crow and me both, looking down. A warm little gust blew as the crow alighted before taking off again. As her flight stirred the pine needles I spied what she'd dropped in the nest. It was my ring. It wasn't the only shiny thing up there—Matilda's grandchild had quite a collection. A key ring, a little length of silver chain, some mismatched earrings, a cat's collar with a bell. I reckoned that, on the ever-fading and most unlikely chance I ever did meet Ev's mother face to face, at least I would be able to tell her Ev had safeguarded what was hers, as best he could, from what my aunt would call the threat of rust, moths, and thieves.

And just so, in a similar spirit, they had cut up and carted off the house in order to safeguard what remained after rust, moths, and four-legged thieves had their way with it. I hear it sits in the capital city of Halifax, inside a big stone building full of other people's paintings, real artists' paintings, some might say. Imagine that, a house inside a house, our little home inside a big, fancy home for art, real art. I don't imagine there are too many fancy art galleries with a murder scene on display. Why, in my mind's eye I still see that dark pool under Ev's head.

For there are aches and pains that don't go away, the hurt of things that happen that no one—no matter how hardhearted, stupid, or absent they are—should ever have to bear.

Which brings me to that baby of mine. Swayed by those old songs of the sweet by-and-by and heavenly shores, I used to dream I would see him again, too, at least feel his presence somehow. Like a pulse of air between a butterfly's wingbeats—something, anything. A person believes what she wants to believe, life is just easier that way. But in the dark of night, under the moon, the truth comes out and shines. I think of that gal, Catherine Dowley, getting out of the car that day, coming in to see me while Ev was chopping wood. The woman who marched in out of the blue and called me her ma, then wrote me a letter. She was the girl who was with that lady, Mrs. Crosby, in Stirrett's store the day I bought the Sunday joint meant to last Mama and me all week.

And here's the sad thing, if you believe all things are possible, that things rise from their ashes. Even if you look at all things with an opened heart and an opened mind, and no longer try to dodge how things really are, it's like Aunt said: *"You still have to pull the plank out of your own eye before you can stoop to pluck the dirt from your neighbour's."*

While I lived, I had a plank the width of a door hampering my sight. But now that plank has been removed, I see the letter come together again, the letter that Catherine wrote me, after saying she was mine. The letter I burned in the stove the day it came. Before me now, pieces of it rise from stove ash and glue themselves back together into sheets of creamy notepaper. The fire's smoke pulls itself down the chimney, through the stovepipe, and out on to the pages. Its grey ink forms sentences in her handwriting, words as bold and brave as can be. I read them spread before me, before they float off into this otherworld to be read, past, present, and future, by the stars however the stars want.

And I had been so sure that seeing my baby boy, no longer through any old glass darkly but face to face, would set crooked things straight. Even drifting away on wings of air, Catherine's words make a lie of him. Just as they did from the day the letter landed in our mailbox and Ev dropped it into my hands and onwards. Even saved from the firebox, its ashes burn forever. The truth of her words scalds me, now that I believe them, can let myself believe them.

For the letter said it was Father, harness maker and father of the timeless timepiece, who arranged everything. Who set it up with the people who took my healthy little baby—a good family, an upright family who took in other unwanted children—and raised her as their own.

My baby girl. Why would she lie? This isn't to say people *don't* lie, that some don't like lies more than they like the truth— I for one can vouch for this. Yet, what was the use of her coming around all those years after? The sin for which Ev had struck me come to haunt us both in the flesh. She wouldn't have wanted to know me as I was or live as I did. Her presence would have poisoned Ev against me for the rest of our days. It would have poisoned me against him, if I had welcomed her into our house.

Into my heart. Ev would've beaten my spirit black and blue, called me names I could never repeat. If I were very lucky, he'd have tried to make up for it by pouring cups of cold tea.

Oh yes, my eyes have opened mightily. Now I *see*. The shadow over my life was not the mistake of putting up with Ev or denying someone her birthright, but failing to see how our fate, hers and mine, and in a way, Ev's, was Father's doing. The daughter of my mistake who should have been the daughter of my heart was the daughter of the fib he told to protect Mama and me—from what, gossip?

Strip away a fib and what you are left with is motherless sorrow, the need for more love than you could ever give or receive. Some get the world they guess up in their dreams and some don't. You make do. It helps to fall in love with the sun as it sinks, the blossom as it falls, the rustle of feathers even as one bird raids another's nest. To stay in love and make do, oh yes, it helps to make fibbing—call it what you want—an art. For the boundless nothing that is behind, before, below, and beside me covers all things. I figure you had best call it love.

EPILOGUE

How *does it end, again? My life? My story? Maybe it never does.* There's that little metal shack that stands on our piece of heaven in Marshalltown; it's the very size of our house and on the very spot where it stood. Is the red behind its steely slats meant to conjure Ev's bingeing temperament, his murder, or my perseverance? The place looks to me like a joyless grey cage. I guess some folks like to remember me that way: caged. Caged inside my marriage to Ev, caged inside a body they saw and some still see as unfit.

What these folks don't see is that these cages made me the bird I was and the bird I am, made me sing in the way I did, the way that brought me happiness and joy and a starry life I wouldn't have known otherwise.

Up on the ridge beside our grave, someone has planted a bush that blooms each spring with big mauve flowers. Our grave, I say: mine and Ev's and his parents'. The bush is fancier than the bushes Mama grew in her garden: snowball bushes, mock orange, spirea, honeysuckle, lilacs. Someone has left a little silver angel bearing the word *Peace* atop our headstone, along with three dried red berries for the birds that might visit. I would like to think maybe it was Carmelita Twohig who left those berries—but no, there's a stone with her name on it just a few rows over. It says she's been here a couple of years now. But never mind Carmelita.

Someone has planted a tulip beside our stone, mine and Ev's and his parents', a white imitation tulip that will last a long, long time. I reckon it's a nice thing to have in winter, to remind us all that even on the dirtiest old days something blooms. That's right, even when fog pushes itself from the bay and over the land and paints everything the same old grey, something down there where you are will keep right on flowering.

AUTHOR'S NOTE

Since Maud Lewis's death in 1970, her story has become so mythologized it's just about impossible to separate hearsay from reality, original information from an ever-deepening well of common knowledge. While certain commercial interests sugar-coat Maud's life, few can gloss the misery she must have suffered living with advanced rheumatoid arthritis under conditions of dreadful poverty. Yet her paintings show a huge creative spirit, joie de vivre, and an astonishing ability to defy adversity.

These remarkable qualities of hers were first made public by photographer Bob Brooks and arts journalist Murray Barnard in their 1965 *Star Weekly* article. Besides her paintings themselves, Brooks's photos of Maud and her husband, Everett, in their tiny home, its every surface adorned with her joyful artwork, are our most vivid record of her. Here's a woman who looks shy and canny, is physically disabled and perhaps bemused but unfazed by the photographer's attention—as happy and content as she claimed to be in interviews and as contemporaries remembered her, and at ease with Everett despite his well-known faults.

Maud appears no less happy in the CBC's 1965 *Telescope* documentary, *The Once-Upon-A-Time-World of Maud Lewis,* in which Everett shares views that probably weren't so unusual at the time but would rightly see him condemned today. As her friend Olive Hayden, the warden's wife at the Marshalltown Almshouse, insisted, "[Maud] was happy. She had what she wanted. They said [Everett] was mean, but.... He might've been mean, but...he wasn't to her. No, I think he really loved her, and she did him" [Elder Transcripts]. And just as Everett's attitudes weren't that uncommon, as others have noted, neither was the poverty that was the couple's "normal" all that rare in rural Nova Scotia in the 1940s, '50s, and early '60s. Simply put, Maud and Everett were products of their time.

Precious few people who knew the couple are still alive or able to share their recollections of either individual. Through a stroke of luck, I was put in contact with ninety-seven-year-old Kay Hooper, one of Maud's friends and a regular visitor to the Lewis home. Hooper attests to the misery Maud was subjected to amidst Everett's drinking and controlling, miserly ways. "It was not a happy place," she told me, calling Maud's living conditions "shocking," "sparse," and "horrible," and suggesting that "Maud was not used to anything better." During her visits, Hooper recalls Maud as "very shy" though "she enjoyed company." Owing to the deformity of her chin, "she had a hard time looking up at you...and was always trying to hide her hands. [In conversations] you had to ask questions to *her*.... She would tuck in her hands and talk...about the weather.... She never painted in front of you." With great fondness, Hooper remembers admiring a beautiful milk pitcher Maud kept money in, Maud dumping out the "two or four dollars" that were in it, giving it to Hooper, and insisting that she take it. As for Everett, Hooper says, "I didn't think much of him, didn't take to him. He would sit quiet in the room, just waiting for the money."

She also recalls Maud standing by the road, thumbing a ride to Yarmouth to escape him. If Maud wasn't abused physically by her husband, without doubt he exploited her financially while depriving her of amenities many of us (though certainly not all) take for granted.

But who can say what Maud really thought of her experience? So much is lost to the vagaries of recycled second- and third-hand memories, and even of public records. To this day, for example, Maud's exact age remains unclear, with various sources listing her birth year as 1901, 1902, and 1903. My decision to abide by the birthdate recorded in her grandmother Isabella Dowley's family Bible—March 7th, 1902—on display at the Yarmouth County Museum, reflects my choice to negotiate a middle ground in writing this version of Maud's story. As with many things in life, I suspect the reality of her experience lies in between abject darkness and cheery sunshine, in the grey areas of shifting light. Not to sugar-coat any aspect of Maud's life, but in dramatizing parts of this shadowy ground, I ask you to remember that, as Margaret Atwood says, all fiction is speculative.

—Carol Bruneau, July 2, 2020

ACKNOWLEDGEMENTS

Many people assisted my work throughout this project. Huge thanks to my publishers, Terrilee Bulger and Heather Bryan, to Jenn Embree for the beautiful cover design, to Kate Watson, Karen McMullin, proofreader Penelope Jackson, and the rest of the Nimbus team for all their support, and most especially to my editor, the visionary Whitney Moran, who planted the seed for a Maud novel, bore with me when I balked, and whose ingenius insights and brilliant guidance have helped make this story so much more than the sum of its parts. You are one powerhouse crew!

In my efforts to portray the world from the perspective of a disabled person, I owe more than I can say to disability activist and author Jen Powley, to whom the novel is dedicated. I'm intensely grateful to her for reading and commenting on an earlier draft, sharing her time and insights so generously and with her typical "brutal" honesty and humour. Jen's guidance has been crucial in shaping my main character's viewpoint.

I'm equally indebted to Kay Hooper for sharing her memories of Maud and Everett, and to those who shared their first-hand research, original interview material, knowledge and insights into the couple's lives, and to the archivists, curators, conservators, and artists whose work ensures that Maud's art lives on. I am extremely grateful to Beth Brooks, daughter of the late Bob Brooks, whose photographs first brought Maud to the public eye, and to Sandra Phinney for their generosity. Without Beth's insights and her kind willingness to share her time and her research for the 1998 NFB documentary *The Illuminated Life of Maud Lewis,* directed and produced by Peter d'Entremont, my project would never have gotten off the ground. The information she shared in conversation originated from her interviews with numerous first-hand sources. My thanks go to Sandra for so enthusiastically sharing her research and writings on Maud, and helping me, as Beth did, to steer a middle course between fact and speculation. I have relied on their wisdom regarding the birth and adoption of Maud's daughter, Maud's relationship with Everett, and Everett's ways with money, and on people's anecdotes gathered in interviews by Phinney on Ev's drinking and Maud's life in Yarmouth. These, along with stories Beth and others gathered in interviews with people who knew Maud and Everett during their married life—among them Larry MacNeil, the son of Maud's secretary, Kay MacNeil; Ursula Sutherland, wife of Digby Royal Bank Manager Hysom Sutherland; Doctor M. R. MacDonald; and Olive Hayden—helped immeasurably. I'm grateful as well to Lisette Gaudet and the Yarmouth County Museum and Archives for all their assistance in providing their files on Maud and for their exhibits that helped me imagine life in Yarmouth when Maud was growing up. For genealogical information and other details about the Dowley and German/Germain families, and about Emery Gordon Allen, the father of Maud's daughter, Ancestry.ca was a godsend.

Like thousands of people, I've been moved by the late Bob Brooks's photographs of Maud and Everett. As well, I've been inspired by the Maud-related works of visual artists Laura Kenney and Steven Rhude.

For cold hard facts, I'm indebted to Jennifer Stairs, Office of the Nova Scotia Judiciary, for providing the court documents regarding Everett Lewis's murder and the perpetrator's conviction. These were critical in crafting my version of Maud's story. In determining the logistics behind Maud's treatment in 1968 for a broken hip, I'm grateful to Carla Adams, Media Relations, Nova Scotia Health Authority, for providing clarification. I'm deeply grateful for the expertise shared by conservator Laurie Hamilton and curator Ray Cronin in their respective books on Maud's painted house and her body of work and art practice. For information on what is correctly called the Marshalltown Almshouse, I've relied on Brenda Thompson's work *A Wholesome Horror: Poor Houses in Nova Scotia.*

Finally, many others provided the encouragement I needed to create a fictional work based on but not limited to facts and notions about Maud's story. I'm deeply grateful to Shawn Brown, Cindy Handren, Kathleen Hall and Kevin Coady, Steve and Jane Roberts, Joan Bruneau, Tim and Martha Leary, Lorri Neilsen-Glenn, Ramona Lumpkin, Binnie Brennan, Kim Pittaway, Nicola Davison, Lesley Crewe, Marilyn Smulders, Sheree Fitch, and Elissa Barnard, whose father wrote the *Star Weekly* article on Maud and Everett, for their kindness and generous support. I'm eternally grateful to Bruce Erskine and our sons, Andrew, Seamus, and especially Angus, who has fed my interest in Maud since a class trip to the AGNS with Mary Evelyn Ternan. Finally, thanks to Lynne Duxbury Smith and to Richard Kaulback, whose childhood memories of visiting the Lewis home conjure an Everett with a kindly twinkle in his eye and, just maybe, something of an unseemly fondness for young girls. Take both attributes as you will. I did, and acknowledge the liberties I've taken in creating this story of Maud. Any inaccuracies or inconsistencies in "the facts" as presented here are mine and mine alone.

NOTES ON
CHAPTER TITLES

A*ll titles in this book have been borrowed from country and gospel* songs Maud may have heard when her radio was co-operating.

"Abide with Me," hymn by Henry Francis Lyte, 1847, set to music while he was dying of tuberculosis.

"A Good Man is Hard to Find," by Bob Wills and His Texas Playboys, 1946.

"Brighten the Corner Where You Are," lyrics by Ina Duley Ogdon, 1913, music by Charles H. Gabriel, 1913, recorded by Red Foley, 1959.

"Ev'ry Precious Moment," by R. Roy Coats, copyright 1968 by Robbins Music Corporation, New York, NY.

"Hello, Central! Give Me Heaven," by Charles H. Harris, 1901, recorded by the Carter Family, 1934.

"I'm Moving On," by Hank Snow and His Rainbow Ranchers, 1950.

"I Saw The Light," words and music by Hank Williams, 1948.

"I've Been Everywhere," written by G. Mack in 1959, recorded by Hank Snow and His Rainbow Ranchers, 1962.

"I Will Lift Up My Eyes," by Margaret Lindsay, copyright 1967 by Robbins Music Corporation, New York, NY.

"Keep on the Sunny Side," lyrics by Ada Blenkhorn, music by J. Howard Entwisle, 1899. Recorded by the Carter Family, 1928. (According to Wikipedia, Blenkhorn was inspired by a phrase used by her disabled nephew who always wanted his wheelchair pushed down "the sunny side" of the street.)

"Let the Lower Lights Be Burning," by P.P. Bliss, recorded by Johnny Cash, 1962.

"Open Up Your Heart," by Buck Owens, 1966.

"Standing on the Promises," by Russell Kelso Carter, a medical doctor who wrote novels as well as hymns, 1886.

"Where We'll Never Grow Old," by Jas. C. Moore, recorded by Jim Reeves, 1962.

"Whispering Hope," by Alice Hawthorne, recorded by Jo Stafford and Gordon MacRae, 1962.

"Wildwood Flower," first recorded by the Carter Family, 1928.

"Work for The Night is Coming," lyrics by Anna Coghill, 1854, music by Lowell Mason, 1864.

BIBLIOGRAPHY

Ancestry.ca. Emery Gordon Allen, John Nelson Dowley, Agnes Mary German/Germain, Ida Germain. ancestry.ca/familytree/person/tree/152047736/person/182020358377/story Accessed December 17, 2019.

Anonymous. "Catherine Dowley," 5 pages, undated. PDF courtesy of Yarmouth County Museum and Archives, Yarmouth, N.S.

———. "Folk Artist's home to be come [sic] exhibit." Yarmouth: *The Vanguard*, June 20, 1984. Courtesy of Yarmouth County Museum and Archives.

Art Gallery of Nova Scotia, Halifax. *Scotiabank Maud Lewis Gallery.* Permanent collection.

Barnard, Murray, text, and Bob Brooks, photographs. "The Little Old Lady who Paints Pretty Pictures." *The Star Weekly*, July 10, 1965. Photocopy courtesy of Yarmouth County Museum and Archives, Yarmouth, N.S.

Beaudry-Cowling, Diane, director, and Barry Cowling, writer. *Maud Lewis: A World Without Shadows.* National Film Board, 1976.

Bergman, Brian. "Paying Tribute to Maud Lewis." *The Canadian Encyclopedia*. Originally published in *MacLean's* magazine, April 14, 1997. thecanadianencyclopedia.ca/en/article/paying_tribute_to_painter_Maud-Lewis. Accessed November 11, 2019.

Black, Dr. John Black. Medical Examiner's Report, Soldiers' Memorial Hospital, Regional Laboratory, Middleton, Nova Scotia, January 1, 1979.

Brooks, Beth, phone interviews by the author, January 22, 2019 and November 12, 2019.

Cronin, Ray. *Our Maud: The Life, Art and Legacy of Maud Lewis*. Halifax, N.S.: Art Gallery of Nova Scotia, 2017.

Dalton, Laurie, curator. *Maud Lewis: A Life Collected*. Wolfville, N.S.: Acadia University Art Gallery, August 3–September 20, 2018.

Dalton, Laurie, curator. *Whose Maud?* Works by Laura Kenney and Steven Rhude. Wolfville, N.S.: Acadia University Art Gallery, June 12–July 28, 2018.

Discover Halifax. "Top 13 Facts About Local Folk-Artist, Maud Lewis." DiscoverHalifaxns.com. Accessed November 11, 2019.

Fillmore, Sarah, curator. *Maud Lewis as Collected by John Risley*. Yarmouth, N.S.: Art Gallery of Nova Scotia, Western Branch, December 1, 2017–June 10, 2018.

Hamilton, Laurie. *The Painted House of Maud Lewis: Conserving a Folk Art Treasure*. Fredericton, N.B. and Halifax, N.S.: Goose Lane Editions and Art Gallery of Nova Scotia, 2001.

Hayden, Olive, interviewed by Sue Amero, Oct. 23, 2000. *Elder Transcripts*. eldertranscripts.ca/pdf/OliveHayden.pdf. Accessed November 11, 2019.

Hayden, Olive. *Working at the Poor Farm.* Interview, Admiral Digby Museum, filmed 2000, published on YouTube November 30, 2010. youtube.com/watch?v=p7juRJTdxb0. Accessed May 30, 2018.

Hooper, Kay, phone interview by the author, December 18, 2019.

Kenins, Laura. "Think You Know the Story of Maud Lewis? Two Nova Scotian artists want you to reconsider the myth." *CBC Arts,* posted March 1, 2019. www.cbc.ca/arts. Accessed November 11, 2019.

Labuschagne, Simone. "Saving Everett; An Interview with Steven Rhude." February 1, 2019. srhude.blogspot.com. Accessed May 30, 2019.

"Maud Lewis," *Wikipedia.* en.wikipedia.org/wiki/Maud_Lewis. Accessed November 11, 2019.

Morton, Erin. *For Folk's Sake: Art and Economy in Twentieth Century Nova Scotia.* Montreal & Kingston: McGill-Queen's University Press, 2016.

Moulton-Barrett, donalee. "Maud's Heart to Ours." *Halifax Chronicle Herald,* September 1984. Photocopy courtesy of Yarmouth County Museum and Archives.

Nichols, Justice John R. Her Majesty the Queen vs. [name redacted by author], Preliminary Inquiry Transcript. Digby, Nova Scotia: July 19, 1979.

Nichols, Justice John R. Warrant of Remand, Province of Nova Scotia. Digby, N.S.: July 19, 1979.

Phinney, Sandra. *Maud Lewis and the "Maudified" House Project: The Story Starts Here.* Saint John, N.B.: Hawthorne Lane Publishing, 2014.

Prahl, Amanda. "The Life and Work of Maud Lewis, Canadian Folk Artist." *ThoughtCo.* November 14, 2018. thoughtco.com/ maud_lewis_biography_4172425. Accessed November 11, 2019.

Ronald, George, director; Peter Kelly, producer; Fletcher Markle, narrator; Thom Benson, executive producer. *Folk Artist Maud Lewis at work in her Nova Scotia home* from *The Once-Upon-A-Time World of Maud Lewis.* CBC *Telescope* Documentary broadcast Nov. 25, 1965, available on CBC Archives. cbc.ca/ player/play/761637443808. Accessed May 22, 2020.

Ruff, Eric, and Laura Bradley, *Images of our Past: Historic Yarmouth Town & County.* Halifax, N.S. and Yarmouth, N.S.: Nimbus Publishing Ltd. and the Yarmouth County Museum, 1997.

Thibeau, Reverend J.C. "For the Thibeau Family: Maud's Yarmouth Neighbours." n.d., n.p., Yarmouth County Museum and Public Archives. Abridged version available online, Thibeau, Reverend J.C. *MAUD's Yarmouth Neighbour.* yarmouth.org/koc/maud/index.htm. Accessed June 27, 2018.

Thompson, Brenda. *A Wholesome Horror: Poor Houses in Nova Scotia.* Halifax, N.S.: SSP Publications, 2017.

Three Dogs in a Garden, "Evertt's [sic] Painting and Murder." threedogsinagarden.blogspot.com/2011/01/evertts-painting-and-murder.html. Accessed April 30, 2019.

Wade, Stephen. "The Maud and Everett Lewis Story." *The Stephen Wade Evangelistic Association Inc.,* Paradise, N.S. n.d. sweainc.com. Accessed May 1, 2019.

Walsh, Aisling, director. *Maudie.* Mongrel Media, 2016.

Woolaver, Lance, and Bob Brooks. *The Illuminated Life of Maud Lewis.* Halifax, N.S.: Nimbus Publishing, 1996.

NICOLA DAVISON

*C*arol Bruneau is the acclaimed author of three short story collections, including *A Bird on Every Tree*, published by Vagrant Press in 2017, and five other novels. Her first novel, *Purple for Sky*, won the 2001 Thomas Head Raddall Atlantic Fiction Award and the Dartmouth Book Award. Her 2007 novel, *Glass Voices*, was a *Globe and Mail* Best Book and has become a book club favourite. Her most recent novel, *A Circle on the Surface*, won the 2019 Jim Connors Dartmouth Book Award. Her reviews, stories, and essays have appeared nationwide in newspapers, journals, and anthologies, and two of her novels have been published internationally. She lives in Halifax, Nova Scotia, with her husband and their dog and badass cat.